THE SIN THAT WAS HIS

By

FRANK L. PACKARD

The Sin That Was His

by **Frank L. Packard**

ISBN: 978-93-58018-35-6

Published by

DOUBLE 9 BOOKS

2/13-B, Ansari Road, Daryaganj
New Delhi – 110002
info@double9books.com
www.double9books.com
Tel. 011-40042856

ABOUT THE AUTHOR

Frank L. Packard (1877-1942) was a Canadian author who wrote primarily in the detective and adventure genres. He was born in Montreal, Canada and worked as a civil engineer before turning to writing full-time. Packard wrote over 30 novels, many of which featured the character of Jimmie Dale, a gentleman thief who used his skills to fight crime. The Jimmie Dale stories were hugely popular in the early 20th century and influenced the development of the modern detective genre. In addition to his novels, Packard also wrote short stories for magazines such as Argosy, Blue Book, and Collier's. His stories often featured tales of adventure, the Canadian wilderness, and the gold rush era. Packard's work was well-received during his lifetime, and he was a prolific writer until his death in 1942. However, his popularity waned in the years following his death, and he is now largely forgotten by modern readers. Nonetheless, his contributions to the development of detective fiction and adventure writing in the early 20th century remain significant.

CONTENTS

CHAPTER I—THREE-ACE ARTIE

OF Arthur Leroy, commonly known throughout the Yukon as Three-Ace Artie, Ton-Nugget Camp knew a good deal—and equally knew very little. He had drifted in casually one day, and, evidently finding the environment remuneratively to his liking, had stayed. He was a bird of passage—tarrying perhaps for the spring clean-up.

He was not exactly elegant in his apparel, for the conditions of an out-post mining camp did not lend themselves to elegance; but he was immeasurably the best dressed and most scrupulously groomed man that side of Dawson. His hands, for instance, were very soft and white; but then, he did no work— that is, of a nature to impair their nicety.

His name was somewhat confusing. It might be either French or English, according to the twist that was given to its pronunciation—and Three-Ace Artie could give it either twist with equal facility. He confessed to being a Canadian—which was the only confession of any nature whatsoever that Three-Ace Artie had ever been known to make. He spoke English in a manner that left no doubt in the world but that it was his native language—except in the mind of Canuck John, the only French Canadian in the camp, who was equally positive that in the person of Three-Ace Artie he had unquestionably found a compatriot born to the French tongue.

A few old-timers around Dawson might have remembered, if it had not been so commonplace an occurrence when it happened, that Leroy, as a very young man, had toiled in over the White Pass; though that being only a matter of some four years ago at this time, Leroy was still a very young man, even if somewhat of a change had taken place in his appearance—due possibly, or possibly not, to the rigours of the climate. Three-Ace Artie since then had grown a full beard. But Leroy's arrival, being but one of so many, the old-timers had found in it nothing to remember.

Other and more definite particulars concerning Three-Ace Artie, however, were in the possession of Ton-Nugget Camp. Three-Ace Artie had no temperance proclivities—but he never drank during business hours. No one had ever seen a glass at his elbow when there was a pack of cards on the table! Frankly a professional gambler, he was admitted to be a good one—and square. He was polished, but not too suave; he was unquestionably possessed of far more than an ordinary education, but he never permitted his erudition to become objectionable; and he had a reputation for coolness and nerve that Ton-Nugget Camp had seen enhanced on several occasions and belied on none. He was of medium height, broad shouldered, and muscular; he had black hair and black eyes; under the beard the jaw was square; unruffled, he was genial; ruffled, he was known to be dangerous; and, still too young to show the markings of an ungracious life, his forehead was unwrinkled, and his skin clear and fresh.

Also, during his three months' sojourn in Ton-Nugget Camp, he was credited, not without reason, in having won considerably more than he had lost. Upon these details rested whatever claim to an intimate acquaintanceship with Three-Ace Artie the camp could boast; for the rest, Ton-Nugget Camp, in common with the Yukon in general, was quite privileged to hazard as many guesses as it pleased!

In a word, such was Three-Ace Artie's status in Ton-Nugget Camp when there arrived one afternoon a young man, little more than a boy, patently fresh from the East. And here, though Ton-Nugget Camp was quick to take the newcomer's measure, and, ignoring the other's claim to the self-conferred title of Gerald Rogers, promptly dubbed him the Kid, it permitted, through lack of observation, a slight detail to escape its notice that might otherwise perhaps have suggested a new and promising field for its guesses concerning Three-Ace Artie.

Though at no more distant a date than a few days previous to his arrival, the Kid had probably never seen a "poke" in his life before, much less one filled with currency in the shape of gold dust, he had, in the first flush of his entry to MacDonald's, and with the life-long air of one accustomed to doing nothing else, flung a very new and pleasantly-filled poke in the general direction of the scales at the end of the bar, and, leaning back against the counter, supporting himself on his elbows, proceeded to "set them up" for all concerned. MacDonald's, collectively and individually, which is to say no small portion of the camp, for MacDonald's was at once hotel, store, bar and general hang-out, obeyed the invitation without undue delay, and was in the act of enjoying the newcomer's hospitality when Three-Ace Artie strolled in.

Some one nearest the bar reached out a glass to the gambler over the intervening heads, the cluster of men broke away that the ceremony of introduction with the stranger might be duly performed—and Ton-Nugget Camp, failing to note the sudden tightening of the gambler's fingers around his glass, the startled flash in the dark eyes that was instantly veiled by half dropped, sleepy lids, heard only Three-Ace Artie's, "Glad to know you, Mr. Rogers," in the gambler's usual and quietly modulated voice.

Following that, however, not being entirely unsophisticated, Ton-Nugget Camp stuck its tongue in its cheek and awaited developments—meanwhile making the most of its own opportunities, for the Kid, boisterous, loose with his money, was obviously too shining a mark for even amateurs to overlook. Ton-Nugget Camp, therefore, was, while expectant, quite content that Three-Ace Artie should, through motives which it attributed to professional delicacy, avoid rather than make any hurried advances toward intimacy with the newcomer; since, not feeling the restraint of any professional ethics itself, Ton-Nugget Camp was enabled to take up a few little collections on its own account via the stud poker route at the expense of the Kid.

Two days passed, during which Three-Ace Artie, besides being little in evidence, refrained entirely from pressing his attentions upon the stranger; but despite this, thanks to the adroitness of certain members of the community and his own all too frequent attendance upon the bar, matters were not flourishing with the Kid. The Kid drank far more than was good for him, played far more than was good for him, and, flushed and fuddled with liquor, played none too well. True, there were those in the camp who offered earnest, genuine and well-meant advice, amongst them a grim old Presbyterian by the name of Murdock Shaw, who was credited with being the head of an incipient, and therefore harmless, reform movement—but this advice the Kid, quite as warmly as it was offered, consigned to other climes in conjunction with its progenitors; and, as a result, all that was left of his original poke at the expiration of those two days was an empty chamois bag from which, possibly by way of compensation, the offensive newness had been considerably worn off.

"If he's got any more," said the amateurs, licking their lips, "here's hopin' that Three-Ace Artie 'll keep on overlookin' the bet!"

And then, the next afternoon, the Kid flashed another poke, quite as new and quite as pleasantly-nurtured as its predecessor—and Three-Ace Artie seemed to awake suddenly to the knock of opportunity at his door.

With just what finesse and aplomb the gambler inveigled the Kid into the game no one was prepared co say—it was a detail of no moment, except to Three-Ace Artie, who could be confidently trusted to take care of such matters, when moved to do so, with the courtly and genial graciousness of one conferring a favour on the other! But, be that as it may, the first intimation the few loungers who were in MacDonald's at the time had that anything was in the wind was the sight of MacDonald, behind the bar, obligingly exchanging the pokes of both men For poker chips. The loungers present thereupon immediately expressed their interest by congregating around the table as Three-Ace Artie and the Kid sat down.

"Stud?" suggested Three-Ace Artie, with an engaging smile.

The Kid, already none too sober, nodded his head.

"And table stakes!" he supplemented, with a somewhat lordly flourish of the replenished glass that he had carried with him from the bar.

"Of course!" murmured the gambler.

It was still early afternoon, but an afternoon of the long-night of the northern winter, sunless, with only a subdued twilight without, and the big metal lamps, hanging from the ceiling, were lighted. In the centre of the room a box-stove alternately crackled and purred, its sheet-iron sides glowing dull red. The bare, rough-boarded room, save for the little group, was empty. Behind the bar, with a sort of curious, cynical smile that supplied no additional beauty to his shrewd, hard-lined visage, MacDonald himself propped his bullet-head in his hands, elbows on the counter, to watch the proceedings.

Three-Ace Artie and the Kid began to play. Occasionally the door opened, admitting a miner who took a brisk, fore-intentioned step or two toward the bar—and catching sight of the game in progress, as though magnet-drawn, immediately changed his direction and joined those already around the table. But neither Three-Ace Artie nor the Kid appeared to pay any attention to the constantly augmenting number of spectators. The game see-sawed, fortune smiling with apparently unbiased fickleness first on one, then on the other. The Kid grew a little more noisy, a little more intoxicated—as MacDonald, from a mere spectator, became an attendant at the Kid's frequent beck and call. Three-Ace Artie was entirely professional—there was no glass at Three-Ace Artie's elbow, when he lost he smiled good-humouredly, when he won he smoothed over the other's discomfiture with self-deprecatory tact; he was unperturbed and cordial, he bet sparingly and in moderation—to enjoy the game, as it were, for the game's own sake, the stakes being, as it were again, simply to supply a little additional zest and tang, and for no other reason whatever!

And, then, little by little, the Kid began to force the game; and, as the stakes grew higher, began to lose steadily, with the result that an hour of play saw most of the chips, instead of a glass, flanking Three-Ace Artie's elbow—and saw a large proportion of Ton-Nugget Camp, to whom the word in some mysterious manner had gone forth, flanking the table five and six deep.

The more the Kid lost, the more he drank. Whatever ease of manner, whatever composure he had originally possessed was gone now. His hair straggled unkemptly over his forehead, his cheeks were flushed, his lips worked constantly on the butt of an unlighted cigarette.

The crowd pressed a little closer, leaned a little further over the table. There was something almost fascinating in the deftness with which the soft, white hands of Three-Ace Artie caressed the cards, there was something almost fascinating, too, in the cool impassiveness of the gambler's poise, and in the sort of languid selfpossession that lighted the dark eyes; but Ton-Nugget Camp had lived too long in familiarity with Three-Ace Artie to be interested in the gambler's personality at that moment—its interest was centred in the game. The play now had all the earmarks of a grand finale. There were big stakes on the table—and the last of the Kid's chips. The crowd raised itself on tiptoes. Both men turned their "hole" cards. Three-Ace Artie reached out calmly, drew the chips toward him, smiled almost apologetically, and, picking up the deck, riffled the cards tentatively—the opposite side of the table was bare of stakes.

For a moment the Kid circled his lips with the tip of his tongue, and flirted his hair back from his forehead with an uncertain, jerky motion of his hand; then he snatched up his glass, spilled a portion of its contents, gulped down the remainder, and began to fumble under his vest, finally wrenching out a money-belt.

"Go on—what do you think!" he said thickly. "I ain't done yet! I'll get mine back, an' yours, too! Table stakes—eh? I'll get you this time—b'God! Table stakes—eh—again? What do you say?"

"Of course!" murmured Three-Ace Artie politely.

And then the crowd shuffled its feet uneasily. Murdock Shaw, who had edged his way close to the table, leaned over and touched the Kid's shoulder.

"I'd cut it out, if I was you, son," he advised bluntly. "You're drunk—and a mark!"

A sort of quick, sibilant intake of breath came from the circle around the table. Like a flash, one of Three-Ace Artie's hands, from the deck of cards, vanished under the table; and the dark eyes, the slumber gone from their depths, narrowed dangerously on Murdock Shaw. Then Three-Ace Artie smiled—unpleasantly.

"It isn't as though you were *new* in the Yukon, Murdock"—there was a deadliness in the quiet, level tones. "What's the idea?"

Like magic, to right and left, on each side of the table, the crowd cleared a line behind the two men—then silence.

The gambler's hand remained beneath the table; his eyes cold, alert, never wavering for the fraction of a second from the miner's face.

Perhaps a minute passed. The miner did not speak or move, save that his lips tightened and the tan of his face took on a deeper hue.

Then Three-Ace Artie spoke again:

"Are you *calling*, Murdock?" he inquired softly.

The miner hesitated an instant, then turned abruptly on his heel.

"When I call you," he said evenly, over his shoulder, "it will break you for keeps—and you won't have long to wait, either!"

The Kid, who had been alternating a maudlin gaze from the face of one man to the other, stood up now, and, hanging to the back of his chair, watched the miner's retreat in a fuddled way.

"Say, go chase yourself!" he called out, in sudden inspiration—and, glancing around for approval, laughed boisterously at his own drunken humour.

The door closed on Murdock Shaw. The Kid slipped down into his chair, dumped a handful of American double-eagles out of the money-belt—and, reaching again for his glass, banged it on the table.

"Gimme another!" he shouted in the direction of the bar. "Hey—Mac—d'ye hear! Gimme another drink!"

Three-Ace Artie's hands were above the table again—the slim, delicate, tapering fingers shuffling, riffling, and reshuffling the cards.

MacDonald approached the table, and picked up the empty glass.

"Wait!" commanded the Kid ponderously, and scowled suddenly in the throes of another inspiration. He pointed a finger at Three-Ace Artie. "Say—give him one, too!" He wagged his head sapiently. "If he wants any more chance at my money, he's got to have one, too! That's what! Old guy's right about that! I'm the only one that's drunk—you've got to drink, too! What'll you have—eh?"

The group had closed in around the table again, and now all eyes were riveted, curiously, expectantly, upon Three-Ace Artie. If the gambler had one fixed principle from which, as Ton-Nugget Camp had excellent reasons for knowing, neither argument nor cajolery had ever moved him, it was that of refusing to drink while he played—but now, while all eyes were on Three-Ace Artie, Three-Ace Artie's eyes were on the pile of American gold that the Kid had displayed. There was a quick little curve to the gambler's lips, that became a slightly tolerant, slightly good-natured smile—and then the crowd nodded significantly to itself.

"Why, certainly!" said Three-Ace Artie pleasantly. "Give me the same, Mac."

"That's the talk!" applauded the Kid.

Three-Ace Artie pushed the cards across the table.

"This is a new game!" announced the Kid. "Cut for deal. Table stakes!"

They cut. Three-Ace Artie won, riffled the cards several times, passed them over to be cut again, and dealt the first card apiece face down.

The Kid examined his card in approved fashion by pulling it slightly over the edge of the table and secretively turning up one corner; then, still face down, he pushed it back, and, MacDonald, returning with the glasses from the bar at that moment, reached greedily for his own and tossed it off. He nodded with heavy satisfaction as Three-Ace Artie drained the other glass. Again he examined his card as before.

"That's a pretty good card!" he stated with owlish gravity. "Worth pretty good bet!" He laid a stack of his gold eagles upon the card.

Three-Ace Artie placed an equivalent number of chips upon his own card, and dealt another apiece—face up now on the table. An eight-spot of spades fell to the Kid; a ten-spot of diamonds to Three-Ace Artie.

"Worth jus' much as before!" declared the Kid—and laid another stack of eagles upon the card.

"Mine's worth a little more this time," smiled Three-Ace Artie—and doubled the bet.

"Sure!" mumbled the Kid. "Sure thing!"

Again Three-Ace Artie dealt—a king of hearts to the Kid; a deuce of hearts to himself.

The Kid's hand seemed to tremble eagerly, as he fumbled with his gold eagles. He glanced furtively at the gambler—and then, as though trying to read in Three-Ace Artie's face how far he might safely egg the other on, he began to drop coin after coin upon his cards.

The crowd stirred a little uncomfortably. The Kid had undoubtedly the better hand so far, but he had made a fool play—a blind man could have read through the back of the card that was so carefully guarded face down on the table. The Kid had a pair of kings against a possible pair of tens or deuces on the gambler's side.

Three-Ace Artie imperturbably "saw" the bet—and coolly dealt the fourth card. Another king fell to the Kid; another deuce to himself.

The Kid's eyes were burning feverishly now. He bet again, laughing, chuckling drunkenly as he swept forward a generous share of his remaining gold—and with a quiet, unostentatiously appraising glance at what was left of the pile of eagles, Three-Ace Artie raised heavily.

Then, for the first time, the Kid hesitated, and a momentary frightened look flashed across his face. He lifted the corner of his "hole" card again and again nervously, as though to assure himself that he had made no mistake—

and finally laughed with raucous confidence again, and, pushing the hair out of his eyes, demanded another drink, and returned the raise.

The onlookers sucked in their breath—but this time approved the Kid's play. The cards showed a pair of deuces and a ten-spot spread out before Three-Ace Artie, a pair of kings and an eight-spot in front of the Kid. But the Kid had already given his hand away, and with a king in the "hole," making three kings, Three-Ace Artie could not possibly win unless his "hole" card was a deuce or a ten, and on top of that that his next and final card should be a deuce or ten as well. It looked all the Kid's way.

Three-Ace Artie again "saw" the other's raise—and dealt the last card.

There was a sudden shuffling of feet, as the crowd leaned tensely forward. A jack fell face up before the Kid—a ten-spot fell before the gambler. Three-Ace Artie showed two pairs—it all depended now on what he held as his "hole" card.

But the Kid, either because he was too fuddled to take the possibilities into account, or because he was drunkenly obsessed with the invincibility of his own three kings, laughed hilariously.

"I got you!" he cried—and bet half of his remaining gold.

Three-Ace Artie's smile was cordial.

"Might as well go all the way then," he suggested—and raised to the limit of the Kid's last gold eagle.

The Kid laughed again. He had played cunningly—quite cunningly. The gambler had fallen into the trap. All his hand showed was two kings.

"I'll see you! I'll see you!"—he was lurching excitedly in his chair, as he pushed the rest of his money forward. "This is the time little old two pairs are no good!" He turned his "hole" card triumphantly. "Three kings" he gurgled—and reached for the stakes.

"Just a minute," objected Three-Ace Artie blandly.

He faced his other card. "I've got another ten here. Full house—three tens and a pair of deuces."

A dead silence fell upon the room. The Kid, lurching in his chair, stared in a dazed, stunned way at the other's cards—and then his face went a deathly white. One hand crept aimlessly to his forehead and brushed across his eyes; and after a moment, leaning heavily upon the table, he stood up, still swaying. But he was not swaying from drunkenness now. The shock seemed to have sobered him, bringing a haggard misery into his eyes. The crowd watched, making no comment. Three-Ace Artie, without lifting his eyes, was calmly engaged in stacking the gold eagles into little piles in front of him. The Kid moistened his lips with his tongue, attempted to speak—and succeeded only in * swallowing hard once or twice. Then, with a pitiful effort to pull himself together, he forced a smile.

"I—I can't play any more," he said. "I'm cleaned out"—and turned away from the table.

The crowd made way for him, following him with its eyes as he crossed the room and disappeared through a back door at the side of the bar, making evidently for his "hotel" room upstairs. Three-Ace Artie said nothing—he was imperturbably pocketing the gold eagles now. The crowd drifted away from the table, dispersed around the room, and some went out. Three-Ace Artie rose from the table and carried the chips back to the bar.

"Guess I'll cash in, Mac," he drawled.

The proprietor pushed the two pokes across the bar.

"Step up, gentlemen!" invited the gambler amiably, wheeling with his back against the bar to face the room.

An air of uneasiness, an awkward tension had settled upon the place. Some few more went out; but the others, as though glad of the relief afforded the situation by Three-Ace Artie's invitation, stepped promptly forward.

Three-Ace Artie's hand encircled a stiff four-fingers of raw spirit.

"Here's how!" he said—and drained his glass.

Somebody "set them up" again; Three-Ace Artie repeated the performance—and MacDonald's resumed its normal poise.

For perhaps half an hour Three-Ace Artie leaned against the bar, joining in a dice game that some one had inaugurated; and then, interest in this lagging, with a yawn and a casual remark about going up to his shack for a snooze, he put on his overcoat, pulled his fur cap well down over his ears, sauntered to the door—and, with a cheery wave of his hand, went out.

But once outside the door, Three-Ace Artie's nonchalance dropped from him, and he stood motionless in the dull light of the winter afternoon peering sharply up and down the camp's single shack-lined street. There was no one in sight. He turned quickly then, and, treading noiselessly in the snow, stole along beside the building to a door at the further end. He opened this cautiously, stepped inside, and, in semidarkness here, halted again to listen. The sounds from the adjoining barroom reached him plainly, but that was all. Satisfied that he was unobserved, he moved swiftly forward to where, at the end of the sort of passageway which he had entered, a steep, ladder-like stairway led upward. He mounted this stealthily, gained the landing above, and, groping his way now along a narrow hallway, suddenly flung open a door.

"Who's there!" came a quick, startled cry from within.

"Don't talk so loud—damn it!" growled Three-Ace

Artie, in a hoarse whisper. "You can hear yourself think through these partitions!" He struck a match, and lighted a candle which he found on the combination table and washing-stand near the bed.

The Kid's face, drawn and colourless, loomed up in the yellow light from the edge of the bed, as he bent forward, blinking in a kind of miserable wonder at Three-Ace Artie.

"You!" he gasped.

Three-Ace Artie closed the door softly.

"Some high-roller, you are, aren't you!" he observed caustically.

The Kid did not answer.

For a full minute Three-Ace Artie eyed the other in silence—then he laughed shortly.

"I don't know which of us is the bigger damn fool—you trying to buy a through ticket to hell; or yours truly for what I'm going to do now! Maybe you have learned your lesson, maybe you haven't; but anyway I am going to take the chance. I'm not here to preach, but I'll push a little personal advice out of long experience your way. The booze and the pasteboards won't get you anywhere—except into the kind of mess you are up against now. If you are hankering for more of it, go to it—that's all. It's your hunt!"

He flung the Kid's poke suddenly upon the table, and piled the gold eagles beside it.

A flush crept into the Kid's cheeks. He leaned further forward, staring helplessly, now at Three-Ace Artie, now at the money on the table.

"W-what do you mean?" he stammered.

"It isn't very hard to guess, is it?" said Three-Ace Artie quietly. "Here's your money—but there's just one little condition tied to it. I can't afford to let the impression get around that I'm establishing any precedents—see? And if the boys heard of this they'd think I was suffering from softening of the brain! You get away from here without saying anything to anybody—and stay away. Bixley, one of the boys, is going over to the next camp this afternoon—and you go with him."

"You—you're giving me back the money?" faltered the Kid.

"Well, it sort of looks that way," smiled Three-Ace Artie.

A certain dignity came to the Kid—and he held out his hand.

"You're a white man," he said huskily. "But I can't accept it. I took it pretty hard down there perhaps, it seemed to get me all of a sudden when the booze went out; but I'm not all yellow. You won it—I can't take it back. It's yours."

"No; it's not mine"—Three-Ace Artie was still smiling. "That's the way to talk, Kid. I like that. But you're wrong—it's yours by rights."

"By rights?" The Kid hesitated, studying Three-Ace Artie's face. "You mean," he ventured slowly, "that the game wasn't on the level—that you stacked the cards?"

Three-Ace Artie shook his head.

"I never stacked a card on a man in my life."

"Then I don't understand what you mean," said the Kid. "How can it be mine by rights?"

"It's simple enough," replied Three-Ace Artie. "I'm paying back a little debt I owe, that's all. I figured the boys had pecked around about deep enough on the outskirts of your pile, and that it was about time for me to sit in and save the rest. I cleaned you out a little faster than I expected, a little faster perhaps than the next man will if you try it again—but not any the less thoroughly. It's the 'next man' I'm trying to steer you away from, Kid."

"Yes, I know"—the Kid spoke almost mechanically. "But a debt?"—his eyes were searching the gambler's face perplexedly now. Then suddenly: "Who are you?" he demanded. "There's something familiar about you. I thought there was the first time I saw you the other afternoon. And yet I can't place you."

"Don't try," said Three-Ace Artie softly. He reached out and laid his hand on the other's shoulder. "It wouldn't do you or me any good. There are some things best forgotten. I'm telling you the truth, that's all you need to know. You're entitled to the money—and another chance. Let it go at that. You agree to the bargain, don't you? You leave here with Bixley this afternoon—and this is between you and me, Kid, and no one else on earth."

For a moment the Kid's gaze held steadily on Three-Ace Artie; then his eyes filled.

"Yes; I'll go," he said in a low voice. "I guess I'm not going to forget this—or you. I don't know what I would have done, and I want to tell you——"

"Never mind that!" interrupted Three-Ace Artie with sudden gruffness. "It's what you do from now on that counts. You've got to hurry now. Any of the boys will show you Bixley's shack, if you don't know where it is. Just tell Bixley what you want, and he'll take you along. He'll be glad of company on the trail. Shake!" He caught the other's hand, wrung it in a hard grip—and turned to the door. "Good luck to you, Kid!" he said—and closed the door behind him.

As cautiously as he had entered, Three-Ace Artie made his way downstairs again; and, once outside, started briskly in the direction of his shack, that he had acquired, bag and baggage, shortly after his arrival in the camp, from a miner who was pulling out. It was some three or four hundred yards from MacDonald's, and as he went along, feet crunching in the snow from his swinging stride, he began quite abruptly to whistle a cheery air. It was too bitterly cold, however, to whistle, so instead he resorted to humming pleasantly to himself.

He stamped the snow from his feet as he reached the shack, opened the door, and went in. A few embers still glowed in the box-stove, and he threw on a stick of wood and opened the damper. He lighted a lamp, and stood for a moment looking around him. There was a bunk at one side of the shack, the table, the stove, a single chair, a few books on a rude shelf, a kit bag in one corner, a skin of some sort on the floor, and a small cupboard containing supplies and cooking utensils. Three-Ace Artie, however, did not appear to be obsessed with the inventory of his surroundings. There was a whimsical smile on his lips, as he pulled off his fur cap and tossed it on the bunk.

"I guess," said Three-Ace Artie, "it will give the Recording Angel quite a shock to chalk one up on the other side of the page for me!"

CHAPTER II—THE TOAST

THREE-ACE ARTIE, sprawled comfortably cally at the book he held in his hand, a copy of Hugo's *Claude Gueux* in French, tossed it to the foot of the bunk, and sat up, dangling his legs over the edge.

A mood that had long been a stranger to him, a mellow mood, as he had defined it to himself, had kept him away from MacDonald's that night. It was the glow of self-benediction, as it were, ever since he had left the boy's room that afternoon, though it had puzzled him to some extent to explain its effect upon himself—that, for instance, the corollary should take the form of a quiet evening, a pipe, and Hugo.

He shrugged his shoulders. It had been so nevertheless. His shoulders lifted again—it was decidedly an incongruous proceeding for one known as Three-Ace Artie!

His thoughts reverted to the Kid. No one had come to the shack since he had returned from the hotel, but he knew the Kid had left the camp, for he had watched from the shack window as Bixley and the boy had passed down the street together. The Kid would not play the fool again for a while, that was certain—whatever he did eventually.

Three-Ace Artie stared introspectively at the lamp, out at full length upon his bunk, yawned, and looked at his watch. It was already after midnight. He glanced a little quizzically.

Kid, of course! He had been conscious of an inward flame for a moment—then for the third time shrugged his shoulders.

"I guess I'll turn in," he muttered.

He bent down to untie a shoe lace—and straightened up quickly again. A footstep sounded from without, there was a knock upon the door, the door opened—and with the inrush of air the lamp flared up. Three-Ace Artie reached out swiftly to the top of the chimney, protecting the flame with the flat of his hand, and, as the door closed again, stared with cool surprise at his visitor. The last time he had seen Sergeant Marden, of the Royal North-West Mounted Police, had been the year before at Two-Strike-Mountain, where each had followed a gold rush—for quite different reasons!

"Hello, sergeant!" he drawled. "I didn't know you were in camp."

"Just got in around supper-time," replied the other. "I've been up on the Creek for the last few weeks."

Three-Ace Artie smiled facetiously.

"Any luck?" he inquired.

"I got my man," said the sergeant quietly.

"Of course!" murmured Three-Ace Artie softly. "You've got a reputation for doing that, sergeant." He laughed pleasantly. "But you haven't dropped in on *me* officially, have you?"

Sergeant Marden, big, thick-set, with a strong, kindly face, with gray eyes that lighted now in a gravely humorous way shook his head.

"No," he answered. "I'm playing the 'old friend' rôle to-night."

"Good!" exclaimed Three-Ace Artie heartily. "Peel off your duds then, and—will you have the bunk, or the chair? Take your choice—only make yourself at home." He stepped over to the cupboard, and, while the sergeant pulled off his cap and mitts, and unbuttoned and threw back his overcoat, Three-Ace Artie procured a bottle of whisky and two glasses, which he set upon the table. "Help yourself, sergeant," he invited cordially.

The sergeant shook his head again, as he drew the chair toward him and sat down.

"I don't think I'll take anything to-night," he said.

"No?"—Three-Ace Artie's voice expressed the polite regret of a perfect host. "Well, fill your pipe then," he suggested hospitably, as he seated himself on the edge of the bunk. He began to fill his own pipe deliberately, apparently wholly preoccupied for the moment with that homely operation—but his mind was leaping in lightning flashes back over the range of the four years that he had spent in the Yukon. What *exactly* did Sergeant Marden of the Royal North-West Mounted want with him to-night? He had known the other for a good while, it was true—but not in a fashion to warrant the sergeant in making a haphazard social call at midnight after what must have been a long, hard day on the trail.

A match, drawn with a long sweep under the table, crackled; Sergeant Marden lighted his pipe, and flipped the match-stub stovewards.

"It looks as though Canuck John wouldn't pull through the night," he said gravely.

"Canuck John!" Three-Ace Artie sat up with a jerk, and glanced sharply at the other. "What's that you say?"

Sergeant Marden removed his pipe slowly from his lips.

"Why, you know, don't you?" he asked in surprise.

"No, I don't know!" returned Three-Ace Artie quickly. "I haven't been out of this shack since late this afternoon; but I saw him this morning, and he was all right then. What's happened?"

"He shot himself just after supper—accident, of course—old story, cleaning a gun," said the sergeant tersely.

"Good God!" cried Three-Ace Artie, in a low, shocked way—and then he was on his feet, and reaching for his cap and coat. "I'll go up there and see him. You don't mind, sergeant, if I leave you here? I guess I knew Canuck John better than any one else in camp did, and—" His coat half on, he paused suddenly, his brows gathering in a frown. "After supper, you said!" he muttered slowly. "Why, that's hours ago!" Then, his voice rasping: "It's damned queer no one came to tell me about this! There's something wrong here!" He struggled into his coat.

"He's been unconscious ever since they found him," said Sergeant Marden, his eyes fixed on the bowl of his pipe as he prodded the dottle down with his forefinger. "The doctor's just come. You couldn't do any good by going up there, and"—his eyes lifted and met Three-Ace Artie's meaningly—"take it all around, I guess it would be just as well if you didn't go. Murdock Shaw and some of the boys are there, and—well, they seem to feel they don't want you."

For a moment Three-Ace Artie stood motionless, regarding the other in a half angry, half puzzled way; then, his weight on both hands, he leaned forward over the table toward Sergeant Marden.

"In plain English, and in as few words as you can put it, what in hell do you mean by that?" he demanded levelly.

"All right, if you want it that way, I'll tell you," said Sergeant Marden quietly. "I guess perhaps the short cut's best. They've given you until to-morrow morning to get out of Ton-Nugget Camp."

"I beg your pardon?" inquired Three-Ace Artie with ominous politeness.

Sergeant Marden produced a poke partially filled with gold dust and laid it on the table.

"What's that?"—Three-Ace Artie's eyes were hard.

"It's the price you paid Sam MacBride for this shack and contents when he went away. The boys say they want to play fair."

And then Three-Ace Artie laughed—not pleasantly. Methodically he removed his overcoat, hung it on its peg, and sat down again on the edge of the bunk.

"Let's see the rest of your hand, sergeant" — his voice was deadly quiet. "I don't quite get the idea."

"I wasn't here myself this afternoon," said Sergeant Marden; "but they seem to feel that the sort of thing that happened kind of gives the community a bad name, and that separating a youngster, when he's drunk, from his last dollar is a bit too raw even for Ton-Nugget Camp. That's about the size of the way it was put up to me."

It seemed to Three-Act Artie that in some way he had not quite heard aright; or that, if he had, he was being made the object of some, unknown to its authors, stupendously ironical joke — and then, as he glanced at the officer's grim, though not altogether unfriendly countenance, and from Sergeant Marden to the bag of gold upon the table, a bitter, furious anger surged upon him. His clenched fist reached out and fell smashing upon the table.

"So that's it, is it!" he said between his teeth. "This is some of Murdock Shaw's work — the snivelling, psalm-singing hypocrite! Well, he can't get away with it! I've a few friends in camp myself."

"Fairweather friends, I should say," qualified the sergeant, busy again with his pipe bowl. "You said yourself that no one had been near the shack here. The camp appears to be pretty well of one mind on the subject."

"Including the half dozen or more who started after the Kid to begin with!" — Three-Ace Artie's laugh was savage, full of menace. "Are they helping to run me out of camp, too!"

"You seem to have got a little of *everybody's* money," suggested Sergeant Marden pointedly. "Anyway, I haven't seen any sign of them putting up a fight for you."

"Quite so!" There was a sudden cold self-possession in Three-Ace Artie's tones. "Well, I can put up quite a fight for myself, thank you. I'm not going! It's too bad Shaw didn't have the nerve to come here and tell me this. I— —"

"I wouldn't let him," interposed the sergeant, with a curious smile. "That's why I came myself."

Three-Ace Artie studied the other's face for an instant.

"Well, go on!" he jerked out. "What's the answer to that?"

"That I am going on to Dawson in the morning, and that I thought perhaps you might be willing to come along."

Three-Ace Artie's under jaw crept out the fraction of an inch, and his eyes narrowed.

"I thought you said you weren't here officially!"

"I'm not — at least, not yet."

"Well, it sounds mighty like an arrest to me!" snarled Three-Ace Artie. He stood up abruptly, and once more leaned over the table. His dark eyes flashed. "But that doesn't go either—not in the Yukon! You can't hold me for anything I've done, and you ought to know better than to think you can do any bluffing with me and get away with it! Murdock Shaw is. evidently running this little game. I gave him a chance to call my hand this afternoon—and he lay down like a whipped pup! That chance is still open to him—but he can't do it by proxy! That's exactly where you and I stand, Marden—don't try the arrest game!"

"I'm not going to—at least, not yet," said the sergeant again. "It's not a question of law. The day may come when the lid goes on out here, but so far the local millennium hasn't dawned. There's no dispute there. I told you I came in here on the 'old friend' basis, and I meant it. I've known you off and on a bit for quite a while; and I always liked you for the reputation you had of playing square. There's no talk of crookedness now, though I must confess you've pulled something a little thinner than I thought it was in you to do. However, let that go. I don't want to butt in on this unless I have to—and that's why I'm trying to get you to come away with me in the morning. If you don't, there'll be trouble, and then I'll have to take a hand whether I want to or not."

"By God!"—the oath came fiercely, involuntarily from Three-Ace Artie's lips. The irony of it all was upon him again. The injustice of it galled and maddened him. And yet—tell them the truth of the matter? He would have seen every last one of them consigned to the bottomless pit first! The turbulent soul of the man was aflame. "Run out of camp, eh!"—it was a devil's laugh that echoed around the shack. "That means being run out of the Yukon! I'd have to get out, wouldn't I—out of the Yukon—ha, ha!—my name would smell everywhere to high heaven!"

"I'm not sure but that's exactly what I would do if I were you," said Sergeant Marden simply. "The fact you've got to face is that you're black-balled—and the easiest way to swallow a nasty dose is to swallow it in a gulp, isn't it?" He got up from his chair and laid his hand on Three-Ace Artie's shoulder. "Look here, Leroy," he said earnestly, "you've got a cool enough head on you not to play the fool, and you're a big enough sport to stand for the cards whatever way they turn. I want you to say that you'll come along with me in the morning—I'll get out of here early before any one is about, or I'll go now if you like, if that will help any. It's the sensible thing to do. Well?"

"I don't know, Marden—I don't know!" Three-Ace Artie flung out shortly.

"Yes, you do," insisted the sergeant quietly. "You know a fight wouldn't get you anywhere—if you got one or two of them, Murdock Shaw for instance, you'd simply be hung for your pains. They mean business, and I don't want any trouble—why make any for me when it can't do you any good? I'm putting it to you in a friendly way; and, besides that, it's common sense, isn't it?" His grip tightened in a kindly pressure on Three-Ace Artie's shoulder. "I'm right, ain't I? What do you say?"

"Oh, you're right enough!"—a hard smile twisted Three-Ace Artie's lips. "There's no argument about that. I'd have to go anyway, I know that—but I'm not keen on going without giving them a run for their money that they'd remember for the rest of their lives!"

"And at the same time put a crimp into your own," said Sergeant Marden soberly. He held out his hand. "You'll come, won't you?"

Twice Three-Ace Artie paced the length of the shack. Logically, as he had admitted, Marden was right; but battling against logic was a sullen fury that prompted him to throw consequences to the winds, and, with his back to the wall, invite Ton-Nugget Camp to a showdown. And then, abruptly, the gambler's instinct to throw down a beaten hand, when bluff would be of no avail and holding it would only increase his loss, turned the scales, and he halted before Sergeant Marden.

"I'll go," he said tersely.

There was genuine relief in the officer's face.

"And I'll stick to my end of the bargain!" the sergeant exclaimed heartily. "When do you want to start?"

"It makes damned little odds to me!" Three-Ace Artie answered gruffly. "Suit yourself."

"All right," said the sergeant. "In that case I'll put in a few hours' sleep, and we'll get away before the camp is stirring." He buttoned up his overcoat, put on his cap, and moved toward the door. "I've got a team of huskies, and there's room on the sled for anything you want to bring along. You can get it ready, and I'll call for you here."

Three-Ace Artie nodded curtly.

Sergeant Marden reached out to open the door, and, with his hand on the latch, hesitated.

"Don't go up there, Leroy," he said earnestly, jerking his head in the direction of the upper end of the camp. "Canuck John is unconscious, as I told you—there's nothing you could do."

But Three-Ace Artie had turned his back. To Canuck John and Sergeant Marden he was equally oblivious for the moment. He heard the door close, heard the sergeant's footsteps outside recede and die away. He was staring now at the bag of gold upon the table. It seemed to mock and jeer at him, and suddenly his hands at his sides curled into clenched and knotted fists—and after a moment he spoke aloud in French.

"It was the first decent thing I ever did in my life"—he was smiling in a sort of horrible mirth. "Do you appreciate that, my very dear friend Raymond? It is exquisite! *Sacré nom de Dieu*, it is magnificent! It was the first decent thing you ever did in your life—think of that, *mon brave!* And see how well you are paid for it! They are running you out of camp!"

He turned and flung himself down on the bunk, his hands still fiercely clenched. Black-balled, Sergeant Marden had called it! Well, it was not the first time he had been black-balled! Here, in the Yukon, the name of Three-Ace Artie was to be a stench to the nostrils; elsewhere, in the city of his birth, he, last of his race, had already dragged an honoured and patrician name in the mire.

A red flame of anger swept his cheeks. What devil's juggling with the cards had brought that young fool across his path, and brought the memories of the days gone by, and brought him an indulgence in weak, mawkish sentimentality! A debt, he had told the boy!

The red flamed into his face again—and yet again. Curse the memories! Once aroused they would not down. Even the old schooldays crowded themselves upon him—and at that he jeered out at himself in bitter raillery. Brilliant, clever in those days, outstripping many beyond his years, as glib with his Latin as with his own French tongue, his father had designed him for the Roman Catholic priesthood, and he, Raymond Chapelle, the son of the rich seigneur, of one of the oldest families in French Canada, instead of becoming a priest of God had become—Three-Ace Artie, the pariah of Ton-Nugget Camp!

Would it not make all hell scream with glee! It brought unholy humour to himself. He—a priest of God! But he had not journeyed very far along that road—even before he had finished school he had had a fling or two! It had been easy enough. There was no mother, and he did not know his father very well. There had been great style and ceremony in that huge, old, lumbering, gray-stone mansion in Montreal—but never a home! His father had seemed concerned about him in one respect only—a sort of austere pride in his accomplishments at school. Produce proof of that, and money was unstinted. It had come very easily, that money—and gone riotously even as a boy. Then he had entered college, and half way through his course his father had died. He had travelled fast after that—so fast that only a blur of wreckage loomed up out of those few years. A passion for gambling, excess without restraint, a *roué* life—and his patrimony, large as it was, was gone. Family after family turned their backs upon him, and his clubs shut their doors in his face! And then the Yukon—another identity—and as much excitement as he could snatch out of his new life!

There was a snarl now on his lips. It had been a furious pace back there in Montreal, but whose business was it save his own! He was not whimpering about it. He could swallow his own medicine without asking anybody else to make a wry face over it for him! Regrets? What should he regret—save that he had lost the money that would enable him to maintain the old pace! Regrets! He would not even be thinking of it now if that young fool had not crossed his path, and he, the bigger fool of the two, had not tried to play the game of the blind leading the blind!

Repay a debt! Fie had not even displayed originality—only a sort of absurd mimicry of the boy's father! He was taunting himself now, mocking at himself mercilessly. What good had it done! How much different would it be with young Rogers than it had been with himself when Rogers' father, an old and intimate friend of his own father's, had taken him home one night just before the final crash, and had talked till dawn in kindly earnestness, pleading with him to change his ways before it was too late! True, it had had its effect. The effect had lasted two days! But somehow, for all that, he had never been able to forget the old gentleman's face, and the gray hairs, and the soft, gentle voice, and the dull glow of the fire in the grate that constantly found a reflection in the moist eyes fixed so anxiously upon him.

What imp of perversity had inspired him to consider that a debt, and prompt him to repay it to the son! Why had he not left well enough alone! What infernal trick of memory had caused him to recognise the boy at the moment of their first meeting! He had known the other in the old days only in the casual way that one of twenty-two would know a boy of fifteen still in short trousers!

He started up from the bunk impulsively, walked to the stove, wrenched the door open, flung in another stick of wood savagely, and began to pace the shack with the sullen fury of a caged beast. The passion within the man was rising to white heat. Run out of Ton-Nugget Camp! The story would spread. A nasty story! It meant that he was run out of the Yukon—his four years here, and not unprofitable years, at an end! It was a life he had grown to like because it was untrammelled; a life in which, at least in intervals, when the surplus cash was in hand, he could live in Dawson for a brief space at a dizzier pace than ever!

He was Three-Ace Artie here—or Arthur Leroy—it did not matter which—one took one's choice! And now—what was he to be next—and where!

Tell them what he had done, crawl to them, beg them to let him stay — never! If he answered them at all, it would be in quite a different way, and — his eyes fixed again upon the bag of gold that Sergeant Marden had left on the table. A bone flung to a cur as he was kicked from the door! The finger nails bit into the palms of Three-Ace Artie's hands.

"Damn you!" he gritted, white-lipped. "Damn every one of you!"

And this was his reward for the only decent thing that he could remember ever having done in his life — the thought with all its jibing mockery was back once more. It added fuel to his fury. It was he, not the Kid, who had had his lesson! And it was a lesson he would profit by! If it was the only decent thing he had ever done — it would be the last! They had intended him for a priest of God in the old days! He threw back his head and laughed until the room reverberated with his hollow mirth. He had come too damnably near to acting the part that afternoon, it seemed! A priest of God! Blasphemy, unbridled, unlicensed, filled his soul. He snatched up the bottle of whisky, and poured a glass full to the brim.

"A toast!" he cried. "On your feet, Raymond! Up, Monsieur Leroy! Artie, Three-Ace Artie — a toast! Drink deep, *mes braves!*" He lifted the glass above his head. "To our liege lord henceforth, praying pardon for our lapse from grace! To his Satanic Majesty — and hell!" He drained the glass to its dregs, and bowed satirically. "I can not do honour to the toast, sire, by snapping the goblet stem." He held up the glass again. "It is only a jelly tumbler, and so — " It struck with a crash against the wall of the shack, as he hurled it from him, and smashed to splinters.

For a moment, clawing at his throat as the raw spirit burned him, staring at the broken glass upon the floor, he stood there; then, with a short laugh, he pushed both table and chair closer to the stove and sat down — and it was as though it were some strange vigil that he had set himself to keep. Occasionally he laughed, occasionally he filled the other glass and drank in gulps, occasionally he thought of Canuck John, who spoke English very poorly and whose eager snatching at the opportunity to speak French had brought about a certain intimacy between them, and, thinking of Canuck John, there came a sort of wondering frown as at the intrusion of some utterly extraneous thing, occasionally as his eyes encountered the bag of gold there came a glitter into their depths and his lips parted, hard drawn, over set teeth; but for the most part he sat with a fixed, grim smile, his hands opening and shutting on his knees, staring straight before him.

Once he got up, and, making the circuit of the shack, collected his personal belongings and packed them into his kit bag — and from under a loose plank in the corner of the room took out a half dozen large and well-filled pokes, tucked them carefully away beneath the clothing in the bag, strapped up the bag, replaced the loosened plank, and returned to his chair.

Sullen, bitter, desperate, soul reckless with the knowledge that all men's hands were against him, as his were against them, he sat there. The hours passed unreckoned and unnoticed. There was no dawn to come, for there was no sun to rise; but it grew a little lighter. A stillness as of the dead hung over Ton-Nugget Camp; and then out of the stillness a dog barked—and became a yapping chorus as others joined in.

He reached out mechanically for the bottle—it was empty. He stared at it for a moment in bewildered surprise. It had been full, untouched when he had placed it on the table. He stood up—steadily, firmly. He stretched out his hand in front of him, and studied it critically—there was not a tremor. His hand dropped to his side. One could absorb a good deal of liquor under mental stress without resultant physical effect! He was not drunk. Only his nerves were raw and on edge. That bag of gold on the table! His eyes narrowed again upon it for the hundredth time. It flaunted itself in his face. It had become symbolic of the unanimous contempt with which Ton-Nugget Camp bade him be gone! Damn their cursed insolence! It was an entirely inadequate reply to go away and simply leave it lying there on the table—and yet what else was there to do? The dogs were barking again. That would be Marden harnessing up his huskies. The sergeant would be along now in another minute or two.

He turned from the table, picked up his overcoat, put it on, and buttoned it to the throat. He put on his cap, jerked his kit bag up from the floor, slung one strap over his shoulder, moved toward the door—and paused to gaze back around the room. The lamp burned on the table, the empty whisky bottle, the glass, the bag of gold beside it; in the stove a knot crackled with a report like a pistol shot. Slowly his eyes travelled around over the familiar surroundings, his home of four months; and slowly the colour mounted in his cheeks—and suddenly, his eyes aflame, a low, tigerish cry on his lips, he flung the kit bag from his shoulder to the ground.

They would tell the story through the Yukon of how he had fleeced and robbed a drunken boy of his last cent on earth—but they would never tell the story of how he had slunk away in the darkness like a whipped and mangy cur! He feared neither God nor devil, norman, nor beast! That had been his lifelong boast, his creed. He feared them now no more than he had ever feared them! He listened. There was a footstep without, but that was Marden's. Not one of all the camp afoot to risk contamination by bidding him goodbye! Well, it was not good-bye yet! Ton-Nugget Camp would remember, his adieu! Passion was rocking the man to the soul, the sense of bitter injury, smarting like a gaping wound, was maddening him beyond all self-control. He tore loose the top button of his coat—and turned sharply to face the door. Here was Marden now. He wanted no quarrel with Mar-den, but——

The door opened. He felt himself mechanically push his cap back on his forehead, felt a sort of unholy joy sweep in a wild, ungovernable surge upon him, felt every muscle of his body stiffen and grow rigid in a fierce and savage elation, and he heard a sound that he meant for a laugh chortle from his lips. It was not Marden standing there—it was Murdock Shaw.

And then he spoke.

"Come in, and shut the door, Murdock," he said in a velvet voice. "I thought my luck was out tonight."

"It's not worth while," the miner answered. "Mar-den's getting ready to go now, and I only came to bring you a message from Canuck John."

"I've got one for you that you'll remember longer!"—Three-Ace Artie's smile was ghastly, as he moved back toward the table in a kind of inimical guarantee that the floor space should be equally divided between them. "Come in, Murdock, if you are a man—*and shut that door.*"

The miner did not move.

"Canuck John is dead," he said tersely.

"What's that to do with me—or you and me!"—there was a rasp in Three-Ace Artie's voice now. "It's you who have started me on the little journey that I'm going to take, you know, and it's only decent to use the time that's left in bidding me good-bye."

"I didn't come here to quarrel with you," Shaw said shortly. "Canuck John regained consciousness for a moment before he died. He couldn't talk much—just a few words. We don't any of us know his real name, or where his home is. From what he said, it seems you do. He said: 'Tell Three-Ace Artie—give goodbye message—my mother and—' And then he died."

Three-Ace Artie's fingers were twisting themselves around the bag of gold that he had picked up from the table.

"I thought so!" he snarled. "You were yellow this afternoon. I thought you hadn't the nerve to come here, unless you figured you were safe some way or another. And so you think you are going to hide behind a dead man and the sanctimonious pathos of a dying message! Well, I'll see you both damned first! Do you hear!" White to the lips with the fury that, gathering all through the night, was breaking now, he started toward the other, his hand clutching the bag of gold.

Involuntarily the miner stepped back still closer to the door.

"That's not the way out for you!" whispered Three-Ace Artie hoarsely. "If you take it, I'll drop you in the snow before you're ten yards up the street! Damn you, we'll play this hand out now for keeps! You've started something, and we'll finish it. You've rid the camp and rid Alaska of a tainted smell, have you? You sneaked around behind my back with your cursed righteousness to give me a push further on the road to hell! I know your kind—and, by God, I know your breed! Four years ago on the White Pass you took a man's last dollar for a hunk of bread. He could pay or starve! You sleek skunk—do you remember? Your conscience has been troubling you perhaps, and so you went around the camp and collected this, did you—*this!*" He held up the bag of gold above his head. "No? You didn't recognise me again? Well, no matter—take it back! Tell Ton-Nugget Camp I gave it back to you—to keep!" In a flash his arm swept forward, and, with all his strength behind it, he hurled the bag at the other's head.

It struck full on the miner's forehead—and dropped with a soft thud on the floor. The man reeled backward, swayed, and clawed at the wall of the shack for support—and while he swayed a red spot dyed his forehead, and a crimson stream ran zigzag down over eye and cheek.

And Three-Ace Artie laughed, and stooped, and picked up his kit bag, and swung one strap over one shoulder as before—Sergeant Marden, stern-faced, was standing on the threshold of the open door.

"I guess my luck is out after all. You win, Murdock!" smiled Three-Ace Artie grimly—and brushed past the sergeant out of the shack.

The dog-team was standing before the door. He dropped his kit bag on the sled, and strode on down the street. Here and there lights were beginning to show from the shack windows. Once a face was pressed against a pane to watch him go by, but no voice spoke to him. It was silent, and it was dark.

Only the snow was white. And it was cold—cold as death.

Presently Sergeant Marden and the dog-team caught up with him.

"He'll need a stitch or two in his head," said the sergeant gruffly.

Raymond Chapelle, alias Arthur Leroy, alias Three-Ace Artie, made no reply. In his soul was anarchy; in his heart a bitter mockery that picked a quarrel with Almighty God.

CHAPTER III—THE CURÉ

RAYMOND CHAPELLE, once known as Three-Ace Artie, and now, if the cardcase in his pocket could be relied upon for veracity, as one Henri Mentone—though the cardcase revealed neither when nor where that metamorphosis had taken place, nor yet again the nature of Monsieur Henri Mentone's pursuits in life—was engaged in the rather futile occupation of staring out through the car window into a black and objectless night. He was not, however, deeply concerned with the night, for at times he shifted his gaze around the smoking compartment, which he had to himself, and smiled cynically. The winter of the Yukon had changed to the springtime of lower French Canada—it was a far cry from Ton-Nugget Camp, from Dawson and the Pacific, to the little village of St. Marleau on the banks of the St. Lawrence, where the river in its miles of breadth was merging with the Atlantic Ocean!

St. Marleau! That was where Canuck John had lived, where the old folks were now—if they were still alive. The cynical smile deepened. The only friend he had was—a dead man! The idea rather pleased him, as it had pleased him ever since he had started for the East. Perhaps there was a certain sentimentality connected with what he was about to do, but not the sickly, fool sentimentality that he had been weak enough to be guilty of with the Kid in Ton-Nugget Camp! He was through with that! Here, if it was sentiment at all, it was a sentiment that appealed to his sporting instincts. Canuck John had put it up to him—and died. It was a sort of trust; and the only man who trusted him was—a dead man. He couldn't throw a dead man down!

He laughed softly, drumming with his carefully manicured fingers on the window pane. Besides, there was too much gossip circulating between the Pacific Coast and Alaska to make it profitable for a gambler who had been kicked out of the Yukon for malpractice to linger in that locality—even if he had shaved off his beard! The fingers, from the window pane, felt in a sort of grimly ruminative way over the smooth, clean-shaven face. So, as well East as anywhere, providing always that he gave Montreal a wide berth—which he had!

Canuck John, of course, had not meant to impose any greater trust than the mere writing of a letter. But, like Murdock Shaw and the rest of Ton-

Nugget Camp, he, Raymond, did not know Canuck John's name. If Canuck John had ever told him, and he had a hazy recollection that the other once had done so, he had completely forgotten it. Of St. Marleau, however, Canuck John had spoken scores of times. That made a letter still possible, of course—to the postmaster of St. Marleau. But it was many years since Canuck John had left there; Canuck John could not write himself and therefore his people would have had no knowledge of his whereabouts, and to write the postmaster that a man known as Canuck John had died in Ton-Nugget Camp was, to say the least of it, open to confusing possibilities in view of the fact that in those many and intervening years Canuck John was not likely to have been the only one who had left his native village to seek a wider field. And since he, Raymond, was coming East in any event, he was rather glad than otherwise that for the moment he had a definite objective in view.

Anyway, Canuck John had been a good sort—and that was all there was to it! And, meanwhile, this filled in, as it were, a hiatus in his own career, for he had not quite made up his mind exactly in what direction, or against whom specifically, he could pit his wits in future—to the best advantage to himself. One thing only was certain, henceforth he would be hampered by no maudlin consideration of ethics, such, for instance, as had enabled him to state truthfully to the Kid that he had never stacked a card in his life. To the winds with all that! He had had his lesson! Fish to his net, hereafter, would be all that came his way! If every man's hand was against him, his own would not remain palsied! For the moment he was in funds, flush, and well provided for; and for the moment it was St. Marleau and his dead friend's sorry legacy—to those who might be dead themselves! That remained to be seen! After that, as far as he was concerned, it was *sauve qui peut*, and—

Monsieur Henri Mentone looked up—and, with no effort to conceal his displeasure, Monsieur Henri Mentone scowled. A young priest had entered the smoking compartment, and was now in the act of settling himself on the opposite seat.

"Good evening," nodded the other pleasantly. "I think we have been travelling companions since Quebec." He produced a cigar, lighted it, and smiled. "It is not a very pleasant night, is it? There appears to be a very high wind."

Raymond Chapelle rattled a newspaper out of his pocket, rattled it open brusquely—and retired behind it.

"It appears to be windy!" he growled uninvitingly.

He glanced at the remainder of his cigar. It was a very good cigar, and he did not care to sacrifice it by giving the other all the elbow room that the entire smoking compartment of the car afforded—as he, otherwise, would not have hesitated an instant to do! If his soul had nurtured any one especial hatred in its late period of bitter and blasphemous fury, it was a hatred of religion and all connected with it. He detested the sight of a priest. It always made him think of that night in Ton-Nugget Camp when memories had got the better of him. A priest of God! He hated them all. And he made no distinction as between creeds. They were all alike. They were Murdock Shaws! And he, if his father had had his way, would now be wearing a *soutane*, and dangling a crucifix from his neck, and sporting one of those damnable round hats like the man in front of him!

"Do you know this country at all?" inquired the priest.

"I do not," Raymond answered curtly from behind his paper.

The other did not appear to notice the rebuff.

"No more do I," he said engagingly. "I have never been below Quebec before, and I am afraid, unfortunately, that I am about to suffer for my ignorance. I am going to St. Marleau."

Raymond lowered his paper, and for the first time gave the other more than a casual glance. He found his *vis-à-vis* to be dark-eyed, of rather pleasant features—this he admitted grudgingly—and a young man of, he judged, about his own age.

"What is the matter with St. Marleau?" Personal interest prompted him to ask the question; nothing could prompt him to infuse even a hint of affability into his tones.

The priest shrugged his shoulders, and smiled whimsically.

"The matter with St. Marleau is that it is on the bank of the river, and that the station is three miles away. I have been talking to the conductor. I did not know that before."

Raymond had not known it before either. The information did not please him. He had taken it as a matter of course that the railroad would set him down at the village itself.

"Well?" he prompted sourly.

"It was what caused me to take a particular interest in the weather"—the priest waved his cigar philosophically. "I shall have to walk, I presume. I am not expected until to-morrow, and the conductor tells me there is nothing but a small station where we stop."

Raymond would have to walk too.

"It is unfortunate!" he observed sarcastically. "I should have thought that you would have provided against any such contingencies by making inquiries before you started."

"That is true," admitted the priest simply. "I am entirely to blame, and I must not complain. I was pleasurably over-excited perhaps. It is my first charge, you see. The curé of St. Marleau, Father Allard, went away yesterday for a vacation—for the summer—his first in many years—he is quite an old man"—the young priest was waxing garrulous, and was no longer interesting. Raymond peered out of the car window with a new and personal concern in the weather. There was no rain, but the howl of the wind was distinctly audible over the roar of the train.

"I was to have arrived to-morrow, as I said"—the priest was rattling on—"but having my preparations all completed to-day and nothing to detain me, I—well, as you see, I am here."

Raymond was picturing realistically, and none too happily, a three-mile walk on a stormy night over a black, rutted country road. The prospect was not a soothing one.

"Monsieur is perhaps a commercial traveller?" ventured the young curé amiably, by way of continuing the conversation.

Raymond folded his paper deliberately, and replaced it in his pocket. There was a quick, twisted smile on his lips, but for the first time his voice was cordiality itself.

"Oh, no," he said. "On the contrary, I make my living precisely as does Monsieur le Curé, except perhaps that I have not always the same certainty of success."

"Ah!" The young priest leaned forward interestingly. "Then you— —"

"Yes," said Raymond, and now a snarl crept into his voice. "I let some one else toil for the money—while I hold out the hat!" He rose abruptly, and flung his cigar viciously in the general direction of the cuspidor. "I am a parasite on my fellow men, monsieur—a gambler," he said evenly, and walked to the door.

Over his shoulder he caught the amazement on the young priest's face, then the quick, deep flush of indignation—and then the corridor shut him off from the other, and he chuckled savagely to himself.

He passed on into the main body of the car, took his bag from the rack over the seat that he had occupied, and went on into the next car in the rear. The priest, he had noticed, had previously been occupying the same car as himself. He wanted no more of the other! And as for making a companion of him on the walk from the station to St. Marleau, he would sooner have walked with the devil! As a matter of fact, he was prepared to admit he would not have been wholly averse to the devil's company. But a priest of God! The cynical smile was back on his lips. They were all alike—he despised them all. But he nevertheless confessed to a certain commiseration; he was sorry for God—the devil was much less poorly served!

CHAPTER IV—ON THE ROAD
TO ST. MARLEAU

RAYMOND descended from the train on the opposite side from the station platform. He proposed that Monsieur le Curé, *pro tem.*, of St. Marleau, should have a start sufficient to afford a guarantee against the possibility of any further association with the other that night!

A furious gust of wind eddied down the length of the train, caught at his travelling bag, and banged it violently against his knees. He swore earnestly to himself, as he picked his way further back across the siding tracks to guard against the chance of being seen from the platform when the train started on again. It was obviously not going to be a pleasant experience, that walk! It was bad enough where he stood, here on the trackside, somewhat sheltered by the train; in the open the wind promised to attain the ferocity of a young tornado!

The train pulled out; and across the tracks a light glimmered from a window, and behind the light a building loomed up black and formless. The light, filtering out on the platform, disclosed two figures—the priest, and, evidently, the station agent.

Raymond sat down on his bag and waited. It was intensely dark, and he was far enough away to be secure from observation. He grinned maliciously, as he watched a shadowy sort of pantomime in which the priest clutched and struggled continually with his *soutane* as the wind kept wrapping it around his legs.

The other might be less infatuated with skirts by the time St. Marleau was reached!

The two figures moved down the platform together, and Raymond lost sight of them in the darkness. He rose, picked up his bag, walked a few yards along the track in the opposite direction to that which they had taken, crossed over the mainline, and clambered upon the platform. Here he stumbled over a trunk. The curé's, presumably! He continued on along the platform slowly — under the circumstances a little information from the station agent would not come in amiss. He jammed his slouch hat firmly down on his head, and yanked the brim savagely over his eyes against the wind. This was likely to prove considerably more than he had bargained for! Three miles of it! And for what! He began to call himself a fool. And then, the station agent returning alone from the lower end of the platform, head down, buffeting the wind, and evidently making for the curé's trunk to house it for the night, Raymond stepped forward and accosted the other.

The man brought himself up with a jerk. Raymond drew the other into the shelter of the station wall. In the meagre light from the window a few yards away, he could make out the man's face but very indistinctly; and the other, in his turn, appeared equally at a disadvantage, save that, possibly, expecting it to be an acquaintance from the village, he found a stranger instead.

"'Cré nom!" ejaculated the man in surprise. "And where did you come from?"

"From the train—naturally," Raymond answered. "You were busy with some one, and I waited."

"Yes, that is so! I see!" The other nodded his head. "It was Father Aubert, the young curé who is come to the village. He has but just started, and if you are going to St. Marleau, and hurry, you will have company over the road."

"Never mind about him!" said Raymond shortly. "I am not looking for that kind of company!"

"Tiens!" exclaimed the man a little blankly. "Not that kind of company—but that is strange! It is a bad night and a lonely walk—and, I do not know him of course, but he seemed very pleasant, the young curé."

"I daresay," said Raymond, and shrugged his shoulders. "But I do not intend to walk at all if I can help it. Is there no horse to be had around here?"

"But, no!"—the other's tones expressed mild reproof at the question. "If there had been, I would have procured it for the curé. There is nothing. It is as near to the village as anywhere."

"And that is three miles!" muttered Raymond irritably.

"It is three miles by the road, true, monsieur; but the village itself is not nearly so far. There is a short cut. If you take the path that leads straight ahead where the road turns off to the left to circle the woods, it will bring you to the brow of the hill overlooking the village and the river, and you will come out just where the road swings in again at the tavern. You save at least a mile."

Raymond brightened.

"Ah! A tavern!" he cried. "That is better! I was beginning to think the cursed——"

"But—wait!" the man laughed suddenly. "It is not what you think! I should not advise you to go there."

"No?" inquired Raymond, "and why not?"

"She is an old hag, an *excommuniée*, old Mother Blondin, who lives there—and her son, who is come back for the past week from God knows where with a scar all over his ugly face, is no better. It is not a tavern at all. That is a name we have for it amongst ourselves. We call it the tavern because it is said that she makes her own *whiskey-blanc* and sells it on the sly, and that there are some who buy it—though when her son is back she could not very well have enough for any customers. He has been drunk for a week, and he is a devil."

"Your Mother Blondin is evidently no fool!" observed Raymond ironically. "And so it is said there are some who buy it—eh? And in turn I suppose she could buy out every farmer in the village! She should have money, your Mother Blondin! Hers is a profitable business."

"Yes," said the other. "For me, that is the way I look at it. It is gossip that her stocking is well lined; but I believe the gossip. It is perhaps well for her if it is so, for she will need it. She is getting old and does not see very well, though, *bon Dieu*, she is still sharp enough with her wits! But"—his shoulders lifted in a shrug—"the way to the village, eh? Well, whether you take the road or the path, you arrive at Mother Blondin's. You go down the hill from there, and the village is on each side of you along the bank of the river. Ask at the first house, and they will show you the way to Madame Dussault's—that is the only place to go. She keeps a boarding house whenever there is anybody to board, for it is not often that any stranger comes to St. Marleau. Are you going to stay long?"

"I don't know," said Raymond pleasantly—and ignored the implied invitation for further confidences.

"Well, if you like," offered the station agent, "you can leave your bag here, and it can go over with the cure's trunk in the morning. He said he would send somebody for it then. You won't find it easy carrying that bag a night like this."

"Oh, it's only a small one; I guess I can manage it all right," said Raymond lightly. He extended his hand—the priest was far enough along by now so that he would not overtake the other; and, though it was still early, not much after eight o'clock, the countryside was not given to keeping late hours, and, if he was to reach St. Marleau before this Dussault household, for instance, had retired for the night, it was time he started. "Much obliged for the information! Goodnight!" he smiled, and picked up his bag—and a moment later, the station behind him, was battling in the face of furious wind gusts along the road.

The Sin That Was His | 37

It was very dark; and the road was execrable, full of ruts and hollows into which he was continually stumbling. He had a flashlight in his bag; but, bad as the walking was, it was, after all, he decided, the lesser of the two evils — if he used the flashlight, he ran a very large risk of inviting the companionship of the priest ahead of him! Also, he had not gone very far before he heartily regretted that he had not foregone the few little conveniences that the bag contained, and had left the thing behind. The wind, as it was, threatened to relieve him of it a score of times. Occasionally he halted and turned his back, and stood still for a breathing spell. His mood, as he went along, became one that combined a sullen stubbornness to walk ten miles, if necessary, once he had started, and an acrimonious and savage jeer at himself for having ever been fool enough to bring about his present discomfiture.

Finally, however, he reached the turn of the road referred to by the station agent, and here he stood for a moment debating with himself the advisability of taking the short cut. His eyes grown accustomed to the darkness, he could distinguish his surroundings with some distinctness, and he made out a beaten track that led off in the same direction which, until then, he had been following; but also, a little beyond this again, he made out a black stretch of wooded land. He shook his head doubtfully. The short cut was a mere path at best, and he might, or might not, be able to follow it through the trees. If he lost it, and it would be altogether too easy a thing to do, his predicament would not be enviable. It was simply a question of whether the mile he might save thereby was worth the risk. He shook his head again — this time decisively.

"I'm not much on the 'straight and narrow' anyhow!" he muttered facetiously — and started on again, following the road.

Gradually the road and the trees began to converge; and presently, the road swerving again, this time sharply toward the river, he found himself travelling through the woods, and injected into the midst of what seemed like the centre of some unearthly and demoniacal chorus rehearsing its parts — the wind shrieked through the upper branches of the trees, and moaned disconsolately through the lower ones; it cried and sobbed; it screamed, and mourned, and sighed; and in the darkness, still blacker shapes, like weird, beckoning arms, the limbs swayed to and fro. And now and then there came a loud, ominous crackle, and then a crash, as a branch, dried and rotten, came hurtling to the ground.

"Damn it," confessed Raymond earnestly to himself, "I don't like this! I wish St. Marleau was where Canuck John is now!"

He quickened his pace — or, rather, tried to do so; but it was much blacker here than out in the open, and besides the road now appeared to be insanely full of twists and turns, and in spite of his efforts his progress was no faster.

It seemed interminable, never-ending. He went on and on. A branch crashed down louder than before somewhere ahead of him. He snarled in consonance with the wind-shrieks and the wind-moans that now came to hold a personal malevolence in their pandemonium for himself. His coat caught once on a projecting branch and was torn. He cursed Canuck John, and cursed himself with abandon. And then abruptly, as the road twisted again, he caught the glimmer of a light through the trees—and his eyes upon the light, rather than upon the ground to pick his way, he stumbled suddenly and pitched forward over something that was uncannily soft and yielding to the touch.

With a startled cry, Raymond picked himself up. It was the body of a man sprawled across the road. He wrenched open his bag, and, whipping out his flashlight, turned it upon the other.

The man lay upon his back, motionless, inert; the white, ghastly face, blood-streaked, was twisted at a sharp angle to the body, disclosing a gaping wound in the head that extended from the temple back across the skull—and a yard away, mute testimony to its tragic work, lay the rotten limb of a tree, devoid of leaves, perhaps ten feet in length and of the thickness of one's two fists, its end jagged and splintered where it had snapped away from its parent trunk.

It was the priest—Father Aubert, the young curé of St. Marleau.

CHAPTER V—THE "MURDER"

RAYMOND stooped to the other's side. He called the man's name—there was no answer. He lifted the priest's head—it sagged limply back again. He felt quickly for the heart beat—there was no sign of life. And then Raymond stood up again.

It was the nature of the man that, the sudden shock of his discovery once over, he should be cool and unperturbed. His nerves were not easily put to rout under any circumstances, and a life in the Great North, where the raw edges were turned only too often, left him, if not calloused, at least composed and, in a philosophical way, unmoved at the sight before him.

"Tough luck—even for a priest!" he muttered, not irreverently. "The man's dead, right enough."

He glanced around him, and his eyes fixed again on the glimmer of light through the trees. That was the tavern undoubtedly—old Mother Blondin's, the *excommuniée*. He shrugged his shoulders, and a grim smile flickered across his lips. She too had her quarrel with the church, but even so she would hardly refuse temporary sanctuary to a dead man. The priest couldn't be left here lying in the road, and if Mother Blondin's son was not too drunk to help carry the body to the house, it would solve the problem until word could be got to the village.

He took up his bag—he could not be cumbered with that when he returned to get the priest—and, the trees sparser here on what was obviously the edge of the woods, with the window light to guide him and his flashlight to open the way, he left the road and began to run directly toward the light.

A hundred yards brought him out into a clearing—and then to his disgust he discovered that, apart possibly from another rent or two in his clothing, he had gained nothing by leaving the road. It had evidently swung straight in toward the house from a point only a few yards further on from where he had left the priest, for he was now alongside of it again!

He grinned derisively at himself, slipped his flashlight into his pocket—and, on the point of starting toward the house, which, with only a small yard in front of it, was set practically on the edge of the road itself, he halted abruptly. There was only one lighted window that he could see, and this was now suddenly darkened by a shadowy form from within, and indistinctly he could make out a face pressed close against the window pane.

Raymond instinctively remained motionless. The face held there, peering long and intently out into the night. It was rather strange! His own approach could not have been heard, for the howl of the wind precluded any possibility of that; and neither could he be seen out here in the darkness. What was it that attracted and seemed to fascinate the watcher at the window? Mechanically, he turned his head to look behind and around him. There was nothing—only the trees swaying in the woods; the scream and screech, and the shrill whistling of the wind; and, in addition now, a rumbling bass, low, yet perfectly distinct, the sullen roar of beating waves. He looked back at the window—the face was gone.

Raymond moved forward curiously. There was no curtain on the window, and a step or two nearer enabled him to see within. It was a typical bare-floored room of the *habitant* class of smaller house that combined a living room and kitchen in one, the front door opening directly upon it. There was a stove at one end, with a box of cordwood beside it; drawn against the wall was a table, upon which stood a lighted lamp; and a little distance from the table, also against the wall, was an old, gray-painted, and somewhat battered *armoire*, whose top was strewn with crockeryware and glass dishes—there was little else in evidence, save a few home-made chairs with thong-laced seats.

Raymond's brows gathered in a puzzled frown. Diagonally across the room from the window and directly opposite the stove was a closed door, and here, back turned, the man who had been peering out of the window—for the man was the only occupant of the room—was crouched with his ear against the panel. His bewilderment growing, Raymond watched the other. The man straightened up after a moment, faced around into the room, and, swaying slightly, a vicious smile of satisfaction on his lips, moved stealthily in the direction of the table.

And now Raymond had no difficulty in recognising the man from the station agent's vivid, if cursory, description. It was Mother Blondin's son. A devil, the agent had called the other—and the man looked it! An ugly white scar straggled from cheek bone to twisted lip, the eyes were narrow and close set, the hair shaggy, and the long arms dangling from a powerful frame made Raymond think of a gorilla.

Reaching the table, the man paused, looked furtively all around the room, and again appeared to be listening intently; then he stretched out his hand and turned the lamp half down.

Raymond's frown deepened. The other was undoubtedly more or less drunk, but that did not explain the peculiar and, as it were, ominous way in which he was acting. What was the man up to? And where was Mother Blondin?

The man moved down the room in the direction of the stove; and, the light dim now, Raymond stepped close to the window for a better view. The man halted at the end of the room, once more looked quickly all about him, gazed fixedly for an instant at the closed door where previously he had held his ear to the panel—and reached suddenly up above his head, the fingers of both hands working and clawing in a sort of mad haste at an interstice in the wall where the rough-squared timbers came imperfectly together.

And then Raymond smiled sardonically. He understood now. It was old Mother Blondin's "stocking"! She had perhaps not been as generous as the son considered she might have been! The man was engaged in the filial occupation of robbing his own mother!

"Worthy offspring—if the old dame doesn't belie her reputation!" muttered Raymond—and stepped to the front door. "However, it's an ill wind that blows nobody good, and, if the priest suffered, Mother Blondin can at least thank my interruption incident thereto for the salvage of her cash." He opened the door and walked in coolly. "Good evening!" he said pleasantly.

The man whirled from the wall—and with a scream, half of pain and half of startled, furious surprise, was jerked back against the wall again. His hand was caught as though in a trap. The hiding place had quite evidently been intended by Mother Blondin for no larger a hand than her own! The man had obviously wormed and wriggled his hand in between the timbers—and his hand would not come out with any greater ease than it had gone in! He wrenched at it, snarling and cursing now, stamping with his feet, and hurling his maledictions at Raymond's head.

"It is not my fault, my friend," said Raymond calmly. "Shall I help you?"

He started forward—and stopped halfway across the room. The man had torn his hand loose, sending a rain of coin clinking to the floor, and, fluttering after it like falling leaves, a score or two of banknotes as well; and now, leaping around, he snatched up a heavy piece of the cordwood, and, swinging it about his head, his face working murderously, sprang toward Raymond.

The bag dropped from Raymond's hand, and his face hardened. He had not bargained for this, but if— —

With a snarl and an oath the man was upon him; the cordwood whistled in its downward sweep, aimed full at his head. He parried the blow with his forearm, and, with a lightning-like movement, side-stepped and sent his right fist crashing to the other's jaw.

It staggered the man for an instant — but only for an instant. Bellowing with rage, dropping the cordwood, heedless of the blows that Raymond battered into his face, by sheer bulk and weight he closed, his arms circling Raymond's neck, his fingers feeling for a throat-hold.

Around the room they staggered, swaying, lurching. The man was half drunk, and, caught in the act of thievery, his fury was demoniacal. Again and again Raymond tried to throw the other off. The man was too big, too powerful for close quarters, and his only chance was an opportunity to use his fists. They panted heavily, the breath of the one hot on the other's cheek; and then, as they swung, Raymond was conscious that the door of the rear room was open, and that a woman was standing on the threshold. It was only a glance he got — of an old hag-like face, of steel-rimmed spectacles, of tumbling and dishevelled gray hair — the man's fingers at last were tightening like a vise around his throat.

But the other, too, had seen the woman.

"*Voleur!* Thief!" he yelled hoarsely. "Smash him on the head with the stick, mother, while I hold him!"

"You devil!" gritted Raymond — and with a wrench, a twist, his strength massed for the one supreme effort, he tore himself loose, hurling the other backward and away from him.

There was a crash of breaking glass as the man smashed into the *armoire*; a wild laugh from the woman in the doorway — and, for the first time, a cry from Raymond's lips. The man snatched up a revolver from the top of the *armoire*.

But quick as the other was, Raymond was quicker as he sprang and clutched at the man's hand. His face was sternly white now with the consciousness that he was fighting for no less than his life. Here, there, now across the room, now back again they reeled and stumbled, struggling for possession of the weapon, as Raymond strove to tear it from his antagonist's grasp. And now the woman, screaming, ran forward and picked up the piece of cordwood, and circling them, screaming still, aimed her blows at Raymond.

One struck him on the head, dazing him a little... his brain began to whirl... he could not wrench the revolver from the man's hand... it seemed as though he had been trying through an eternity... his hands seemed to be losing their strength... another desperate jerk from the other like that and his hold would be gone, the revolver in the unfettered possession of this whisky-maddened brute, whose lips, like fangs, were flecked with slaver, in whose eyes, bloodshot, burned the light of murder... his fingers were slipping from their grip, and — —

There was a blinding flash; the roar of the report; the revolver clattered to the floor; a great, ungainly bulk seemed to Raymond to waver and sway before him in most curious fashion, then totter and crash with an impact that shook the house—or was it that ghastly, howling wind!—to the ground.

Raymond reeled back against the *armoire*, and hung there gasping, panting for his breath, sweeping his hand again and again across his forehead. He was abominably dizzy. The room was swinging around and around; there were two figures, now on the ceiling, now on the floor—a man who lay flat on his back with his arms and legs grotesquely extended, and whose shirt was red-splotched; and a hag with streaming gray hair, who rocked and crooned over the other.

"Dead! Dead! Dead!"—the wail rose into a high and piercing falsetto. The hag was on her feet and running wildly for the front door. "Murder! Thief! Murder! Murder!"

The horrible screeching died away; and a gust of wind, swirling in through the door that blew open after the woman, took up the refrain: "Murder—murder—*murder!*"

His head ached and swam. He was conscious that he should set his wits at work, that he should think—that somehow he was in peril. He groped his way unsteadily to where his bag lay on the floor. As he reached it, the wind blew the lamp out. He felt around inside the bag, found his flask, and drank greedily.

The stimulant cleared his brain. He stood up, and stared around him in the darkness. His mind was active enough now—grimly active. If he were caught, he would swing for murder! He had only acted in self-defence, he had not even fired the shot, the revolver had gone off in the man's own hand—but there wasn't a chance for him, if he were caught. The old hag's testimony that he had come there as a thief—that was what undoubtedly she believed, and undoubtedly what she would swear—would damn him. And—cursed irony!—that conversation with the station agent, innocent enough then, would corroborate her now! Nor had he any reputation to fall back upon to bolster up his story if he faced the issue and told the truth. Reputation! He could not even give a plausible account of himself without making matters worse. A gambler from the Klondike! The *roué* of Montreal! Would that save him!

His only hope was to run for it—and at once. It could not be very far to the village, and it would not be long before that precious old hag had alarmed the community and returned with the villagers at her heels. But where would he go? There were no trains! It would be a man-hunt through the woods, and with so meagre a start that sooner or later they would get him. And even if he evaded them at first he would have no chance to get very far away from that locality, and ultimately he would have to reckon on the arrival of the police. It was probable that old Mother Blondin could not recognise him again, for the light had been turned down and she was partially blind; and he was certain that the station agent would not know his face again either — but both could, and would, supply a general description of his dress, appearance and build that would serve equally as well to apprehend him in that thinly populated country where, under such circumstances, to be even a stranger was sufficient to invite suspicion.

Well, if to run for it was his only chance, he would take it! He stooped for his bag, and, in the act, stood suddenly motionless in a rigid sort of way. No! There was perhaps another plan! It seemed to Raymond that he held his breath in suspense until his brain should pass judgment upon it. The priest! The dead priest, only a little way off out there on the road! No — it was not visionary, nor wild, nor mad. If they *found* the man that they supposed had murdered the old woman's son, they would not search any further. That was absurdly obvious! The priest was not expected until to-morrow. The only person who knew that the priest had arrived, and who knew of his, Raymond's, arrival, was the station agent. But the quarry once run to earth, there would be no reason for anybody, as might otherwise be the case in a far-flung pursuit, going to the station on a night like this. The priest's arrival therefore would not become known to the villagers until the next morning at the earliest, and quite probably not until much later, when some one from the village should drive over to meet the train by which he was expected to arrive. As a minimum, therefore, that gave him ten or twelve hours' start — and with ten or twelve hours free from pursuit, he could take very good care of the "afterwards"! Yes, it was the way! The only way! From what the priest had said in the train, it was evident that he was a total stranger here, and so, being unknown, the deception would not be discovered until the station agent told his story. Furthermore, the wound in the priest's head from the falling limb of the tree would be attributed to the blow the old hag had struck *him* on the head with the cordwood! The inference, plausible enough, would be that he had run from the house wounded, only to drop at last to the ground on the spot where the priest, *dressed as the murderer*, was found! And besides — yes — there was other evidence he could add! The revolver, for instance!

Quick now, his mind made up, Raymond snatched the flashlight from his pocket, swept the ray around the floor, located the weapon, and, running to it, picked it up and put it in his pocket.

Every second was counting now. It might be five, or ten, or fifteen minutes before they got back from the village, he did not know—but every moment was priceless. There was still work to be done out there on the road, even after he was through here!

He was across the room now by the rear wall, gathering up the coins and bills that the dead man had scattered on the floor. These, like the revolver, he transferred to his pocket. A thief, had been their cry. That was the motive! Well, he would corroborate it! There would be no mistake—until to-morrow—about their having found the guilty man!

His hand was a slimmer hand than Blondin's—it slipped easily into the chink between the timbers. It was like a hollow bowl inside, and there was more money there. He scooped it out. Twice his hand went in again, until the hiding place was empty; and then, running back across the room, he grabbed up his bag, and rushed from the house.

An instant he paused to listen as he reached the road; but there was only the howl of the storm, no sound that he could hear as yet from the direction of the village—though, full of ominous possibilities, he did not know how far away the village was!

He ran on again at top speed, flashing his way along with his light, the wind at his back aiding him now. It would not matter if a stray gleam were seen by any one, if he could only complete his work in time—it would only be proof, instead of inference, that the murderer had run from the house along the road to the spot where he was found.

He reached the priest, set down his bag, and, taking up the broken limb of the tree, carried it ten yards away around the turn of the road, and flung it in amongst the trees; then he was back once more, and bending over the priest. He worked swiftly now, but coolly and with grim composure, removing the priest's outer garments. He noted with intense relief that there was no blood on the clerical collar—that the blood, due to the twisted position of the other's head, had trickled from the cheek directly to the ground. It would have been an awkward thing—blood on the collar!

It was not easy work. The limp form seemed a ton-weight in his arms, as he lifted it now this way, now that, to get off the other's clothes. And at times he recoiled from it, though the stake he was playing for was his life. It was unnerving business, and the hideous moaning of the wind made it worse. And mostly he must work by the sense of touch, for he could not hold the flashlight and still use both hands. But it was done at last, and now he took off his own clothes, and hastily donned the priest's.

He must be careful now—a single slip, something overlooked in his pockets perhaps might ruin everything, and the ten or twelve hours' start, that was all he asked for, would be lost; but, equally, the pockets must not be too bare! He was hurriedly going through his discarded garments now. Mother Blondin's money and the revolver, of course, must be found there.

The cardcase, yes, that could not do any harm... there were no letters, no one ever wrote to him... the trifling odds and ends must be left in the pockets too, they lent colour if nothing else... but his own money was quite a different matter, and he had the big sum in bills of large denominations with him that he had exchanged for the pokes of gold dust which he had brought from the Yukon. He tucked this money securely away under the *soutane* he was now wearing, and once more bent over the priest.

He had now to dress the priest in his, Raymond's, clothes. It was not readily accomplished; it was even more difficult than it had been to undress the man; and besides, as he worked now, he found himself fighting to maintain his coolness against a sort of reckless haste to have done with it that was creeping upon him. It seemed that he had been hours at the work, that with every second now the villagers in full cry must come upon him. Curse it, could he never button that collar and knot that tie! Why did the man's head wobble like that! The vest now! Now the coat!

He stood up finally at the end, and flirted his hand across his brow. His forehead was clammy wet. He shivered a little; then, lips tight, he pulled himself together. He must make certain, absolutely certain that he had done nothing, or left nothing undone to rob him of those few precious hours that were so necessary to his escape.

He nodded after a moment in a kind of ghastly approval—he had even hung the other's crucifix around his neck! There remained only the exchange of hats, and—yes, the bag—was there anything in the bag that would betray him? He dropped his own hat on the ground a yard away from the priest's head where the other's hat had rolled, picked up the priest's hat, and put it on—then bent down over the bag.

He lifted his head suddenly, straining his ears to listen. What was that! Only the howl and unearthly moaning of the wind? It must have been, and his nerves were becoming over-strung, for the wind was blowing from the direction of the village, and it seemed as though the sound he had thought he heard, that he could not have defined, had come from the other direction. But the bag! Was there anything in it that he should not leave? He turned the flashlight into its interior, began to rummage through its contents—and then, kneeling there, it was as though he were suddenly frozen into that posture, bereft of all power of movement.

It was only a lantern—but it seemed as though he were bathed in a blistering flood of light that poured full upon him, that burst suddenly, without warning, from around the turn of the road in the direction away from the village. He felt the colour ebb from his face; he knew a sickly consciousness of doom. He was caught—caught in the priest's clothes! Shadowy outlined there, was a horse and wagon. A woman, carrying the lantern, was running toward him—a man followed behind. The wind rose in demoniacal derision—the damnable wind that, responsible for everything that night, had brought this crowning disaster upon him!

A girl's voice rang out anxiously:

"What is it? Oh, what is it? What has happened?" Raymond felt himself grow unnaturally calm. He leaned solicitously over the priest's form.

"I do not know"—he was speaking with sober concern. "I found this man lying here as I came along. He has a wound of some sort in his head, and I am afraid that he is dead."

The man, stepping forward, crossed himself hurriedly.

The girl, with a sharp little cry, knelt down on the other side of the priest—and in the lantern's glimmer Raymond caught a glimpse of great dark eyes, of truant hair, wind-tossed, that blew about a young, sweet face that was full now of troubled sympathy.

"And you," she said quickly; "you are the new curé, monsieur. The station agent told us you had come, and we drove fast, my uncle and I, to try and catch up with you."

Raymond's eyes were on the priest's form. There was no need to simulate concern now, it was genuine enough, and it was as if something cold and icy were closing around his heart. He was not sure—great God, it was not possible!—but he thought—he thought the priest had moved. If that were so, he was doubly trapped! Cries came suddenly from the direction of the village, from the direction of old Mother Blondin's house. He heard himself acknowledging her remark with grave deliberation.

"Yes," he said, "I am Father Aubert."

CHAPTER VI—THE JAWS OF THE TRAP

VOLEUR! Thief! Murder! Murder!" — it rose a high, piercing shriek, and the wind seemed to catch up the words and eddy them around, and toss them hither and thither until the storm and the night and the woods were full of ghouls chanting and screaming and gibbering their hideous melody: "*Voleur!* Thief! Murder! Murder!"

The girl, from the other side of the prostrate priest, rose in quick alarm to her feet, and lifted the lantern high above her head to peer down the road.

"Listen!" she cried. "What does it mean? See the lights there! Listen!"

The lantern lifted now, Raymond could no longer see the priest's face. He slipped his hand in desperately under the man's vest. He had felt there once before for the heart beat when he had first stumbled upon the other. In God's name, where was his nerve! He needed it now more than he had ever needed it in all his dare-devil career before. He had *thought* the priest had moved. If the man were alive, he, Raymond, was not only in a thousandfold worse case than if he had run for it and taken his chances — he had forfeited whatever chance there might have been. The mere fact that he had attempted to disguise himself, to assume the priest's garments as a means of escape, damned him utterly, irrevocably upon the spot. His hand pressed hard against the other's body. Yes, there was life there, a faint fluttering of the heart. No — no, it was only himself — a tremor in his own fingers. And then a miserable sense of disaster fell upon him. The wind howled, those shrieks still rang out, there came hoarse shouts and the pound of running feet, but above it all, distinct, like a knell of doom, came a low moan from the priest upon the ground.

Sharply, as though it were being suddenly seared and burned, Raymond snatched away his hand; and his hand struck against something hard, and mechanically he gripped at it. The man was *alive!* The glare of lanterns, many of them, flashed from the turn of the road. The village was upon the scene. The impulse seized him to run. There was the horse and wagon standing there. His lips tightened. Madness! That would be but the act of a fool! It was his wits, his brain, his nerve that was his only hope now — that cool, callous nerve that had never failed him in a crisis before.

A form, unkempt, with gray, streaming, dishevelled hair, rushed upon him and the priest, and thrust a lantern into the faces of them both. It was the old hag, old Mother Blondin.

"Here he is! Here he is!" she screamed. "It is he!" —her voice kept rising until, in a torrent of blasphemous invective, it attained an ear-splitting falsetto.

It seemed to Raymond that a hundred voices were all talking at once; that the villagers now, as they closed in and clustered around him, were as a multitude in their numbers; and there was light now, a blaze of it, from a host of accursed lanterns jiggling up and down, each striving to thrust itself a little further forward than its fellow. And then upon Raymond settled a sort of grim, cold, ironical composure. The stakes were very high.

"If you want your life, play for it!" urged a voice within him.

The old hag, in an abandoned paroxysm of grief, rage and fury, was cursing, and shaking her lantern and her doubled fist at the priest; and, not content with that, she now began to kick viciously at the unconscious form.

Raymond rose from his knees, and laid one hand quietly upon her arm.

"Peace, my daughter!" he said softly. "You are in the presence of Holy Church, and in the presence perhaps of death."

She whirled upon him, her wrinkled old face, if possible, contorted more furiously than before.

"Holy Church!" she raved. "Holy Church! Ha, ha! What have I to do with Holy Church that kicked me from its doors! Will Holy Church give me back my son? And what have you to do with this, you smooth-faced hypocrite! It is the law I want, not you to stand there and mumble while you smugly paw your crucifix!"

It came quick and sharp—an angry sibilant murmur from the crowd, a threatening forward movement. Mechanically, Raymond's fingers fell away from the crucifix. It was the crucifix, dangling from his neck, that he had unconsciously grasped as he had snatched away his hand from the priest's body—and it was the crucifix that, equally unconscious of it, he had been grasping ever since. Strange that in his agitation he should have grasped at a crucifix! Strange that the act and his unconscious poise, as he held the crucifix, should have lent verisimilitude to the part he played, the rôle in which he sought sanctuary from death!

His hand raised again. The murmuring ceased; the threatening stir was instantly checked. And then Raymond took the old woman by the shoulders, and with kindly force placed her in the arms of the two nearest men.

"She does not know what she is saying," he said gently. "The poor woman is distraught. Take her home. I do not understand, but she speaks of her son being given back to her, and — —"

"It is a murder, *mon père*," broke in one of the men excitedly. "She came running to the village a few minutes ago to tell us that her son had been killed. It is this man here in the road who did it. She recognises him, you see. There is the wound in his head, and she said she struck him there with a piece of wood while he was struggling with her son."

The old woman was in hysteria now, alternately sobbing and laughing, but no longer struggling.

"Murdered! Her son—murdered!" Raymond gasped in a startled way. "Ah, then, be very good to her! It is no wonder that she is beside herself."

They led her laughing and crying away.

"The law! The law! I demand the law on him!"—her voice, now guttural, now shrill, quavering, virulent, out of control, floated back. "*Sacré nom de Dieu*, a life for a life, he is the murderer of my son!"

And now, save for the howling of the storm, a silence fell upon the scene. Raymond glanced quickly about him. What was it now, what was it—ah, he understood! They were waiting for *him*. As though it were the most obvious thing in the world to do, as though no one would dream of doing anything else, the villagers, collectively and singly, laid the burden of initiative upon his clerically garbed shoulders. Raymond dropped upon his knees again beside the priest, pretending to make a further examination of the other's wound. He could gain a moment or two that way, a moment in which to think. The man, though still unconscious, was moaning constantly now. At any moment the priest might regain his senses. One thing was crucial, vital— in some way he must manouvre so that the other should not be removed from his own immediate surveillance until he could find some loophole of escape. Once the man began to talk, unless he, Raymond, were beside the other to stop the man's mouth, or at least to act as interpreter for the other's ramblings—the man was sure to ramble at first, or at least people could be made to believe so—he, Raymond, would be cornered like a rat in a trap, and, more to be feared even than the law, the villagers, in their fury at the sacrilege they would consider he had put upon them in the desecration of their priest, would show him scant ceremony and little mercy.

He was cool enough now, quite cool—with the grim coolness of a man who realises that his life depends upon his keeping his head. Still he bent over the priest. He heard a girl's voice speaking rapidly—that would be the girl with the great dark eyes who had come upon him with the lantern, for there was no other woman here now since he had got rid temporarily of that damnable old hag.

"... It is Father Aubert, the new curé. Labbée, at the station, told us he had arrived unexpectedly. We have brought his trunk that he was going to send for in the morning, and we drove fast hoping to catch up with him so that he would not have to walk all the way. We found him here kneeling beside that man there, that he had stumbled over as he came along. Labbée told us, too, of the other. He said the man seemed anxious to avoid Monsieur le Curé, and hung around the station until Father Aubert had got well started toward St. Marleau. He must have taken the path to the tavern, or he would not have been here ahead of Monsieur le Curé, and — — "

Raymond reached into the open travelling bag on the ground beside him, took out the first article coming to hand that would at all serve the purpose, a shirt, and, tearing it, made pretense at binding up the priest's head.

"My thanks to you, mademoiselle!" he muttered soberly under his breath. "If it were not for the existence of that path — — !" He shrugged his shoulders, and, his head lowered, a twisted smile flickered upon his lips.

The girl had ceased speaking. They were all clustered around him, watching him. Short exclamations, bearing little evidence of good will toward the unconscious man, came from first one and then another.

"... *Meurtrier!*... He will hang in any case! ... The better for him if he dies there!... What does it matter, the blackguard!..."

Raymond rose to his feet.

"No," he said reprovingly. "It is not for us to think in that way. For us, there is only a very badly wounded man here who needs our help and care. We will give that first, and leave the rest in the hands of those who have the right to judge him if he lives. See now, some of you lift him as carefully as possible into the wagon. I will hold his head on my lap, and we will get to the village as quickly as we can."

It was a strange procession then that began to wend its way toward the village of St. Marleau. The wagon proved to be a sort of buckboard, and Raymond, clambering upon it, sitting with his back propped against the seat, held the priest's head upon his knees. Upon the seat itself the girl and her uncle resumed their places. With the unconscious man stretched out at full length there was no room for the trunk; but, eager to be of service to their new curé, so kind and gentle and tender to even a criminal for whom the law held nothing in reserve but the gallows and a rope, who was tolerant even of Mother Blondin in her blasphemies, the villagers quarrelled amongst themselves for the privilege of carrying it.

They moved slowly — that the wounded man might not be too severely jarred. Constantly the numbers around the wagon were augmented. Women began to appear amongst them. The entire village was aroused. St. Marleau in all its history had known no such excitement before. A murder in St. Marleau —

and the murderer caught, and dying they said, was being brought back to the village in the arms of the young curé, who had, a cause even for added excitement, arrived that evening instead of to-morrow as had been expected. Tongues clacked and wagged. It was like a furious humming accompaniment to the howling of the wind. But out of respect to the curé who held the dying man on his knees, they did not press too closely about the wagon.

They passed the "tavern," which was lighted now in every window, and some left the wagon at this point and went to the "tavern," and others who had collected at the "tavern" joined the wagon. They began to descend the hill. And now along the road below, to right and left, lights twinkled from every house. They met people coming up the hill. There were even children now.

Head bent over the priest, that twisted smile was back on Raymond's lips. The man moaned at intervals, but showed no further sign of returning consciousness. Would the other live—or die? Raymond's hands, hidden under the priest's head, were clenched. It was a question of his own life or the other's now—wasn't it? What hell-inspired ingenuity had flung him into this hideous maze in which at every twist and turn, as he sought some avenue of escape, he but found, instead, the way barred against him, his retreat cut off, and peril, like some soulless, immutable thing, closing irrevocably down upon him! He dared not leave the priest; he dared not surrender the other for an instant—lest consciousness should return. *But if the man died!*

Raymond's face, as a ghastly temptation came, was as white as the upturned face between his knees. If the man died it would be simple enough. For a few days, for whatever time was necessary, he could play the rôle of priest, and then in some way—his brain was not searching out details now, there was only the sure confidence in himself that he would be equal to the occasion if only the chance were his—then in some way, without attendant hue and cry, without the police of every city in America loosed upon him, since the "murderer" of the old hag's son would be dead, he could disappear from St. Marleau. But the man was not dead—yet. And why should he even think the man would die! Because he *hoped* for it? His lips twitched; and his hands, with a slow, curious movement, unclenched, and clenched again—and then with a sort of mental wrench, his brain, alert and keen, was coping with the immediate situation, the immediate danger.

The girl and her uncle were talking earnestly together on the seat. And now, for all that he had not thrust himself forward in what had so far transpired, the man appeared to be of some standing and authority in the neighbourhood, for, turning from the girl, he called sharply to one of the crowd. A villager hurried in response to the side of the wagon, and Raymond, listening, caught snatches of the terse, low-toned instructions that were given.

The doctor at Tournayville, and at the same time the police... yes—to-night... at once....

"*Bien sur!*" said the villager briskly, and disappeared in the crowd.

Then the girl spoke. Raymond could not hear very distinctly, but it was something about her mother being unprepared, and from that about a room downstairs, and he guessed that they were discussing where they would take the wounded man.

He straightened up suddenly. That was a subject which concerned him very intimately. There was only one place where the priest could go, and that was where he, Raymond, went. They were on the village street now, and, twisting his head around to look ahead, he could make out the shadowy form of the church steeple close at hand.

"Monsieur," he called quietly to the man on the seat, "we will take this poor fellow to the *presbytère*, of course."

"Oh, but, Father Aubert"—the girl turned toward him quickly—"we were just speaking of that. It would not be at all comfortable for you. You see, even your own room there will not be ready for you, since you were not expected to-night, and you will have to take Father Allard's, so that if this man went there, too, there would be no bed at all for you."

"I hardly think I shall need any bed to-night, mademoiselle," Raymond said gravely. "The man appears to be in a very critical condition. I know a little something of medicine, and I could not think of leaving him until—I think I heard your uncle say they were going to Tournayville for a doctor—until the doctor arrives."

"Yes, Monsieur le Curé," said the man, screwing around in his seat, "that is so. I have sent for the doctor, and also for the police—but it is eight miles to Tournayville, and on a night like this there will be a long while to wait, even if the doctor is to be found at once."

"You have done well, monsieur," commended Raymond—but under his breath, with a savage, ironical jeer at himself, he added: "And especially about the police, curse you!"

"But, Monsieur le Curé," insisted the girl anxiously, "I am sure that— —"

"Mademoiselle is very kind, and it is very thoughtful of her," Raymond interposed gratefully; "but under the circumstances I think the *presbytère* will be best. Yes; I think we must decide on the *presbytère*.

"But, yes, certainly—if that is Monsieur le Curé's wish," agreed the man. "Monsieur le Curé should know best. Valérie, jump down, and run on ahead to tell your mother that we are coming."

Valérie! So that was the girl's name! It seemed a strangely incongruous thought that here, with his back against the wall, literally fighting for his life, the name should seem somehow to be so appropriate to that dark-eyed face, with its truant, wind-tossed hair, that had come upon him so suddenly out of the darkness; that face, sweet, troubled, in distress, that he had glimpsed for an instant in the lantern's light. Valérie! But what was her other name? What had her mother to do with the *presbytère*, that the uncle should have sent her on with that message? And who was the uncle, this man here, and what was his name? And how much of all this was he, as Father Aubert, supposed already to know? The curé of the village, Father Allard—what correspondence, for instance, had passed between him and Father Aubert? A hundred questions were on his lips. He dared not ask a single one. They had turned in off the road now and were passing by the front of the church. He lowered his head close down to the priest's. The man still moaned in that same low and, as it were, purely mechanical way. Some one in the crowd spoke:

"They are taking him to the *presbytère*."

At the rear of the wagon, amongst the bobbing lanterns, surrounded by awe-struck children and no less awe-struck women, he saw the trunk being trundled along by two men, each grasping one end by the handle. The crowd took up its spokesman's lead.

... To the *presbytère*.... They are going to the *presbytère*.... The curé is taking him to the *presbytère*...

"Yes, damn you!" gritted Raymond between his teeth. "To the *presbytère*— for the devil's masquerade!"

CHAPTER VII—AT THE PRESBYTÈRE

IT was Valerie who held the lamp; and beside her in the doorway stood a gentle-faced, silverhaired, slim little old lady—and the latter was another Valerie, only a Valerie whom the years in their passing had touched in a gentle, kindly way, as though the whitening hair and the age creeping upon her were but a crowning. And Raymond, turning to mount the stoop of the *presbytère*, as some of the villagers lifted the wounded priest from the wagon, drew his breath in sharply, and for an instant faltered in his step. It was as though, framed there in the doorway, those two forms of the women, those two faces that seemed to radiate an innate sanctity, were like guardian angels to bar the way against a hideous and sacrilegious invasion of some holy thing within. And Valerie's eyes, those great, deep, dark eyes burned into him. And her face, that he saw now for the first time plainly, was very beautiful, and with a beauty that was not of feature alone—for her expression seemed to write a sort of creed upon her face, a creed that frankly mirrored faith in all around her, a faith that, never having been startled, or dismayed, or disillusioned, and knowing no things for evil, accepted all things for good.

And Raymond's step faltered. It seemed as though he had never seen a woman's face like that—that it was holding him now in a thrall that robbed his surroundings momentarily of their danger and their peril.

And then, the next instant, that voice within him was speaking again.

"You fool!" it whispered fiercely. "What are you doing! If you want your life, play for it! Look around you! A false move, a rational word from the lips of that limp thing they are carrying there behind you, and these people, who believe where you mock, who would kneel if you but lifted your hand in sign of benediction, would turn upon you with the merciless fury of wild beasts! You fool! You fool! Do you like the feel of hemp, as it tightens around your neck!"

And then Raymond lifted his head, and his eyes, and with measured pace walked forward up the steps to where the two women stood.

Valérie's introduction was only another warning to him to be upon his guard—she seemed to imply that he naturally knew her mother's name.

"Father Aubert, this is my mother," she said.

With a sort of old-world grace, the elder woman bowed.

"Ah, Monsieur le Curé," she said quickly, "what a terrible thing to have happened! Valérie has just told me. And what a welcome to the parish for you! Not even a room, with that *pauvre* unfortunate, *misérable* and murderer though he is, and — —"

"But it is a welcome of the heart, I can see that," Raymond interposed, and smiled gravely, and took both of the old lady's hands in his own. "And that is worth far more than the room, which, in any case, I shall hardly need to-night. It is you, not I, who should have cause to grumble, for, to my own unexpected arrival, I bring you the added trouble and inconvenience of this very badly wounded and, I fear, dying man."

"But—that!" she exclaimed simply. "But Monsieur le Curé would never have thought of doing otherwise! Valérie meant only kindness, but she should not have made any other suggestion. It is for nothing else, if not this, the *presbytère! Le pauvre misérable*" —she crossed herself reverently—"even if he has blood that thought of doing otherwise! Valérie meant only kindness, but she should not have made any other suggestion. It is for nothing else, if not this, the *presbytère! Le pauvre misérable*" —she crossed herself reverently— "even if he has blood that is not his own upon him."

They were coming up the steps, carrying the wounded priest.

"This way!" said the little old lady softly. "Valérie, dear, hold your lamp so that they can see. Ah, *le pauvre misérable*; ah, Monsieur le Curé!"

The girl leading, they passed down a short hallway, entered a bedroom at the rear of the house, and Valérie set the lamp upon the table.

Raymond motioned to the men to lay the priest upon the bed. He glanced quietly about him, as he moved to the priest's side. He must get these people away—there were reasons why he should be alone. Alone! His brain was like some horrible, swirling vortex. Why alone? For what reasons? Not that hellish purpose that had flashed so insidiously upon him out there on the ride down to the *presbytère!* Not that! Strange how outwardly calm, how deadly calm, how composed and self-possessed he was, when such a thought had even for an instant's space found lodgment in his soul. It was well that he was calm, he would need to be calm—he was doing what that inner monitor had told him to do—he was playing the game—he was playing for his life. Well, he had only to dismiss these men now, who hung so curiously awe-struck about the bed, and then get rid of the women—no, they had gone now; Valérie, with her beautiful face, and those great dark eyes; and the mother, whose gray hair did not seem to bring age with it at all, and—no, they were back again—no, they were not—those were not women's steps entering the room.

He had been making pretence at loosening the priest's collar, and he looked up now. The trunk! He had forgotten all about the trunk. The newcomers were two men carrying the trunk. They set it down against the wall near the door. It was a little more than probable that they had seized the opportunity afforded by the trunk to see what was going on in the room. They would be favoured amongst their fellows without! They, too, hats in hand, stared, curious and awe-struck, toward the bed.

"Thank you, all of you," Raymond heard himself saying in a low tone. "But go now, my friends, go quietly; madame and her daughter will give me any further assistance that may be needed."

They filed obediently from the room—on tiptoe—their coarse, heavy boots squeaking the more loudly therefor. Raymond's hands sought the priest's collar again, to loosen it this time with a definite object in view. He had changed only his outer garments with the other. He dared not have the priest undressed until he had made sure that there were no tell-tale marks on the underclothing; a laundry number, perhaps, that the police would pounce instantly upon. He found himself experiencing a sort of facetious soul-grin—detectives always laid great stress upon laundry marks!

Again he was interrupted. With the collar in his hand, his own collar, that he had removed now from the priest's neck, he turned to see Valérie and her mother entering the room. They were very capable, those two—too capable! They were carrying basins of water, and cloths that were obviously intended for bandages. He had not meant to use any bandages, he had meant to—what?

He forced a grave smile of approval to his lips, and nodded his head.

The elder woman glanced about her a little in surprise.

"Oh, are the men gone!" she exclaimed. "*Tiens!* The stupids! But I will call one of them back, and he will help you undress *le pauvre*, Father Aubert."

It was only an instant before Raymond answered; but it seemed, before he did so, that he had been listening in a kind of panic for long minutes dragged out interminably to that inner voice that kept telling him to play the game, play the game, and that only fools lost their heads at insignificant little unexpected denouements. She was only suggesting that the man should be undressed; whereas the man must under no circumstances be undressed until—until— —

"I think perhaps we had better not attempt it in his condition until the doctor arrives, madame," he said slowly, thoughtfully, as though his words were weighted with deliberation. "It might do far more harm than good. For the present, I think it would be better simply to loosen his clothing, and make him as comfortable as possible in that way."

"Yes; I think so, too," said Valérie—she had moved a little table to the bedside, and was arranging the basins of water and the cloths upon it.

"Of course!" agreed the little old lady simply. "Monsieur le Curé knows best."

"Yes," said Valérie, speaking in hushed tones, as she cast an anxious look at the white, blood-stained face upon the bed, "and I think it is a mercy that Father Aubert knows something about medicine, for otherwise the doctor might be too late. I will help you, Monsieur le Curé—everything is ready."

He knew nothing about medicine—there was nothing he knew less about! What fiend had prompted him to make such a claim!

"I am afraid, mademoiselle," he said soberly, "that my knowledge is far too inadequate for such a case as this."

"We will be able to do something at least, father"—there was a brave, troubled smile in her eyes as she lifted them for an instant to his; and then, bending forward, with deft fingers she removed the torn piece of shirt from the wounded man's head.

And then, between them, while the mother watched and wrung out the cloths, they dressed the wound, a ghastly, unsightly thing across the side of the man's skull—only it was Valerie, not he, who was efficient. And strangely, as once before, but a little while before, when out there in front of the house, it was Valerie, and not the man, and not the wound, and not the peril in which he stood that was dominant, swaying him for the moment. There was a wondrous tenderness in her hands as she worked with the bandages, and sometimes her hands touched his; and sometimes, close together, as they leaned over the bed together, her hair, dark, luxuriant, brushed his cheek; and the low-collared blouse disclosed a bare and perfect throat that was white like ivory; and the half parted lips were tender like the touch of her fingers; and in her face at sight of the gruesome wound, bringing an added whiteness, was dismay, and struggling with dismay was a wistful earnestness and resolution that was born of her woman's sympathy; and she seemed to steal upon and pervade his senses as though she were some dream-created vision, for she was not reality at all since his subconsciousness told him that in actual reality no one existed at all except that moaning thing upon the bed—that moaning thing upon the bed and himself—himself, who seemed to be swinging by a precarious hold, from which even then his fingers were slipping away, over some bottomless abyss that yawned below him. "Valérie! Valérie!" He was repeating her name to himself, as though calling to her for aid from the edge of that black gulf, and— —

"Fool!" jeered that inner voice. "Have you never seen a pretty girl before? She'd be the first to turn upon you, if she knew!"

"You lie!" retorted another self.

"Where's Three-Ace Artie gone?" inquired the voice with cold contempt.

Raymond straightened up. Valérie, turning from the bed, gathered the basins and soiled cloths together, and moved quietly from the room.

"Will he live, father?"—it was the little gray-haired woman, Valérie's mother, Valérie's older self, who was looking up into his face so anxiously, whose lips quivered a little as she spoke.

Would the man *live!* A devil's laugh seemed suddenly to possess Raymond's soul. They would be alone together, that gasping, white-faced thing on the bed, and himself; they would be alone together before the doctor came—he would see to that. There had been interruption, confusion... his brain itself was confusion... extraneous thoughts had intervened... but they would be *alone* presently. And—great God!—what hellish mockery!—she asked *him* if this man would *live!*

"I am afraid"—he was not looking at her; his hand, clutching at the skirt of the *soutane* he wore, closed and tightened and clenched—"I am afraid he will not live."

"Ah, *le pauvre!*" she whispered, and her eyes filled with tears. "Ah, Monsieur le Curé, I do not know these things so well as you. It is true that he is a very guilty man, but is not God very good and tender and full of compassion, father? Oh, I should not dare to say these things, for it is you who know what is right and best"—she had caught his sleeve, and was leading him across the room. "And Mother Church, Monsieur le Curé, is very merciful and very tender and very compassionate too—and, oh—and, oh— can there not be mercy and love even for such as he—must he lose his soul too, as well as his life?"

Raymond, in a blind, wondering way, stared at her. The tears were streaming down her cheeks now. They had halted before a low, old-fashioned cupboard, an *armoire* much like the *armoire* in the old hag's house, and now she opened the doors in the lower portion, and took out a worn and rusty black leather bag, and set it upon the top of the *armoire*.

"It is only to show you where it is, father, if—if it might be so—even for him—the Sacrament"—and, turning, she crossed the room, and meeting Valérie upon the threshold drew the girl away with her, and closed the door softly.

It was a bag such as the parish priests carried with them on their visits to the sick and dying. Raymond eyed it sullenly. The Sacrament!

"What have I to do with that!" he snarled beneath his breath.

"Are you not a priest of God?"

He whirled like a flash, startled, sweeping his glances around the room. And then he laughed in smothered, savage relief. It was only that voice within that chose a cursed mockery this time to put him upon his guard.

He was staring now at the sprawled form on the bed, at a red stain that was already creeping through the fresh bandages. His face grew hard and set; a flush came and died away, leaving it an ashen gray.

And then he stepped to the door—and listened—and locked it.

CHAPTER VIII—THOU SHALT NOT KILL

IT seemed as though the stillness of death were already in the room; a stillness that was horrible and unnerving in contrast with the shrill swirling of the wind without, and the loud roar and pound of the waves breaking upon the shore close at hand beneath the windows.

His face still set as in a rigid mould, features drawn in hard, sharp lines, then ashen gray now even upon the lips, Raymond crossed from the door to the nearer of the two windows. It was black outside, inky black, unnaturally black, relieved only by a wavering, irregular line of white where the waves broke into foam along the rocky beach—and this line, as it wavered, and wriggled, and advanced, and receded seemed to lend an uncanny ghostlike aspect to the blackness, and, as he strained his eyes out of the window, he shuddered suddenly and drew back. But the next instant he snarled fiercely to himself. Was he to lose his nerve because it was black outside, and because the waves were running high and creaming along the shore! He would have something shortly that would warrant him in losing his nerve if he faltered now—the hemp around his neck, rasping, chafing at his throat, the horrible prickling as the rough strands grew taut!

He clutched at his throat mechanically, rubbing it with his fingers mechanically—and, as fiercely as before, snarled again. Enough of this! He was neither fool nor child. There was a sure way out from that dangling noose, cornered, trapped though he was—and he knew the way now. He reached up and drew down the window shade, and passed quickly to the other window and drew down the shade there as well.

And then he turned, and stepped to the bed, and bent over the priest.

There was the underclothing first. He must make sure of that—that there would be no marks of identification—that there would be nothing to rise up against him, a mute and mocking witness to his undoing. He loosened the man's clothing. It would not be necessary to take off the outer garments. It was much easier here with the man on a bed, and a light in the room than it had been out there on the road, and—ah! Lips compressed, he nodded sharply to himself. The undergarments were new. That precluded laundry marks— unless the man had had some marking put upon them himself. No, there was nothing—nothing but the maker's tag sewn in on the shirt at the back of the neck. He turned the priest over on the bed to complete his examination. There was nothing on any other part of the garments. The socks, then, perhaps? He pulled up the trousers' legs hurriedly. No, there was nothing there, either. He reached out to turn the priest over again—and paused. He could snip that maker's tag from the neck of the shirt just as easily in the position in which the man now lay, and—and the man's face would not be staring up at him. There was a cursed, senseless accusation in that white face, and the lip muscles twitched as though the man were about to shout aloud, to scream out—murder! If only the fool had died out there in the woods, and would stop that infernal low moaning noise, and those strangling inhalations as he gasped for breath!

Automatically, Raymond's fingers sought his penknife in its accustomed place in his vest pocket—and slipped down a smooth, unobstructed surface. His eyes followed his fingers in a sort of dazed, perplexed way, and then he laughed a little huskily. The *soutane!* He had forgotten for the moment that he was a priest of God! It was the other who wore the vest, it was in the other's pocket that the knife was to be found. He had forgotten the devil's masquerade in the devil's whispering that was in his soul!

He snatched the knife from the vest pocket, opened it, cut away the cloth tag, and with infinite pains removed the threads that had held the tag in place. He returned the knife to the vest pocket, and tucked the little tag away in one of his own pockets; then hastily rearranged the other's clothing again, and turned the man back into his original position upon the bed.

And now! He glanced furtively all around the room. His hands crept out, and advanced toward the priest. It was a very easy thing to do. No one would know. No one but would think the man had died naturally. *Died!* It was the first time he had allowed his mind to frame a concrete expression that would fit the black thing that was in his soul.

A bead of sweat spurted out from his forehead. His hands somehow would not travel very fast, but they were all the time creeping nearer to the priest's throat. He had only to keep on forcing them on their way... and it was not very far to go... and, once there, it would only take an instant. God, if that white face would not stare up at him like that... the eyes were closed of course... but still it stared.

Raymond touched his lips with the tip of his tongue, and again and again circled the room with his eyes. Was that somebody there outside the window? Was that a step out there in the passageway? Were those *voices* that chattered and gibbered from everywhere?

He jerked back his hands, and they fell to his sides, and he shivered. What was it? What was the matter? What was it that he had to do? It wasn't murder. That was a lie! The man wouldn't live anyhow, but he might live long enough to talk. It was his life or the other's, wasn't it? If he were caught now, there was no power on earth could save him. On earth? What did he mean by that? What other power was there? It was only a trite phrase he had used.

What was he hesitating about? It was the only chance he had.

"Get it done! Get it done, and over with, you squeamish fool!" prodded that inner voice savagely.

His hands crept out again. Of course! Of course! He knew that. He must get it done and over with. Only—only, great God, why did his hands tremble so! He lifted one of them to his forehead and drew it away dripping wet. What did that voice want to keep nagging him for! He knew what he had to do. It was the only way. If the priest were dead, he, Raymond, would be safe. There would be no question as to who the murderer of Blondin was—and the priest would be buried and that would be the end of it. And—yes! He had it all now. It was almost too simple! He, Raymond, as the curé of the village, after a day or two, would meet with an accident. A boating accident—yes, that was it! They would find an upturned boat and his hat floating on the water perhaps—but they would never find the body! He need only, in the interval of those few days, gather together from somewhere some clothes into which he could change, hide in the woods after the "accident," and at night make his final escape.

"Of course!" snapped the voice impatiently. "I've been telling you that all along! There would be no further investigation as to the murder; and only a sorrowful search along the shore, free from all suspicion, for the body of Father Aubert. Well, why don't you act? Are you going to fling your life away? Are you afraid? Have you forgotten that it is growing late, that very soon now the doctor and the police will be here?"

Afraid! No; he wasn't afraid of God or devil, or man or beast—that was his creed, wasn't it? Only that damnable face still stared up at him, and he couldn't get his hands near enough to—to do the work.

Slowly, inch by inch, his face as white and set as chiselled marble, his hands crept forward again. How soft the bare, exposed throat looked that was almost at his finger tips now. Would it *feel* soft to the touch, or—he swayed unsteadily, and crouched back, that cold shiver passing over him. It was strange that he should shiver, that he should find it cold. His brain was afire, and it whirled, and whirled, and whirled; and devils laughed in his soul— and yet he stood aghast at the abhorrent deed.

Wait! He would be able to think clearly in an instant. He must do it—or die himself. Yes, yes; it was the *touch* of his flesh against the other's flesh from which he shrank, the *feel* of his fingers on the other's throat that held him back—that was it! Wait! He would remedy that. That would have been a crude, mad way in any case. What had he been thinking of! It would have left a mark. It would have been sure to have left a mark. Perhaps they would not have noticed it, but it would have invited the risk. There was a better way, a much better way—and a way in which that face wouldn't be able to stare up at him any more, a way in which he wouldn't hear that moaning, and that rattling, and that struggling for breath. The man was almost dead now. It was only necessary to take that other pillow there, and hold it tightly over the other's face. *That* wouldn't leave any mark. Yes, the pillow! Why hadn't he thought of that before! It would have been all over by now.

Once more his hands began to creep up and outward. He leaned far over the bed, reaching for the pillow—and something came between the pillow and his hands. He glanced downward in a startled way. It was the crucifix hanging from his neck. With a snarl, he swung it away. It came back and struck against his knuckles. He tried to wrench it from his neck. It would not come—but, instead, one hand slipped through the chain, and pushed the crucifix outward, and for an instant held it there between him and that white, staring face. He pulled his hand away. And the crucifix swung backward and forward. And he reached again for the pillow, and the crucifix was still between. And his hands, trembling, grew tangled in the chain.

"Thou shalt not kill!"—it was not that inner voice; it was a voice like the girl's, like Valerie's, soft and full of a divine compassion. And her fingers in tenderness seemed to be working with that bandaged head; and the dark eyes, deep and steadfast, were searching his soul. "Thou shalt not kill!"

And with a low, horror-stricken cry, Raymond staggered backward from the bed, and dropped into a chair, and buried his face in his hands.

CHAPTER IX—UNTIL THE DAWN

THE man upon the bed moaned continuously now; the wind swirled around the corners of the house; the waves pounded in dull, heavy thuds upon the shore without—but Raymond heard none of it. It seemed as though he were exhausted, spent, physically weak, as from some Titanic struggle. He did not move. He sat there, head bowed, his hands clasped over his face.

And then, after a long time, a shudder shook his frame—and he rose mechanically from his chair. The door was locked, and subconsciously he realised that it should not be found locked when that somebody—who was it?—yes, he remembered now—the doctor from Tournayville, and the police—it should not be found locked when the doctor and the police arrived, because they would naturally ask him to account for the reason of it. He crossed to the door, unlocked it, and returned to the chair.

And now he stared at the crucifix upon his breast. For the second time that night it had played a strange and unaccountable rôle. He lifted his hand to his head. His head still ached from the blow the old hag had struck him with the piece of wood. That was what was the matter. His head ached and he could not therefore think logically, otherwise he would not be fool enough to hold the crucifix responsible for—for preventing him from what he had been about to do a little while ago.

His face grew cynical in its expression. The crucifix had nothing to do with it, nor had the vision of the girl's eyes, nor had the imagined sound of Valérie's voice—those things were, all of them, but the form his true self had taken to express itself when he had so madly tormented himself with that hellish purpose. If it had not been things like that, it would have been something else. He could not have struck down a wounded and defenceless man, he could not have committed murder in cold blood like that. He had recoiled from the act, because it was an act that was beyond him to perform, that was all. That man there on the bed was as safe, as far as he, Raymond, was concerned, as though they were separated by a thousand miles.

"Sophistry!" sneered that inner voice. "You are a weak-kneed fool, and very far from a heroic soul that has been tried by fire! Well, you will pay for it!" Raymond cast a quick startled glance at the bed, and half rose from his seat. What — again? Was that thought back again? He sank back in the chair, gripping the chair-arms until his knuckles cracked.

"I won't!" he mumbled hoarsely. "By God — I won't! Maybe — maybe the man will die."

And then impulsively he was on his feet, and pacing the room, a sweep of anger upon him.

"What had I to do with all this!" he cried, in low, fierce tones. "And look at me!" — he had halted before the dresser, and was glaring into the mirror. "*Look at me!*" A face whose pallor was enhanced by the black clerical garb gazed contortedly back at him; the crucifix, symbol of peace, hung from about his neck. He tucked it hastily inside the *soutane*. "Look at me!" he cried, and clenched his fist and shook it at the mirror. "Three-Ace Artie! That's you there, Three-Ace Artie! God or the devil has stacked the cards on you, and — —"

He swung sharply about — listening; and, on the instant, with grave demeanour, his face soberly composed, faced the doorway.

The door opened, and two men stepped into the room. One was a big man, bearded, with a bluff and hearty cast of countenance that seemed peculiarly fitting to his immense breadth of shoulder; the other, a sort of foil as it were, was small, sharp featured, with roving black eyes that, as he stood on the threshold and on tiptoe impatiently peered over the big man's shoulder, darted quick little glances in all directions about him. The small man closed the door with a sort of fussily momentous air.

"*Tiens*, Monsieur le Curé" — the big man extended his hand to Raymond. "I am Doctor Arnaud. And this is Monsieur Dupont, the assistant chief of police of Tournayville. Hum!" — he glanced toward the bed. "Hum!" — he dropped Raymond's hand, and moved quickly to the bedside.

Raymond shook hands with the little man.

"Bad business! Bad business!" — the assistant chief of police of Tournayville continued to send his darting glances about the room, and the while he made absurd clucking noises with his tongue. "Yes, very bad — very bad! I came myself, you see."

There was much about the man that afforded Raymond an immense sense of relief. He was conscious that he infinitely preferred Monsieur Dupont, assistant chief of the Tournayville police, to Sergeant Marden, of the Royal North-West Mounted.

"Yes," said Raymond quietly, "I am afraid it is a very serious matter."

"Not at all! Not at all!" clucked Monsieur Dupont, promptly contradicting himself. "We've got our man — eh — what?" He jerked his hand toward the bed. "That's the main thing. Killed Théophile Blondin, did he? Well, quite privately, Monsieur le Curé, he might have done worse, though the law does not take that into account—no, not at all, not at all. Blondin, you understand, Monsieur le Curé, was quite well known to the police, and he was"—Monsieur Dupont pinched his nose with his thumb and forefinger as though to escape an unsavoury odour—"you understand, Monsieur le Curé?"

"I did not know," replied Raymond. "You see, I only——"

"Yes, yes!" interrupted Monsieur Dupont. "Know all that! Know all that! They told me on the drive out. You arrived this evening, and found this man lying on the road. Rude initiation to your pastorate, Monsieur le Curé. Too bad!" He raised his voice. "Well, Doctor Arnaud, what is the verdict—eh?"

"Come here and help me," said the doctor, over his shoulder. He was replacing the bandage, and now he looked around for an instant at Raymond. "I can't improve any on that. It was excellent—excellent, Monsieur le Curé."

"The credit is not mine," Raymond told him. "It was Mademoiselle Valérie. But the man, doctor?"

"Not a chance in a thousand"—the doctor shook his head. "Concussion of the brain. We'll get his clothes off, and make him comfortable. That's about all we can do. He'll probably not last through the night."

"I will help you," offered Raymond, stepping forward.

"It's not necessary, Monsieur le Curé," said the doctor. "Monsieur Dupont here can——"

"No," interposed Monsieur Dupont. "Let Monsieur le Curé help you. We will kill two birds with one stone that way. We have still to visit the Blondin house. We do not know this man's name. We know nothing about him. While you are undressing him, I will search through his clothing. Eh? Perhaps we shall find something. I do not swallow whole all the story I have heard. We shall see what we shall see."

Raymond glanced swiftly at Monsieur Dupont. Because the man clucked with his tongue and had an opinion of himself, he was perhaps a very long way from being either stupid or a fool. Monsieur Dupont might not prove so preferable to Sergeant Marden as he had been so quick to imagine.

"Yes," agreed Raymond. "Monsieur Dupont is right, I am sure. I will assist you, doctor, while he makes his search."

Monsieur Dupont stepped briskly around to the far side of the bed, and peered intently into the unconscious man's face, as he waited for Raymond and the doctor to hand him the first article of clothing. He kept clucking with his tongue, and once his eyes narrowed significantly.

Raymond experienced a sense of disquiet. Was the man simply posing for effect, or was he acting naturally—or was there something that had really aroused the other's suspicions. He handed the priest's coat, or, rather, his own, to Monsieur Dupont.

Monsieur Dupont began to go through the pockets — like one accustomed to the task.

"Hah, hah!" he ejaculated suddenly. "Monsieur le Curé, Monsieur le Docteur, I call you both to witness! All this loose money in the side pocket! The side pocket, mind you, and the money loose! It bears out the story that they say Mother Blondin tells about the robbery. I was not quite ready to believe it before. See!" He dumped the money on the bed. "You are witnesses." He gathered up the money again and replaced it in the pocket. "And here" — from another pocket he produced the revolver — "you are witnesses again." He broke the revolver. "Ah — h'm — one shot fired! You see for yourselves? Yes, you see. Very well! Continue, messieurs! There may be something more, though it would certainly appear that nothing more was necessary." He nodded crisply at both Raymond and the doctor.

The vest yielded up the cardcase. Monsieur Dupont shuffled over the dozen or so of neatly printed cards that it contained.

"Là, là!" said he sharply. "Our friend is evidently a smooth one. One of the clever kind that uses his brains. Very nice cards — very plausible sort of thing, eh? Yes, they are. Very! Henri Mentone, eh? Henri Mentone, alias something — from nowhere. Well, messieurs, is there still by any chance something else?"

There was nothing else. Monsieur Dupont, however, was not satisfied until he had examined, even more minutely than Raymond had previously done, the priest's undergarments. The doctor turned from the bed. Monsieur Dupont rolled all the clothing into a bundle, and tucked it under his arm.

"Well, let us go, doctor!" jerked out Monsieur Dupont. "If he dies, he dies — eh? In any case he can't run away. If he dies, there is Mother Blondin to consider, eh? She struck the blow. They would not do much to her perhaps, but she would have to be held. It is the law. If he does not die, that is another matter. In any case I shall remain in the village to keep an eye on them both — yes? Well then, well then — eh? — let us go!"

The doctor glanced hesitantly toward the bed.

"I have done all that is possible for the moment," he said; "but perhaps I had better call madame. She and mademoiselle have insisted on sitting up out there in the front room."

Raymond's head was bowed.

"Do not call them," he said gravely. "If the man is about to die, it is my place to stay, doctor."

"Yes—er—yes, that is so," acquiesced the doctor. "Very well then, I'll pack them off to bed. I shan't be long at Mother Blondin's. Must pay an official visit—I'm the coroner, Monsieur le Curé. I'll be back as soon as possible, and meanwhile if he shows any change" —he nodded in the direction of the bed— "send for me at once. I'll arrange to have some one of the men remain out there within call."

"Very well," said Raymond simply. "You will be gone—how long, doctor?"

"Oh, say, an hour—certainly not any longer."

"Very well," said Raymond again.

He accompanied them to the door, and closed it softly behind them as they stepped from the room. And now he experienced a sort of cool complacency, an uplift, the removal as of some drear foreboding that had weighed him down. The peril in a very large measure had vanished. The policeman had swallowed the bait, hook and all; and the doctor had said there was not one chance in a thousand that the man would live until morning. Therefore the problem resolved itself simply into a matter of two or three days in which he should continue in the rôle of curé—after that the "accident," and this accursed St. Marleau could go into mourning for him, if it liked, or do anything else it liked! He would be through with it!

But those two or three days! It was not altogether a simple affair, that. If only he could go now—at once! Only that, of course, would arouse suspicion— even if the man did not regain consciousness, and did not blurt out something before he died. But why should he keep harping on that point? Any fool could see that his safest game was to play the hand he held until the "murderer" was dead and buried, and the matter legally closed forever. He had already decided that a dozen times, hadn't he? Well then, these two or three days! He must plan for these two or three days. There were things he should know, that he would be expected to know—not mere church matters; his Latin, the training of the old school days, a prayer-book, and his wits would carry him through anything of such a nature which might intervene in that short time. But, for instance, the mother of Valérie—who was she? How did she come to be in charge of the *presbytère?* What was her name—and Valérie's? It would be very strange indeed if, coming there for the summer to supply for Father Allard, he was not acquainted with all such details.

Raymond's glance fell upon the trunk. The next instant he was hunting through his pockets, but making an awkward business of it thanks to the unaccustomed skirt of his *soutane.* A bunch of keys, however, rewarded his efforts. He stepped over to the trunk, trying first one key and then another. Finally, he found the right one, unlocked the trunk—and, suddenly, his hand upon the uplifted lid, the blood left his face, and he stood as though paralysed, staring at the doorway. He was caught—caught in the act. True, she had knocked, but she had opened the door at the same time. The little old lady, Valerie's mother, was standing there looking at him—and the trunk was open.

"Monsieur le Curé," she said, "it is only to tell you that we have made up a couch for you in the front room that you can use when the doctor returns."

He found his voice. Somehow she did not seem at all surprised that he had the trunk open.

"It is very kind and thoughtful of you, madame."

"*Mais, non!*" she exclaimed, with a smile. "But, no! And if you need anything before the doctor gets back, father, you have only to call. We shall hear you."

"I will call if I need you"—Raymond was conscious that he was speaking, but that the words came only in a queer, automatic kind of way.

She poked her head around the door for a sort of anxious, pitying, quick-flung glance at the bed; then looked questioningly at Raymond.

Raymond shook his head.

"*Ah, le pauvre! Le pauvre misérable!*" she whispered. "Good-night, Monsieur le Curé. Do not fail to call if you want us."

The door closed. As once before in a night of vigil, in that far-north shack, Raymond stretched out his hand before him to study it. It was not steady now—it trembled and shook. He looked at the trunk—and then a low, hollow laugh was on his lips. A fool and a child he was, and his nerves must be near the breaking point. Was there anything strange, was there anything surprising in the fact that Monsieur le Curé should be discovered in the act of opening Monsieur le Curé's trunk! And it had brought a panic upon him— and his hand was shaking like an old man's. He was in a pretty state, when coolness was the only thing that stood between him and—the gallows! Damn that cursed moaning from the bed! Would it never cease!

For a time he stood there without moving; and then, his composure regained, the square jaw clamped defiantly against his weakness, he drew up a chair, and, sitting down, began to rummage through the trunk.

"François Aubert—eh?" he muttered, as he picked up a prayerbook and found the fly-leaf autographed. "So my name is François! Well, that is something!" He opened another book, and, on the fly-leaf again, read an inscription. "'To my young friend'—eh? and from the Bishop! The Bishop of Montigny, is it? Well, that also is something! I am then personally acquainted with this Monsignor Montigny! I will remember that! And—ha, these!—with any luck, I shall find what I want here."

He took up a package of letters, ran them over quickly—and frowned in disappointment. They were all addressed in a woman's hand. He was not interested in that. It was the correspondence from Father Allard that he wanted. He was about to return the letters to the trunk and resume his search, when he noticed that the topmost envelope bore the St. Marleau postmark. He opened it hurriedly—and his frown changed to a nod of satisfaction. It was, after all, what he wanted. Father Allard was blessed with the services of a secretary, that was the secret—Father Allard's signature was affixed at the bottom of the neatly written page.

Raymond leaned back in his chair, and proceeded to read the letters. Little by little he pieced together, from references here and there, the information that he sought. It was a sort of family arrangement, as it were. The old lady was Father Allard's sister, and her name was Lafleur; and the husband was dead, since, in one instance, Father Allard referred to her as the "Widow Lafleur," instead of his customary "my sister, Madame Lafleur." And the uncle, who it now appeared was the notary and likewise the mayor of the village, was Father Allard's brother.

Raymond returned the letters to the trunk, and commenced a systematic examination of the rest of its contents, which, apart from a somewhat sparse wardrobe, consisted mainly of books of a theological nature. He was still engaged in this occupation, when he heard the front door open and close. He snatched the prayer-book out of the trunk, shut down the lid, and, with a finger between the closed pages of the book, stood up as the doctor came briskly into the room.

"I'm back a little ahead of time, you see," announced Doctor Arnaud with a pleasant nod, and stepped at once across the room to the wounded man.

For perhaps five minutes the doctor remained at the bedside; then, closing his little black bag, he laid it upon the table, and turned to Raymond.

"Now, father," he said cheerily, "I understand there's a couch all ready for you in the front room. I'll be here for the balance of the night. You go and get some sleep."

Raymond motioned toward the bed.

"Is there any change?" he asked.

The doctor shook his head.

"Then," said Raymond quietly, "my place is still here." He smiled soberly. "The couch is for you, doctor."

"But," protested the doctor, "I — —"

"The man is dying. My place is here," said Raymond again. "If you are needed, I have only to call you from the next room. There is no reason why both of us should sit up."

"Hum — *tiens* — well, well!" — the doctor pulled at his beard. "No, of course, not — no reason why both should sit up. And if you insist — —"

"I do not insist," interposed Raymond, smiling again. "It is only that in any case I shall remain."

"You are a fine fellow, Monsieur le Curé," said the bluff doctor heartily. He clapped both hands on Raymond's shoulders. "A fine fellow, Monsieur le Curé! Well, I will go then — I was, I confess it, up all last night." He moved over to the door — and paused on the threshold. "It is quite possible that the man may revive somewhat toward the end, in which case — Monsieur Dupont has suggested it — a little stimulation may enable us to obtain a statement from him. You understand? So you will call me on the instant, father, if you notice anything."

"On the instant," said Raymond — and as the door closed behind the doctor, he went back to his seat in the chair.

The man would die, the doctor had said so again. That was assured. Raymond fingered the prayer-book that he still held abstractedly. That was assured. It seemed to relieve his brain from any further necessity of thinking, thinking, thinking — his brain was very weary. Also he was physically weary and tired. But he was safe. Perhaps a few days of this damnable masquerade, but then it would be over.

He began to turn the pages of the prayer-book — and then, with a whimsical shrug of his shoulders, he began to read. He must put the night in somehow, therefore why not put it in to advantage? To refresh his memory a little with the ritual would be a safeguard against those few days that he must still remain in St. Marleau — as Father François Aubert!

He read for a little while, then got up and went to the bed to look at the white face upon it, to listen to the laboured breathing that stood between them both — and death. He could see no change. He returned to his chair, and resumed his reading.

At intervals he did the same thing over again — only at last, instead of reading, he dozed in his chair. Finally, he slept — not heavily, but fitfully, lightly, a troubled sleep that came only through bodily exhaustion, and that was full of alarm and vague, haunting dreams.

The night passed. The morning light began to find its way in through the edges of the drawn window shades. And suddenly Raymond sat upright in his chair. He had heard a step along the hall. The prayer-book had fallen to the floor. He picked it up. What was that noise—that low moaning from the bed? Not dead! The man wasn't dead yet! And—yes—it was daylight!

The door opened. It was Valerie. How fresh her face was—fresh as the morning dew! What a contrast to the wan and haggard countenance he knew he raised to hers!

And she paused in the doorway, and looked at him, and looked toward the bed, and back again to him, and the sweet face was beautiful with a woman's tenderness.

"Ah, how good you are, Monsieur le Curé, and how tired you must be," she said.

CHAPTER X—KYRIE ELEISON

ST. MARLEAU was agog. St. Marleau was hysterical. St. Marleau was on tiptoe. It was in the throes of excitement, and the excitement was sustained by expectancy. It wagged its head in sapient prognostication of it did not quite know what; it shook its head in a sort of amazed wonder that such things should be happening in its own midst; and it nodded its head with a profound respect, not unmixed with veneration, for its young curé—the good, young Father Aubert, as St. Marleau, old and young, had taken to calling him, since it would not have been natural to have called him anything else.

The good, young Father Aubert! Ah, yes—was he not to be loved and respected! Had he not, for three nights and two days now, sacrificed himself, until he had grown pale and wan, to watch like a mother at the bedside of the dying murderer, who did not die! It was very splendid of the young curé; for, though Madame Lafleur and her daughter beseeched him to take rest and to let them watch in his stead, he would not listen to them, saying that he was stronger than they and better able to stand it, and that, since it was he who had had the stranger brought to the *presbytère*, it was he who should see that no one else was put to any more inconvenience than could be avoided.

Ah, yes,—it was most certainly the good, young Father Aubert! For, on the short walks he took for the fresh air, the very short walks, always hurrying back to the murderer's bedside, did he not still find time for a friendly and cheery word for every one he met? It was a habit, that, of his, which on the instant twined itself around the heart of St. Marleau, that where all were strangers to him, and in spite of his own anxiety and weariness, he should be so kindly interested in all the little details of each one's life, as though they were indeed a part of his own. How could one help but love the young curé who stopped one on the village street, and, man, woman or child, laid his hand in frank and gentle fashion upon one's shoulder, and asked one's name, and where one lived, and about one's family, and for the welfare of those who were dear to one? And did not both Madame Lafleur and her daughter speak constantly of how devout he was, that he was never without a prayer-book in his hand? Ah, indeed, it was the good, young Father Aubert!

But this in no whit allayed the hysteria, the excitement and the expectancy under which St. Marleau laboured. A murder in St. Marleau! That alone was something that the countryside would talk about for years to come. And it was not only the murder; it was—what was to happen next! It was Mother Blondin's son who had been murdered by the stranger, and Mother Blondin, though not under arrest, was being watched by the police, who waited for the man in the *presbytère* to die. It was Mother Blondin who had struck the murderer, and if the murderer died then she would be responsible for the man's death. What, then, would they do with Mother Blondin?

St. Marleau, not being well versed in the law, did not know; it knew only that the assistant chief of the Tournayville police had installed himself in the Tavern where he could see that Mother Blondin did not run away, since the man at the *presbytère* did not need any police watching, and that this assistant chief of the Tournayville police was as dumb as an oyster, and looked only very wise, like one who has great secrets locked in his bosom, when questions were put to him.

And then, another thing—the funeral of Théophile Blondin. It was only this morning—the third morning after the murder—that that had been decided. Mother Blondin had raved and cursed and sworn that she would not let the body of her son enter the church. But Mother Blondin was not, perhaps, as much heretic as she wanted, or pretended, to be. Mother Blondin, perhaps, could not escape the faith of the years when she was young; and, while she scoffed and blasphemed, in her soul God was stronger than she, and she was afraid to stand between her dead son and the rites of Holy Church in which, through her own wickedness, she could not longer participate. But, however that might be, the people of St. Marleau, that is those who were good Christians and had respect for themselves, were concerned little with such as Mother Blondin, or, for that matter, with her son—but the funeral of a man who had been murdered right in their midst, and that was now to take place! Ah, that was quite another matter!

And so St. Marleau gathered in a sort of breathless unanimity that morning to the tolling of the bell, as the funeral procession of Théophile Blondin began to wend its way down the hill—and within the sacred precincts of the church the villagers, as best they might, hushed their excitement in solemn and decorous silence.

And at the church door, in surplice and stole, the altar boy beside him, as the cortège approached, stood Raymond Chapelle—the good, young Father Aubert.

He was very pale; the dark eyes were sunk deep in their sockets from three sleepless nights, and from the torment of constant suspense, where each moment in the countless hours had been pregnant with the threat of discovery, where each second had swung like some horrible pendulum hesitating between safety — and the gallows. He could not escape this sacrilege that he was about to commit. There was no escape from it. They had thought it strange, perhaps, that he had not said mass on those two mornings that were gone. It was customary; but he knew, too, that it was not absolutely obligatory — and so, through one excuse and another, he had evaded it. And even if it had been obligatory, he would still have had to find some way out, to have taken the law temporarily, as it were, into his own hands — for he would not have dared to celebrate the mass. Dared? Because of the sacrilege, the meddling with sacred things? Ah, no! What was his creed — that he feared neither God nor devil, nor man nor beast! What was that toast he had drunk that night in Ton-Nugget Camp — he, and Three-Ace Artie, and Arthur Leroy, and Raymond Chapelle! No; it was not *that* he feared — it was this sharp-eyed altar boy, this lad of twelve, who at the mass would be always at his elbow. But he was no longer afraid of the boy, for now he was ready. He had realised that he could not escape performing some of the offices of a priest, no matter what happened to that cursed fool lying over yonder there in the *presbytère* upon the bed, who seemed to get better rather than worse, and so — he had overheard Madame Lafleur confide it to the doctor — he had been of a devoutness rarely seen. Through the nights and through the days, spurred on by a sharper, sterner prod than his father's gold in the old school days had been, he had poured and studied over the ritual and the theological books that he had found in the priest's trunk, until now, committing to memory like a parrot, he was thoroughly master of anything that might arise — especially this burial of Théophile Blondin which he had foreseen was not likely to be avoided, in spite of the attitude of that miserable old hag, the mother.

Raymond's head was slightly bowed, his eyes lowered — but his eyes, nevertheless, were allowing nothing to escape them. They were extremely clumsy, and infernally slow out there in bringing the casket into the church! He would see to it that things moved with more despatch presently! There was another reason why he had not dared to act as a priest in the church before — that man over there in the *presbytère* upon the bed. He had, on that first morning, not dared to leave the other, and it had been the same yesterday morning. True, to avert suspicion, he had gone out sometimes, but never far, never out of call of the *presbytère* — which was a very different matter from being caught in the midst of a service where his hands would have been tied and he could not have instantly returned. It was strange, very strange about the wounded priest, who, instead of dying, appeared to be stronger, though he lay in a sort of comatose condition — and now the doctor even held out hopes of the man's recovery! Suppose — suppose the priest should regain consciousness now, at this moment, while he was in the act of conducting the funeral, in the other's stead, over the body of the man for whose murder, in *his*, Raymond's, stead, the other was held guilty! He was juggling with ghastly dice! But he could not have escaped this—there was no way to avoid this funeral of the son of that old hag who had run screaming, "murder—murder—murder," into the storm that night.

He raised his head. It was the gambler now, steel-nerved, accepting the chances against him, to all outward appearances impassive, who stood there in the garb of priest. He was cool, possessed, sure of himself, cynical of all things holy, disdainful of all things spiritual, contemptuous of these villagers around him that he fooled—as he would have been contemptuous of himself to have hesitated at the plunge, desperate though it was, that was his one and only chance for liberty and life.

Ha! At last—eh? They had brought Théophile Blondin to the door!

And then Raymond's voice, rich, full-toned, stilled that queer, subdued, composite sound of breathings, of the rustle of garments, of slight, involuntary movements—of St. Marleau crowded in the pews in strained, tense waiting.

"'*Si iniquitates observaveris, Domine; Domine quis sustinebit?*—If Thou, O Lord, wilt mark iniquities; Lord, who shall abide it?"

It was curious that the service should begin like that, curious that he had not before found any meaning or significance in the words. He had learned them like a parrot. "If Thou, O Lord, wilt mark iniquities...." He bowed his head to hide the tightening of his lips. Bah, what was this! Some inner consciousness inanely attempting to suggest that there was not only significance in the words, but that the significance was personal, that the very words from his lips, performing the office of priest, desecrating God's holy place, was iniquity, black, blasphemous and abhorrent in God's sight—if there were a God!

Ah, that was it—if there were a God! He was reciting now the *De Profundis* in a purely mechanical way. "Out of the depths...."

If there were a God—yes, that was it! He had never believed there was, had he? He did not believe it now—but he would make one concession. What he was doing was not in intent blasphemous, neither was it to mock—it was to save his life. He was a man with a halter strangling around his neck. And if there was a God, who then had brought all this about? Who then was responsible, and who then should accept the consequences? Not he! He had not sought from choice to play the part of priest! He had not sought the life of this dead man in the coffin there in front of him! He had not sought to—yes, curse it, it was the word to use—kill the drunken, besotted, worthless fool!

A cold anger came, steadying his nerves. It was too bad that in some way he could not wreck a vengeance on the corpse for all this—the miserable, rum-steeped hound who had got him into this hellish fix.

They were bearing the body into the church toward the head of the nave. He was at the *Subvenite* now. "'...Kyrie eleison."

The boyish treble, hushed yet clear, of young Gauthier Beaulieu, the altar boy, rose from beside him in the responses:

"'Christe eleison"

"Lord, have mercy.... From the gate of hell,"

"Deliver his soul, O Lord."

Again! That sense of solemnity, that personal implication in the words! It was coincidence, nothing more. No; it was not even that! He was simply twisting the meaning, allowing himself to be played with by a warped imagination. He was not a weak fool, was he, to let this get the better of him? And, besides, he would hurry through with it, and since he would say neither office nor mass it would not take long. It must be hot this summer morning, though he had not noticed it particularly when he had left the *presbytère*. The church seemed heavy and oppressive. Strange how the pews were all lined with eyes staring at him!

The tread of feet up the aisle died away. The bier was set at the head of the nave, and lighted candles placed around it. There fell a silence, utter and profound.

Why was it now that his lips scarcely moved, that his voice was scarcely audible; why that sudden foreboding, intangible yet present everywhere, at his temerity, at his unhallowed, hideous perversion of sanctity in that he should pray as a priest of God, in the habiliments of one of God's ministers, in God's church—ay, it was a devil's masquerade, for he, if never before, stood branded now, sealing that blasphemous toast, a disciple of hell.

"'Non intres in judicium cum servo tuo, Domine....' Enter not into judgment with Thy servant, O Lord...."

And so he denied God, did he? And so he was callous and indifferent, and scoffed at the possibility of a church, simply because it was a church, being the abiding place of a higher, holier, omnipotent presence? Why, then, that hoarseness in his throat—why, then, did he not shout his parrot words high to the vaulted roof in triumphant defiance? Why that struggle with his will to finish the prayer?

From the little organ loft in the gallery over the door, floated now the notes of the *Responsory*, and the voices of the choir rolled solemnly through the church:

"'*Libera me, Domine, de morte æterna....*' Deliver me, O Lord, from eternal death...."

Death! Eternal death! What was death? There was a dead man there in the casket—dead because he and the man had fought together, and the other had been killed. And he was burying, in a church, as a priest, he, who was the one upon whom the law would set its claws if it but knew, the man that he had killed! It came suddenly, with terrific force, blotting out those wavering candle flames around the coffin, the scene of that night. The wind was howling; that white-scarred face was cheek to cheek with him; they lunged and staggered around that dimly lighted room, he and the man who lay dead there in the coffin. They struggled for the revolver; that old hag circled about them like a swirling hawk—that blinding flash—the acrid smell of powder—the room revolving around and around—and the dead man, who was here in the coffin now, had lain sprawled out there on the floor. He shivered—and cursed himself fiercely the next instant—it seemed as though the casket suddenly opened, and that ugly, venomous, scarred face lifted up and leered at him.

"'*Dies ilia, dies iræ...,*'" came the voices of the choir. "That day, a day of wrath...."

His jaws clenched. He pulled himself together. That was Valerie up there playing the little organ; Valerie with the great, dark eyes, and the beautiful face; Valerie, who thought it so unselfish of him because he had had a couch made up in the room in order that he might not leave the wounded man. The wounded man! Following the order of the service, Raymond was putting incense into the censer while the *Responsory* was being sung, and his fingers gripped hard upon the vessel. Again that thought to torture and torment him! Had he not enough to do to go through with this! Who was with the wounded man now? That officious, nosing fool, who preened himself on the strength of being assistant-chief of police of some pitiful little town that no one outside of its immediate vicinity had ever heard of before? Or was it Madame Lafleur? But what, after all, did it matter who was there—if the man should happen to regain his senses? Ha, ha! Would it not be a delectable sight if that police officer should arrest him, strip these priestly trappings from him just as he left the church! It would be quite a dramatic scene, would it not—quite too damnably dramatic! He was swinging with that infernal pendulum between liberty and death. He was, at that moment, if ever a man was, or had been, the sport of fate. He had not liked the looks of the wounded priest half an hour ago when he had left the *presbytère* for the sacristy—it had seemed as though the man were beginning to look *healthy*.

"'*Kyrie eleison....*'" The *Responsory* was over. In a purely mechanical way again he was proceeding with the service. As the ritual prescribed, he passed round the bier with sprinkler and censer—and presently he found himself reciting the last prayer of that part of the service held within the church; and then the bier was being lifted and borne down the aisle again.

Out into the sunlight, to the smell of the fields, to the breeze from the river wafting upon his cheek! He drew in a deep breath—and almost at the same instant passed his hand heavily across his eyes. He had thought that stifling heat, that overwhelming oppressiveness all in the atmosphere of the church; but here was the sunlight, and here the fields, and here the soft breeze blowing from the water—yet that sense of foreboding, a prescience, a weight upon him that sank deep to the soul, remained with him still.

Slowly the procession passed around the green in front of the church, and through the gate of the whitewashed fence into the little burial ground beyond on the river's bank. They were chanting *In Paradisum*, but Valerie was no longer with the choir, for now, as they passed through the gate, he saw her, a slim figure all in white, hurry across the green toward the *presbytère*.

What was this before him! It was not the smell of fields, but the smell of freshly turned earth—a grave. The grave of Théophile Blondin, the man whom he had fought with—and killed. And he was a priest of God, burying Théophile Blondin. What ghastly, hellish travesty! What were those words returning to his memory, coming to him out of the dim past when he was still a boy, and still susceptible to the teachings of the fathers who had sought to guide him into the church—God is not mocked.

"God is not mocked! God is not mocked!"—the words seemed to echo and reverberate around him, they seemed to be thundered in a voice of vengeance. "God is not mocked!"—and he was *blessing* the grave of Théophile Blondir!

Did these people, gathered, clustered about him, not hear that voice! Why did they not hear it? It was not the *Benedictus* that was being sung that prevented them from hearing it, for he could scarcely hear the *Benedictus*.

Raymond's lips moved. "I am not mocking God," he whispered. "I do not believe in God, but I am not mocking. I am asking only for my life. I am taking only the one chance I have. I did not intend to kill the fool—he killed himself. I am no murderer. I——" He shivered suddenly again, as once in the church he had shivered before. His hands outstretched seemed to be creeping again toward a bare throat that lay exposed upon a bed, the feel of soft, pulsing flesh seemed upon his finger tips. And then a diabolical chortle seemed to rattle in his ears. So murder was quite foreign to him, eh? And he did not believe in God? And he was quite above and apart from all such nonsense? And therein, of course, lay the reason why the tumbling of this dead thing into a grave left him so cool and imperturbable; and why the solemn words of the service had no meaning; and why it was a matter of supreme unconcern to him, provided he was not caught at it, that he took God's words upon his lips, and God's garb upon his shoulders!

White-faced, Raymond lifted his head. The *Benedictus* was ended, and now the words came slowly from his lips in a strange, awed, almost wondering way.

"'*Requiem oternam.... Ego sum resurrectio et vita....*' I am the Resurrection and the Life: he that believeth in Me, although he be dead, shall live: and every one who liveth, and believeth in Me, shall never die."

His voice faltered a little, steadied by a tremendous effort of will, and went on again, low-toned, through the responses and short prayer that closed the service. "'*Kyrie eleison*'... not into temptation.... '*Requiem oternam.*'... '*Requiescat in pace*'... through the mercy of God.... 'Amen.'"

Forgotten for the moment was that grim pendulum that hovered over the bed in the *presbytère* yonder, and by the side of the grave Raymond stood and looked down on the coffin of Théophile Blondin. The people began to disperse, but he was scarcely conscious of it. It seemed that he had run the gamut of every human emotion since he had met the funeral procession at the church door; but here was another now—an incomprehensible, quiet, chastened, questioning mood. They were very beautiful words, these, that he was repeating to himself. He did not believe them, but they were very beautiful, and to one who did believe they must offer more than all of life could hold.

"'I am the resurrection and the life... he that be-lieveth in Me... shall never die.'"

There was another gateway in the little whitewashed fence, a smaller one that gave on the sacristy at the side and toward the rear of the church. Slowly, head bowed, absorbed, unconscious of the rôle he played so well, Raymond walked toward the gate, and through it, and, raising his head, paused. A shrivelled and dishevelled form crouched there against the palings. It was old Mother Blondin.

And Raymond stared—and suddenly a wave of immeasurable pity, mingling a miserable sense of distress, swept upon him. In there was forbidden ground to her; and in there was her son—killed in a fight with him. She had come around here to the side, unobserved, unless Dupont were lurking somewhere about, to be as near at the last as she could. An old hag, wretched, dissolute—but human above all things else, huddling before the dying embers of mother-love. She did not look up; her forehead was pressed close against the fence as she peered inside; a withered, dirty hand clutched fiercely at a paling on each side of her face.

Raymond stepped toward her, and spontaneously laid his hand upon her shoulder. And strange words were on his lips, but they were sincere words out of a heart torn and troubled and dismayed, out of a soul that had recoiled as before some tremendous cataclysm. And his words were the words he had been repeating over and over to himself.

"'I am the resurrection and the life...' My poor, poor woman, let me help you. See, you must not mourn that way alone. Come, let me take you back to your home— —"

She rose to her feet, and looked at him, and for an instant the hard, set, wrinkled face seemed to soften, and into the blear eyes seemed to spring a mist of tears—then her face contorted into livid fury, and she struck at his hand, flinging it from her shoulder.

"You go to hell!" she snarled. "You, and all like you, you go to hell!"

She was gone—shuffling around the corner of the church.

And then Raymond laughed a little. It was like a dash of cold water in the face. He had been a fool—a fool all morning, a fool to let mere words, mere environment have any influence upon him, a fool to sentimentality in talking to her like that, mawkish to have used the words! He would have said what she had said to any one else, if he had been in her place—only more bitterly, more virulently, if that were possible.

He shrugged his shoulders, and moved on toward the sacristy to divest himself of his surplice and stole—and again he paused, this time in the doorway, and turned around, as a voice cried out his name.

"Father Aubert!"

It was Valérie, running swiftly toward him from the *presbytère*.

And Raymond stood still and waited. Intuitively he knew. Something had happened in the *presbytère* at last. He was the gambler again, cool, imperturbable, steel-nerved, with the actual crisis upon him. It was the turn of the card, the throw of the dice, that was all. Was it life—or death? It was Valérie who was to pronounce the sentence. She reached him, breathless, flushed. He smiled at her.

"Monsieur le Curé—Father Aubert," she panted, "come quickly! He can speak! He has regained consciousness!"

CHAPTER XI—"HENRI MENTONE"

VALERIE'S flushed face was lifted eagerly to his. She had caught impetuously at the sleeve of his *soutane*, and was urging him forward. And yet he was walking with deliberate measured tread across the green toward the *presbytère*. Strange how the blood seemed to be hammering feverishly at his temples! Every impulse prompted him to run, as a man running for his life, to reach the *presbytère*, to reach that room, to shut the door upon himself and that man whose return to consciousness meant—what? But it was too late to run now. Too late! Already the news seemed to have spread. Those who had been the last to linger at the grave of Théophile Blondin were gathering, on their way out from the little burying ground, around the door of the *presbytère*. It would appear bizarre, perhaps, that the curé should come tearing across the green with vestments flying simply because a man had regained consciousness! Ha, ha! Yes, very bizarre! Why should their curé run like one demented just because a man had regained consciousness! If the man were at his last gasp now, were just about to die—that would be different! He found a bitter mirth in that. Yes, decidedly, they would understand that! But as it was, they would think their curé had gone suddenly mad, perhaps, or they would think, perhaps—something else.

The dice were thrown, the card was turned—against him. His luck was out. It was like walking tamely to where the noose dangled and awaited his neck to walk toward those gaping people clustered around the door, to walk into the *presbytère*. But it was his only chance. Yes, there was a chance—one chance left. If he could hold out until evening, until darkness!

Until evening, until darkness—with the night before him in which to attempt his escape! But there were still eight hours or more to evening. There were only a few more steps to go before he reached the *presbytère*. The distance was pitifully short. In those few steps he must plan everything; plan that that accursed noose swaying before his eyes should — —

"*Dies illa, dies iræ*—that day, a day of wrath." What brought those words flashing through his mind! He had said them once that morning—but a little while ago—in church—as a priest—at Théophile Blondin's funeral. Damn it, they were not meant for him! They did not mean to-day. They were not premonitory. He was not beaten yet!

In the shed behind the *presbytère* there was a pair of the old sacristan's overalls, and an old coat, and an old hat. He had noticed them yesterday. They would serve his purpose—a man in a pair of overalls and a dirty, torn coat would not look much like a priest. Yes, yes; that would do, it was the way—when night came. He would have the darkness, and he would hide the next day, and the day after, and travel only by night. It invited pursuit of course, the one thing that next to capture itself he had struggled and plotted to avoid, but it was the only chance now, and, if luck turned again, he might succeed in making his way out of the country—when night came.

But until then! What until then? That was where his danger lay now—in those hours until darkness.

"Yes!" whispered Raymond fiercely to himself. "Yes—if only you keep your head!"

What was the matter with him? Had he forgotten! It was what he had been prepared to face that night when he had brought the priest to the *presbytère*, should the man then have recovered sufficiently to speak. It should be still easier now to make any one believe that the man was wandering in his mind, was not yet lucid or coherent after so long a lapse from consciousness. And the very story that the man would tell must sound like the ravings of a still disordered mind! He, Raymond, would insist that the man be kept very quiet during the day; he, Raymond, would stay beside the other's bed. Was he not the curé! Would they not obey him, show deference to his judgment and his wishes—until night came!

They were close to the *presbytère* now, close to the little gaping crowd that surrounded the door; and, as though conscious for the first time that she was clinging to his arm, Valérie, in sudden embarrassment at her own eagerness, hurriedly dropped her hand to her side. And, at the act, Raymond looked at her quickly, in an almost startled way. Strange! But then his brain was in turmoil! Strange that extraneous things, things that had nothing to do with the one grim purpose of saving his neck should even for an instant assert themselves! But then they—no, she—had done that before. He remembered now... when they were putting on that bandage.

When that crucifix had tangled up his hands, and she had seemed to stand before him to save him from himself... those dark eyes, that pure, sweet face, the tender, womanly sympathy—the antithesis of himself! And to-night, when night came, when the night he longed for came, when the night that meant his only chance for life came, he—what was this!—this sudden pang of yearning that ignored, with a most curious authority, as though it had the right to ignore, the desperate, almost hopeless peril that was closing down upon him, that seemed to make the coming of the night now a thing he would put off, a thing to regret and to dread, that bade him search for some other way, some other plan that would not necessitate—

"A fool and a pretty face!"—it was the gibe and sneer and prod of that inward monitor. "See all these people who are so reverently making way for you, and eying you with affection and simple humility, see the rest of them coming back from all directions because the *murderer* is about to tell his story—well, see how they will make way for you, and with what affection and humility they will eye you when you come out of that house again, if all the wits the devil ever gave you are not about you now!"

He spoke to her quietly, controlling his voice:

"You have not told me yet what he said, mademoiselle?"

She shook her head.

"He did not say much—only to ask where he was and for a drink of water."

He had no time to ask more. They had reached the group before the *presbytère* now, and the buzz of conversation, the eager, excited exchange of questions and answers was hushed, as, with one accord, men and women made way for their curé. And Raymond, lifting his hand in a kindly, yet authoritative gesture, cautioning patience and order, mounted the steps of the *presbytère*.

And then, inside the doorway, Raymond quickened his step. From the closed door at the end of the short hallway came the low murmur of voices. It was Madame Lafleur probably who was there with the other now. How much, how little had the man said—since Valérie had left the room? Raymond's lips tightened grimly. It was fortunate that Madame Lafleur had so great a respect for the cloth! He had nothing to fear from her. He could make her believe anything. He could twist her around his finger, and—he opened the door softly—and stood, as though turned suddenly rigid, incapable of movement, upon the threshold—and his hand upon the doorknob closed tighter and tighter in a vise-like grip. Across the room stood, not Madame Lafleur, but Monsieur Dupont, the assistant chief of the Tournayville police, and in Monsieur Dupont's hand was a notebook, and upon Monsieur Dupont's lips, as he turned and glanced quickly toward the door, there played an enigmatical smile.

"Ah! It is Monsieur le Curé!" observed Monsieur Dupont smoothly. "Well, come in, Monsieur le Curé—come in, and shut the door. I promise you, you will find it interesting. What? Yes, very interesting!"

"Oh, Monsieur Dupont is here!"—the words seemed to come to Raymond as from some great distance behind him.

He turned. It was Valérie. Of course, it was Valérie! He had forgotten. She had naturally followed him along the hall to the door. What did this Dupont mean by what he had said? What had Dupont already learned—that was so *interesting!* It would not do to have Valérie here, if—if he and Dupont— —

"Perhaps, Mademoiselle Valérie," he said gravely, "it would be as well if you did not come in. Monsieur Dupont appears to be officially engaged."

"But, of course!" she agreed readily. "I did not know that any one was here. I left the man alone when I ran out to find you. I will come back when Monsieur Dupont has gone."

And Raymond smiled, and stepped inside the room, and closed the door, and leaned with his back against it.

"Well, Monsieur le Curé"—Monsieur Dupont tapped with his pencil on the notebook—"I have it all down here. All! Everything that he has said."

Raymond had not even glanced toward the bed—his eyes, cool, steady now, were on the officer, watching the other like a hawk.

"Yes?" he prompted calmly.

"And"—Monsieur Dupont made that infernal clucking noise with his tongue—"I have—nothing! Did I not tell you it was interesting? Yes, very interesting! Very!"

Was the man playing with him? How clever was this Dupont? No fool, at any rate! He had already shown that, in spite of his absurd mannerisms. Raymond's hand began to toy with the crucifix on his breast, while his fingers surreptitiously loosened several buttons of his *soutane*.

"Nothing?"—Raymond's eyebrows were raised in mild surprise. "But Mademoiselle Valérie told me he had regained consciousness."

"Yes," said Monsieur Dupont, "I heard her say so to some one as she left the house. I was keeping an eye on that *vieille sauvage*, Mother Blondin. But this—ah! Quite a more significant matter! Yes—quite! You will understand, Monsieur le Curé, that I lost no time in reaching here?"

And now for the first time Raymond looked swiftly toward the bed. It was only for the barest fraction of a second that he permitted his eyes to leave the police officer; but in that glance he had met coal black eyes, all pupils they seemed, fixed in a sort of intense penetration upon him. The man was still lying on his back, he had noticed that—but it was the eyes, disconcerting, full of something he could not define, boring into him, that dominated all else. He stepped nonchalantly toward Monsieur Dupont.

"It is astonishing that he has said nothing," he murmured softly. "Will you permit me, Monsieur Dupont"—he held out his hand—"to see your book?"

"The book? H'm! Well, why not?" Monsieur Dupont shrugged his shoulders as he placed the notebook in Raymond's hand. "It is not customary — but, why not!"

And then upon Raymond came relief. It surged upon him until he could have laughed out hysterically, laughed like a fool in this Monsieur Dupont's face — this Monsieur Dupont who was the assistant chief of the police force of Tournayville. It was true! Dupont had at least told the truth. So far Dupont had learned nothing. Raymond's face was impassive as he scrutinised the page before him. Written with a flourish on the upper line, presumably to serve as a caption, were the words:

"The Murderer, Henri Mentone," and beneath: "Evades direct answers. Hardened type — knows his way about. Pretends ignorance. Stubborn. Wily rascal — yes, very!"

Raymond handed the notebook back to Monsieur Dupont.

"It is perhaps not so strange after all, Monsieur Dupont," he remarked with a thoughtful air. "We must not forget that the poor fellow has but just recovered consciousness. He is hardly likely to be either lucid or rational."

"Bah!" ejaculated Monsieur Dupont grimly. "He is as lucid as I am. But I am not through with him yet! He is not the first of his kind I have had upon my hook!" He leaned toward the bed. "Now, then, my little Apache, you will answer my questions! Do you understand? No more evasions! None at all! They will do you no good, and — —"

Raymond's hand fell upon Monsieur Dupont's shoulder. Though he had not looked again until now, he was conscious that those eyes from the bed had never for an instant swerved from his face. Now he met them steadily. He addressed Monsieur Dupont, but he spoke to the man on the bed.

"Have you warned him, Monsieur Dupont," he said soberly, "that anything he says will be used against him? And have you told him that he is not obliged to answer? He is weak yet and at a disadvantage. He would be quite justified in waiting until he was stronger, and entirely competent to weigh his own words."

Monsieur Dupont was possessed of an inconsistency all his own.

"*Tonnerre!*" he snapped. "And what is the use of warning him when he will not answer at all?"

"You appear not quite to have given up hope!" observed Raymond dryly.

"H'm!" Monsieur Dupont scowled. "Very well, then" — he leaned once more over the bed, and addressed the man — "you understand? It is as Monsieur le Curé says. I warn you. You are not obliged to answer. Now then — your name, your age, your birthplace?"

Raymond shifted his position to the foot of the bed.

Damn those eyes! Move where he would, they never left his face. The man had paid no attention to Monsieur Dupont. Why, in God's name, why did the man keep on staring and gazing so fixedly at him—and why had the man refused to answer Dupont's questions—and why had not the man with his first words poured out his story eagerly!

"Well, well!" prodded Monsieur Dupont. "Did you not hear—eh? Your name?"

The man's eyes followed Raymond.

"Where am I?" he asked faintly.

It was too querulous, that tone, too genuinely weak and peevish to smack of trickery—and suddenly upon Raymond there came again that nervous impulse to laugh out aloud. So that was the secret of it, was it? There was a sort of sardonic humour then in the situation! The suggestion, the belief he had planned to convey to shield himself—that the man was still irrational—was, in fact, the truth! But how long would that condition last? He must put an end to this—get this cursed Dupont away!

"Where am I?" muttered the man again.

"*Tiens!*" clucked Monsieur Dupont. "You see, Monsieur le Curé! You see? Yes, you see. He plays the game well—with finesse, eh?" He turned to the man. "Where are you, eh? Well, you are better off where you are now than where you will be in a few days! I promise you that! Now, again—your name?"

The man shook his head.

"Monsieur Dupont," said Raymond, a little severely. "You will arrive at nothing like this. The man is not himself. To-morrow he will be stronger."

"Bah! Nonsense! Stronger!" jerked out Monsieur Dupont derisively. "Our fox is quite strong enough! Monsieur le Curé, you are not a police officer—do not let your pity deceive you. And permit me to continue!" He slipped his hand into his pocket, and adroitly flashed a visiting card suddenly before the man's eyes. "Well, since you cannot recall your name, this will perhaps be of assistance! You see, Monsieur Henri Mentone, that you get yourself nowhere by refusing to answer!" Once more the man shook his head.

"So!" Monsieur Dupont complacently returned the card to his pocket. "Now we will continue. You see now where you stand. Your age?"

Again the man shook his head.

"He does not know!" remarked Monsieur Dupont caustically. "Very convenient memory! Yes—very! Well, will you tell us where you came from?"

The Sin That Was His | 89

For the fourth time the man shook his head—and at that instant Raymond edged close to Monsieur Dupont's side. What was that in those eyes now—that something that was creeping into them—that *dawning* light, as they searched his face!

"He does not know that, either!" complained Monsieur Dupont sarcastically. "Magnificent! Yes—very! He knows nothing at all! He— —"

With a low cry, the man struggled to his elbow, propping himself up in bed.

"Yes, I know!"—his voice, high-pitched, rang through the room. "I know now!" He raised his hand and pointed at Raymond. "*I know you!*"

Raymond's hand was thrust into the breast of his *soutane*, where he had unbuttoned it beneath the crucifix—and Raymond's fingers closed upon the stock of an automatic in his upper left-hand vest pocket.

"Poor fellow!" murmured Raymond pityingly. "You see, Monsieur Dupont"—he moved still a little closer—"you have gone too far. You have excited him. He is incoherent. He does not know what he is saying."

Monsieur Dupont was clucking with his tongue, as he eyed the man speculatively.

"Yes, yes; I know you now!" cried the man again. "Oh, monsieur, monsieur!"—both hands were suddenly thrust out to Raymond, and there was a smile on the trembling lips, an eager flush dyeing the pale cheeks. "It is you, monsieur! I have been very sick, have I not? It—it was like a dream. I—I was trying to remember—your face. It is your face that I have seen so often bending over me. Was that not it, monsieur—monsieur, you who have been so good—was that not it? You would lift me upon my pillow, and give me something cool to drink. And was it not you, monsieur, who sat there in that chair for long, long hours? It seems as though I saw you there always—many, many times."

It was like a shock, a revulsion so strong that for the moment it unnerved him. Raymond scarcely heard his own voice.

"Yes," he said—his forehead was damp, as he brushed his hand across it.

Monsieur Dupont blew out his cheeks.

"*Nom d'un nom!*" he exploded. "Ah, your pardon, Monsieur le Curé! But it is mild, a very mild oath, is it not—under the circumstances? Yes—very! I admire cleverness—yes, I do! The man has a head! What an appeal to the emotions! Poignant! Yes, that's the word—poignant. Looking for sympathy! Trying to make an ally of you, Monsieur le Curé!"

"Get rid of the fool! Get rid of the fool!" prompted that inward monitor impatiently.

Raymond, with a significant look, plucked at Monsieur Dupont's sleeve, and led the other across the room away from the bed.

"Do you think so?" he asked, in a lowered voice.

"Eh?" inquired Monsieur blankly. "Think what?"

"What you just said—that he is trying to make an ally of me."

"Oh, that—*zut!*" sniffed Monsieur Dupont. "But what else?"

"Then suppose"—Raymond dropped his voice still lower—"then suppose you leave him with me until tomorrow. And meanwhile—you understand?"

Monsieur Dupont pondered the suggestion.

"Well, very well—why not?" decided Monsieur Dupont. "Perhaps not a bad idea—perhaps not. And if it does not succeed"—Monsieur Dupont shrugged his shoulders—"well, we know everything anyhow; and I will make him pay through the nose for his tricks! But he is under arrest, Monsieur le Curé, you understand that? There is a cell in the jail at Tournayville that— —"

"Naturally—when he is able to be moved," agreed Raymond readily. "We will speak to the doctor about that. In the meantime he probably could not walk across this room. He is quite safe here. I will be responsible for him."

"And I will put a flea in the doctor's ear!" announced Monsieur Dupont, moving toward the door. "The assizes are next week, and after the assizes, say, another six weeks and"—Monsieur Dupont's tongue clucked eloquently several times against the roof of his mouth. "We will not keep him waiting long!" Monsieur Dupont opened the door, and, standing on the threshold where he was hidden from the bed, laid his forefinger along the side of his nose. "You are wrong, Monsieur le Curé"—he had raised his voice to carry through the room. "But still you may be right! You are too softhearted; yes, that is it—soft-hearted. Well, he has you to thank for it. I would not otherwise consider it—it is against my best judgment. I bid you good-bye, Monsieur le Curé!"

Raymond closed the door—but it was a moment, standing there with his back to the bed, before he moved. His face was set, the square jaws clamped, a cynical smile flickering on his lips. It had been close—but of the two, as between Monsieur Dupont and himself and the gallows, Monsieur Dupont had been the nearer to death! He saw Monsieur Dupont in his mind's-eye sprawled on the floor. It would not have been difficult to have stopped forever any outcry from that weak thing upon the bed. And then the window; and after that—God knew! And it would have been God's affair! It was God Who had instituted that primal law that lay upon every human soul, the law of self-preservation; and it was God's choosing, not his, that he was here! Who was to quarrel with him if he stopped at nothing in his fight for life! Well,

Dupont was gone now! That danger was past. He had only to reckon now with Valérie and her mother—until night came. He raised his hand heavily to his forehead and pushed back his hair. Valérie! Until night came! Fool! What was Valérie to him! And yet—he jeered at himself in a sort of grim derision—and yet, if it were not his one chance for life, he would not go to-night. He could call himself a fool, if he would; that ubiquitous and caustic other self, that was the cool, calculating, unemotional personification of Three-Ace Artie, could call him a fool, if it would—those dark eyes of Valérie's—no, not that—it was not eyes, nor hair, nor lips, they were only part of Valérie—it was Valérie, like some rare fragrance, fresh and pure and sweet in her young womanhood, that— —

"Monsieur!"—the man was calling from the bed.

And then Raymond turned, and walked back across the room, and drew a chair to the bedside, and sat down. And Raymond smiled—but not at the bandaged, outstretched form before him. A fool! Well, so be it! The fool would sit here for the rest of the morning, and the rest of the afternoon, and listen to the babbling wanderings of another fool who had not had sense enough to die; and he would play this cursed rôle of saint, and fumble with his crucifix, and mumble his * Latin, and keep this Mademoiselle Valérie, who meant nothing to him, from the room—until to-night. And—what was this other fool saying?

"Monsieur—monsieur, who was that man who just went out?"

Raymond answered mechanically:

"It was Monsieur Dupont, the assistant chief of the Tournayville police."

"What was he doing here?" asked the other slowly, as though trying to puzzle out the answer to his own question. "Why was he asking me all those questions?"

Raymond, tight-lipped, looked the man in the eyes.

"We've had enough of this, haven't we?" he challenged evenly. "I thought at first you were still irrational. You're not—that is now quite evident. Well—we are alone—what is your object? You had a chance to tell Dupont your story!"

A pitiful, stunned look crept into the man's face. He stretched out his hand over the coverlet toward Raymond. "You—you, too, monsieur!" he said numbly. "What does it mean? What does it mean?"

It startled Raymond. There was trickery here, it could be nothing else—and yet there was sincerity too genuine to be assumed in the other's words and acts. Raymond sat back in his chair, and for a long minute, brows knitted, studied the man. It was possible, of course, that the other might not have recognised him—they had only been together for a few moments in the smoking compartment of the train, and, dressed now as a priest, that might well be the case—but why not the story then?—why not the simple statement that he was the new curé coming to the village, that he had been struck down and—bah! What was the man's game! Well, he would force the issue, that was all! He leaned over the bed; and, his hand upon the other's, his fingers closed around the man's wrist until, beneath their tips, they could gauge the throb of the other's pulse. And his eyes, steel-hard, were on the other.

"I am the curé," he said, in a low, level tone, "of St. Marleau—while Father Allard is away. My name is—*François Aubert*."

"And mine," said the man, "is"—he shook his head—"mine is"—his face grew piteously troubled—"it is strange—I do not remember that either."

There had been no tell-tale nervous flutter of the man's pulse. Raymond's hand fell away from the other's wrist. What was this curious, almost uncanny presentiment that was creeping upon him! Was it possible that the man was telling the *truth!* Was it possible that—his own brain was whirling now—he steadied himself, forcing himself to speak.

"Did you not read the card that Dupont showed you?"

"Yes," said the other. "Henri Mentone—is that my name?"

"Do you not know!"—Raymond's tone was suddenly sharp, incisive.

"No," the other answered. "No, I cannot remember." He reached out his arms imploringly to Raymond again. "Oh, monsieur, what does it mean? I do not know where I am—I do not know how I came here."

"You are in the *presbytère* at St. Marleau," said Raymond, still sharply. Was it true; or was the man simply magnificent in duplicity? No—there could be no reason, no valid reason for the man to play a part?—no reason why he should have withheld his story from Dupont. It was not logical. He, Raymond, who alone knew all the story, knew that. It must be true—but he dared not yet drop his guard. He must be sure—his life depended on his being sure. He was speaking again—uncompromisingly: "You were picked up unconscious on the road by the tavern during the storm three nights ago—you remember the storm, of course?"

Again that piteously troubled look was on the other's face.

"No, monsieur, I do not remember," he said tremulously.

"Well, then," persisted Raymond, "before the storm—you surely remember that! Where you came from? Where you lived? Your people?"

"Where I came from, my—my people"—the man repeated the words automatically. He swept his hand across his bandaged head. "It is gone," he whispered miserably. "I—it is gone. There—there is nothing. I do not remember anything except a girl in this room saying she would run for the curé, and then that man came in." A new trouble came into his eyes. "That man—you said he was a police officer—why was he here? And—you have not told me yet—why should he ask me questions?"

There was still a card to play. Raymond leaned again over the man.

"All this will not help you," he said sternly. "Far better that you should confide in me! The proof against you is overwhelming. You are already condemned. You murdered Théophile Blondin that night, and stole Mother Blondin's money. Mother Blondin struck you that blow upon the head as you ran from the house. You were found on the road; and in your pockets was Mother Blondin's money—and her son's revolver, with which you shot him. In a word, you are under arrest for murder."

"Murder!"—the man, wide-eyed, horror-stricken, was staring at Raymond—and then he was clawing himself frantically into an upright position in the bed. "No, no! Not that! It cannot be true! Not—*murder!*" His voice rose into a piercing cry, and rang, and rang again through the room. He reached out his arms. "You are a priest, monsieur—by that holy crucifix, by the dear Christ's love, tell me that it is not so! Tell me! Murder! It is not true! It cannot be true! No, no—no! Monsieur—father—do you not hear me crying to you, do you not—" His voice choked and was still. His face was buried in his hands, and great sobs shook his shoulders.

And Raymond turned his head away—and Raymond's face was gray and drawn. There was no longer room for doubt. That blow upon the skull had blotted out the man's memory, left it—a blank.

CHAPTER XII—HIS BROTHER'S KEEPER

FATHER ALLARD'S desk had been moved into the front room. Raymond, on a very thin piece of paper, was tracing the signature inscribed on the fly-leaf of the prayer-book—François Aubert. Before him lay a number of letters written that morning by Valérie—parish letters, a letter to the bishop—awaiting his signature. Valérie, who had been private secretary to her uncle, was now private secretary to—François Aubert!

The day before yesterday he had signed a letter in this manner, and Valérie, who was acquainted with the signature from her uncle's correspondence, had had no suspicions. Raymond placed his tracing over the bottom of one of the letters, and, bearing down heavily as he wrote, obtained an impression on the letter itself. The impression served as a guide, and he signed—François Aubert.

It was simple enough, this expedient in lieu of a piece of carbon paper that he had no opportunity to buy, and for which, from the notary perhaps, Valérie's other uncle, who alone in the village might be expected to have such a thing, he had not dared to make the request; but it was tedious and laborious—and besides, for the moment, his mind was not upon his task.

He signed another, and still another, his face deeply lined as he worked, wrinkles nesting in strained little puckers around the corners of his eyes—and suddenly, while there were yet two of the letters to be signed, he sat back in his chair, staring unseeingly before him. From the rear room came that footstep, slow, irregular, uncertain. It was Henri Mentone. Dupont's "flea" in the doctor's ear had had its effect. Henri Mentone was taking his exercise—from the bed to the window, from the window to the door, from the door to the bed, and over again. In the three days since the man had recovered consciousness, he had made rapid strides toward recovering his strength as well, though he still spent part of the day in bed—this afternoon, for instance, he was to be allowed out for a little while in the open air.

Raymond's eyes fixed on the open window where the morning sunlight streamed into the room. Yes, the man was getting on his feet rapidly enough to suit even Monsieur Dupont. The criminal assizes began at Tournayville the day after to-morrow. And the day after to-morrow Henri Mentone was to stand his trial for the murder of Théophile Blondin!

Raymond's fingers tightened upon the penholder until it cracked warningly, recalling him to himself. He had not gone that night. Gone! He laughed mockingly. The man had lost his memory! Who would have thought of that—and what it meant? If the man had died, or even if the man had talked and so *forced* him to accept pursuit as his one and only chance, the issue would have been clear cut. But the man, curse him, had not died; nor had he told his story—and to all appearances at least, except for still being naturally a little weak, was as well as any one. Gone! Gone—that night! Great God, they would *hang* the fool for this!

The sweat beads crept out on Raymond's forehead. No, no—not that! They thought the man was shamming now, but they would surely realise before it was too late that he was not. They would convict him of course, the evidence was damning, overwhelming, final—but they would not hang a man who could not remember. No, they wouldn't hang him. But what they would do was horrible enough—they would sentence the man for life, and keep him in the infirmary perhaps of some penitentiary. For life—that was all.

The square jaw was suddenly out-thrust. Well, what of it! He, Raymond, was safe as it was. It was his life, or the other's. In either case it would be an innocent man who suffered. As far as actual murder was concerned, he was no more guilty than this priest who had had nothing to do with it. Besides, they would hang him, Raymond, and they wouldn't hang the other. Of course, they didn't believe the man now! Why should they? They did not know what he, Raymond, knew; they had only the evidence before them that was conclusive enough to convict a saint from Heaven! Ha, ha! Why, even the man himself was beginning to believe in his own guilt! Sometimes the man was as a caged beast in an impotent fury; and—and sometimes he would cling like a frightened child with his arms around his, Raymond's, neck.

It was warm here in the room, warm with the bright, glorious sunlight of the summer morning. Why did he shiver like that? And this—why *this*? The smell of incense; those organ notes rising and swelling through the church; the voices of the choir; the bowed heads everywhere! He surged up from his chair, and, rocking on his feet, his hands clenched upon the edge of the desk. Before what dread tribunal was this that he was being called suddenly to account! Yesterday—yesterday had been Sunday—and yesterday he had celebrated mass. His own voice seemed to sound again in his ears: "*Introibo ad altare Dei*—I will go in unto the Altar of God.... *Ab homme iniquo et dolosoerue me*—Deliver me from the unjust and deceitful man.... *In quorum manibus iniquitates sunt*—In whose hands are iniquities.... *Hic est enim Calix sanguinis mei novi et æterni testamenti: mysterium fidei*—For this is the Chalice of My Blood of the new and eternal testament: the mystery of faith...." No—no, no! He had not profaned those holy things, those holy vessels. He had not done it! It was a lie! He had fooled even Gauthier Beaulieu, the altar boy.

He sank back into his chair like a man exhausted, and drew his hand across his eyes. It was nothing! He was quite calm again. Those words, the church, those holy things had nothing to do with Henri Mentone. If any one should think otherwise, that one was a fool! Had Three-Ace Artie ever been swayed by "mystery of faith"—or been called a coward! Yes, that was it—a coward! It was true that he had as much right to life as that pitiful thing in the back room, but it was he who had put that other's life in jeopardy! That creed—that creed of his, born of the far Northland where men were men, fearing neither God nor devil, nor man, nor beast—it was better than those trembling words which had just been upon his lips. True, he was safe now, if he let them dispose of this Henri Mentone—but to desert the other would be a coward's act. Well, what then—what then! Confess—and with meek, uplifted eyes, like some saintly martyr, stand upon the gibbet and fasten the noose around his own neck? *No!* Well then, what—*what?* The tormented look was back in Raymond's eyes. There was a way, a way by which he could give the man a chance, a way by which they both might have their chance, only the difficulties so far had seemed insurmountable—a problem that he had not yet been able to solve—and the time was short. Yes, the way was there, if only— —.

With a swift movement, incredibly swift, alert in an instant, his hand swept toward the desk. Some one was knocking at the door. His fingers closed on the thin piece of paper that had served him in tracing the signature of Francois Aubert, and crushed it into a little ball in the palm of his hand. The door opened. There were dark eyes there, dark hair, a slim figure, a sweet, quiet smile, a calm, an untroubled peace, a pervading radiance. It was unreal. It could not exist. There was only a ghastly turmoil, agony, dismay and strife everywhere—his soul told him so! This was Valérie. God, how tired he was, how weary! Once he had seen those arms supporting that wounded man's head so tenderly—like a soothing caress. If he might, just for a moment, know that too, it would bring him—rest.

She came lightly across the room and stood before the desk.

"It is for the letters, Monsieur le Curé," she smiled. "I am going down to the post-office." She picked up the little pile of correspondence; and, very prettily business-like, began to run through it.

Impulsively Raymond reached out to take the letters from her—and, instead, his hand slipped inside his *soutane*, and dropped the crushed ball of paper into one of his pockets. It was too late, of course! She would already have noticed the omission of the two signatures.

"There are two there that I have not yet signed," observed Raymond casually.

"Yes; so I see!" she answered brightly. "I was just going to tell you how terribly careless you were, Monsieur le Curé! Well, you can sign them now, while I am putting the others in their envelopes. Here they are."

He took the two letters from her hand—and laid them deliberately aside upon the desk.

"It was not carelessness," he said laughingly; "except that I should not have allowed them to get mixed up with the others. There are some changes that I think I should like to make before they go. They are not important—to-morrow will do."

"Of course!" she said. Then, in pretended consternation: "I hope the mistakes weren't mine!"

"No—not yours"—he spoke abstractedly now. He was watching her as she folded the letters and sealed the envelopes. How quickly she worked! In a minute now she would go and leave him alone again to listen to those footfalls from the other room. He wanted rest for his stumbling brain; and, yes—he wanted her. He could have reached out and caught her hands, and drawn that dark head bending over the desk closer to him, and held her there—a prisoner. He brushed his hands hurriedly over his forehead. A prisoner! What did he mean by that? Oh, yes, the thought was born of the idea that he was already a jailor. He had been a jailor for three days now—of that man there, who was too weak to get away. He had appointed himself jailor—and Monsieur Dupont had confirmed the appointment. What had that to do with Valérie? He only wanted her to stay because—a fool, was he!—because he wanted to torture himself a little more. Well, it was exquisite torture then, her presence, her voice, her smile! Love? Well, what if he loved! Days and days their lives had been spent together now. How long was it? A week—no, it must be more than a week—it seemed as though it had been as long as he could remember. Yes, he loved her! He knew that now—scoff, sneer and gibe if that inner voice would! He loved her! He loved Valérie! Madness? Well, what of that, too! Did he dispute it! Yes, it was madness—and in more ways than one! He was fighting for his life in this devil's masquerade, and he might win; but he could not fight for or win his love. That was just dangled before his eyes as the final Satanic touch to this hell-born conspiracy that engulfed him! He was in the garb of a priest! How those hell demons must shake their very souls out with laughter in their damnable glee! He could not even touch her; he could say no word, his tongue was tied; nor look at her—he was in the garb of a priest! He—what was this! A fire seemed in his veins. Her hand in his! Across the desk, her hand had crept softly into his!

"Monsieur—Monsieur le Curé—you are ill!" she cried anxiously.

And then Raymond found himself upon his feet, his other hand laid over hers—and he forced a smile.

"I—no"—Raymond shook his head—"no, Mademoiselle Valérie, I am not ill."

"You are worn out, then!" she insisted tremulously. "And it is our fault. We should have made you let us help you more. You have been up night after night with that man, and in the daytime there was the parish work, and you have never had any rest. And yesterday in the church you looked so tired—and—and——"

The dark eyes were misty; the sweet face was very close to his. If he might bend a little, just a very little, that glad wealth of hair would brush his cheek.

"A little tired, perhaps—yes—mademoiselle," he said, in a low voice. "But it is nothing!" He released her hand, and, turning abruptly from the desk, walked to the window.

She had followed him with her eyes, turned to look after him—he sensed that. There was silence in the room. He did not speak. He did not dare to speak until—ah!—this should bring him to his senses quickly enough!

He was staring out through the window. A buck-board had turned in from the road, and was coming across the green toward the *presbytère*. Dupont and Doctor Arnaud! They were coming for Henri Mentone now—*now!* He had let the time slip by until it was too late—because he had not been able to fight his way through the odds against him! And then there came a wan smile to Raymond's lips. No! His fears were groundless. Three-Ace Artie would have seen that at once! The buckboard was single-seated, there was room only for two—and Monsieur Dupont could be well trusted to look after his own comfort when he took the man away.

He drew back from the window, and faced around—and the thrill that had come from the touch of her hand was back again, as he caught her gaze upon him. What was it that was in those eyes, that was in her face? She had been looking at him like that, he knew, all the time that he had been standing at the window. They were still misty, those eyes—she could not hide that, though she lowered them hurriedly now. And that faint flush tinging her cheeks! Did it mean that she—Fool! He knew what it meant! It meant that if he cared to seek for any added self-torture with his madman's imaginings, he could find it readily to hand. She—to have any thought but that prompted by her woman's sympathy, her tender anxiety for another's trouble! She—who thought him a priest, and, pure in her faith as in her soul, would have recoiled in horror from— —

He steadied his voice.

"Monsieur Dupont and the doctor have just arrived," he said.

She looked up, her face serious now.

"They have come for Henri Mentone?"

"No, not yet, I imagine," he answered; "since they have only a one-seated buckboard."

"I will be glad when he has gone!" she exclaimed impulsively.

"Glad?"

"Yes—for your sake," she said. "He has brought you to the verge of illness yourself." She was looking down again, shuffling the sealed envelopes abstractedly. "And it is not only I who say so—it is all St. Marleau. St. Marleau loves you for it, for your care of him, Monsieur le Curé—but also St. Marlbau thinks more of its curé than it does of one who has taken another's life."

Raymond did not reply—he was listening now to the footsteps of Monsieur Dupont and the doctor, as they passed by along the hallway outside. Came then a sharp, angry voice raised querulously from the rear room—that was Henri Mentone. Monsieur Dupont's voice snapped in reply; and then the voices merged into a confused buzz and murmur. He glanced quickly at Valérie. She, too, was listening. Her head was turned toward the door, he could not see her face.

He walked slowly across the room to her side by the desk.

"You do not think, mademoiselle," he asked gravely, "that it is possible the man is telling the truth, that he really cannot remember anything that happened that night—and before?"

She shook her head.

"Every one knows he is guilty," she said thoughtfully. "The evidence proves it absolutely. Why, then, should one believe him? If there was even a little doubt of his guilt, no matter how little, it might be different, and one might wonder then; but as it is—no."

"And it is not only you who say so" —he smiled, using her own words— "it is all St. Marleau?"

"Yes, all St. Marleau—and every one else, including Monsieur le Curé, even if he has sacrificed himself for the man," she smiled in return. Her brows puckered suddenly. "Sometimes I am afraid of him," she said nervously. "Yesterday I ran from the room. He was in a fury."

Raymond's face grew grave.

"Ah! You did not tell me that, mademoiselle," he said soberly.

"And I am sorry I have told you now, if it is going to worry you," she said quickly. "You must not say anything to him. The next time I went in he was so sorry that it was pitiful."

In a fury—at times! Was it strange! Was it strange if one did not sit unmoved to watch, fettered, bound, impotent, a horrible doom creeping inexorably upon one! Was it strange if at times, all recollection blotted out, conscious only that one was powerless to avert that creeping terror, one should experience a paroxysm of fury that rocked one to the very soul—and at times in anguish left one like a helpless child! He had seen the man like that—many times in the last few days. And he, too, had seen that same terror creep like a dread thing out of the night upon himself to hover over him; and he could see it now lurking there, ever present—but he, Raymond, could fight!

The door of the rear room opened and closed; and Monsieur Dupont's voice resounded from the hall.

"Where is Monsieur le Curé? Ho, Monsieur le Curé!"

Valérie looked toward him inquiringly.

"Shall I tell them you are here?" she asked.

Raymond nodded mechanically.

"Yes—if you will, please."

He leaned against the desk, his hands gripping its edge behind his back. What was it now that this Monsieur Dupont wanted? He was never sure of Dupont. And this morning his brain was fagged, and he did not want to cope with this infernal Monsieur Dupont! He watched Valérie walk across the room, and disappear outside in the hall.

"Monsieur le Curé is here," he heard her say. "Will you walk in?" And then, at some remark in the doctor's voice which he did not catch: "No; he is not busy. I was just going to take his letters to the postoffice. He heard Monsieur Dupont call."

And then, as the two men stepped in through the doorway, Raymond spoke quietly:

"Good morning, Monsieur Dupont! Good morning, Doctor Arnaud!"

"Hah! Monsieur le Curé!" Monsieur Dupont wagged his head vigorously. "He is in a very pretty temper this morning, our friend in there—eh? Yes, very pretty! You have noticed it? Yes, you have noticed it. It would seem that he is beginning to realise at last that his little tricks are going to do him no good!"

Raymond waved his hand toward chairs.

"You will sit down?" he invited courteously.

"No" — Doctor Arnaud smiled, as he answered for them both. "No, not this morning, Monsieur le Curé. We are returning at once to Tournayville. I have an important case there, and Monsieur Dupont has promised to have me back before noon."

"Yes," said Monsieur Dupont, "we stopped only to tell you" — Monsieur Dupont jerked his hand in the direction of the rear room — "that we will take him away to-morrow morning. Doctor Arnaud says he will be quite able to go. We will see what the taste of a day in jail will do for him before he goes into the dock — what? He is very fortunate! Yes, very! There are not many who have only one day in jail before they are tried! Yes! To-morrow morning! You look surprised, Monsieur le Curé, that it should be so soon. Yes, you look surprised!"

"On the contrary," observed Raymond impassively, "when I saw you drive up a few minutes ago, I thought you had come to take him away at once."

"But, not at all!" Monsieur Dupont indulged in a significant smile. "No — not at all! I take not even that chance of cheating the court out of his appearance — I do not wish to house him for months until the next assizes. I take no chances on a relapse. He has been quite safe here. Yes — quite! He will be quite safe for another twenty-four hours in your excellent keeping, Monsieur le Curé — since he is still too weak to run far enough to have it do him any good!"

"You pay a high compliment to my vigilance, Monsieur Dupont," said Raymond, with a faint smile.

"Hah!" cried Monsieur Dupont. "Hah!" — he began to chuckle. "Do you hear that, Monsieur le Docteur Arnaud? I thought it had escaped him! He has a sense of humour, our estimable curé! You see, do you not? Yes, you see. Well, we will go now!" He pushed the doctor from the room. "*Au revoir* Monsieur le Curé! It is understood then? To-morrow morning! *Au revoir* — till to-morrow!"

Monsieur Dupont bowed, and whisked himself out of sight. Raymond went to the door, closed it, and mechanically began to pace up and down the room. He heard Monsieur Dupont and the doctor clamber into the buckboard, and heard the buckboard drive off. There was moisture upon his forehead again. He swept it away. To-morrow morning! He had until to-morrow morning in which to act — if he was to act at all. But the way! He could not see the way. It was full of peril. The risk was too great to be overcome! He dared not even approach that man in there with any plan. There was something horribly sardonic in that! If he was to act, he must act now, at once — there was only the afternoon and the night left.

"You are safe as it is," whispered that inner voice insidiously. "The man's condemnation by the law will dispose of the killing of Théophile Blondin forever. It will be as a closed book. And then—have you forgotten?—there is your own plan for getting away after a little while. It cannot fail, that plan. Besides, they will not sentence the man to hang, they will be sure to see that his memory is really gone; whereas they will surely hang you if you are caught—as you will be, if you are fool enough to attempt the impossible now. What did you ever get out of being quixotic? Do you remember that little affair in Ton-Nugget Camp?"

"My God, what shall I do?" Raymond cried out aloud. "If—if only I could see the way!"

"But you can't!" sneered the voice viciously. "Haven't you tried hard enough to satisfy even that remarkably tender conscience that you seem to have picked up somewhere so suddenly! You—who were going to kill the man with your own hands! Let well enough alone!"

It was silent now in the rear room. Raymond halted in the centre of the floor and listened. There were no footsteps; no sound of voice—only silence. He laughed a little harshly. What was the man doing? Planning his *own* escape! Again Raymond laughed in bitter mirth. God speed to the man in any such plans—only the man, as Monsieur Dupont had most sagaciously suggested, would not get very far alone. But still it would be humorous, would it not, if the man should succeed alone, where he, Raymond, had utterly failed so far to work out any plan that would accomplish the same end! There was the open window to begin with, the man had been told now probably that he was to be taken away to-morrow morning, and—why was there such absolute stillness from that other room? The partitions were very thin, and—Raymond, as mechanically as he had set to pacing up and down the room, turned to the door, passed out into the hall, and walked softly along to the door of the rear room. He listened there again. There was still silence. He opened the door, stepped across the threshold—and a strange white look crept into his face, and he stood still.

Upon the floor at the bedside knelt Henri Mentone, and at the opening of the door the man did not look up. There was no fury now; it was the child, helpless in despair and grief. His hands were outflung across the coverlet, his head was buried in his arms—and there was no movement, save only a convulsive tremor that shook the thin shoulders. And there was no sound.

And the whiteness deepened in Raymond's face—and, as he looked, suddenly the scene was blurred before his eyes.

And then Raymond stepped back into the hall, and closed the door again, and on Raymond's lips was a queer, twisted smile.

"To-morrow morning, I think you said, Monsieur Dupont," he whispered. "Well, to-morrow morning, Monsieur Dupont—he will be gone."

CHAPTER XIII—THE CONFEDERATE

THERE had been a caller, there had been parish matters, there had been endless things through endless hours which he had been unable to avoid—except in mind. He had attended to them subconsciously, as it were; his mind had never for an instant left Henri Mentone. And it was beginning to take form now, a plan whereby he might effect the other's escape.

Sitting at his desk, he looked at his watch as he heard Valérie and her mother go upstairs. It was a quarter past three. Later on in the afternoon, in another hour or thereabouts Madame Lafleur would take Henri Mentone for a few steps here and there about the green, or sit with him for a little fresh air on the porch of the *presbytère*. Raymond smiled ironically. As jailor he had delegated the task to Madame Lafleur—since, as he had told both Valérie and her mother at the noonday meal, he was going out to make pastoral visits that afternoon. Meanwhile—he had just looked into Henri Mentone's room—the man was lying on his bed asleep. If he worked quickly now—while Valérie and her mother were upstairs, and the man was lying on his bed!

He picked up a pen, and drew a piece of paper toward him. Everything hinged on his being able to procure a confederate. He, the curé of St. Marleau, must procure a confederate by some means, and naturally without the confederate knowing that Monsieur le Curé was doing so—and, almost as essential, a confederate who had no love for Monsieur le Curé! It was not a very simple matter! That was the problem with which he had racked his brains for the last three days. Not that the minor details were lacking in difficulties either; he, as the curé, must not appear even remotely in the plan; he, as the curé, dared not even suggest escape to Henri Mentone—but he could overcome all that if only he could secure a confederate. That was the point upon which everything depended.

His pen poised in his hand, he stared across the room. Yes, he saw it now—a gambler's chance. But the time was short now, short enough to make him welcome any chance. He would go to Mother Blondin's. He might find a man there such as he sought, one of those who already had offended the law by frequenting the dissolute old hag's illicit still. He could ask, of course, who these men were without exciting any suspicion, and if luck failed him that afternoon he would do so, and it would be like a shot still left in his locker; but if, in his rôle of curé, he could actually trap one of them drinking there, and incense the man, even fight with him, it would make success almost certain. Yes, yes — he could see it all now — clearly — afterwards, when it grew dark, he would go to the man in a far different rôle from that of a curé, and the man would be at his disposal. Yes, if he could trap one of them there — but before anything else Henri Mentone must be prepared for the attempt.

Raymond began to write slowly, in a tentative sort of way, upon the paper before him. Henri Mentone, remembering nothing of the events of that night, must be left in no doubt as to the genuineness and good faith of the note, or of the vital necessity of acting upon its instructions. At the expiration of a few minutes, Raymond read over what he had written. He scored out a word here and there; and then, on another sheet of paper, in a scrawling, illiterate hand, he wrote out a slangy, ungrammatical version of the original draft. He read it again now:

"The memory game won't go, Henri. They've got you cold, but they don't know there was two of us in it at the old woman's that night, so keep up your nerve, for I ain't for laying down on a pal. I got it fixed for a getaway for you to-night. Keep the back window open, and be ready at any time after dark — see? Leave the rest to me. If that mealy-mouthed priest gets in the road, so much the worse for him. I'll take care of him so he won't be any trouble to any one except a doctor, and mabbe not much to a doctor — get me? I'd have been back sooner, only I had to beat it for you know where to get the necessary coin. Here's some to keep you going in case we have to separate in a hurry to-night. — — Pierre."

Raymond nodded to himself. Henri Mentone might not relish the suggestion of any violence offered to the "mealy-mouthed priest," for he had come to look upon Father François Aubert as his only friend, and, except in his fits of fury, to cling dependently upon him; but then there would be no violence offered to Father François Aubert, and the suggestion supplied a final touch of authenticity to the note, since Henri Mentone would realise that escape was impossible unless in some way the curé could be got out of the road.

Raymond destroyed the original draft, and took out his pocketbook. He smiled curiously, as he examined its contents. It was the gold of the Yukon, the gold of Ton-Nugget Camp, that he had changed into banknotes of large denominations. He selected two fifty-dollar bills. It was not enough to carry the man far, or to take care of the man until he was on his feet, nor were fifty-dollar bills the most convenient denomination for a man under the present circumstances; but that was not their purpose — they would act as a guarantee of one "Pierre" and "Pierre's" plan, and to-night he would give the man more without stint, and supplement it with some small bills from his roll of "petty cash." He folded the money in the note, found a small piece of string in one of the drawers of the desk, stood up, took his hat, tiptoed softly across the room, out into the hall, and from the hall to the front porch.

Here, he stood quietly for a moment, looking about him; and then, satisfied that he was unobserved, that neither Valérie nor her mother had noticed his exit, he walked quickly around to the back of the house—and paused again, this time beneath the open window of Henri Mentone's room. Here, too, but even more sharply now, he looked about him—then stooped ana picked up a small stone. He tied the note around this, and, crouched low by the window, called softly: "Henri! Henri!"

He heard a rustle, the creak of the bed, as though the man, startled and suddenly roused, were jerking himself up into an upright position.

"It is Pierre!" Raymond called again. "*Courage, mon vieux!* Have no fear! All is arranged for tonight. But do not come to the window—we must be careful. Here—*voici!*"—he tossed the note in over the sill. "Until dark—tu comprends, Henri? I will be back then. Be ready!"

He heard the man cry out in a low voice, and the creak of the bed again, and the man's step on the floor—and, stooping low, Raymond darted around the corner of the house.

A moment later he was standing again in the hallway of the *presbytère*.

"Oh, Madame Lafleur!" he called up the stairs. "It is only to tell you that I am going out now."

"Yes, Monsieur le Curé—yes. Very well, Monsieur le Curé," she answered.

Raymond closed the front door behind him, and, walking sedately across the green and past the church, gained the road. It was Mother Blondin's now, but he would not go by the station road—further along the village street, where the houses thinned out and were scattered more apart, he could climb up the little hill without being seen, and by walking through the woods would come out on the path whose existence had once already done him such excellent service. And the path, as an approach to Mother Blondin's this afternoon, offered certain very important strategical advantages.

But now for the moment he was in the heart of the village, and from the doorways and garden patches of the little squat, curved-roof, whitewashed houses of rough-squared logs that flanked the road on either side, voices called out to him cheerily as he walked along. He answered them—all of them. He was even conscious, in spite of the worry of his mind, of a curious and not altogether unwelcome wonder. They were simple folk, these people, big-hearted and kindly, free and open-handed with the little they had, and they appeared to have grown fond of him in the few days he had been in St. Marleau, to look up to him, to trust him, to have faith in him, and to accept him as a friend, offering a frank friendship in return.

His hands were clasped behind his back as he walked along, and suddenly his fingers laced tightly over one another. The pleasurable wonder of it was gone. He was playing well this rôle of saint! He was a gambler—Three-Ace Artie of Ton-Nugget Camp; a gambler—too unclean even for the Yukon. But he was no hypocrite! He would have liked to have torn these saintly trappings from his body, wrenched off his *soutane* and hurled it in the faces of these people, and bade them keep their friendship and their trust—tell them that he asked for nothing that they gave because they believed him other than he was. He was no hypocrite—he was a man fighting desperately for that for which every one had a right to fight, for which instinct bade even an insect fight—his life! He did not despise this proffered friendship, the smile of eye and lip, the ring of genuine sincerity in the voices that called to him—but they were not his, they were not meant for Three-Ace Artie, they were not meant for Raymond Chapelle. Somehow—it was a grotesque thought—he envied himself in the rôle of curé for these things. But they were not his. It was strange even that he, in whose life there had been naught but riot and ruin, should still be able to simulate so well the better things, to carry through, not the rôle of priest, that was a matter of ritual, a matter of keeping his head and his nerve, but the far kindlier and intimate rôle of *father* to the parish! Yes, it was very strange, and——

"*Bon jour*, Monsieur le Curé!"

Raymond halted. It was Madame Bouchard, the carpenter's wife. With a sort of long-handled wooden paddle, she was removing huge loaves of bread from the queer-looking outdoor oven which, though built of a mixture of stone and brick, resembled very much, through being rounded over at the top, an exaggerated beehive. A few yards further in from the edge of the road Bouchard himself was at work upon a boat in front of his shop. Above the shop was the living quarters of the family, and here, on a narrow veranda, peering over, a half dozen scantily clad and very small children clung to the railings.

Raymond sniffed the air luxuriously.

"*Tiens*, Madame Bouchard!" he cried. "Your husband is to be envied! The smell of the bread is enough to make one hungry!"

The carpenter laid down his tools, and looked up, laughing.

"*Salut*, Monsieur le Curé!" he called.

"If Monsieur le Curé would like one"—Madame Bouchard's cheeks had grown a little rosy—"I—I will send one to the *presbytère* for him."

Raymond had eaten of St. Marleau bread before. The taste was sour, and it required little short of a deftly wielded axe to make any impression upon the crust.

"You are too good, too generous, Madame Bouchard," he said, shaking his forefinger at her chidingly. "And yet"—he smiled broadly—"if there is enough to spare, there is nothing I know of that would delight me more."

"Of course, she can spare it!" declared the carpenter heartily, coming forward. "Stanislaus will carry you two presently. And, *tiens*, Monsieur le Curé, you like to row a boat—eh?"

Raymond, on the point of shaking his head, checked himself. A boat! One of these days—soon, if this devil's trap would only open a little—there was his own escape to be managed. He had planned that carefully... a boating accident... the boat recovered... the curé's body swept out somewhere in those twenty-five miles of river breadth that stretched away before him now, and from there—who could doubt it!—to the sea.

"Yes," he said; "I am very fond of it, but as yet I have not found time."

"Good!" exclaimed the carpenter. "Well, in two or three days it will be finished, the best boat in St. Marleau—and Monsieur le Curé will be welcome to it as much as he likes. It is a nice row to the islands out there—three miles—to gather the sea-gull eggs—and the islands themselves are very pretty. It is a great place for a picnic, Monsieur le Curé."

"Excellent!" said Raymond enthusiastically. "That is exactly what I shall do." He clapped the carpenter playfully upon the shoulder. "So—eh, Monsieur Bouchard,—you will lose no time in finishing the boat!" He turned to Madame Bouchard. "*Au revoir*, madame—and very many thanks to you. I shall think of you at supper to-night, I promise you!" He waved his hand to the children on the veranda, and once more started along the road.

Madame Bouchard's voice, speaking to her husband, reached him. The words were not intended for his ears, and he did not catch them all. It was something about—"the good, young Father Aubert."

A wan smile crept to Raymond's lips. For the moment at least, he was in a softened, chastened mood. "The good, young Father Aubert"—well, let it be so! They would never know, these people of St. Marleau. Somehow, he was relieved at that. He did not want them to know. Somehow, he, too, wanted for himself just what they would have—a memory—the memory of a good, young Father Aubert.

At a bend in the road, where the road edged in against the slope of the hill, hiding him from view, Raymond clambered up the short ascent. In a clump of small cedars at the top, he paused and looked back. The great sweep of river, widening into the Gulf of St. Lawrence, with no breath of air to stir its surface, shimmered like a mirror under the afternoon sun. A big liner, outward bound, and perhaps ten miles from shore, seemed as though it were painted there. To the right, close in, was the little group of islands, with bare, rounded, rocky peaks, to which the carpenter had referred. About him, from distant fields, came the occasional voice of a man calling to his horses, the faint whir of a reaper, and a sort of pervading, drowsy murmur of insect life. Below him, nestled along the winding road, were the little whitewashed houses, quiet, secure, tranquil, they seemed to lie there; and high above them all, as though to typify the scene, to set its seal upon it, from the steeple of the church there gleamed in the sunlight a golden cross, the symbol of peace — such as he wore upon his breast!

With a quick intake of his breath, a snarl smothered in a low, confused cry, as he glanced involuntarily downward at his crucifix, he gathered up the skirts of his *soutane*, and, as though to vent his emotion in physical exertion, began to force his way savagely through the bushes and undergrowth.

He had other things to do than waste time in toying with visionary sentiment! There was one detail in that scene of *peace* he had not seen — that man in the rear room of the *presbytère* who was going to trial for the murder of Théophile Blondin, because he was decked out in the clothes of one Raymond Chapelle, alias Henri Mentone. It would be well perhaps for Raymond Chapelle to remember that, and to remember nothing else for the remainder of the afternoon!

He went on through the woods, heading as nearly as he could judge in a direction that would bring him out at the rear of the tavern. And now he laughed shortly to himself. Peace! There would be a peace that would linger long in somebody's memory at Mother Blondin's this afternoon, if only luck were with him! He was on a priestly mission — to console, bring comfort to the old hag for the loss of her son — and, quite incidentally, to precipitate a fight with any of the loungers who might be burying their noses in Mother Blondin's home-made *whiskey-blanc!* He laughed out again. St. Marleau would talk of that, too, and applaud the righteousness of the good, young Father Au^ bert — but he would attain the object he sought. He, the good, young Father Aubert, the man with a rope around his neck, whose hands were against everyman's, had too many friends in St. Marleau — he needed an *enemy* now! It was the one thing that would make the night's work sure.

He reached the edge of the wood to find himself even nearer the tavern than he had expected — and to find, too, that he would not have to lie long in wait for a visitor to Mother Blondin's. There was one there already. So far then, he could have asked for no better luck. He caught the sound of voices —

the old hag's, high-pitched and querulous; a man's, rough and domineering. Looking cautiously through the fringe of trees that still sheltered him, Raymond discovered that he was separated from Mother Blondin's back door by a matter of but a few yards of clearing. The door was open, and a man, heavy-built, in a red-checkered shirt, a wide-brimmed hat of coarse straw, was forcing his way past the shrivelled old woman. As the man turned his head sideways, Raymond caught a glimpse of the other's face. It was not a pleasant face. The eyes were black, narrow and shifty under a low brow; and a three days' growth of black stubble on his jaws added to his exceedingly dirty and unkempt appearance.

Mother Blondin's voice rose furiously.

"You will pay first!" she screamed. "I know you too well, Jacques Bourget! Do you understand? The money! You will pay me first!"

"Or otherwise you will tell the police, eh?" the man guffawed contemptuously. He pushed his way inside the house, and pushed a table that stood in the centre of the room roughly back against the wall. "You shut your mouth!" he jeered at her—and, stooping down, lifted up a trap door in the floor. "Now trot along quick for some glasses, so you can keep count of all we both drink!"

"You are a thief, a robber, a *crapule*, a—" she burst into a stream of blasphemous invective. Her wrinkled face grew livid with ungovernable rage. She shook a bony fist at him. "I will show you what you will get for this! You think I am alone—eh? You think I am an old woman that you can rob as you like—eh? You think my whisky is for your guzzling throat without pay—eh? Well, I will show you, you——"

The man made a threatening movement toward her, and she retreated back out of Raymond's sight—evidently into an inner room, for her voice, as virago-like as ever, was muffled now.

"Bring me a glass, and waste no time about it!" the man called after her. "And if you do not hold your tongue, something worse will happen to you than the loss of a drop out of your bottle!"

The man turned, and descended to the cellar through the trapdoor.

"Yes," said Raymond softly to himself. "Yes, I think Monsieur Jacques Bourget is the man I came to find."

He stepped out from the trees, walked noiselessly across to the house, and, reaching the doorway, remained standing quietly upon the threshold. He could hear the man moving about in the cellar below; from the inner room came Mother Blondin's incessant mutterings, mingled with a savage rattling of crockery. Raymond smiled ominously—and then Raymond's face grew stern with well-simulated clerical disapproval.

The man's head, back turned, showed above the level of the floor. Into the doorway from the inner room came Mother Blondin—and halted there, her withered old jaw sagging downward in dumfounded surprise until it displayed her almost toothless gums. The man gained his feet, turned around—and, with a startled oath, dropped the bottle he was carrying. It crashed to the floor, broke, and the contents began to trickle back over the edge of the trapdoor.

"*Sacristi!*" shouted the man, his face flaring up into an angry red. He thrust his head forward truculently from his shoulders, and glared at Raymond. "*Sacré nom de Dieu*, it is the saintly priest!" he sneered.

"My son," said Raymond gravely, "do not blaspheme! And have respect for the Church!"

"Bah!" snarled the man. "Do you think I care for you—or your church!" He looked suddenly at Mother Blondin. "Hah!"—he jumped across the room toward her. "So that is what you meant by not being alone—eh? I did not understand! You would trick me, would you! You would sell me out for the price of a drink—and—ha, ha—to a priest! Well"—he had her now by the shoulders—"I will take a turn at showing you what I will do! Eh—why did you not warn me he was here?" He caught her head, and banged it brutally against the wall. "Eh—why did——"

Raymond, too, was across the room. It was strange! Most strange! He had intended to seek an occasion to quarrel. The occasion was made for him. He had no longer any desire to quarrel—he was possessed of an overwhelming desire to get his fingers around the throat of this cur who banged that straggling, dishevelled gray hair against the wall. He was not quite sure that it was himself who spoke. No, of course, it was not! It was Monsieur le Curé— the good, young Father Aubert. He was between them now, only Mother Blondin had fallen to the floor.

"My son," he said placidly, "since you will not respect the Church for one reason, I will teach you to respect it for another." He pointed to old Mother Blondin, who, more terrified than hurt perhaps, was getting to her knees, moaning and wringing her hands. "You have heard, though I fear you may have forgotten it, of the Mosaic law. An eye for an eye, my son. I intend to do to you exactly what you have done to this woman."

The man, drawn back, eyed him first in angry bewilderment, and then with profound contempt.

"You'd better get out of here!" he said roughly.

"Presently—when I have thrown you out"—Raymond was calmly tucking up the skirts of his *soutane*. "And"—the flat of his hand landed with a stinging blow across the other's cheek — "you see that I do not take even you off your guard."

The man reeled back — and then, with a bull-like roar of rage, head down, rushed at Raymond.

It was not Monsieur le Curé now — it was Raymond Chapelle, alias Arthur Leroy, alias Three-Ace Artie, cold, contained, quick and lithe as a panther, and with a panther's strength. A crash — a lightning right whipped to the point of Bourget's jaw — and Bourget's head jolted back quivering on his shoulders like a tuning fork. And like a flash, before the other could recover, a left and right smashed full again into Bourget's face.

With a scream, Mother Blondin crawled and scuttled into the doorway of the inner room. The man, bellowing with mad dismay, his hands outstretched, his fingers crooked to tear at Raymond's flesh if they could but reach it, rushed again.

And now Raymond, wary of the other's strength and bulk, gave ground; and now he side-stepped and swung, battering his blows into Bourget's face; and now he ran craftily from the other. Chairs and table crashed to the floor; their heels crunched in the splinters of the broken bottle. The man's face began to bleed profusely from both nose and a cut lip. They were not tactics that Bourget understood. He clawed, he kept his head down, he rushed in blind clumsiness — and always Raymond was just beyond his reach.

Again and again they circled the room, Bourget, big, lumbering, awkward, futilely expending his strength, screaming oaths with gasping breath. And again and again, springing aside as the man charged blindly by, Raymond with a grim fury rained in his blows. It was something like that other night — here in Mother Blon-din's. She was shrieking again now from the doorway:

"Kill him! The *misérable!* Hah, Jacques Bourget, are you a jack-in-the-box only to bob your head backward every time you are hit! I did not bring the priest here! *Sacré nom,* you cannot blame me! I had nothing to do with it! *Sacré nom — sacré nom — sacré nom — kill him!*"

Kill who? Who did she mean — the man or himself? Raymond did not know. She was just a blurred object of rage and tumbled hair dancing in a frenzy up and down there in the doorway. He ran again. Bourget, like a stunned fool, was covering his face with his arms as he dashed forward. Ah, yes, Bourget was trying to crush him back into the corner there, and — no! — the maniacal rush had faltered, the man was swaying on his feet. And then Raymond, crouched to elude the man, sprang instead at the other's throat, his hands closed like a vise, and with the impact of his body both lurched back against the wall by the rear doorway.

"My son," panted Raymond, "you remember—an eye for an eye"—he smashed the man's head back against the wall—and then, gathering all his strength, flung the other from him out through the open door.

The fight was out of the man. For a moment he lay sprawled on the grass. Then he raised himself up, and got upon his knees. His face was bruised and blood-stained almost beyond recognition. He shook both fists at Raymond.

"By God, I'll get you for this!"—the man's voice was guttural with unbridled passion. "I'll get you, you censer-swinging devil! I'll twist your neck with the chain of your own crucifix! Damn you to the pit! You're not through with me!"

"Go!" said Raymond sternly. "Go—and be glad that I have treated you no worse!"

He shut the door in the man's face; and, turning abruptly, walked across the floor to where Mother Blondin, quiet for the moment, gaped at him from the threshold of the other room.

"He will not trouble you any more, Madame Blondin, I imagine," he said quietly. "See, it is over!" He smiled at her reassuringly—he needed to know now only where the man lived. "I should be sorry to think he was one of my parishioners. Where does he come from?"

"He is a farmer, and he lives in the house on the point a mile and a quarter up the road"—the answer had come automatically; she was listening, without looking at Raymond, to the threats and oaths that Jacques Bourget, as he evidently moved away for his voice kept growing fainter, still bawled from without. And then hate and sullen viciousness was in her face again. Her hair had tumbled to her shoulders and straggled over her forehead. She jabbed at it with both hands, sweeping it from her eyes, and leered at him fiercely. "You dirty spy!" she croaked hoarsely. "I know you—I know all of you priests! You are all alike! Sneaks! Sneaks! Meddlers and sneaks! But you'll get to hell some day—like the rest of us! Ha, ha—to hell! You can't fool the devil! I know you. That's what you sneaked up here for—to spy on me, to find something against me that the police weren't sharp enough to find, so that you could get rid of me, get me out of St. Marleau! I know! They've been trying that for a long time!"

"To turn you over to the police," said Raymond gently, "would never save you from yourself. I came to talk to you a little about your son—to see if in any way I could help you, or be of comfort to you."

She stared at him for an instant, wondering and perplexed; and then the snarl was on her lips again.

"You lie! No priest comes here for that! I am an *excommuniée*."

"You are a woman in sorrow," Raymond said simply.

She did not answer him—only drew back into the other room.

Raymond followed her. It was the room where he had fought that night—with Théophile Blondin. His eyes swept it with a hurried glance. There was the *armoire* from which Théophile Blondin had snatched the revolver—and there was the spot on the floor where the dead man had fallen. And here was the old hag with the streaming hair, as it had streamed that night, who had run shrieking into the storm that he had murdered her son. And the whole scene began to live itself over again in his mind in minute detail. It seemed to possess an unhealthy fascination that bade him linger, and at the same time to fill him with an impulse to rush away from it. And the impulse was the stronger; and, besides, it would be evening soon, and there was that man in the *presbytère*, and there was much to do, and he had his confederate now—one Jacques Bourget.

"I shall not stay now"—he smiled, as he turned to Mother Blondin, and held out his hand. "You are upset over what has happened. Another time. But you will remember, will you not, that I would like to help you in any way I can?"

She reached out her hand mechanically to take his that was extended to her, and suddenly, muttering, jerked it back—and Raymond, appearing not to notice, smiled again, and, crossing the room, went out through the front door.

He went slowly across the little patch of yard, and on along the road in the direction of the village, and now his lips thinned in a grim smile. Yes, St. Marleau would hear of this, his chivalrous protection of Mother Blondin—and place another halo on his head! The devil's sense of humour was of a brand all its own!

The more he twisted and squirmed and wriggled to get out of the trap, desperate to the extent that he would hesitate at nothing, the more he became—the good, young Father Aubert! Even that dissolute old hag, whose hatred for the church and all pertaining to it was the most dominant passion in her life, was not far from the point where she would tolerate a priest—if the priest were the good, young Father Aubert!

He reached the point where the road began to descend the hill, and, pausing, looked back. Yes—even Mother Blondin, the *excommuniée!* She was standing in the doorway, dirty, unkempt, disreputable, and, shading her eyes with her hand, was gazing after him. Yes, even she—whose son had been killed in a fight with him.

And Raymond, fumbling suddenly with his hat, lifted it to Mother Blondin, and went on down the hill.

CHAPTER XIV—THE HOUSE ON THE POINT

IT was late, a good half hour after the usual supper time, when Raymond returned to the *presbytère*. He had done a very strange thing. He had gone into the church, and sat there in the silence and the quiet of the sacristy—and twilight had come unnoticed. It was the quiet he had sought, respite for a mind that had suddenly seemed nerve-racked to the breaking point as he had come down the hill from Mother Blondin's. It had been dim, and still, and cool, and restful in there—in the church. There was still Valerie, still the priest who had not died, still his own peril and danger, and still the hazard of the night before him; all that had not been altered; all that still remained—but in a measure, strangely, somehow, he was calmed. He was full of apologies now to Madame Lafleur, as he sat down to supper.

"But it is nothing!" she said, placing a lamp upon the table. She sat down herself; and added simply, as though, indeed, no reason could be more valid: "I saw you go into the church, Monsieur le Curé."

"Yes," said Raymond, his eyes now on Valerie's empty seat. "And where is Mademoiselle Valerie? Taking our *pauvre* Mentone his supper?"

"Oh, no!" she answered quickly. "I took him his supper myself a little while ago—though I do not know whether he will eat it or not. Valerie went over to her uncle's about halfpast five. She said something about going for a drive."

Raymond cut his slice of cold pork without comment. He was conscious of a dismal sense of disappointment, a depression, a falling of his spirits again. The room seemed cold and dead without Valérie there, without her voice, without her smile. And then there came a sense of pique, of irritation, unreasonable no doubt, but there for all that. Why had she not included him in the drive? Fool! Had he forgotten? He could not have gone if she had—he had other things to do than drive that evening!

"Yes," said Madame Lafleur, significantly reverting to her former remark, as she handed him his tea, "yes, I do not know if the poor fellow will eat anything or not."

Raymond glanced at her quickly. What was the matter? Had anything been discovered! And then his eyes were on his plate again. Madame Lafleur's face, whatever her words might be intended to convey, was genuinely sympathetic, nothing more.

"Not eat?" he repeated mildly. "And why not, Madame Lafleur?"

"I am sure I do not know," she replied, a little anxiously. "I have never seen him so excited. I thought it was because he was to be taken away to-morrow morning. And so, when we went out this afternoon, I tried to say something to him about his going away that would cheer him up. And would you believe it, Monsieur le Curé, he just stared at me, and then, as though I had said something droll, he—fancy, Monsieur le Curé, from a man who was going to be tried for his life—he laughed until I thought he would never stop. And after that he would say nothing at all; and since he has come in he has not been for an instant still. Do you not hear him, Monsieur le Curé?"

Raymond heard very distinctly. His ears had caught the sounds from the moment he had entered the *presbytère*. Up and down, up and down, from that back room came the stumbling footfalls; then silence for a moment, as though from exhaustion the man had sunk down into a chair; and then the pacing to and fro again. Raymond's lips tightened in understanding, as he bent his head over his plate. Like himself, the man in there was waiting—for darkness!

"He is over-excited," he said gravely. "And being still so weak, the news that he is to go to-morrow, I am afraid, has been too much for him. I have no doubt he was verging on hysteria when he laughed at you like that, Madame Lafleur."

"I—I hope we shall not have any trouble with him," said Madame Lafleur nervously. "I mean that I hope he won't be taken sick again. He did not look at the tray at all when I took it in; he kept his eyes on me all the time, as though he were trying to read something in my face."

"Poor fellow!" murmured Raymond.

Madame Lafleur nodded her gray head in sympathetic assent.

"Ah, yes, Monsieur le Curé—the poor fellow!" she sighed. "It is a terrible thing that he has done; but it is also terrible to think of what he will have to face. Do you think it wrong, Monsieur le Curé, to wish almost that he might escape?"

Escape! Curse it—what was the matter with Madame Lafleur to-night? Or was it something the matter with himself?

"Not wrong, perhaps," he said, smiling at her, "if you do not connive at it."

"Oh, but, Monsieur le Curé!" she exclaimed reprovingly. "What a thing to say! But I would never do that! Still, it is all very sad, and I am heartily glad that I am not to be a witness at the trial like you and Valérie. And they say that Madame Blondin, and Monsieur Labbée, the station agent, and a lot of the villagers are to go too."

"Yes, I believe so," Raymond nodded.

Madame Lafleur, in quaint consternation, suddenly changed the subject.

"Oh, but I forgot to tell you!" she cried. "The bread! Madame Bouchard sent you two loaves all fresh and hot. Do you like it?"

The bread! He had been conscious neither that the bread was sour, nor that the crust was unmanageable. He became suddenly aware that the morsel in his mouth was not at all like the baking of Madame Lafleur.

"You are all too good to me here in St. Marleau," he protested.

He checked her reply with a chiding forefinger, and a shake of his head — and presently, the meal at an end, pushed back his chair, and strolled to the window. He stood there for a moment looking out. It was dark now — dark enough for his purpose.

"It is a beautiful night, Madame Lafleur," he said enthusiastically. "I am almost tempted to go out again for a little walk."

"But, yes, Monsieur le Curé — why not!" Madame Lafleur was quite anxious that he should go. Madame Lafleur was possessed of that enviable disposition that was instantly responsive to the interests and pleasures of others.

"Yes — why not!" smiled Raymond, patting her arm as he passed by her on his way to the door. "Well, I believe I will."

But outside in the hall he hesitated. Should he go first to the man in the rear room? He had intended to do so before he went out — to probe the other, as it were, to satisfy himself, perhaps more by the man's acts and looks than by words, that Henri Mentone had entered into the plans for the night. But he was satisfied of that now. Madame Lafleur's conversation had left no doubt but that the man's unusual restlessness and excitement were due to his being on the *qui vive* of expectancy. No, there was no use, therefore, in going to the man now, it would only be a waste of valuable time.

This decision taken, Raymond walked to the front door and down the steps of the porch. Here he turned, and, choosing the opposite side of the house from the kitchen and dining room, where he might have been observed by Madame Lafleur, yet still moving deliberately as though he were but sauntering idly toward the beach, made his way around to the rear of the *presbytère*. It was quite dark. There were stars, but no moon. Behind here, between the back of the house and the shed, there was no possibility of his being seen. The only light came from Henri Mentone's room, and the shades there were drawn.

He opened the shed door silently, stepped inside, and closed the door behind him. He struck a match, held it above his head – and almost instantly extinguished it, as he located the sacristan's overalls, and the old coat and hat.

And now Raymond worked quickly. He stripped off his *soutane*, drew on the overalls, turning the bottoms well up over his own trousers, slipped on the coat, tucked the hat into one of the coat pockets, and put on his *soutane* again. It was very simple – the *soutane* hid everything. He smiled grimly, as he, stepped outside again – the Monsieur le Curé who came out, was the Monsieur le Curé who had gone in.

Raymond chose the beach. The village street meant that he would be delayed by being forced to stop and talk with any one he might meet, to say nothing of the possibility of having the ruinous, if well meaning, companionship of some one foisted upon him – while, even if seen, there would be nothing strange in the fact that the curé should be taking an evening walk along the shore.

He started off at a brisk pace along the stretch of sand just behind the *presbytère*. It was a mile and a quarter to the point – to Jacques Bourget's. At the end of the sandy stretch Raymond went more slowly – the shore line as a promenade left much to be desired – there was a seemingly interminable ledge of slate rock over which he had need to pick his way carefully. He negotiated this, and was rewarded with another short sandy strip – but only to encounter the slate rocks again with their ubiquitous little pools of water in the hollows, which he must avoid warily.

Sometimes he slipped; once he fell. The grim smile was back on his lips. There seemed to be something ironical even in these minor difficulties that stood between him and the effecting of the other's escape! There seemed to be a world of irony in the fact that he who sought escape himself should plan another's rather than his own! It was the devil's toils, that was all, the devil's damnable ingenuity, and hell's incomparable sense of humour! He had either to desert the man; or stand in the man's place himself, and dangle from the gallows for his pains; or get the man away. Well, he had no desire to dangle from the gallows – or to desert the man! He had chosen the third and only course left open to him. If he got the man away, if the man succeeded in making his escape, it would not only save the man, but he, Raymond, would have nothing thereafter to fear – the Curé of St. Marleau in due course would meet with his deplorable and fatal accident! True, the man would always live in the shadow of pursuit, a thing that he, Raymond, had been willing to accept for himself only as a last resort, but there was no help for that in the other's case now. He would give the man more money, plenty of it. The man should be across the border and in the States early to-morrow, then New York, and a steamer for South America. Yes, it should unquestionably succeed. He had worked out all those details while he was still racking his brain for a "Jacques Bourget," and he would give the man minute instructions at the last moment when he gave him more money—that hundred dollars was only an evidence of good faith and of the loyalty of one "Pierre." The only disturbing factor in the plan was the man's physical condition. The man was still virtually an invalid—otherwise the police would have been neither justified in so doing, nor for a moment have been willing to leave him in the *presbytère,* as they had. Monsieur Dupont was no fool, and it was perfectly true that the man had not the slightest chance in the world of getting away—alone. But, aided as he, Raymond, proposed to aid the other, the man surely would be able to stand the strain of travelling, for a man could do much where his life was at stake. Yes, after all, why worry on that score! It was only the night and part of the next day. Then the man could rest quietly at a certain address in New York, while waiting for his steamer. Yes, unquestionably, the man, with his life in the balance, would be able to manage that.

Raymond was still picking his way over the ledges, still slipping and stumbling, and now, recovering from a fall that had brought him to his knees, he gave his undivided attention to his immediate task. It seemed a very long mile and a quarter, but at the expiration of perhaps another twenty minutes he was at the end of it, and halted to take note of his surroundings. He could just distinguish the village road edging away on his left; while ahead of him, but a little to his right, out on the wooded point, he caught the glimmer of a light through the trees. That would be Jacques Bourget's house.

He now looked cautiously about him. There was no other house in sight. His eyes swept the road up and down as far as he could see—there was no one, no sign of life. He listened—there was nothing, save the distant lapping of the water far out, for the tide was low on the mud flats.

A large rock close at hand suggested a landmark that could not be mistaken. He stepped toward it, took off his *soutane,* and laid the garment down beside the rock; he removed his clerical collar and his clerical hat, and placed them on top of the *soutane,* taking care, however, to cover the white collar with the hat—then, turning down the trouser legs of the overalls, and turning up the collar of the threadbare coat, he took the battered slouch hat from his pocket and pulled it far down over his eyes.

"Behold," said Raymond cynically, "behold Pierre—what is his other name? Well, what does it matter? Pierre—Desforges. Desforges will do as well as any—behold Pierre Desforges!"

He left the beach, went up the little rise of ground that brought him amongst the trees, and made his way through the latter toward the lighted window of the house. Arrived here, he once more looked about him.

The house was isolated, far back from the road; and, in the darkness and the shadows cast by the trees, would have been scarcely discernible, save that it was whitewashed, and but for the yellow glow diffused from the window. He approached the door softly, and listened. A woman's voice, and then a man's, snarling viciously, reached him. "... *le sacré maudit curé!*"

Raymond laughed low. Jacques Bourget and his wife appeared to have an engrossing topic of conversation, if they had been at it since afternoon! Also Jacques Bourget appeared to be of an unforgiving nature!

There was no veranda, not even a step, the door was on a level with the ground; and, from the little Raymond could see of the house now that he was close beside it, it appeared to be as down-at-the-heels and as shiftless as its proprietor. He leaned forward to avail himself of the light from the window, and, taking out a roll of bills, of smaller denominations than those which he carried in his pocketbook, he counted out five ten-dollar notes.

Jacques Bourget from within was still in the midst of a blasphemous tirade. Raymond rapped sharply on the door with his knuckles. Bourget's voice ceased instantly, and there was silence for a moment. Raymond rapped again — and then, as a chair leg squeaked upon the floor, and there came the sound of a heavy tread approaching the door, he drew quickly back into the shadows at one side.

The door was flung open, and Bourget's face, battered and cut, an eye black and swollen, his lip puffed out to twice its normal size, peered out into the darkness.

"Who's there?" he called out gruffly.

"S-sh! Don't talk so loud!" Raymond cautioned in a guarded voice. "Are you Jacques Bourget?"

The man, with a start, turned his face in the direction of Raymond's voice. Mechanically he dropped his own voice.

"Mabbe I am, and mabbe I'm not," he growled suspiciously. "What do you want?"

"I want to talk to you if you are Jacques Bourget," Raymond answered. "And if you are Jacques Bourget I can put you in the way of turning a few dollars tonight, to say nothing of another little matter that will be to your liking."

The man hesitated, then drew back a little in the doorway.

"Well, come in," he invited. "There's no one but the old woman here."

"The old woman is one old woman too many," Raymond said roughly. "I'm not on exhibition. You come out here, and shut the door. You've nothing to be afraid of—the only thing I have to do with the police is to keep away from them, and that takes me all my time."

"I ain't worrying about the police," said Bourget shrewdly.

"Maybe not," returned Raymond. "I didn't say you were. I said I was. I've got a hundred dollars here that— —"

A woman appeared suddenly in the doorway behind Bourget.

"What is it? Who is it, Jacques?" she shrilled out inquisitively.

Bourget, for answer, swore at her, pushed her back, and, slamming the door behind him, stepped outside.

"Well, what is it? And who are you?" he demanded.

"My name is Desforges—Pierre Desforges," said Raymond, his voice still significantly low. "That doesn't mean anything to you—and it doesn't matter. What I want you to do is to drive a man to the second station from here to-night—St. Eustace is the name, isn't it?—and you get a hundred dollars for the trip."

"What do you mean?" Bourget's voice mingled incredulity and avarice. "A hundred dollars for that, eh? Are you trying to make a fool of me?"

Raymond held the bills up before the man's face. "Feel the money, if you can't see it!" he suggested, with a short laugh. "That's what talks."

"*Bon Dieu!*" ejaculated Bourget. "Yes, it is so! Well, who am I to drive? You? You are running away! Yes, Î understand! They are after you—eh? I am to drive you, eh?"

"No," said Raymond. He drew the man close to him in the darkness, and placed his lips to Bourget's ear. "*Henri Mentone.*"

Bourget, startled, sprang back.

"*What! Who!*" he cried out loudly.

"I told you not to talk so loud!" snapped Raymond. "You heard what I said."

Bourget twisted his head furtively about.

"No, '*cré nom—no!*" he said huskily. "It is too much risk! If one were caught at that—eh? *Bien non, merci!*"

"There's no chance of your being caught"—Raymond's voice was smooth again. "It is only nine miles to St. Eustace—you will be back and in bed long before daylight. Who is to know anything about it?"

"Yes, and you!"—Bourget was still twisting his head about furtively. "What do I know about you? What have you to do with this?"

"I will tell you," said Raymond, and into the velvet softness of his voice there crept an ominous undertone; "and at the same time I will tell you that you will be very wise to keep your mouth shut. You understand? If I trust you, it is to make you trust me. Henri Mentone is my pal. I was there the night Théophile Blondin was killed. But I made my escape. I do not desert a pal, only I had no money. Well, I have the money now, and I am back. And I am just in time—eh? They say he is well enough to be taken away in the morning."

"*Mon Dieu*, you were there at the killing!" muttered Bourget hoarsely. "No—I do not like it! No—it is too much risk!" His voice grew suddenly sharp with undisguised suspicion. "And why did you come to me, eh? Why did you come to me? Who sent you here?"

"I came because Mentone must be driven to St. Eustace—because he is not strong enough to walk," said Raymond coolly. "And no one sent me here. I heard of your fight this afternoon. The curé is telling around the village that if he could not change the aspect of your heart, there was no doubt as to the change in the aspect of your face."

"*Sacré nom!*" gritted Bourget furiously. "He said that! I will show him! I am not through with him yet! But what has he to do with this that you come here? Eh? I do not understand."

"Simply," said Raymond meaningly, "that Monsieur le Curé is the one with whom we shall have to deal in getting Mentone away."

"Hah!" exclaimed Bourget fiercely. "Yes—I am listening now! Well?"

"He sits a great deal of the time in the room with Mentone," explained Raymond, with a callous laugh. "Very well. Mentone has been warned. If this fool of a curé knows no better than to sit there all night tonight, I will find some reason for calling him outside, and in the darkness where he will recognise no one we shall know what to do with him, and when we are through we will tie him and gag him and throw him into the shed where he will not be found until morning. On the other hand, if we are able to get Mentone away without the curé knowing it, you will still not be without your revenge. He is responsible for Mentone, and if Mentone gets away through the curé's negligence, the curé will get into trouble with the police."

"I like the first plan better," decided Bourget, with an ugly sneer. "He talks of my face, does he! *Nom de Dieu*, he will not be able to talk of his own! And a hundred dollars—eh? You said a hundred dollars? Well, if there is no more risk than that in the rest of the plan, *sacré nom*, you can count on Jacques Bourget". . .

"There is no risk at all," said Raymond. "And as to which plan—we shall see. We shall have to be guided by the circumstances, eh? And for the rest—listen! I will return by the beach, and watch the *presbytère*. You give me time to get back, then harness your horse and drive down there—drive past the *presbytère*. I will be listening, and will hear you. Then after you have gone a little way beyond, turn around and come back, and I will know that it is you. If you drive in behind the church to where the people tie their horses at mass on Sundays, you can wait there without being seen by any one passing by on the road. I will come and let you know how things are going. We may have to wait a while after that until everything is quiet, but in that way we will be ready to act the minute it is safe to do so."

"All that is simple enough," Bourget grunted in agreement. "And then?"

"And then," said Raymond, "we will get Mentone out through the window of his room. There is a train that passes St. Eustace at ten minutes after midnight—and that is all. The St. Eustace station, I understand, is like the one here—far from the village, and with no houses about. He can hide near the station until traintime; and, without having shown yourself, you can drive back home and go to bed. It is your wife only that you have to think of—she will say nothing, eh?"

"*Baptême!*" snorted Bourget contemptuously. "She has learned before now when to keep her tongue where it belongs! And you? You are coming, too?"

"Do you think I am a fool, Bourget?" inquired Raymond shortly. "When they find Mentone is gone, they will know he must have had an accomplice, for he could not get far alone. They will be looking for two of us travelling together. I will go the other way. That makes it safe for Mentone—and safe for me. I can walk to Tournayville easily before daylight; and in that way we shall both give the police the slip."

"*Diable!*" grunted Bourget admiringly. "You have a head!"

"It is good enough to take care of us all in a little job like to-night's," returned Raymond, with a shrug of his shoulders. "Well, do you understand everything? For if you do, there's no use wasting any time."

"Yes—I have it all!" Bourget's voice grew vicious again. "That *sacré maudit curé!* Yes, I understand."

Raymond thrust the banknotes he had been holding into Bourget's hand.

"Here are fifty dollars to bind the bargain," he said crisply. "You get the other fifty at the church. If you don't get them, all you've got to do is drive off and leave Mentone in the lurch. That's fair, isn't it?"

Bourget shuffled back to the edge of the lighted window, counted the money, and shoved it into his pocket.

"*Bon Dieu!*" Bourget's puffed lip twisted into a satisfied grin. "I do not mind telling you, my Pierre Desforges, that it is long since I have seen so much."

"Well, the other fifty is just as good," said Raymond in grim pleasantry. He stepped back and away from the house. "At the church then, Bourget—in, say, three-quarters of an hour."

"I will be there," Bourget answered. "Have no fear—I will be there!"

"All right!" Raymond called back—and a moment later gained the beach again.

At the rock, he once more put on his *soutane*; and, running now where the sandy stretches gave him opportunity, scrambling as rapidly as he could over the ledges of slate rock, he headed back for the *presbytère*.

It was as good as done! There was a freeness to his spirits now—a weight and an oppression lifted from him. Henri Mentone would stand in no prisoner's dock the day after to-morrow to answer for the murder of Théophile Blondin! And it was very simple—now that Bourget's aid had been enlisted. He smiled ironically as he went along. It would not even be necessary to pommel Monsieur le Curé into a state of insensibility! Madame Lafleur retired very early—by nine o'clock at the latest—as did Valérie. As soon as he heard Bourget drive up to the church, he would go to the man to allay any impatience, and as evidence that the plan was working well. He would return then to the *presbytère*—it was a matter only of slipping on and off his *soutane* to appear as Father Aubert to Madame Lafleur and Valérie, and as Pierre Desforges to Jacques Bourget. And the moment Madame Lafleur and Valérie were in bed, he would extinguish the light in the front room as proof that Monsieur le Curé, too, had retired, run around to the back of the house, get Henri Mentone out of the window, and hand him over to Bourget, explaining that everything had worked even more smoothly than he had hoped for, that all were in bed, and that there was no chance of the escape being discovered until morning. Bourget, it was true, was very likely to be disappointed in the measure of the revenge wrecked upon the curé, but Bourget's feelings in the matter, since Bourget then would have no choice but to drive Henri Mentone to St. Eustace, were of little account.

And as far as Henri Mentone was concerned, it was very simple too. The man would have ample time and opportunity to get well out of reach. He, Raymond, would take care that the man's disappearance was not discovered any earlier than need be in the morning! It would then be a perfectly natural supposition—a supposition which he, Raymond, would father—that the man, in his condition, could not be far away, but had probably only gone restlessly and aimlessly from the house; and at first no one would even think of such a thing as escape. They would look for him around the *presbytère*, and close at hand on the beach. It would be impossible that, weak as he was, the man had gone far! The search would perhaps be extended to the village by the time Monsieur Dupont arrived for his vanished prisoner. Then they would extend the search still further, to the adjacent fields and woods, and it would certainly be noontime before the alternative that the man, aided by an accomplice, had got away became the only tenable conclusion. But even then Monsieur Dupont would either have to drive three miles to the station to reach the telegraph, or return to Tournayville—and by that time Henri Mentone would long since have been in the United States.

And after that—Raymond smiled ironically again—-well after that, it would be Monsieur Dupont's move!

CHAPTER XV—HOW HENRI MENTONE RODE WITH JACQUES BOURGET

IT was eight o'clock—the clock was striking in the kitchen—as Raymond entered the *presbytère* again. He stepped briskly to the door of the front room, opened it, and paused—no, before going in there to wait, it would be well first to let Madame Lafleur know that he was back, to establish the fact that it was *after* his return that the man had escaped, that his evening walk could in no way be connected with what would set all St. Marleau by the ears in the morning. And so he passed on to the dining room, which Madame Lafleur used as a sitting room as well. She was sewing beside the table lamp.

"Always busy, Madame Lafleur!" he called out cheerily, from the threshold. "Well, and has Mademoiselle Valérie returned?"

"Ah, it is you, Monsieur le Curé!" she exclaimed, dropping her work on her knees. "And did you enjoy your walk? No, Valérie has not come back here yet, though I am sure she must have got back to her uncle's by now. Did you want her for anything, Monsieur le Curé—to write letters? I can go over and tell her."

"But, no—not at all!" said Raymond hastily. He indicated the rear room with an inclination of his head. "And our *pauvre* there?"

Madame Lafleur's sweet, motherly face grew instantly troubled.

"You can hear him tossing on the bed yourself, Monsieur le Curé. I have just been in to see him. He has one of his bad moods. He said he wanted nothing except to be left alone. But I think he will soon be quiet. Poor man, he is so weak he will be altogether exhausted—it is only his mind that keeps him restless."

Raymond nodded.

"It is a very sad affair," he said slowly, "a very sad affair!" He lifted a finger and shook it playfully at Madame Lafleur. "But we must think of you too—eh? Do not work too late, Madame Lafleur!"

She answered him seriously.

"Only to finish this, Monsieur le Curé. See, it is an altar cloth—for next Sunday." She held it up. "It is you who work too hard and too late."

It was a cross on a satin background. He stared at it. It had been hidden on her lap before. He had not been thinking of—a cross. For the moment, assured of Henri Mentone's escape, he had been more light of heart than at any time since he had come to St. Mar-leau; and, for the moment, he had forgotten that he was a meddler with holy things, that he was—a priest of God! It seemed as though this were being flaunted suddenly now as a jeering reminder before his eyes; and with it he seemed as suddenly to see the chancel, the altar of the church where the cloth was to play its part—and himself kneeling there—and, curse the vividness of it! he heard his own lips at their sacrilegious work: "*Lavabo inter innocentes manus meas: et circumdabo altare tuum, Domine....* I will wash my hands among the innocent: and I will compass Thine altar, O Lord." And so he stared at this cross she held before him, fighting to bring a pleased and approving smile to the lips that fought in turn for their right to snarl a defiant mockery.

"Ah, you like it, Monsieur le Curé!" cried Madame Lafleur happily. "I am so glad."

And Raymond smiled for answer, and went from the room.

And in the front room he lighted the lamp upon his desk, and stood there looking down at the two letters that still awaited the signature of— Francois Aubert. "I will wash my hands among the innocent"—he raised his hands, and they were clenched into hard and knotted fists. Words! Words! They were only words. And what did their damnable insinuations matter to him! Others might listen devoutly and believe, as he mouthed them in his surplice and stole—but for himself they were no more than the mimicry of sounds issuing from a parrot's beak! It was absurd then that they should affect him at all. He would better laugh and jeer at them, and all this holy entourage with which he cloaked himself, for these things were being made to serve his own ends, were being turned to his own account, and—it was Three-Ace Artie now, and he laughed hoarsely under his breath—for once they were proving of some real and tangible value! Madame Lafleur, and her cross, and her altar cloth! He laughed again. Well, while she was busy with her churchly task, that she no doubt fondly believed would hurry her exit through the purgatory to come, he would busy himself a little in getting as speedily as possible out of the purgatory of the present. These letters now. While he was waiting, and there was an opportunity, he would sign them. It would be easier to say that he had decided not to make any changes in them after all, than to have new ones written and then have to find another opportunity for signing the latter. He reached for the prayer-book to make a tracing of the signature that was on the fly-leaf—and suddenly drew back his hand, and stood motionless, listening.

From the road came the rumble of wheels. The sound grew louder. The vehicle passed by the *presbytère*, going in the direction of Tournayville. The sound died away. Still Raymond listened—even more intently than before. Jacques Bourget did not own the only horse and wagon in St. Marleau, but Bourget was to turn around a little way down the road, and return to the church. A minute, two passed, another; and then Raymond caught the sound of a wheel-tire rasping and grinding against the body of a wagon, as though the latter were being turned in a narrow space—then presently the rattle of wheels again, coming back now toward the church. And now by the church he heard the wagon turn in from the road.

Raymond relaxed from his strained attitude of attention. Jacques Bourget, it was quite evident, intended to earn the balance of his money! Well, for a word then between Pierre Desforges and Jacques Bourget—pending the time that Madame Lafleur and her altar cloth should go to bed. The letters could wait.

He moved stealthily and very slowly across the room. Madame Lafleur must not hear him leaving the house. He would be gone only a minute—just to warn Bourget to keep very quiet, and to satisfy the man that everything was going well. He could strip off his *soutane* and leave it under the porch.

Cautiously he opened the door, an inch at a time that it might not creak, and stepped out into the hall on tiptoe—and listened. Madame Lafleur's rocking chair squeaked back and forth reassuringly. She had perhaps had enough of her altar cloth for a while! How could one do fine needle work—and rock! And why that fanciful detail to flash across his mind! And—his face was suddenly set, his lips tight-drawn together—*what was this!* These footsteps that had made no sound in crossing the green, but were quick and heavy upon the porch outside! He drew back upon the threshold of his room. And then the front door was thrust open. And in the doorway was Dupont, Monsieur Dupont, the assistant chief of the Tournayville police, and behind Dupont was another man, and behind the man was—yes—it was Valerie.

"*Tiens! 'Cré nom d'un chien!*" clucked Monsieur Dupont. "Ha, Monsieur le Curé, you heard us—eh? But you did not hear us until we were at the door—and a man posted at the back of the house by that window there, eh? No, you did not hear us. Well, we have nipped the little scheme in the bud, eh?"

Dupont *knew!* Raymond's hand tightened on the door jamb—and, as once before, his other hand crept in under his crucifix, and under the breast of his *soutane* to his revolver.

"I do not understand"—he spoke deliberately, gravely. "You speak of a scheme, Monsieur Dupont? I do not understand."

"Ah, you do not understand!" — Monsieur Duponts face screwed up into a cryptic smile. "No, of course, you do not understand! Well, you will in a moment! But first we will attend to Monsieur Henri Mentone! Now then, Marchand" — he addressed his companion, and pointed to the rear room — "that room in there, and handcuff him to you. You had better stay where you are, Monsieur le Curé. Come along, Marchand!"

Dupont and his companion ran into Henri Mentone's room. Raymond heard Madame Lafleur cry out in sudden consternation. It was echoed by a cry in Henri Mentone's voice. But he was looking at Valérie, who had stepped into the hall. She was very pale. What had she to do with this? What did it mean? Had she discovered that he — no, Dupont would not have rushed away in that case, but then — His lips moved: "You — Valérie!" How very pale she was — and how those dark eyes, deep with something he could not fathom, sought his face, only to be quickly veiled by their long lashes.

"Do not look like that, Monsieur le Curé — as though I had done wrong." she said in a low, hurried tone. "I am sorry for the man too; but the police were to have taken him away to-morrow morning in any case. And if I went for Monsieur Dupont to-night, it was — —"

"You went for Monsieur Dupont?" — he repeated her words dazedly, as though he had not heard aright. "It was you who brought Monsieur Dupont here just now — from Tournayville! But — but, I do not understand at all!"

"Valérie! Valérie!" — it was Madame Lafleur, pale and excited, who had rushed to her daughter's side. "Valérie, speak quickly! What are they doing? What does all this mean?"

Valérie's arm stole around her mother's shoulder.

"I — I was just telling Father Aubert, mother," she said, a little tremulously. "You — you must not be nervous. See, it was like this. You had just taken the man for a little walk about the green this afternoon — you remember? When I came out of the house a few minutes later to join you, I saw what I thought looked like some money sticking out from one end of a folded-up piece of paper that was lying on the grass just at the bottom of the porch steps. I was sure, of course, that it was only a trick my imagination was playing on me, but I stooped down and picked it up. It was money, a great deal of money, and there was writing on the paper. I read it, and then I was afraid. It was from some friend of that man's in there, and was a plan for him to make his escape to-night."

"Escape!" — Madame Lafleur drew closer to her daughter, as she glanced apprehensively toward the rear room.

Dupont's voice floated menacingly out into the hall—came a gruff oath from his companion—the sound of a chair over-turned—and Henri Mentone's cry, pitched high.

In a curiously futile way Raymond's hand dropped from the breast of his *soutane* to his side. Valérie and her mother seemed to be swirling around in circles in the hall before him. He forced himself to speak naturally:

"And then?"

Valérie's eyes were on her mother.

"I did not want to alarm you, mother," she went on rapidly; "and so I told you I was going for a drive. I ran to uncle's house. He was out somewhere. I could go as well as any one, and if Henri Mentone had a friend lurking somewhere in the village there would be nothing to arouse suspicion in a girl driving alone; and, besides, I did not know who this friend might be, and I did not know who to trust. I told old Adèle that I wanted to go for a drive, and she helped me to harness the horse."

And now, as Raymond listened, those devils, that had chuckled and screeched as the lumpy earth had thudded down on the lid of Théophile Blondin's coffin, were at their hell-carols again. It was not just luck, just the unfortunate turn of a card that the man had dropped the money and the note. It was more than that. It seemed to hold a grim, significant premonition—for the future. Those devils did well to chuckle! Struggle as he would, they had woven their net too cunningly for his escape. It was those devils who had torn his coat that night in the storm, as he had tried to force his way through the woods. It was *his* coat that Henri Mentone was wearing. He remembered now that the lining of the pocket on the inside had been ripped across. It was those devils who had seen to that—for this—knowing what was to come. A finger seemed to wag with hideous jocularity before his eyes—the finger of fate. He looked at Valerie. It was nothing for her to have driven to Tournayville, she had probably done it a hundred times before, but it seemed a little strange that Henri Mentone's possible escape should have been, apparently, so intimate and personal a matter to her.

"You were afraid, you said, Mademoiselle Valerie," he said slowly. "Afraid—that he would escape?"

She shook her head—and the colour mounted suddenly in her face.

"Of what then?" he asked.

"Of what was in the note," she said, in a low voice. "I knew I had time, for nothing was to be done until the *presbytère* was quiet for the night; but the plan then was to—to put you out of the way, and——"

His voice was suddenly hoarse.

"And you were afraid—for me? It was for me that you have done this?"

She did not answer. The colour was still in her cheeks—her eyes were lowered.

"The blessed saints!" cried Madame Lafleur, crossing herself. "The devils! They would do harm to Father Aubert! Well, I am sorry for that man no longer! He——"

They were coming along the hall—Henri Mentone handcuffed to Monsieur Dupont's companion, and Monsieur Dupont himself in the rear.

"Monsieur le Curé!" Henri Mentone called out wildly. "Monsieur le Curé, do not——"

"Enough! Hold your tongue!" snapped Monsieur Dupont, giving the man a push past Raymond toward the front door. "Do you appeal to Monsieur le Curé because he has been good to you—or because you intended to knock Monsieur le Curé on the head to-night! Bah! Hurry him along, Marchand!" Monsieur Dupont paused before Valérie and her mother. "You will do me a favour, mesdames? A very great favour—yes? You will retire instantly to bed—instantly. I have my reasons. Yes, that is right—go at once." He turned to Raymond. "And you, Monsieur le Curé, you will wait for me here, eh? Yes, you will wait. I will be back on the instant."

The hall was empty. In a subconscious sort of way Raymond stepped back into his room, and, reaching the desk, stood leaning heavily against it. His brain would tolerate no single coherent thought. Valérie had done this for fear of harm to him, Valérie had... there was Jacques Bourget who if he attempted now to... it was no wonder that Henri Mentone had been restless all evening, knowing that he had lost the note, and not daring to question... the day after to-morrow there was to be a trial at the criminal assizes... Valérie had not met his eyes, but there had been the crimson colour in her face, and she had done this to save *him*... were they still laughing, those hell-devils... were they now engaged in making Valérie love him, and making her torture her soul because she was so pure that no thought could strike her more cruelly than that love should come to her for a priest? Ah, his brain was logical now! His hands clenched, and unclenched, and clenched again. Impotent fury was upon him. If it were true! Damn them to the everlasting place from whence they came! But it was not true! It was but another trick of theirs to make him writhe the more—to make *him* believe she cared!

A footstep! He looked up. Monsieur Dupont was back.

"*Tiens!*" cried Monsieur Dupont. "Well, you have had an escape, Monsieur le Curé! An escape! Yes, you have! But I do not take all the credit. No, I do not. She is a fine girl, that Valérie Lafleur. If she were a man she would have a career—with the police. I would see to it! But you do not know yet what it is all about, Monsieur le Curé, eh?"

"There was a note and money that Mademoiselle Valérie said she found"—Raymond's voice was steady, composed.

"*Zut!*" Monsieur Dupont laid his forefinger along the side of his nose impressively. "That is the least of it! There is an accomplice—two of them in it! You would not have thought that, eh, Monsieur le Curé? No, you would not. Very well, then—listen! I have this Mentone safe, and now I, Dupont, will give this accomplice a little surprise. There will be the two of them at the trial for the murder of Théophile Blondin! The grand jury is still sitting. You understand, Monsieur le Curé? Yes, you understand. You are listening?"...

"I am listening," said Raymond gravely—and instinctively glanced toward the window. It might still have been Jacques Bourget who had turned down there on the road; or, if not, then the man would be along at any minute. In either case, he must find some way to warn Bourget. "I am listening, Monsieur Dupont," he said again. "You propose to lay a trap for this accomplice?"

"It is already laid," announced Monsieur Dupont complacently. "They will discover with whom they are dealing! I returned at once with Mademoiselle Valérie. I brought two men with me; but you will observe, Monsieur le Curé, that I did not bring two teams—nothing to arouse suspicion—nothing to indicate that I was about to remove our friend Mentone to-night. It would be a very simple matter to secure a team here when I was ready for it. You see, Monsieur le Curé? Yes, you see. Very well! My plans worked without a hitch. Just as we approached the church, we met a man named Jacques Bourget driving alone in a buckboard. Nothing could be better. It was excellent. I stopped him. I requisitioned him and his horse and his wagon in the name of the law. I made him turn around, and told him to follow us back here after a few minutes. You see, Monsieur le Curé? Yes, you see. Monsieur Jacques Bourget is now on his way to Tournayville with one of my officers and the prisoner."

Raymond's fingers were playing nonchalantly with the chain of his crucifix. Raymond's face was unmoved. It was really funny, was it not! No wonder those denizens of hell were shrieking with abandoned glee in his ears. This time they had a right to be amused. It was really very funny—that Jacques Bourget should be driving Henri Mentone away from St. Marleau! Well, and now—what?

"You are to be congratulated, Monsieur Dupont," he murmured. "But the accomplice—the other one, who is still at large?"

"Ah, the other one!" said Monsieur Dupont, and laid his hand confidentially on Raymond's arm. "The other—heh, *mon Dieu*, Monsieur le Curé, but you wear heavy clothes for the summertime!"

It was the bulk of the sacristan's old coat! There was a smile in Raymond's eyes, a curious smile, as he searched the other's face. One could never be sure of Monsieur Dupont.

"A coat always under my *soutane* in the evenings"—Raymond's voice was tranquil, and he did not withdraw his arm.

"A coat—yes—of course!" Monsieur Dupont nodded his head. "Why not! Well then, the other—listen. All has been done very quietly. No alarm raised. None at all! I have sent Madame Lafleur and her daughter to bed. The plan was that the accomplice should come to the back window for Mentone. But they would not make the attempt until late—until all in the village was quiet. That is evident, is it not? Yes, it is evident. Very good! You sleep here in this room, Monsieur le Curé? Yes? Well, you too will put out your light and retire at once. I will go into Mentone's room, and wait there in the dark for our other friend to come to the window. I will be Henri Mentone. You see? Yes, you see. It is simple, is it not? Yes, it is simple. Before morning I will have the man in a cell alongside of Henri Mentone. Do you see any objections to the plan, Monsieur le Curé?"

"Only that it might prove very dangerous—for you," said Raymond soberly. "If the man, who is certain to be a desperate character, attacked you before you— —"

"Dangerous! Bah!" exclaimed Monsieur Dupont. "That is part of my business. I do not consider that! I have my other officer outside there now by the shed. As soon as the man we are after approaches the window, the officer will leap upon him and overpower him. And now, Monsieur le Curé, to bed—eh? And the light out!"

"At once!" agreed Raymond. "And I wish you every success, Monsieur Dupont! If you need help you have only to call; or, if you like, I will go in there and stay with you."

"No, no—not at all!" Monsieur Dupont moved toward the door. "It is not necessary. Nothing can go wrong. We may have to wait well through the night, and there is no reason why you should remain up too. *Tiens!* Fancy! Imagine! Did I not tell you that Mentone was a hardened rascal? Two of them! Well, we will see if the second one can remember any better than the first! The light, Monsieur le Curé—do not forget! He will not come while there is a sound or a light about the house!" Monsieur Dupont waved his hand, and the door closed on Monsieur Dupont.

Raymond, still leaning against the desk, heard the other walk along the hall, and enter the rear room—and then all was quiet. He leaned over and blew out the lamp. Nothing must be allowed to frustrate Monsieur Dupont's plans!

And then, in the darkness, for a long time Raymond stood there. And thinking of Monsieur Dupont's dangerous vigil in the other room, he laughed; and thinking of Valérie, he knew a bitter joy; and thinking of Henri Mentone, his hands knotted at his sides, and his face grew strained and drawn. And after that long time was past, he fumbled with his hands outstretched before him like a blind man feeling his way, and flung himself down upon the couch.

CHAPTER XVI—FOR THE MURDER OF THÉOPHILE BLONDIN

THEY sat on two benches by themselves, the witnesses in the trial of Henri Mentone for the murder of Théophile Blondin. On one side of Raymond was Valérie, on the other was Mother Blondin; and there was Labbée, the station agent, and Monsieur Dupont, and Doctor Arnaud. And on the other bench were several of the villagers, and two men Raymond did not know, and another man, a crown surveyor, who had just testified to the difference in time and distance from the station to Madame Blondin's as between the road and the path—thus establishing for the prosecution the fact that by following the path there had been ample opportunity for the crime to have been committed by one who had left the station after the curé had already started toward the village and yet still be discovered by the curé on the road near the tavern. The counsel appointed by the court for the defence had allowed the testimony to go unchallenged. It was obvious. It did not require a crown surveyor to announce the fact—even an urchin from St. Marleau was already aware of it. The villagers too had testified. They had testified that Madame Blondin had come running into the village screaming out that her son had been murdered; and that they had gone back with her to her house and had found the dead body of her son lying on the floor.

It was stiflingly hot in the courtroom; and the courtroom was crowded to its last available inch of space.

There were many there from Tournayville—but there was all of St. Marleau. It was St. Marleau's own and particular affair. Since early morning, since very early morning, Raymond had seen and heard the vehicles of all descriptions rattling past the *presbytère*, the occupants dressed in their Sunday clothes. It was a *jour de fête*. St. Marleau did not every day have a murder of its own! The fields were deserted; only the very old and the children had not come. They were not all in the room, for there was not place for them all—those who had not been on hand at the opening of the doors had been obliged to content themselves with gathering outside to derive what satisfaction they could from their proximity to the fateful events that were transpiring within; and they had at least seen the prisoner led handcuffed from the jail that adjoined the courthouse, and had been rewarded to the extent of being able to view with intense and bated interest people they had known all their lives, such as Valérie, and Mother Blondin, and the more privileged of their fellows who had been chosen as witnesses, as these latter disappeared inside the building!

Raymond's eyes roved around the courtroom, and rested upon the judge upon the bench. His first glance at the judge, taken at the moment the other had entered the room, had brought a certain, quick relief. Far from severity, the white-haired man sitting there in his black gown had a kindly, genial face. He found his first impressions even strengthened now. His eyes passed on to the crown prosecutor; and here, too, he found cause for reassurance. The man was middle-aged, shrewd-faced, and somewhat domineering. He was crisp, incisive, and had been even unnecessarily blunt and curt in his speech and manner so far — he was not one who would enlist the sympathy of a jury. On the other hand — Raymond's eyes shifted again, to hold on the clean-cut, smiling face of the prisoner's counsel — Lemoyne, that was the lawyer's name he had been told, was young, pleasant-voiced, magnetic. Raymond experienced a sort of grim admiration, as he looked at this man. No man in the courtroom knew better than Lemoyne the hopelessness of his case, and yet he sat there confident, smiling, undisturbed.

Raymond's eyes sought the floor. It was a foregone conclusion that the verdict would be guilty. There was not a loophole for defence. But they would not hang the man. He clung to that. Lemoyne could at least fight for the man's life. They would not hang a man who could not remember. They had beaten him, Raymond, the night before last; and at first he had been like a man stunned with the knowledge that his all was on the table and that the cards in his hand were worthless — and then had come a sort of philosophical calm, the gambler's optimism — the hand was still to be played. They would sentence the man for life, and — well, there was time enough in a lifetime for another chance. Somehow — in some way — he did not know now — but in some way he would see that there was another chance. He would not desert the man.

Again he raised his eyes, but this time as though against his will, as though they were impelled and drawn in spite of himself across the room. That was Raymond Chapelle, alias Arthur Leroy, alias Three-Ace Artie, alias Henri Mentone, sitting there in the prisoner's box; at least, that gaunt, thin-faced, haggard man there was dressed in Raymond Chapelle's clothes — and *he*, François Aubert, the priest, the curé, in his *soutane*, with his crucifix around his neck, sat here amongst the witnesses at the trial of Raymond Chapelle, who had killed Théophile Blondin in the fight that night. One would almost think the man *knew!* How the man's eyes burned into him, how they tormented and plagued him! They were sad, those eyes, pitiful—they were helpless—they seemed to seek him out as the only *friend* amongst all these bobbing heads, and these staring, gaping faces.

"Marcien Labbée!"—the clerk's voice snapped through the courtroom. "Marcien Labbée!" The clerk was a very fussy and important short little man, who puffed his cheeks in and out, and clawed at his white side-whiskers. "Marcien Labbée!"

The station agent rose from the bench, entered the witness box, and was sworn.

With a few crisp questions, the crown prosecutor established the time of the train's arrival, and the fact that the curé and another man had got off at the station. The witness explained that the curé had started to walk toward the village before the other man appeared on the platform.

"And this other man"—the crown prosecutor whirled sharply around, and pointed toward Henri Mentone—"do you recognise him as the prisoner at the bar?"

Labbée shook his head.

"It was very dark," he said. "I could not swear to it."

"His general appearance then? His clothes? They correspond with what you remember of the man?"

"Yes," Labbée answered. "There is no doubt of that."

"And as I understand it, you told the man that Monsieur le Curé had just started a moment before, and that if he went at once he would have company on the walk to the village?"

"Yes."

"What did he say?"

"He said that he was not looking for that kind of company."

There was a sudden, curious, restrained movement through the courtroom; and, here and there, a villager, with pursed lips, nodded his head. It was quite evident to those from St. Marleau at least that such as Henri Mentone would not care for the company of their curé.

"You gave the man directions as to the short cut to the village?"

"Yes."

"You may tell the court and the gentlemen of the jury what was said then."

Labbée, who had at first appeared a little nervous, now pulled down his vest, and looked around him with an air of importance.

"I told him that the path came out at the tavern. When I said 'tavern,' he was at once very interested. I thought then it was because he was glad to know there was a place to stay—it was such a terrible night, you understand? So I told him it was only a name we gave it, and that it was no place for one to go. I told him it was kept by an old woman, who was an *excommuniée*, and who made whisky on the sly, and that her son was——"

"*Misérable!*"—it was Mother Blondin, in a furious scream. Her eyes, under her matted gray hair, glared fiercely at Labbée.

"Silence!" roared the clerk of the court, leaping to his feet.

Raymond's hand closed over the clenched, bony fist that Mother Blondin had raised, and gently lowered it to her lap.

"He will do you no harm, Madame Blondin," he whispered reassuringly. "And see, you must be careful, or you will get into serious trouble."

Her hand trembled with passion in his, but she did not draw it away. It was strange that she did not! It was strange that he felt pity for her when so much was at stake, when pity was such a trivial and inconsequent thing! This was a murder trial, a trial for the killing of this woman's son. It was strange that he should be holding the *mother's* hand, and—it was Raymond who drew his hand away. He clasped it over his other one until the knuckles grew white.

"And then?" prompted the crown prosecutor.

"And then, I do not remember how it came about," Labbée continued, "he spoke of Madame Blondin having money—enough to buy out any one around there. I said it was true that it was the gossip that she had made a lot, and that she had a well-filled stocking hidden away somewhere."

"*Crapule!*"—Mother Blondin's voice, if scarcely audible this time, had lost none of its fury.

The clerk contented himself with a menacing gesture toward his own side-whiskers. The crown prosecutor paid no attention to the interruption.

"Did the man give any reason for coming to St. Marleau?"

"None."

"Did you ask him how long he intended to remain?"

"Yes; he said he didn't know."

"He had a travelling bag with him?"

"Yes."

"This one?"—the crown prosecutor held up Raymond's travelling bag from the table beside him.

"I cannot say," Labbée replied. "It was too dark on the platform."

"Quite so! But it was of a size sufficient, in your opinion, to cause the man inconvenience in carrying it in such a storm, so you offered to have it sent over with Monsieur le Curé's trunk in the morning?"

"Yes."

"What did he say?"

"He said he could carry it all right."

"He started off then with the bag along the road toward St. Marleau?"

"Yes."

The crown prosecutor glanced inquiringly toward the prisoner's counsel. The latter shook his head.

"You may step down, Monsieur Labbée," directed the crown prosecutor. "Call Madame Blondin!" There was a stir in the courtroom now. Heads craned forward as the old woman shuffled across the floor to the witness box—Mother Blondin was quite capable of anything—even of throwing to the ground the Holy Book upon which the clerk would swear her! Mother Blondin, however, did nothing of the sort. She gripped at the edge of the witness box, mumbling at the clerk, and all the while straining her eyes through her steel-bowed spectacles at the prisoner across the room. And then her lips began to work curiously, her face to grow contorted—and suddenly the courtroom was in an uproar. She was shaking both scranny fists at Henri Mentone, and screaming at the top of her voice.

"That is the man! That is the man!"—her voice became ungovernable, insensate, it rose shrilly, it broke, it rose piercingly again. "That is the man! The law! The law! I demand the law on him! He killed my son! He did it! I tell you, he did it! He——"

Chairs and benches were scraping on the floor. Little cries of nervous terror came from the women; involuntarily men stood up the better to look at both Mother Blondin and the accused. It was a sensation! It was something to talk about in St. Marleau over the stoves in the coming winter. It was something of which nothing was to be missed.

"Order! Silence! Order!" bawled the clerk.

Valérie had caught Raymond's sleeve. He did not look at her. He was looking at Henri Mentone—at the look of dumb horror on the man's face—and then at a quite different figure in the prisoner's dock, whose head was bent down until it could scarcely be seen, and whose face was covered by his hands. He tried to force a grim complacence into his soul. It was absolutely certain that *he* had nothing to fear from the trial. Nothing! The other Henri Mentone, the other priest, was answering for the killing of that night, and— who was this speaking? The crown prosecutor? He had not thought the man could be so suave and gentle.

"Try and calm yourself, Madame Blondin. You have a perfect right to demand the punishment of the law upon the murderer of your son, and that is what we are here for now, and that is why I want you to tell us just as quietly as possible what happened that night."

She stared truculently.

"Everybody knows what happened!" she snarled at him. "He killed my son!"

"How did he kill your son?" inquired the crown prosecutor, with a sudden, crafty note of scepticism in his voice. "How do you know he did?"

"I saw him! I tell you, I saw him! I heard my son shout '*voleur*' and cry for help"—Mother Blon-din's words would not come fast enough now. "I was in the back room. When I opened the door he was fighting my son. He tried to steal my money. Some of it was on the floor. My son cried for help again. I ran and got a stick of wood. My son tried to get his revolver from the *armoire*. This man got it away from him. I struck the man on the head with the wood, then he shot my son, and I ran out for help."

"And you positively identify the prisoner as the man who shot your son?"

"Yes, yes! Have I not told you so often enough!"

"And this"—the crown prosecutor handed her a revolver—"do you identify this?"

"Yes; it was my son's."

"You kept your money in a hiding place, Madame Blondin, I understand—in a hollow between two of the logs in the wall of the room? Is that so?"

"Yes; it is so!"—Mother Blondin's voice grew shrill again. "But I will find a better place for it, if I ever get it back again! The police are as great thieves as that man! They took it from him, and now they keep it from me!"

"It is here, Madame Blondin," said the lawyer soothingly, opening a large envelope. "It will be returned to you after the trial. How much was there?"

"I know very well how much!" she shrilled out suspiciously. "You cannot cheat me! I know! There were all my savings, years of savings—there was more than five hundred dollars."

A little gasp went around the courtroom. Five hundred dollars! It was a fortune! Gossip then had not lied—it had been outdone!

"Now this hiding place, Madame Blondin—you had never told any one about it? Not even your son?"

"No."

"It would seem then that this man must have known about it in some way. Had you been near it a short time previous to the fight?"

"I told you I had, didn't I? I told Monsieur Dupont all that once." Mother Blondin was growing unmanageable again. "I went there to put some money in not five minutes before I heard my son call for help."

"Your son then was not in the room when you went to put this money away?"

"No; of course, he wasn't! I have told that to Monsieur Dupont, too. I heard him coming downstairs just as I left the room."

"That is all, Madame Blondin, thank you, unless——" The crown prosecutor turned again toward the counsel for the defence.

Lemoyne rose, and, standing by his chair without approaching the witness box, took a small penknife from his pocket, and held it up.

"Madame Blondin," he said gently, "will you tell me what I am holding in my hand?"

Mother Blondin squinted, set her glasses further on her nose, and shook her head.

"I do not know," she said.

"You do not see very well, Madame Blondin?"—sympathetically.

"What is it you have got there—eh? What is it?" she demanded sharply.

Lemoyne glanced at the jury—and smiled. He restored the penknife to his pocket.

"It is a penknife, Madame Blondin—one of my own. An object that any one would recognise—unless one did not see very well. Are you quite sure, Madame Blondin—quite sure on second thoughts—that you see well enough to identify the prisoner so positively as the man who was fighting with your son?"

The jury, with quick meaning glances at one another, with a new interest, leaned forward in their seats. There was a tense moment—a sort of bated silence in the courtroom. And then, as Mother Blondin answered, some one tittered audibly, the spell was broken, the point made by the defence swept away, turned even into a weapon against itself.

"If you will give me a stick of wood and come closer, close enough so that I can hit you over the head with it," said Mother Blondin, and cackled viciously, "you will see how well I can see!"

Madame Blondin stepped down.

And then there came upon Raymond a thrill, a weakness, a quick tightening of his muscles. The clerk had called his name. He walked mechanically to the witness stand. It was coming now. He must be on his guard. But he had thought out everything very carefully, and—no, almost before he knew it, he was back in his seat again. He had been asked only if he had followed the road all the way from the station, to describe how he had found the man, and to identify the prisoner as that man. He was to be recalled. Le-moyne had not asked him a single question.

"Mademoiselle Valérie Lafleur!" called the clerk.

"Oh, Monsieur le Curé!" she whispered tremulously. "I—I do not want to go. It—it is such a terrible thing to *have* to say anything that would help to send a man to death—I—-"

"Mademoiselle Valérie Lafleur!" snapped the clerk. "Will the witness have the goodness to— —"

Raymond did not hear her testimony; he knew only that she, too, identified the man as the one she had seen lying unconscious in the road, and that the note she had found was read and placed in evidence—in his ears, like a dull, constant dirge, were those words of hers with which she had left him—"it is such a terrible thing to have to say anything that would help to send a man to death." Who was it that was sending the man to death? Not he! He had tried to save the man. It wasn't death, anyway. The man's guilt would appear obvious, of course—Lemoyne, the lawyer, could not alter that; but he had still faith in Lemoyne. Lemoyne would make his defence on the man's condition. Lemoyne would come to that.

"My son!" croaked old Mother Blondin fiercely, at his side. "My son! What I know, I know! But the law—the law on the man who killed my son!"

"Pull yourself together, you fool!" rasped that inner voice. "Do you want everybody in the courtroom staring at you. Listen to the incomparable Dupont telling how clever he was!"

Yes, Dupont was on the stand now. Dupont was testifying to finding the revolver and money in the prisoner's pockets. He verified the amount. Dupont had his case at his fingers' tips, and he sketched it, with an amazing conciseness for Monsieur Dupont, from the moment he had been notified of the crime up to the time of the attempted escape. He was convinced that, in spite of all precautions, the prisoner's accomplice had taken alarm—since he, Dupont, had sat the night in the room waiting for the unknown's appearance, and neither he nor his deputy, who had remained until daylight hiding in the shed where he could watch the prisoner's window, had seen or heard anything. On cross-examination he admitted that pressure had been brought to bear upon the prisoner in an effort to trip the man up in his story, but that the prisoner had unswervingly held to the statement that he could remember nothing.

The voices droned through the courtroom. It was Doctor Arnaud now identifying the man. They were always identifying the man! Why did not he, the saintly curé of St. Marleau—no, it was Three-Ace Artie—why did not he, Three-Ace Artie, laugh outright in all their faces! It was not hard to identify the man. He had seen to that very thoroughly, more thoroughly than even he had imagined that night in the storm when all the devils of hell were loosed to shriek around him, and he had changed clothes with a *dead* man. A dead man—yes, that was the way it should have been! Did he not remember how limply the man's neck and head wagged on the shoulders, and how the body kept falling all over in grotesque attitudes instead of helping him to get its clothes off! Only the dead man had come to life! That was the man over there inside that box with the little wood-turned decorations all around the railing—no, he wouldn't look—but that man there who was the colour of soiled chalk, and whose eyes, with the hurt of a dumb beast in them, kept turning constantly in this direction, over here, here where the witnesses sat.

"Doctor Arnaud"—it was the counsel for the defence speaking, and suddenly Raymond was listening with strained attention—"you have attended the prisoner from the night he was found unconscious in the road until the present time?"

"Yes, monsieur."

"You have heard me in cross-examination ask Mademoiselle Lafleur and Monsieur Dupont if at any time during this period the prisoner, by act, manner or word, swerved from his statement that he could remember nothing, either of the events of that night, or of prior events in his life. You have heard both of these witness testify that he had not done so. I will ask you now if you are in a position to corroborate their testimony?"

"I am," replied Doctor Arnaud. "He has said nothing else to my knowledge."

"Then, doctor, in your professional capacity, will you kindly tell the court and the gentlemen of the jury whether or not loss of memory could result from a blow upon the head."

"It could—certainly," stated Doctor Arnaud. "There is no doubt of that, but it depends on the——"

"Just a moment, doctor, if you please; we will come to that"—Lemoyne, as Raymond knew well that Le-moyne himself was fully aware, was treading on thin and perilous ice, but on Lemoyne's lips, as he interrupted, was an engaging smile. "This loss of memory now. Will you please help us to understand just what it means? Take a hypothetical case. Could a man, for example, read and write, do arithmetic, say, appear normal in all other ways, and still have lost the memory of his name, his parents, his friends, his home, his previous state?"

"Yes," said Doctor Arnaud. "That is quite true. He might lose the memory of all those things, and still retain everything he has acquired by education."

"That is a medical fact?"

"Yes, certainly, it is a medical fact."

"And is it not also a medical fact, doctor, that this condition has been known to have been caused by a blow — I will not say so slight, for that would be misleading — but by a blow that did not even cause a wound, and I mean by wound a gash, a cut, or the tearing of the flesh?"

"Yes; that, too, is so."

Lemoyne paused. He looked at Henri Mentone, and suddenly it seemed as though a world of sympathy and pity were in his face. He turned and looked at the jury — at each one of the twelve men, but almost as though he did not see them. There was a mist in his eyes. It was silent again in the courtroom. His voice was low and grave as he spoke again.

"Doctor Arnaud, are you prepared to state professionally under oath that it is impossible that the blow received by the prisoner at the bar should have caused him to lose his memory?"

"No." Doctor Arnaud shook his head. "No; I would not say that."

Lemoyne's voice was still grave.

"You admit then, Doctor Arnaud, that it is possible?"

Doctor Arnaud hesitated. "Yes," he said. "It is possible, of course."

"That is all, doctor" — Lemoyne sat down.

"One moment!" — the crown prosecutor, crisp, curt, incisive, was on his feet. "Loss of memory is not insanity, doctor?"

"No."

"Is the prisoner in your professional judgment insane?"

"No," declared Doctor Arnaud emphatically. "Most certainly not!"

With a nod, the crown prosecutor dismissed the witness.

A buzz, whisperings, ran around the room. Raymond's eyes were fixed sombrely on the floor. Relief had come with Lemoyne's climax, but now in Doctor Arnaud's reply to the crown prosecutor he sensed catastrophe. A sentence for life was the best that could be hoped for, but suppose — suppose Lemoyne should fail to secure even that! No, no — they would not hang the man! Even Doctor Arnaud had been forced to admit that he might have lost his memory. That would be strong enough for any jury, and — they were calling his name again, and he was rising, and walking a second time to the witness stand. Surely all these people *knew*. Was not his face set, and white, and drawn! See that ray of sunlight coming in through that far window, and how it did not deviate, but came straight toward him, and lay upon the crucifix on his breast, to draw all eyes upon it, upon that Figure on the Cross, the Man Betrayed. God, he had not meant this! He had thought the priest already dead that night. It was a dead man he had meant should answer for the killing of that ugly, scarred-faced, drunken blackguard, Théophile Blondin. That couldn't do a dead man any harm! It was a dead man, a dead man, a dead man — not this living, breathing one who — —

"Monsieur le Curé," said the crown prosecutor, "you were present in the prisoner's room with Monsieur Dupont and Doctor Arnaud, when Monsieur Dupont made a search of the accused's clothing?"

"Yes," Raymond answered.

"Do you identify this revolver as the one taken from the prisoner's pocket?"

What was it Valérie had said — that it was such a terrible thing to have to say anything that would help to send a man to death? But the man was not going to death. It was to be a life sentence — and afterwards, after the trial, there would be time to think, and plot, and plan.

"It is the same one," said Raymond in a low voice.

"You also saw Monsieur Dupont take a large number of loose bills from the prisoner's pocket?"

"Yes."

"Do you know their amount?"

"No. Monsieur Dupont did not count them at the time."

"There were a great many, however, crumpled in the pocket, as though they had been hastily thrust there?"

"Yes."

Why did that man in the prisoner's dock look at him like that — not in accusation — it was worse than that — it was in a sorrowful sort of wonder, and a numbed despair. Those devils were laughing in his ears — he was telling the *truth!*

"That is all, I think, Monsieur le Curé," said the crown prosecutor abruptly.

All! There came a bitter and abysmal irony. Puppets! All were puppets upon a set stage — from the judge on the bench to that dismayed thing yonder who wrung his hands before the imposing majesty of the law! All! That was all, was it — the few words he had said? Who then was the author of every word that had been uttered in the room, who then had pulled the strings that jerked these automatons about in their every movement! Ah, here was

Lemoyne this time, the prisoner's counsel. This time there was to be a cross-examination. Yes, certainly, he would like to help Lemoyne, but Lemoyne must not try to trap him. Lemoyne, too, was a puppet, and therefore Lemoyne could not be expected to know how very true it was that "Henri Mentone" was on trial for his life, and that "Henri Mentone" would fight for that life with any weapon he could grasp, and that Lemoyne would do the prisoner an ill turn to put "Henri Mentone" on the defensive! Well—he brushed his hand across his forehead, and fixed his eyes steadily on Lemoyne—he was ready for the man.

"Monsieur le Curé"—Lemoyne had come very close to the witness stand, and Lemoyne's voice was soberly modulated—"Monsieur le Curé, I have only one question to ask you. You have been with this unfortunate man since the night you found him on the road, you have nursed him night and day as a mother would a child, you have not been long in St. Marleau, but in that time, so I am told, and I can very readily see why, you have come to be called the good, young Father Aubert by all your parish. Monsieur le Curé, you have been constantly with this man, for days and nights you have scarcely left his side, and so I come to the question that, it seems to me, you, of all others, are best qualified to answer." Lemoyne paused. He had placed his two hands on the edge of the witness box, and was looking earnestly into Raymond's face. "Monsieur le Curé, do you believe that when the prisoner says that he remembers nothing of the events of that night, that he has no recollection of the crime of which he is accused—do you believe, Monsieur le Curé, that he is telling the truth?"

There had been silence in the courtroom before—it was a silence now that seemed to palpitate and throb, a *living* silence. Instinctively the crown prosecutor had made as though to rise from his chair; and then, as if indifferent, had changed his mind. No one else in the room had moved. Raymond glanced around him. They were waiting—for his answer. The word of the good, young Father Aubert would go far. Lemoyne's eyes were pleading mutely—for the one ground of defence, the one chance for his client's life. But Lemoyne did not need to plead—for that! They must not hang the man! They were waiting—for his answer. Still the silence held. And then Raymond raised his right hand solemnly.

"As God is my judge," he said, "I firmly believe that the man is telling the truth."

Benches creaked, there was the rustle of garments, a sort of unanimous and involuntary long-drawn sigh; and it seemed to Raymond that, as all eyes turned on the prisoner, they held a kindlier and more tolerant light. And then, as he walked back to the other witnesses and took his seat, he heard the crown prosecutor speak—as though disposing of the matter in blunt disdain:

"The prosecution rests."

Valérie laid her hand over his.

"I am so glad—so glad you said that," she whispered.

Monsieur Dupont leaned forward, and clucked his tongue very softly.

"Hah, Monsieur le Curé!" He wagged his head indulgently. "Well, I suppose you could not help it—eh? No, you could not. I have told you before that you are too soft-hearted."

There were two witnesses for the defence—Doctor Arnaud's two fellow-practitioners in Tournayville. Their testimony was virtually that of Doctor Arnaud in cross-examination. To each of them the crown prosecutor put the same question—and only one. Was the prisoner insane? Each answered in the negative.

And then, a moment later, Lemoyne, rising to sum up for the defence, walked soberly forward to the jury-box, and halted before the twelve men.

"Gentlemen of the jury," he began quietly, "you have heard the professional testimony of three doctors, one of them a witness for the prosecution, who all agree that the wound received by the prisoner might result in loss of memory. You have heard the testimony of that good man, the curé of St. Marleau, who gave his days and nights to the care and nursing of the one whose life, gentlemen, now lies in your hands; you have heard him declare in the most solemn and impressive manner that he believed the prisoner had no remembrance, no recollection of the night on which the crime was committed. Who should be better able to form an opinion as to whether, as the prosecution pretends, the prisoner is playing a part, or as to whether he is telling the truth, than the one who has been with him from that day to this, and been with him in the most intimate way, more than any one else? And I ask you, too, to weigh well and remember the character of the man, whom his people call the good, young Father Aubert, who has so emphatically testified to this effect. His words were not lightly spoken, and they were pure in motive. You have heard other witnesses—all witnesses for the defence, gentlemen—assert that they have seen nothing, heard nothing, that would indicate that the prisoner was playing a part. Gentlemen, every scrap of evidence that has been introduced but goes to substantiate the prisoner's story. Is it possible, do you believe for an instant, that a man could with his first conscious breath assume such a part, and, sick and wounded and physically weak, play it through without a slip, or sign, or word, or act that would so much as hint at duplicity? But that is not all. Gentlemen, I will ask you to come with me in thought to a scene that occurred this morning an hour before this trial began, and I would that the gift of words were mine to make you see that scene as I saw it." He turned and swept out his hand toward the prisoner. "That man was in his cell, on his knees beside his cot. He did not look up as I entered, and I did not disturb him. We were alone together there. After a few minutes he raised his head. There was agony in his face such as I have never seen before on a human countenance. I spoke to him then. I told him that professional confidence was sacred, I warned him of the peril in which he stood, I pleaded with him to help me save his life, to tell me all, everything, not to tie my hands. Gentlemen of the jury, do you know his answer? It was a simple one—and spoken as simply. 'When you came in I was asking God to give me back my memory before it was too late.' That is what he said, gentlemen."

There were tears in Lemoyne's eyes—there were tears in other eyes throughout the courtroom. There was a cry in Raymond's heart that went out to Le-moyne. He had not failed! He had not failed! Le-moyne had not failed!

"Gentlemen, he did not know." Lemoyne's voice rose now in impassioned pleading—and he spoke on with that eloquence that is born only of conviction and in the soul. It was the picture of the man's helplessness he drew; the horror of an innocent man entangled in seemingly incontrovertible evidence, and doomed to a frightful death. He played upon the emotions with a master touch—and as the minutes passed sobs echoed back from every quarter of the room—and in the jury box men brushed their hands across their eyes. And at the end he was very quiet again, and his words were very low.

"Gentlemen of the jury, I believe in my soul that this man is innocent. I ask you to believe that he is innocent. I ask you to believe that if he could tell of the events of that night he would stand before you a martyr to a cruel chain of circumstance. And I ask you to remember the terrible responsibility that rests upon you of passing judgment upon a man, helpless, impotent, and alone, and who, deprived of all means of self-defence, has only you to look to—for his life."

There was buoyancy in Raymond's heart. Lemoyne had not failed! He had been magnificent—triumphant! Even the judge was fumbling awkwardly with the papers on his desk. What did it matter now what the crown prosecutor might say? No one doubted perhaps that the man was guilty, but the spell that Lemoyne had cast would remain, and there would be mercy. A chill came, a chill like death—if it were not so, what would he have to face!

"Gentlemen of the jury"—the crown prosecutor was speaking now—"I should do less than justice to my learned friend if I did not admit that I was affected by his words; but I should also do less than justice to the laws of this land, to you, and to myself if I did not tell you that emotion has no place in the consideration of this case, and that fact alone must be the basis of your verdict. I shall not keep you long. I have only a few words to say. The court will instruct you that if the prisoner is sane he is accountable to the law for his crime. We are concerned, not with his loss of memory, though my learned friend has made much of that, but with his sanity. The court will also instruct you on that point. I shall not, therefore, discuss the question of the prisoner's mental condition, except to recall to your minds that the medical testimony has been unanimous in declaring that the accused is not insane; and except to say that, in so far as loss of memory is concerned, it is plainly evident that he was in full possession of all his faculties at the time the murder was committed, and that I am personally inclined to share the opinion of his accomplice in crime—a man, gentlemen, whom we may safely presume is even a better judge of the prisoner's character than is the curé of St. Marleau—who, from the note you have heard read, has certainly no doubt that the prisoner is not only quite capable of attempting such a deception, but is actually engaged in practising it at the present moment.

"I pass on to the facts' brought out by the evidence. On the night of the crime, a man answering the general description of the prisoner arrived at the St. Marleau station. It was a night when one, and especially a stranger, would naturally be glad of company on the three-mile walk to the village. The man refused the company of the curé. Why? He, as it later appears, had very good reasons of his own! It was such a night that it would be all one would care to do to battle against the wind without being hampered by a travelling bag. He refused the station agent's offer to keep the bag until morning and send it over with the curé's trunk. Why? It is quite evident, in view of what followed, that he did not expect to be there the next morning! He drew from the station agent, corroborating presumably the information previously obtained either by himself or this unknown accomplice, the statement that Madame Blondin was believed to have a large sum of money hidden away somewhere in her house. That was the man, gentlemen, who answers the general description of the prisoner. Within approximately half an hour later Madame Blondin's house is robbed, and, in an effort to protect his mother's property, Théophile Blondin is shot and killed. The question perhaps arises as to how the author of this crime knew the exact hiding place where the money was kept. But it is not material, in as much as we know that he was in a position to be in possession of that knowledge. He might have been peering in through the window when Madame Blondin, as she testified, was at the hiding place a few minutes before he broke into her house—or his accomplice, still unapprehended, may, as I have previously intimated, already have discovered it.

"And now we pass entirely out of the realm of conjecture. You have heard the testimony of the murdered man's mother, who both saw and participated in the struggle. The man who murdered Théophile Blondin, who was actually seen to commit the act, is identified as the prisoner at the bar. He was struck over the head by Madame Blondin with a stick of wood, which inflicted a serious wound. We can picture him running from the house, after Madame Blondin rushed out toward the village to give the alarm. He did not, however, get very far—he was himself too badly hurt. He was found lying unconscious on the road a short distance away. Again the identification is complete—and in his pocket is found the motive for the crime, Madame Blondin's savings—and in his pocket is found the weapon, Théophile Blondin's revolver, with which the murder was committed. Gentlemen, I shall not take up your time, or the time of this court needlessly. No logical human being could doubt the prisoner's guilt for an instant. I ask you, gentlemen of the jury, to return a verdict in accordance with the evidence."

Raymond did not look up, as the crown prosecutor sat down. "No logical human being could doubt the prisoner's guilt for an instant." That was true, wasn't it? No human being—save only *one*. Well, he had expected that—it was even a tribute to his own quick wit. Puppets! Yes, puppets—they were all puppets—all but himself. But if there was guilt, there was also mercy. They would show mercy to a man who could not remember. How many times had he said that to himself! Well, he had been right, hadn't he? He had more reason to believe it now than he had had to believe it before. Lemoyne had, beyond the shadow of a doubt, convinced every one in the courtroom that the man could not remember.

"Order! Attention! Silence!" rapped out the clerk pompously.

The judge had turned in his seat to face the jury.

"Gentlemen of the jury," he said impassively, "it is my province to instruct you in the law as it applies to this case, and as it applies to the interpretation of the evidence before you. There must be no confusion in your minds as to the question of the prisoner's mental condition. The law does not hold accountable, nor does it bring to trial any person who is insane. The law, however, does not recognise loss of memory as insanity. There has been no testimony to indicate that the prisoner is insane, or even that he was not in an entirely normal condition of mind at the time the crime was committed; there has been the testimony of three physicians that he is not insane. You have therefore but one thing to consider. If, from the evidence, you believe that the prisoner killed Théophile Blondin, it is your duty to bring in a verdict of guilty; on the other hand, the prisoner is entitled to the benefit of any reasonable doubt as to his guilt that may exist in your minds. You may retire, gentlemen, for your deliberations."

There was a hurried, whispered consultation amongst the twelve men in the jury box. It brought Raymond no surprise that the jury did not leave the room. It brought him no surprise that the figure with the thin, pale face, who was dressed in Raymond Chapelle's clothes, should be ordered to stand and face those twelve men, and hear the word "guilty" fall from the foreman's lips. He had known it, every one had known it—it was the judge now, that white-haired, kindly-faced man, upon whom he riveted his attention. A sentence for life... yes, that was terrible enough... but there was a way... there would be some way in the days to come... he had fastened this crime upon a dead man to save his own life... not on this living one whose eyes now he could not meet across the room, though he could feel them upon him, feel them staring, staring at his naked soul... he would find some way... there would be time, there was all of time in a sentence for life... he would not desert the man, he would— — -

"Henri Mentone"—the judge was speaking again—"you have been found guilty by a jury of your peers of the murder of one Théophile Blondin. Have you anything to say why the sentence of this court should not be passed upon you?"

There was no answer. What was the man doing? Was he crying? Trembling? Was there that old nameless horror in the face? Were his lips quivering as a child's lips quiver when it is broken-hearted? Raymond dared not look; dared not look anywhere now save at the white-haired, kindly-faced—yes, he was kindly-faced—judge. And then suddenly he found himself swaying weakly, and his shoulder bumped into old Mother Blondin. Not that—great God—not that! That kindly-faced man was putting a *black hat* on his head, and standing up. Everybody was standing up. He, too, was standing up, only he was not steady on his feet. Was Valérie's hand on his arm in nervous terror, or to support him! Some one was speaking. The words were throbbing through his brain. Yes, throbbing—throbbing and clanging like hammer blows—that was why he could not hear them all.

"... the sentence of this court... place of confinement... thence to the place of execution... hanged by the neck until you are dead, and may God have mercy on your soul."

And then Raymond looked; and through the solemn silence, and through the doom that hung upon the room, there came a cry. It was Henri Mentone. The man's hands were stretched out, the tears were streaming down his cheeks. And was this mockery—or a joke of hell! Then why did not everybody howl and scream with mirth! The man was calling upon himself to save himself! No, no—he, Raymond, was going mad to call it mockery or mirth. It was ghastly, horrible, pitiful beyond human understanding, it tore at the heart and the soul—the man was doing what that Figure upon the Cross had once been bade to do—his own name was upon his own lips, he was calling upon himself to save himself. And the voice in agony rang through the crowded room, and people sobbed.

"Father—Father Francois Aubert, help me, do not leave me! I do not know—I do not understand. Father—*Father François Aubert*, help me—I do not understand!"

And Raymond, groping out behind him, flung his arm across the back of the bench, and, sinking down, his head fell forward, and his face was hidden.

"*Tiens*," said Mother Blondin sullenly, as though forced to admit it against her will, "he has a good heart, even if he is a priest."

CHAPTER XVII—THE COMMON CUP

IT seemed as though it were an immeasurable span of time since that voice had rung through the courtroom. He could hear it yet—he was hearing it always. "Father—Father François Aubert—help me—I do not know—I do not understand." And sometimes it was pitiful beyond that of any human cry before; and sometimes it was dominant in its ghastly irony. And yet that was only yesterday, and it was only the afternoon of the next day now.

There were wild roses, and wild raspberries growing here along the side of the road, and the smoke wreathed upward from the chimneys of the whitewashed cottages, and the water lapped upon the shore—these things were unchanged, undisturbed, unaffected, untouched. It seemed curiously improper that it should be so—that the sense of values was somehow lost.

He had come from the courtroom with his brain in a state of numbed shock, as it were, like a wound that has taken the nerve centres by surprise and had not yet begun to throb. It was instinct, the instinct to fight on, the instinct of self-preservation that had bade him grope his way to Lemoyne, the counsel for the defence. "I have friends who have money," he had said. "Appeal the case—spare no effort—I will see that the expenses are met." And after that he had driven back to St. Marleau, and after that again he had lived through a succession of blurred hours, obeying mechanically a sense of routine—he had talked to the villagers, he had eaten supper with Valérie and her mother, he had gone to bed and lain awake, he had said mass in the church that morning—mass!

Was it the heat of the day! His brow was feverish. He took off his hat, and turned to let the breeze from the river fan his face and head. It was only this afternoon, a little while ago, that he had emerged from that numbed stupor, and now the hurt and the smarting of the wound had come. His brain was clear now—*terribly* clear. Better that the stupor, which was a kindly thing, had remained! He had said mass that morning. "*Lavabo inter innocentes manus meas*—I will wash my hands among the innocent." In the sight of holy God, he had said that; at God's holy altar as he had spoken, symbolising his words, he had washed his fingers in water. It had not seemed to matter so much then, he had even mocked cynically at those same words the night that Madame

Lafleur had shown him the altar cloth—but that other voice, those other words had not been pounding at his ears then, as now. And now they were joined together, his voice and that other voice, his words and those other words: "I will wash my hands among the innocent—hanged by the neck until you are dead, and may God have mercy on your soul."

He stood by the roadside hatless. Through the open doorway of a cottage a few yards away he could see old grandmother Frenier, who was exceedingly poor, and deaf, and far up in the eighties, contentedly at work with her spinning-wheel; on the shore, where the tide was half out and the sand of the beach had merged into oozy mud, two bare-footed children overturned the rocks of such size as were not beyond their strength, laughing gleefully as they captured the sea-worms, whose nippers could pinch with no little degree of ferocity, and with which, later, no doubt, they intended to fish for tommy-cods; also there was sunlight, and sparkling water, and some one driving along the road toward him in a buckboard; and he could hear Bouchard in the carpenter shop alternately hammering and whistling—the whistling was out of tune, it was true, but what it lacked in melody it made up in spirit. This was reality, this was actuality, happiness and peace, and contentment, and serenity; and he, standing here on the road, was an integral part of the scene—no painter would leave out the village curé standing hatless on the road—the village curé would, indeed, stand out as the central figure, like a benediction upon all the rest. Why then should he not in truth, as in semblance, enter into this scene of tranquillity? Where did they come from, those words that were so foreign to all about him, where had they found birth, and why were they seared into his brain so that he could not banish them? Surely they were but an hallucination—he had only to look around him to find evidence of that. Surely they had no basis in fact, those words—"hanged by the neck until you are dead, and may God have mercy on your soul."

They seemed to fade slowly away, old grandmother Frenier and her spinning-wheel, and the children puddling in the mud, and the buckboard coming along the road; and he no longer heard the whistling from the carpenter shop—it seemed to fade out like a picture on a cinema screen, while another crept there, at first intangible and undefined, to supplant the first. It was sombre and dark, and a narrow space, and a shadowy human form. Then there came a ray of light—sunlight, only the gladness and the brightness were not in the sunlight because it had first to pass through an opening where there were iron bars. But the ray of light, nevertheless, grew stronger, and the picture took form. There were bare walls, and bare floors, and a narrow cot—and it was a cell. And the shadowy form became more distinct—it was a man, whose back was turned, who stood at the end of the cell, and whose hands were each clutched around one of the iron bars, and who seemed to be striving to thrust his head out into the sunlight, for his head, too, was pressed close against the iron bars. And there was something horribly familiar in the figure. And then the head turned slowly, and the sunlight, that was robbed of its warmth and its freedom, slanted upon a pale cheek, and ashen lips, and eyes that were torture-burned; and the face was the face of the man who was—to be hanged by the neck until he was dead, and upon whose soul that voice had implored the mercy of God.

Raymond stared at his hat which was lying in the road. How had it got there? He did not remember that he had dropped it. He had been holding it in his hand. This buckboard that was approaching would run over it. He stooped and picked it up, and mechanically began to brush away the dust. That figure in the buckboard seemed to be familiar, too. Yes, of course, it was Monsieur Dupont, the assistant chief of the Tournayville police—the man who always answered his own questions, and clucked with his tongue as though he were some animal learning to talk. But Monsieur Dupont mattered little now. It was not old grandmother Frenier and her spinning-wheel that was reality—it was Father François Aubert in the condemned cell of the Tournayville jail, waiting to be hanged by the neck until he was dead for the murder of Théophile Blondin.

Raymond put on his hat with forced calmness. He must settle this with himself; he could not afford to lose his poise—either mentally or physically. He laid no claim to the heroic or to the quixotic—he did not want to die in the stead of that man, or in the stead of any other man. Neither was he a coward—no man had ever called Raymond Chapelle, or Arthur Leroy, or Three-Ace Artie a coward. He was a gambler—and there was still a chance. There was the appeal. He was gambling now for both their lives. He would lay down no hand, he would fight as he had always fought—to the end— while a chance remained. There was still a chance—the appeal. It was long odds, he knew that—but it was a chance—and he was a gambler. He could only wait now for the turn of the final card. He would not tolerate consideration beyond that point—not if with all his might he could force his brain to leave that "afterwards" alone. It was weeks yet to the date set for the execution of Henri Mentone for the murder of Théophile Blondin, and it would be weeks yet before the appeal was acted upon. He could only wait now—here—here in St. Marleau, as the good young Father Aubert. He could not run away, or disappear, like a pitiful coward, until that appeal had had its answer. Afterwards—no, there was no "afterwards"—not *now!* Now, it was the ubiquitous Monsieur Dupont, the short little man with the sharp features, and the roving black eyes that glanced everywhere at once, who was calling to him, and clambering out of the buckboard.

"You are surprised to see me, eh, Monsieur le Curé?" clucked Monsieur Dupont. "Yes, you are surprised. Very well! But what would you say, eh, if I told you that I had come to arrest Monsieur le Curé of St. Marleau? Eh—what would you say to that?"

Arrest! Curious, the cold, calculating alertness that swept upon him at that word! What had happened?

Was the game up—now? Curious, how he measured appraisingly—and almost contemptuously—the physique of this man before him. And then, under his breath, he snarled an oath at the other. Curse Monsieur Dupont and his perverted sense of humour! It was not the first time Monsieur Dupont had startled him. Monsieur Dupont was grinning broadly—like an ape!

"I imagine," said Raymond placidly, "that what I would say, Monsieur Dupont, would be to inquire as to the nature of the charge against Monsieur le Curé of St. Marleau."

"And I," said Monsieur Dupont, "would at once reply—assault. Assault—bodily harm and injury—assault upon the person of one Jacques Bourget."

"Oh!" said Raymond—and smiled. "Yes, I believe there have been rumours of it in the village, Monsieur Dupont. Several have spoken to me about it, and I even understand that the Curé of St. Marleau pleads guilty."

And then Monsieur Dupont puckered up his face, and burst into a guffaw.

"'Cré nom—ah, pardon—but it is excusable, one bad little word, eh? Yes, it is excusable. But imagine—fancy! The good, young Father Aubert—and Jacques Bourget! I would have liked to have seen it. Yes, I would! Monsieur le Curé, you do not look it, but you are magnificent. Monsieur le Curé, I lift my hat to you. Bon Dieu—ah, pardon again—but you were not gentle with Jacques Bourget, whom one would think could eat you alive! And you told me nothing about it—you are modest, eh? Yes, you are modest."

"I have had no opportunity to be modest." Raymond laughed, "since, so I understand, Bourget encountered some of the villagers on his way home that afternoon, and gave me a reputation that, to say the least of it, left me with little to be modest about."

"I believe you," chuckled Monsieur Dupont. "I believe you, Monsieur le Curé, since I, too, got the story from Jacques Bourget himself. He desired to swear out a warrant for your arrest. You have not seen Bourget for several days, eh, Monsieur le Curé? No, you have not seen him. But I know very well how to handle such as he! He will swear out no warrant. On the contrary, he would very gladly feed out of anybody's hand just now—even yours, Monsieur le Curé. I have the brave Jacques Bourget in jail at the present moment."

"In jail?" Raymond's puzzled frown was genuine. "But——"

"Wait a minute, Monsieur le Curé"—Monsieur Dupont's smile was suddenly gone. He tapped Raymond impressively on the shoulder. "There is more in this than appears on the surface, Monsieur le Curé. You see? Yes, you see. Well then, listen! He talked no longer of a warrant when I threatened him with arrest for getting whisky at Mother Blondin's. I had him frightened. And that brings us to Mother Blondin, which is one of the reasons I am here this afternoon—but we will return to Mother Blondin's case in a moment. You remember, eh, that I caught Bourget driving on the road the night Mentone tried to escape, and that I made him drive the prisoner to Tournayville? Yes, you remember. Very good! This morning his wife comes to Tournayville to say that he has not been seen since that night. We make a search. He is not hard to find. He has been drunk ever since—we find him in a room over one of the saloons just beginning to get sober again. Also, we find that since that night Bourget, who never has any money, has spent a great deal of money. Where did Bourget get that money? You begin to see, eh, Monsieur le Curé? Yes, you begin to see." Monsieur Dupont laid his forefinger sagaciously along the side of his nose. "Very good! I begin to question. I am instantly suspicious. Bourget is very sullen and morose. He talks only of a warrant against you. I seize upon that story again to threaten him with, if he does not tell where he got the money. I put him in jail, where I shall keep him for two or three days to teach him a lesson before letting him go. It is another Bourget, a very lamblike Bourget, Monsieur le Curé, before I am through; though I have to promise him immunity for turning king's evidence. Do you see what is coming, Monsieur le Curé? No, you do not. Most certainly you do not! Very well then, listen! I am on the track of Mentone's accomplice. Bourget was in the plot. It was Bourget who was to drive Mentone away that night—to the St. Eustace station—after they had throttled you. Now, Monsieur le Curé"—Monsieur Dupont's eyes were afire; Monsieur Dupont assumed an attitude; Monsieur Dupont's arms wrapped themselves in a fold upon his breast—"now, Monsieur le Curé, what do you say to that?"

"It is amazing!"—Raymond's hands, palms outward, were lifted in a gesture eminently clerical. "Amazing! I can hardly credit it. Bourget then knows who this accomplice is?"

"No—*tonnerre*—that is the bad luck of it!" scowled Monsieur Dupont. "But there is also good luck in it. I am on the scent. I am on the trail. I shall succeed, shall I not? Yes, certainly, I shall succeed. Very well then, listen! It was dark that night. The man went to Bourget's house and called Bourget outside. Bourget could not see what the fellow looked like. He gave Bourget fifty dollars, and promised still another fifty as soon as Bourget had Mentone in the wagon. And it was on your account, Monsieur le Curé, that he went to Bourget."

Raymond was incredulous.

"On mine?" he gasped.

"Yes, certainly—on yours. It was to offer Bourget a chance to revenge himself on you. You see, eh? Yes, you see. He said he had heard of what you had done to Bourget. Very well! We have only to analyse that a little, and instantly we have a clue. You see where that brings us, eh, Monsieur le Curé?" Raymond shook his head.

"No, I must confess, I don't," he said.

"Hah! No? *Tiens!*" ejaculated Monsieur Dupont almost pityingly. "It is easy to be seen, Monsieur le Curé, that you would make a very poor police officer, and an equally poor criminal—the law would have its fingers on you while you were wondering what to do. It is so, is it not? Yes, it is so. You are much better as a priest. As a priest—I pay you the compliment, Monsieur le Curé—you are incomparable. Very good! Listen, then! I will explain. The fellow said he had heard of your fight with Bourget. Splendid! Excellent! He must then have heard of it from *some one*. Therefore he has been seen in the neighbourhood by some one besides Bourget. Who is that 'some one' who has talked with a stranger, and who can very likely tell us what that stranger looks like, where Bourget cannot? I do not say that it is certain, but that it is likely. It may not have been so dark when he talked to this 'some one'—eh? In any case it is enough to go on. Now, you see, Monsieur le Curé, why I am here—I shall begin to question everybody; and for your part, Monsieur le Curé, you can do a great deal in letting the parish know what we are after."

Raymond looked at Monsieur Dupont with admiration. Monsieur Dupont had set himself another "vigil"!

"Without doubt, Monsieur Dupont!" he assured the other heartily. "Certainly, I will do my utmost to help you. I will have a notice posted on the church door."

"Good!" cried Monsieur Dupont, with a gratified smile. "And now another matter—and one that will afford you satisfaction, Monsieur le Curé. In a day or so, I will see that Mother Blondin is the source of no more trouble in St. Marleau—or anywhere else."

"Mother Blondin?" repeated Raymond—and now he was suddenly conscious that he was in some way genuinely disturbed.

"Yes," said Monsieur Dupont. "Twice in the past we have searched her place. We knew she sold whisky. But she was too sharp for us—and those who bought knew how to keep their mouths shut. But with Bourget as a witness, it is different, eh? You see? Yes, you see. She is a fester, a sore. We will clean up the place; we will put her in jail. The air around here will be the sweeter for it, and——"

"No," said Raymond soberly. "No, Monsieur Dupont" — his hands reached out and clasped on Monsieur Dupont's shoulders. He knew now what was disturbing him. It was that surge of pity for the proscribed old woman, that sense of miserable distress that he had experienced more than once before. The scene of that morning, when she had clung to the palings of the fence outside the graveyard while they shovelled the earth upon the coffin of her son, rose vividly before him. And it was he again who was bringing more trouble upon her now through his dealings with Jacques Bourget. Yes, it was pity — and more. It was a swiftly matured, but none the less determined, resolve to protect her. "No, Monsieur Dupont, I beg of you" — he shook his head gravely — "no, Monsieur Dupont, you will not do that."

"Heh! No? And why not?" demanded Monsieur Dupont in jerky astonishment. "I thought you would ask for nothing better. She is already an *excommuniée*, and — —-"

"And she has suffered enough," said Raymond earnestly. "It would seem that sorrow and misery had been the only life she had ever known. She is too old a woman now to have her home taken from her, and herself sent to jail. She is none too well, as it is. It would kill her. A little sympathy, a little kindness, Monsieur Dupont — it will succeed far better."

"Bah!" sniffed Monsieur Dupont. "A little sympathy, a little kindness! And will that stop the whisky selling that the law demands shall be stopped, Monsieur le Curé?"

"I will guarantee that," said Raymond calmly.

"You!" Monsieur Dupont clucked vigorously with his tongue. "You will stop that! And besides other things, do you perform miracles, Monsieur le Curé? How will you do that?"

"You must leave it to me" — Raymond's hands tightened in friendly fashion on Monsieur Dupont's shoulders — "I will guarantee it. If that is a miracle, I will attempt it. If I do not succeed I will tell you so, and then you will do as you see fit. You will agree, will you not, Monsieur Dupont? — and I shall be deeply grateful to you."

Monsieur Dupont shrugged his shoulders helplessly.

"I have to tell you again that you are too soft-hearted, Monsieur le Curé. Yes, there is no other name for it — soft-hearted. And you will be made a fool of. I warn you! Well — very well! Try it, if you like. I give you a week. If at the end of a week — well, you understand? Yes, you understand."

"I understand," said Raymond; and, with a final dap on Monsieur Dupont's shoulders, he dropped his hands. "And I am of the impression that Monsieur le Curé is not the only one who is — soft-hearted."

"Bah! Nothing of the sort! Nothing of the sort!" snorted Monsieur Dupont in a sort of pleased repudiation, as he climbed back into the buckboard. "It is only to open your eyes." He picked up the reins. "I shall spend the rest of the day around here on that other business. Do not forget about the notice, Monsieur le Curé."

"It shall be posted on the church door this afternoon," Raymond promised.

He stood for a moment looking after Monsieur Dupont, as the other drove off; and then, turning abruptly, he walked rapidly along in the opposite direction, and, reaching the station road that led past old Mother Blondin's door, began to climb the hill. Yes, decidedly he would post a notice on the church door for Monsieur Dupont! If in any way he could aid Monsieur Dupont to lay hands on this accomplice of Henri Mentone, he—the derision that had crept to his lips faded away, and into the dark eyes came a sudden weariness. There was humour doubtless in the picture of Monsieur Dupont buttonholing every one he met, as he flitted indefatigably all over the country in pursuit for his mare's nest; but, somehow, he, Raymond, was not in the mood for laughter—for even a grim laughter.

There was a man waiting to be hanged; and, besides the man waiting to be hanged, there was—Valérie.

There was Valérie who, come what would, some day, near or distant, whether he escaped or not, must inevitably know him finally for the man he was. Not that it would change her life, it was only those devils of hell who tried to insinuate that she cared; but to him it was a thought pregnant with an agony so great that he could *pray*—he who had thought never to bow the knee in sincerity to God—yes, that he could pray, without mimicry, without that hideous profanation upon his lips, that he might not stand despised, a contemptuous thing, a sacrilegious profligate, in the eyes of the woman whom he loved.

He clenched his hands. He was not logical. If he cared so much as that why—no, here was specious argument! He *was* logical. His love for Valerie, great as it might be, great as it was, in the final analysis was hopeless. If he escaped, he could never return to the village, he could never return to her—to be recognised as the good, young Father Aubert; if he did not escape, if he—no, that was the "afterwards," he would not consent to think of that—only if he did not escape there would be more than the hopelessness of this love to concern him, there would be death. Yes, he was logical. The love he knew for Valérie was but to mock him, to tantalise him with a vista of what, under other circumstances, he might have claimed by right of his manhood's franchise—if he had not, years ago, from a boy almost, bartered away that franchise to the devil. Well, was he to whimper now, and turn, like a craven thing, from the bitter dregs that, while the cup was still full and the dregs yet afar off, he had held in bald contempt and incredulous raillery! The dregs were here now. They were not bitter on his lips, they were bitter in his soul; they were bitter almost beyond endurance—but was he to whimper! Yes, he was logical.

All else might be hopeless; but it was not hopeless that he might save his life. He had a right to fight for that, and he would fight for it as any man would fight—to the last.

He had climbed the hill now, and was approaching old Mother Blondin's door. Logical! Yes, he was logical—but life was not all logic. In the abstract logic was doubtless a panacea that was all-embracing; in the presence of the actual it shrank back a futile thing from the dull gnawing of the heart and the misery of the soul. Perhaps that was why he was standing here at Mother Blondin's door now. God knew, she was miserable enough; God knew, that the dregs too were now at her lips! They were not unlike—old Mother Blondin and himself. Theirs was a common cup.

He knocked upon the door—and, as he knocked, he caught sight of the old woman's shrivelled face peering at him none too pleasantly from the window. And then her step, sullen and reluctant, crossed the floor, and she held the door open grudgingly a little way; and the space thus opened she blocked completely with her body.

"What do you want?" she demanded sourly.

"I would like to come in, Madame Blondin," Raymond answered pleasantly. "I would like to have a little talk with you."

"Well, you can't come in!" she snarled defiantly. "I don't want to talk to you, and I don't want you coming here! It is true I may have been fool enough to say you had a good heart, but I want nothing to do with you. You are perhaps not as bad as some of them; but you are all full of tricks with your smirking mouths! No priest would come here if he were not up to something. I am an *excommuniée*—eh? Well, I am satisfied!" Her voice was beginning to rise shrilly. "I don't know what you want, and I don't want to know; but you can't wheedle around me just because Jacques Bourget knocked me down, and you——"

"It is on account of Jacques Bourget that I want to speak to you," Raymond interposed soothingly. "Bourget has been locked up in jail."

She stared at him, blinking viciously behind her glasses.

"Ah! I thought so! That is like the whole tribe of you! You had him arrested!"

"No," said Raymond. "I did not have him arrested. You remember the note that was read out at the trial, Madame Blendin—about the attempted escape of Henri Mentone?"

"Well?"—Madame Blondin's animosity at the sight of a *soutane* was forgotten for the moment in a newly aroused interest. "Well—what of it? I remember! What of it?"

"It seems," said Raymond, "that Monsieur Dupont has discovered that Bourget was to help in the escape."

Madame Blondin cackled suddenly in unholy mirth. "And so they arrested him, eh? Well, I am glad! Do you hear? I am glad! I hope they wring his neck for him! He would help the murderer of my son to escape, would he? I hope they hang him with the other!"

"They will not hang him," Raymond replied. "He has given all the information in his possession to the police, and he is to go free. But it was because of that afternoon here that he was persuaded to help in the escape. He expected to revenge himself on me: and that story, too, Madame Blondin, is now known to the police. Bourget has confessed to buying whisky here, and is ready to testify as a witness against you."

"*Le maudit!*" Mother Blondin's voice rose in a virulent scream. "I will tear his eyes out! Do you hear? I will show Jacques Bourget what he will get for telling on me! He has robbed me! He never pays! Well, he will pay for this! He will pay for this! I will find some one who will cut his tongue out! They are not all like Jacques Bourget, they are— —"

"You do not quite understand, Madame Blondin," Raymond interrupted gravely. "It is not with Jacques Bourget that you are concerned now, it is with the police. Monsieur Dupont came to the village this afternoon—indeed, he is here now. He said he had evidence enough at last to close up this place and put you in jail, and that he was going to do so. You are in a very serious situation, Madame Blondin"—he made as though to step forward—"will you not let me come in, as a friend, and talk it over with you, and see what we can do?"

Mother Blondin's hand was like a claw in its bony thinness, as it gripped hard over the edge of the door.

"No, you will not come in!" she shouted. "You, or your Monsieur Dupont, or the police—you will not come in! Eh—they will take my home from me— all I've got—they will put me in jail"—she was twisting her head about in a sort of pitiful inventory of her surroundings. "They have been trying to run me out of St. Marleau for a long time—all the *good* people, the saintly people—you, and your hypocrites. They cross to the other side of the road to get out of old Mother Blondin's way! And so at last, between you, you have beaten an old woman, who has no one to protect her since you have killed her son! It is a victory—eh! Go tell them to ring the church bells—go tell them—go tell them! And on Sunday, eh, you will have something to preach about! It will make a fine sermon!"

And somehow there came a lump into Raymond's throat. There was something fine in this wretched, tattered, unkempt figure before him—something of the indomitable, of the unconquerable in her spirit, misapplied though it was. Her voice fought bravely to hold its defiant, infuriated ring, to show no sign of the misery that had stolen into the dim old eyes, and was quivering on the wrinkled lips, but the voice had broken—once almost in a sob.

"No, no, Madame Blondin"—he reached out his hand impulsively to lay it over the one that was clutched upon the door—"you must not——"

She snatched her hand away—and suddenly thrust her head through the partially open doorway into his face.

"It is not Bourget, it is not Jacques Bourget!" she cried fiercely. "It is you! If you had not come that afternoon when you had no business to come, this would not have happened. It is you, who——"

"That is true," said Raymond quietly. "And that is why I am here now. I have had a talk with Monsieur Dupont, and he will give you another chance."

She still held her face close to his.

"I do not believe you!" she flung out furiously. "I do not believe you! It is some trick you are trying to play! I know Monsieur Dupont! I know him! He would give no one a chance if he could help it! I have been too much for him for a long time, and if he had evidence against me now he would give me not a minute to sell any more of—of what he thinks I sell here!"

"That also is true," said Raymond, as quietly as before. "He could not very well permit you to go on breaking the law if he could prevent it. But in exchange for his promise, I have given him a pledge that you will not sell any more whisky."

She straightened up—and stared at him, half in amazement, half in crafty suspicion.

"Ah, then, so it is you, and not Monsieur Dupont, who is going to stop it—eh?" she exclaimed, with a shrill laugh. "And how do you intend to do it—eh? How do you intend to do it? Tell me that!"

"I think it will be very simple," said Raymond—and his dark eyes, full of a kindly sympathy, looked into hers. "To save your home, and you, I have pledged myself to Monsieur Dupont that this will stop, and so—well, Madame

Blondin, and so I have come to put you upon your honour to make good my pledge." She craned her head forward again to peer into his face. She looked at him for a long minute without a word. Her lips alternately tightened and were tremulous. The fingers of her hand plucked at the door's edge. And then she threw back her head in a quavering, jeering laugh.

"Ha, ha! Old Mother Blondin upon her honour—think of that! You, a smooth-tongued priest—and me, an *excommuniée*! Ha, ha! Think of that! And what did Monsieur Dupont say, eh—what did Monsieur Dupont say?"

"He said what I know is not true," said Raymond simply. "He said you would make a fool of me."

"Ah, he said that!"—she jerked her head forward again sharply. "Well, Monsieur Dupont is wrong, and you are right. I would not do that, because I could not—since you have already made one of yourself! Ha, ha! Old Mother Blondin upon her *honour*! Ha, ha! It is a long while since I have heard that— and from a priest—ha, ha! How could any one make a fool of a fool!" Her voice was high-pitched again, fighting for its defiance; but, somehow, where she strove to infuse venom, there seemed only a pathetic wistfulness instead. "And so you would trust old Mother Blondin—eh? Well"—she slammed the door suddenly in his face, and her voice came muffled through the panels— "well, you are a fool!"

The bolt within rasped into place—and Raymond, turned away, and began to descend the hill.

Mother Blondin for the moment was in the grip of a sullen pride that bade her rise in arms against this fresh outlook on life; but Mother Blondin would close and bolt yet another door, unless he was very much mistaken— the rear door, and in the faces of her erstwhile and unhallowed clientele!

Yes, he had pity for the old woman who had no kin now, and who had no friends. Pity! He owed her more than that! So then—there came a sudden thought—so then, why not? He would not long be curé of St. Marleau, but while he was—well, he was the curé of St. Marleau! He could not remove the ban of excommunication, that was beyond the authority of a mere curé, it would require at least Monsignor the Bishop to do that; but he could remove the ban—of ostracism! Yes, decidedly, the good, young Father Aubert could do that! He was vaguely conscious that there were degrees of excommunication, and he seemed to remember that Valérie had said it was but a minor one that had been laid upon Mother Blondin, and that the villagers of their own accord had drawn more and more aloof. It would, therefore, not be very difficult.

He quickened his step, and, reaching the bottom of the hill, made his way at once toward the carpenter shop. He could see Madame Bouchard hoeing in the little garden patch between the road and the front of the shop. It was Madame Bouchard that he now desired to see.

"*Tiens! Bon jour*, Madame Bouchard!" he called out to her, as he approached. "I am come a penitent! I did not deserve your bread! I am sure that you are vexed with me! But I have not seen you since to thank you."

She came forward to where Raymond now leaned upon the fence.

"Oh, Monsieur le Curé!" she exclaimed laughingly. "How can you say such things! Fancy! The idea! Vexed with you! It is only if you really liked it?"

"H'm!" drawled Raymond teasingly, pretending to deliberate. "When do you bake again, Madame Bouchard?"

She laughed outright now.

"To-morrow, Monsieur le Curé—and I shall see that you are not forgotten."

"It is a long way off—to-morrow," said Raymond mournfully; and then, with a quick smile: "But only one loaf this time, Madame Bouchard, instead of two."

"Nonsense!" she returned. "It is a great pleasure. And what are two little loaves!"

"A great deal," said Raymond, suddenly serious. "A very great deal, Madame Bouchard; and especially so if you send one of the two loaves to some one else that I know of."

"Some one else?"

"Yes," said Raymond. "To Mother Blondin."

"To—Mother Blondin!"—Madame Bouchard stared in utter amazement. "But—but, Monsieur le Curé, you are not in earnest! She—she is an *excommuniée*, and we—we do not— —"

"I think it would make her very glad," said Raymond softly. "And Mother Blondin I think has— —"

It was on the tip of his tongue to say that Mother Blondin was not likely now to sell any more whisky at the tavern, but he checked himself. It was Mother Blondin who must be left to tell of that herself. If he spread such a tale, she would be more likely than not to rebel at a situation which she would probably conceive was being thrust forcibly down her throat; and, in pure spite at what she might also conceive to be a self-preening and boastful spirit on his part for his superiority over her, sell all the more, no matter what the consequences to herself. And so he changed what he was about to say. "And Mother Blondin I think has known but little gladness in her life."

"But—but, Monsieur le Curé," she gasped, "what would the neighbours say?"

"I hope," said Raymond, "that they would say they too would send her loaves—of kindness."

Madame Bouchard leaned heavily upon her hoe.

"It is many years, Monsieur le Curé, since almost I was a little girl, that any one has willingly had anything to do with the old woman on the hill."

"Yes," said Raymond gently. "And will you think of that, Madame Bouchard, when you bake to-morrow—the many years—and the few that are left—for the old woman on the hill."

The tears had sprung to Madame Bouchard's eyes. He left her standing there, leaning on the hoe.

He went on along the road toward the *presbytère*. It had been a strange afternoon—an illogical one, an imaginary one almost. It seemed to have been a jumble of complexities, and incongruities, and unrealities—there was the man who was to be hanged by the neck until he was dead; and Monsieur Dupont who, through a very natural deduction and not because he was a fool, for Monsieur Dupont was very far from a fool, was now vainly engaged like a dog circling around in a wild effort to catch his own tail; and there was Mother Blondin who had another window to gaze from; and Madame Bouchard who had still another. Yes, it had been a strange afternoon—only now that voice in the courtroom was beginning to ring in his ears again. "Father—Father François Aubert—help me—I do not understand." And the gnawing was at his soul again, and again his hat was lifted from his head to cool his fevered brow.

And as he reached the church there came to him the sound of organ notes, and instead of crossing to the *presbytère* he stepped softly inside to listen—it would be Valérie—Valérie, and Gauthier Beaulieu, the altar boy, probably, who often pumped the organ for her when she was at practice. But as he stepped inside the music ceased, and instead he heard them talking in the gallery, and in the stillness of the church their voices came to him distinctly.

"Valérie"—yes, that was the boy's voice—"Valérie, why do they call him the good, young Father Aubert?"

"Such a question!" Valérie laughed. "Why do you call him that yourself?"

"I don't—any more," asserted the boy. "Not after what I saw at mass this morning."

Raymond drew his breath in sharply. What was this! What was this that Gauthier Beaulieu, the altar boy, had seen at mass! He had fooled the boy—the boy could not have seen anything! He drew back, opening the door cautiously. They were coming down the stairs now—but he must hear—hear what it was that Gauthier Beaulieu had seen.

"Why, what do you mean, Gauthier?" Valérie asked.

"I mean what I say," insisted the boy doggedly. "It is not right to call him that! When he was kneeling there this morning, and I guess it was the bright light because the stained window was open, for I never saw it before, I saw his hair all specked with white around his temples. And a man with white in his hair isn't young, is he! And I saw it, Valérie—honest, I did!"

"Your eyes should have been closed," said Valérie. "And——"

Raymond was crossing the green to the *presbytère*.

CHAPTER XVIII—THE CALL IN THE NIGHT

IT was very dark here in the front room, and somehow the darkness seemed tangible to the touch, like something oppressive, like the folds of a pall that was spread over him, and which he could not thrust aside. And it was still, and very quiet—save for the voices, and save that it seemed he could hear that faltering, irregular step from the rear room, where there was no longer any step to hear.

Surely it would be daylight soon—the merciful daylight. The darkness and the night were meant only for sleep, and it was an eternity since he had slept—no, not an eternity, only a week—it was only a week since he had slept. No, that was not true either—there had been hours, not many of them, but there had been hours when his eyes had been closed and he had not been conscious of his surroundings, but those hours had been even more horrible than when he had tossed on his bed awake. They had brought neither rest nor oblivion—they were full of dreams that were hideous—and the dreams would not leave him when he was awake—and the sleep when it came was a curse because the dreams remained to cast an added blight upon his wakefulness—and he had come even to fight against sleep and to resist it because the dreams remained.

Dreams! There was always the dream of the Walled Place which—no! Not that—*now!* Not that! Yes! The dream of the Walled Place. See—it went like this: He was in a sort of cavernous gloom in which he could not see very distinctly, but he was obsessed with the knowledge that there were hidden things from which he must escape. So he would run frantically around and around, following four square walls which were so high that the tops merged into the gloom; and the walls, as he touched them with his hands, seeking an opening, were wet with a slime that grew upon them. Then, looming out of the centre of this place, he would suddenly see what it was that he was running away from. There was a form, a human form, with something black over its head, that swayed to and fro, and was suspended from a bar that reached across from one wall to another; and on the top of this bar there roosted a myriad winged creatures like gigantic bats, only their eyes blazed, and they had enormous claws—and suddenly these vampires would rise with a terrifying crackling of their wings, and shrill, abominable screams, and swirl and circle over him, drawing nearer and nearer until his blood ran cold—and then, shrieking like a maniac, he would run again around and around the walls, beating at the slime until his hands bled. And the screaming things with outstretched talons followed him, and he stumbled and fell, and fell again, and shrieked out in his terror of these inhuman vultures that had roosted above the swaying thing with the black-covered head—and just as they were settling upon him there was an opening in the wall where there had been no opening before, and with his last strength he struggled toward it—and the way was blocked. The opening had become a gate that was all studded with iron spikes which if he rushed upon it would impale him, and which Valerie was closing—and as she closed it her head was averted, and one hand was thrown across her eyes, its palm toward him, as though she would not look upon his face.

Raymond's hands were wet with perspiration. They slipped from the arms of his chair, and hung downward at his sides. What time was it? It had been midnight when he had risen fully dressed from his bed in the rear room—that he occupied now that they had taken the man away to jail—and had come in here to sit at the desk. Since then the clock had struck many times, the half hours, and the hours. Ah—listen! It was striking again. One—two—three! Three o'clock! It was still a long way off, the daylight—the merciful daylight. The voices did not plague him so constantly in the warmth of the sunshine. Three o'clock! It would be five o'clock before the dawn came.

They had changed, those voices, in the last week—at least there was a new voice that had come, and an old one that did not recur so insistently. "Father—Father François Aubert—help me—I do not understand"—yes, that was still dinning forever in his ears; but, instead of that voice which said some one was to be hanged by the neck until dead, the new voice had quite a different thing to say. It was the voice of the "afterwards." Hark! There it was now: "What fine and subtle shade of distinction is there between being hanged and imprisoned for life; what difference does it make, what difference could it make, what difference will it make—why do you temporise?"

He had fought with all his strength against that "afterwards"—and it was stronger than he. He could not evade the issue that was flung at him, and flung again and again until his brain writhed in agony with it. He was a gambler, but he was not a blind gambler. He did not want the man to lose his life, or his freedom for all of life—he did not want to lose his own life. While the appeal was pending *something* might happen, a thousand things might happen, there was always, always a chance. He would not throw away that chance—only a fool who had lost his nerve would do that. But he was not blind. The chance was one where the odds against him staggered him—

there was so little chance that, fight as he would to escape it, logic and plain common sense had forced upon him the "afterwards." And these days while the appeal was pending were like remorseless steps that led on and on to end only upon the brink of a yawning chasm, whose depth and whose blackness were as the depth and blackness of hell, and over which he sprang suddenly erect, his head flung back, the strong jaws clamped like a vise. Who had brought this torture upon him? He could not sleep! He knew no repose! God, or devil, or power infernal—who was it? Neither sleep nor repose might be his, but he was unbroken yet, and he could still fight! He asked only that— that the author of this torment stand before him—and fight! Why should he, unless the one meagre hope that something might happen in the meantime be fulfilled, why should he stand faced with the choice of swinging like a felon from the gallows, or of allowing that other innocent man to go to his doom? Yes, why should he submit to this torture, when that scarred-faced blackguard had brought his death upon himself—why should he submit to it, when it was so easy to escape it all! Once, that night in Ton-Nugget Camp, he had flung down the gauntlet in the face of God, and in the face of hell, and in the face of man, and in the face of beast. Was he a weakling and a fool now who had not sense enough to seize his opportunity to be quit of this, and to go his way, and live again the full, red-blooded, reckless life that he had lived since he was a boy, and that now, a young man still, beckoned to him with allurements as yet untasted! To-morrow—no, to-day when the daylight came—he had only to borrow Bouchard's boat, and the boat upturned would be found, and St. Mar-leau would mourn the loss of the good, young Father Aubert whose body had been swept out to sea, and the law would take its course on the man in the condemned cell, and Three-Ace Artie would be as free and untrammelled as the air—yes, and a coward, and a crawling thing, and—the paroxysm of fury passed. He sagged against the desk. This was the "afterwards"—but why should it come now! Between now and then there was a chance that something might intervene. He had only been trying to delude himself when he had said that in a life sentence there was all of time to plan and plot—he knew that. And he knew, too, that he was no more content that the man should be imprisoned for life than that the man should hang— that one was the equal of the other. He knew that this "all of time" was ended when the appeal was decided. He knew all that—that voice would not let him juggle with myths any more. But that moment had not come yet—there were still weeks before it would come—and in those weeks there lay a hope, a chance, a gambling chance that something might happen. And even in the appeal there lay a hope too, not that the sentence might be commuted to life imprisonment, that changed nothing now, but that they might perhaps after all consider the man's condition sufficient reason for not holding him to account for murder, and might therefore, instead, place him under medical treatment somewhere until, if ever, he recovered. He, Raymond, had not struck the man, he had not in even a remote particular been responsible for the man's wound, or the ensuing condition, and if the man were turned over to medical supervision the man automatically ceased to have any claim upon him.

But that was not likely to happen—it was only one of those thousand things that *might* happen—nothing was likely to happen except that the man would be hanged. And when that time came, if the appeal were lost and every one of those thousand chances swept away, and the only thing that could save the man's life would be to—God, would he never stop this! Would his mind never, even through utter exhaustion, cease its groping in this horrible turmoil! On, on, on! His brain was remorselessly driven on! It was like—like a slave that, already lacerated and bleeding, was lashed on again to renewed effort by some monstrous, brutal and inhuman master!

Yes, when that time came, and if that chance were gone, and supposing he gave himself up to stand in the other's place, could he in any way evade the rope, wriggle away from that dangling noose? Was there a loophole in the evidence anywhere? If only in some way he could prove that the act had been committed in self-defence! He had feared to risk such a plea that night, because he had feared that his own past would condemn him out of hand; and, moreover, however that might have been, the man lying in the road, whom he had thought dead, had seemed to offer the means of washing his hands for good and all of the whole matter. Self-defence! Ha, ha! Listen to those devils laugh! It was his own hand that had tied the knot in the noose so that it would never slip—it was he who had so cunningly supplied all the attendant details that irrevocably placed the stamp of robbery and murder upon the doings of that night. Here there was no delusion; here, where delusion was sought again, there was no delusion—if he gave himself up he would hang—hang by the neck until he was dead—and, since he had desecrated God's holy places, he would hang without the mercy of God upon his soul. Well, what odds did that make—whether there was mercy of God upon his soul-or not! Was there anything in common between—no, that was not what he had to think about now—it was quite another matter.

Suppose, when he was forced to fling down his hand finally, that instead of giving himself up, or instead of making it appear that the good, young Father Aubert was dead—suppose that he simply made an escape from St. Marleau such as he had planned for Henri Mentone that night? He could at least secure a few hours' start, and then, from somewhere, before it was too late, send back, say, a written confession. He could always do that. Surely that would save the man. They would hunt for him, Raymond, as they would hunt for a wild beast that had run amuck, and they would hunt for him for the rest of his life, and in the end they might even catch him—but that was the chance he would have to accept. Yes, here was another way—only why did not this way bring rest, and repose, and satisfaction, and sleep? And why ask the question? He knew—he knew why! It was—Valérie. It was not a big way, it was not a man's way—and in Valerie's eyes at the last, not absolving him, not even that she might endure the better, for it could not intimately affect her, there was left to him only the one redeeming act, the one thing that would lift him above contempt and loathing, and that was that she should know him—for a *man*.

Life, the mere act of breathing, of knowing a concrete existence, was not everything; it did not embrace everything, it was not even a state that was not voluntarily to be surrendered to greater things, to— —

"A fool and a woman's face, and blatant sophistry, and mock heroics!" — that inner monitor, with its gibe and sneer, was back again. Its voice, too, must make itself heard!

He raised his hands and pressed them tight against his throbbing temples. This was hell's debating society, and he must listen to the arguments and decide upon their merits and pronounce upon them, for he was the presiding officer and the decision remained with him! How they gabbled, and shrieked, and whispered, and jeered, and interrupted each other, and would not keep order—those voices! Though now for the moment that inner voice kept drowning all the others out.

"You had your chance! If you hadn't turned squeamish that night when all you needed to do was to hold a pillow over the man's face for a few minutes, you wouldn't have had any of this now! How much good will it do you what *she* thinks—when they get through burying you in lime under the jail walls!"

It was dark, very dark here in the room. That was the window over there in that direction, but there was not even any grayness showing, no sign yet of daylight—no sign yet of daylight. Why would they not let him alone, these voices, until the time came when he *must* act? That was all he asked. In the interval something might—his hands dropped to his sides, and he half slipped, half fell into his chair, and his head went forward over the desk. Was all that to begin over again—and commence with the dream of the Walled Place! No, no; he would not let it—*he would not let it!*

He would think about something else; force himself to think—rationally— about something else. Well then, the man in the condemned cell, whom he had not dared refuse to visit, and whom he had gone twice that week to see? No—-not that, either! The man was always sitting on that cursed cot with his hands clasped dejectedly between his knees, and the iron bars robbed the sunlight of warmth, and it was cold, and the man's eyes haunted him. No — not that, either! He had to go and see the man again to-morrow — and that was enough — and that was enough!

Well then, Mother Blondin? Yes, that was better! He could even laugh ironically at that — at old Mother Blondin. Old Mother Blondin was falling under the spell of the example set by the good, young Father Aubert! Some of the old habitués, he had heard, were beginning to grumble because it was becoming difficult to obtain whisky at the tavern. The Madame Bouchards were crowding the habitues out; and the old woman on the hill, even if with occasional sullen and stubborn relapses, was slowly yielding to the advances of St. Marleau that he had inaugurated through the carpenter's v/ife. Ah — he had thought to laugh at this, had he! Laugh! He might well keep his head buried miserably in his arms here upon the desk! Laugh! It brought instead only a profound and bitter loneliness. He was alone, utterly alone, isolated and cut off in a world where there was the sound of no human voice, the touch of no human hand, alone — amidst people whose smiles greeted him on every hand, amidst people who admired and loved him, and listened reverently to the words of God that fell from his lips. But they loved, and admired, and gave their friendship, not to the man he was, but to the man they thought he was — to the good, young Father Aubert. That was what was actuating even Mother Blondin! And the life that he had led as the good, young Father Aubert was being held up to him now as in a mental mirror that lay bare to his gaze his naked soul. They loved him, these people; they had faith in him — and a pure, unswerving faith in the religion, and in the God as whose holy priest he masqueraded!

Raymond's lips twisted in pain. The love of these people struck to the heart, and the pang hurt. It would have been a glad thing to have won this love — for himself. And he was requiting what they gave in their ignorance by defiling what meant most in life to them — the holy things they worshipped. It was strange — strange how of late he had sought, in a sort of pitiful atonement for the wrong he had done them, to put sincerity into the words that, before, he had only mumbled at the church altar! Yes, he had earned their love and their respect, and he was the good, young Father Aubert, and the life he had led amongst them was a blasphemous lie — but it had not been the motives of a hypocrite that had actuated him. It had not been that the devil desired to pose as a saint. He stood acquitted before even God of that. He had sought only, fought only, asked only — for his life.

A sham, a pretence, a lie — it was abhorrent, damnable — it was not even Three-Ace Artie's way — and he was chained to it in every word and thought and act. There — that thing that loomed up through the darkness there a few inches from him—that was one of the lies. That was a typewriter he had rented in Tour-nayville and had brought back when returning from his last visit to the jail. Personal letters had begun to arrive for Father François Aubert. He might duplicate a signature, but he could not imitate pages of the man's writings. And he could not dictate a letter to-the man's *mother*—and meet Valérie's eyes.

Valérie! Out in that world where he was set apart, out in that world of inhuman isolation, this was the loneliness that was greatest of all. Valérie! Valérie! It seemed as though he were held in some machiavellian bondage, free to move and act, free in all things save one—he could not pass the border of his prison-land. But he, Raymond Chapelle, could look out over the border of his prison-land, and watch this woman, whose face was pure and beautiful, as she walked about, and talked, and was constantly in the company of a young priest, who was the good, young Father Aubert, the Curé of St. Marleau. And because he had watched her hungrily for many days, and knew the smile that came so gladly to the sweet lips, and because he had looked into the clear, steadfast eyes, and listened to her voice, and because she was just Valérie, he had come to the knowledge of a great love—and a great, torturing, envious jealousy of this man, cloaked in priestly garb, who was forever at her side.

His lips moved, but no sound came from them. Valérie! Valérie! Why had she not come into his life before! Before—when? Before that night at Mother Blondin's? Was he not man enough to look the truth in the face! That night was only a culminating incident of a life that went back many years to the days when—when there had been no Valérie either! But it was too late to think of that now—now that Valérie had come, come as a final, terrible punishment, holding up before him, through bitter contrast, the hollow worthlessness of the stakes that, when the choice had been freely his, he had chosen to play for!

Valérie! Valérie! His soul was calling out to her. A life with Valérie! What would it not have meant? The dear love that she might have given him—the priceless love that he might have won! Gone! Gone forever! No, it was not gone, for it had never been. He thanked God for that. Yes, there must be a God who had brought this about, for while he flouted this God in the dress of this God's priest, this God utilised that very act to save Valérie, who trusted this God, from the misery and sorrow and hopelessness that must have come to her with love. She could not love a priest; there could be no thought of such a thing for Valérie. This God had set that barrier there—to protect her. Yes, he thanked God for that; he thanked God he had not brought this hurt upon her—and those minions of hell, who tried to tantalise, and with their insidious deviltry tried to make him think otherwise, were powerless here. But that did not appease the yearning; that did not answer the cry of his heart and soul.

Valérie! Valérie! Valérie! He was calling to her with all his strength from the border of that prison-land. Valérie! Valérie! Would his voice not reach her! Would she not turn her head and smile! Valérie! Valérie! He wanted her now in his hour of agony, in this hour of terrible loneliness, in this hour when his brain rocked and reeled on the verge of madness.

How still it was—and how dark! There were no voices now—only the voice of his soul calling, calling, calling for Valérie—calling for what he could never have—calling for the touch of her hand to guide him—calling for her smile to help him on his way. Yes, Valérie—he was calling Valérie—he was calling to her from the depths of his being. Out into the night, out into the everywhere, he was flinging his piteous, soundless cry, and God, if God would, might listen, and know that His revenge was taken; and hell might listen, and shriek its mirth—they would not silence him.

Valérie! Valérie! No, there was no answer. There would never be an answer—but he would always call. Through the years to come, if there were those years to reckon with, he would call as he was calling now. Valérie! Valérie! Valérie! She would not hear—she would not answer—she would not know. But he would call—because he loved her.

A sob shook his bowed shoulders. A hand in agony gathered and crushed a fold of flesh from the forehead that lay upon it. Valérie! Valérie! He did not cry out. He made no sound. It was still, still as the living death in that prison-land—and then—and then he was swaying to his feet, and clutching with both hands at the desk, for support. Valérie! The door was open, and a soft light filled the room. Valérie! Valérie was standing there on the threshold, holding a lamp in her hand. It was phantasm! A vision! It was not real! It was not Valérie! His mind was a broken thing at last! It was not Valérie—but that was Valérie's voice—that was Valérie's voice.

The lamp shook a little unsteadily in her hand.

"Did you call?" she asked.

He did not answer—only looked at her, as though in truth she were a vision that had come to him. She was in dressing-gown; and her hair, loosely knotted, framed her face in dark, waving tresses; and her eyes were wide, startled and perplexed, as they fixed upon him.

"I—I thought I heard you call," she faltered.

All the gladness, all the joy in life, all that the world could hold seemed for an instant his. All else was forgotten—all else but that singing in his heart—all else but that fierce, elemental, triumphant, mighty joy lifting him high to a pinnacle that reared itself supreme, commanding and immortal, far beyond the reach of that sea of torment which had engulfed him. Valérie had heard him call—and she had answered—and she was here. Valérie was here—

she had come to him. Valérie had heard him call—and she was here. And then beneath his feet that pinnacle, so supreme, commanding and immortal, seemed to dissolve away, and that sea of torment closed over him again, and all those voices that plagued him, mocking, jeering, screaming, shrieking, were like a horrible requiem ringing in his ears. She had heard him call—and he had made no sound—only his soul had spoken.. And she had answered. And she was here—here now—standing there on the threshold. *Why?* He dared not answer. It was a blessed thing, a wonderful, glorious thing—-and it was a terrible thing, a thing of misery and despair. What was he doing now—*answering* that "why"! No, no—it was not true—it could not be true. He had thanked God that it could not be so. It was not that—*that* was not the reason she had heard him call—that was not the reason she was here. It was not! It was not! It was only those insidious— —

He heard himself speaking; he was conscious that his voice by some miracle was low, grave, contained. "No, Mademoiselle Valérie, I did not call."

The colour was slowly leaving her cheeks, and into her eyes came creeping confusion and dismay.

"It—it is strange," she said nervously. "I was asleep, and I thought I heard you call for—for help, and I got up and lighted the lamp, and— —"

Was that his laugh—quiet, gentle, reassuring? Was he so much in command of himself as that? Was it the gambler, or the priest, or—great God!—the lover now? She was here—she had come to him.

"It was a dream, Mademoiselle Valérie," he was saying. "A very terrible dream, I am afraid, if I was the subject of it; but, see, it is nothing to cause you distress, and to-morrow you will laugh over it."

She did not reply at once. She was very pale now; and her lips, though tightly closed, were quivering. Nor did she look at him. Her eyes were on the floor. Her hand mechanically drew and held the dressing-gown closer about her throat.

He had not moved from the side of the desk, nor she from the threshold of the door—and now she looked up suddenly, and held the lamp in her hand a little higher, and her eyes searched his face.

"It must be very late—very, very late," she said steadily. "And you have not gone to bed. There is something the matter. What is it? Will you tell me?"

"But, yes!" he said—and smiled. "But, yes—I will tell you. It is very simple. I think perhaps I was overtired. In any case, I was restless and could not sleep, and so I came in here, and—well, since I must confess—I imagine I finally fell asleep in my chair."

"Is that all?" she asked — and there was a curious insistence in her voice. "You look as though you were ill. Are you telling me all?"

"Everything!" he said. "And I am not ill, Mademoiselle Valérie" — he laughed again — "you would hear me complain fast enough if I were! I am not a model patient."

She shook her head, as though she would not enter into the lightness of his reply; and again her eyes sought the floor. And, as he watched her, the colour now came and went from her cheeks, and there was trouble in her face, and hesitancy, and irresolution.

"What is it, Mademoiselle Valérie?" — his forced lightness was gone now. She was frightened, and nervous, and ill at ease — that she should be standing here like this at this hour of night, of course. Yes, that was it. Naturally that would be so. He lifted his hand and drew it heavily across his forehead. She was frightened. If he might only take her in his arms, and draw her head to his shoulder, and hold her there, and soothe her! It seemed that all his being cried to him to do that. "Well, why don't you?" — that inner voice was flashing the suggestion quick upon him — "well, why don't you? You could do it as a priest, in the rôle of priest, you know — like a father to one of his flock. Go ahead, here's your chance — be the priest, be the priest! Don't you want to hold her in your arms — be the priest, be the priest!"

She had not answered his question. He found himself answering it for her.

"What is it, Mademoiselle Valérie? You must not let a dream affect you, you know. It is gone now. And you can see that — —"

"It is strange" — she spoke almost to herself. "I — I was so sure that I heard you call."

Why was he not moving toward her? Why was he clinging in a sort of tenacious frenzy to the desk? Why was he not obeying the promptings of that inner voice? It would be quite a natural thing to do what that voice prompted — and Valérie, Valérie who would never be his, would for a moment, snatched out of all eternity, be in his arms.

"But you must not let such a thing as a dream affect you" — he seemed to be speaking without volition of his own, and he seemed stupidly able to say but the same thing over again. "And, see, it is over, and you are awake now to find that no one is really in trouble after all."

And then she raised her head — and suddenly, but as though she were afraid even of her own act, as though she still fought against some decision she had forced upon herself, she walked slowly forward into the room, and set the lamp down upon the desk.

"Yes, there is some one in trouble" — the words came steadily, but scarcely above a whisper; and her hand was tense about the white throat now, where before it had mechanically clutched at the dressing-gown. "I am in trouble — Father Aubert."

"You — Valérie!" He was conscious, even in his startled exclamation, of a strange and disturbing prescience. Father Aubert — he could not remember when she had called him that before — *Father* Aubert. It was very rarely that she called him that, it was almost always Monsieur le Curé. And he — her name — he had called her Valérie — not Mademoiselle Valérie — but Valérie, as once before, when she had stood out there in the hall the night they had taken that man away, her name had sprung spontaneously to his lips.

"Yes," she said, and bowed her head. "I am in trouble, father; for I have sinned."

"Sinned — Valérie" — the words were stumbling on his lips. How fast that white throat throbbed! Valérie, pure and innocent, meant perhaps to confess to — *Father* Aubert. Well, she should not, and she would not! Not that! She should not have to remember in the "afterwards" that she had bared her soul at the shrine of profanity. Back again into his voice he forced a cheery, playful reassurance. "It cannot be a very grievous sin that Mademoiselle Valérie has been guilty of! Of that, I am sure! And to-morrow — —"

"No, no!" she cried out. "You do not know! See, be indulgent with me now, father — I am in trouble — in very deep and terrible trouble. I — I cannot even confess and ask you for absolution — but you can help me — do not try to put me off — I — I may not have the courage again. See, I — I am not very brave, and I am not very strong, and the tears are not far off. Help me to do what I want to do."

"Valérie!" he scarcely breathed her name. Help her to do what she wanted to do! There was another prescience upon him now; but one that he could not understand, save that it seemed to be pointing toward the threshold of a moment that he was to remember all his life.

"Sit down there in your chair, father, please" — her voice was very low again. "Sit there, and let me kneel before you."

He stepped back as from a blow.

"No, Valérie, you shall not kneel to me" — he did not know what he was saying now. Kneel! Valérie kneel to him! "You shall not kneel to me, I — —"

"*Yes!*" The word came feverishly. The composure that she had been fighting to retain was slipping from her. "Yes — I must! I must!" She was close upon him, forcing him back toward the chair. Her eyes, dry and wide before, were swimming with sudden tears. "Oh, don't you understand! Oh, don't you understand! I am not kneeling to you as a man, I am kneeling to you as — as a — a *priest* — a priest of God — for — for I have sinned."

She was on her knees — and, with a mental cry of anguish, Raymond slipped down into the chair. Yes, he understood — now — at last! He understood what, pray God, she should never realise he understood! She — Valérie — cared. And she was trying now — God, the cruelty of it! — and she was trying now to save herself, to protect herself, by forcing upon herself an actual physical acceptance of him as a priest. No! It was not so! It could not be so! He did *not* understand!

He would not have it so! He would not! It was only hell's trickery again — only that — and — —

"Lay your hands on my head, father." She caught his hands and lifted them, and laid them upon her bowed head — and as his hands touched her she seemed to tremble for an instant, and her hands tightened upon his. "Hold them there for a little while, father," she murmured — and took her own hands away, and clasped them before her hidden face.

Raymond's countenance was ashen as he bent forward. What had that voice prompted him to do? Be the priest? Well, he was being the priest now — and he knew torment in the depths of a sacrilege at last before which his soul shrank back appalled. The soft hair was silken to the touch of his hands, and yet it burned and seared him as with brands of fire. It was Valérie's hair. It was Valérie's head that was bowed before him. It was Valérie, the one to whom his soul had called, who was kneeling to him — as a priest of God — to save herself!

"Say the *Pater Noster* with me, father," she whispered.

He bent his head still lower — lower now that she might not by any chance glimpse his face. Like death it must look. He pressed his hands in assent upon her head — but it was Valérie's voice alone that faltered through the room.

".... *Sanctificetur nomen tuum* — hallowed be Thy name... *fiat voluntas tua* — Thy will be done.... *et dimitte nobis débita nostra* — and forgive us our trespasses... *et ne nos inducas in tentationem* — and lead us not into temptation... *sed libera nos a malo* — but deliver us from evil... Amen."

The lamp burned upon the desk; it lighted up the room — but before Raymond's eyes was only a blur, and nothing was distinct. And there was silence — silence for a long time.

And then Valérie spoke again.

"I am stronger now," she said. "I — I think God showed me the way. You have been very good to me to-night — not to question me — just to let me have my way. And now bless me, father, and I will go."

Bless Valérie—ask God's blessing on Valérie—would that be profanation? God's blessing on Valérie! Ay, he could ask that! Profligate, sinner, sham and mocker, he could ask that in reverence and sincerity—God's blessing upon Valérie—because he loved her.

"God keep you, Valérie," he said, and fought the tremor from his voice. "God keep you, Valérie—and bless you—and guard you through all your life."

She rose from her knees, and turning quickly because her cheeks were wet, picked up the lamp, and walked to the door. At the threshold she paused, but did not look back.

"Good-night, father," she said simply.

"Good-night, Valérie," he answered.

It was dark again in the room. He had risen from his chair as Valérie had risen from her knees—and now his hand felt out for the chair again, and he sank down, and, as when she had come to him, his head was buried again in his arms upon the desk.

Valérie cared! Valérie loved him! Valérie, too, had been through her hour of torment. "Not as a man—as a priest, a priest of God." No, he would not believe that, he would not let himself believe that. It could not be so! She was troubled, in distress—about something else. What time was it now? Not daylight yet—the merciful daylight—no sign of daylight yet? If it were true—what then? If she cared—what then?

If Valérie loved him—what then? What was he to do in the "afterwards"? It would not be himself alone who was to bear the burden then. It was not true, of course; he would not believe it, he would not let himself believe it. But if it were true how would Valérie endure the hanging by the neck until he was dead of the man she loved, or the knowledge of what he was, or the death by accident—of the man she loved!

He did not stir now. He made no sound, no movement—and his head lay in his outflung arms. And time passed, and through the window crept the gray of dawn—and presently it was daylight—the merciful daylight—and the night was gone. But he was scarcely conscious of it now. It grew lighter still, and filled the room—that merciful daylight. And his brain, sick and stumbling and weary, reeled on and on, and there was the dream of the Walled Place again, and Valérie was closing the gate that was studded with iron spikes—and there was no way out.

And then very slowly, like a man rousing from a stupor, his head came up from the desk, and he listened. From across the green came the sound of the church bells ringing for early mass. And as he listened the bells seemed to catch up the tempo of some refrain. What was it? Yes, he knew now. It was the opening of the mass—the words he would have to go in there presently and say. Were they mocking him, those bells! Was this what the daylight, the merciful daylight had brought—only a crowning, pitiless, merciless jeer! His face, strained and haggard, lifted suddenly a little higher. Was it only mockery, or could it be—see, they seemed to peal more softly now—could it be that they held another meaning—like voices calling in compassion to him because he was lost? No—his mind was dazed—it could not mean that—for him. But listen! They were repeating it over and over again. It was the call to mass, for it was daylight, and the beginning of a new day. Listen!

"*Introibo ad altare Dei*—I will go in unto the Altar of God."

CHAPTER XIX—THE TWO SINNERS

INTROIBO ad altare Dei — I will go in unto the Altar of God." It had been days, another week of them, since the morning when he had raised his head to that call for early mass,' and his brain, stumbling and confused, had set those words in a refrain to the tempo of the pealing bells.

It was midnight now — another night — the dreaded night. They were not all like that other night, not all so pitiless — that would have been beyond physical endurance. But they were bad, all the nights were bad. They seemed cunningly just to skirt the border edge of strain that could be endured, and cunningly just to evade the breaking point.

It was midnight. On the table beside the bed stood the lighted lamp; and beside the lamp, topped by a prayer-book, was a little pile of François Aubert's books; and the bed was turned neatly down, disclosing invitingly the cool, fresh sheets. These were Madame Lafleur's kindly and well-meant offices. Madame La-fleur knew that he did not sleep very well. Each evening she came in here and set the lamp on the table, and arranged the books, and turned down the bed.

This was the same rocking-chair he sat in now that he had sat in night after night, and watched a man with bandaged head lying on that same bed — watched and waited for the man to die. The man was not there any more — there were just the cool, fresh sheets. The man was in Tournayville. He had seen the man again that afternoon — and now it was the man who was waiting to die.

"I will go in unto the Altar of God." With a curious hesitancy he reached out and took the prayer-book from the table, and abstractedly began to finger its pages. What did those words mean? They had been with him incessantly, insistently, since that morning when he had groped for their meaning as between the bitterest of mockeries and a sublime sincerity. They did not mock him now, they held no sting of irony. It was very strange. They had not mocked him all that week. He had been glad, eager, somehow, to repeat them to himself. Did they mean — peace?

Peace! If he could have peace—even for to-night. If he could lie down between those cool, fresh sheets—and sleep! He was physically weary. He had made himself weary each night in the hope that weariness might bring a dreamless rest. He had thrown himself feverishly into the rôle of the Curé of St. Marleau; he had walked miles and driven miles; there was not a cottage in the parish upon whose door he had not knocked, and with whose occupants he had not shared-the personal joys and sorrows of the moment; and he had sat with the sick—with old Mother Blondin that morning, for instance, who seemed quite ill and feeble, and who in the last few days had taken to her bed. Yes, it was strange! He had done all this, too, with a certain sincerity that was not alone due to an effort to find forgetfulness during the day and weariness that would bring repose at night. He had found neither the forgetfulness nor the repose; but he had found a sort of wistful joy in the kindly acts of the good, young Father Aubert!

He had found neither the forgetfulness nor the repose. He could not forget the "afterwards"—the day that must irrevocably come—unless something, some turn of fate, some unforeseen thing intervened. *Something!* It was a pitiful thing to cling to—a pitiful thing even for a gambler's chance! But he clung to it now more desperately, more tenaciously than ever before. It was not only his life now, it was not only the life of the condemned man in that cell—it was Valérie. He might blindfold his mental vision; he might crush back, and trample down, and smother the thought, and refuse to admit it—but in his soul he believed she cared. And if she cared, and if that "something" did not happen, and he was forced, in whatever way he finally must choose, to play the last card—there was Valérie. If she cared—there was Valérie to suffer too! If he hanged instead of that man—there was Valérie! If he confessed from a safe distance after flight—there was Valérie to endure the shame! If the good, young Father Aubert died by "accident"—there was the condemned man in the death cell to pay the penalty—and Valérie to know the grief! Choice! What choice was there? Who called this ghastly impasse a choice! He could only wait—wait and cling to that hope, which in itself, because it was so paltry a thing to lean on, but added to the horror and suspense of the hours and days that stretched between now and the "afterwards."

"Something" might happen—yes, something might happen—but nothing had happened yet—nothing yet—and his brain, day and night, would not stop mangling and tearing itself to pieces—and would not let him rest—and there was no peace—none—not even for a few short hours.

His fingers were still mechanically turning the pages of the prayer-book. "I will go in unto the Altar of God." Why did those words keep on running insistently through his mind? Did they suggest—peace?

Well, if they did, why wasn't there something practical about them, something tangible, something he could lay material hands upon, and sense, and feel? The Altar, of God! Was there in very reality a God? He had chosen once to deny it contemptuously; and he had chosen once to despise religion as cant and chicanery cleverly practised upon the gullible and the weak-minded to the profit of those who pretended to interpret it! But there were beautiful words here in this book; and religion, if this were religion, must therefore be beautiful too — if one could believe. He remembered those words at the burial of Théophile Blondin — years, an eternity ago that was — "I am the resurrection and the life... he that believeth in Me... shall never die." He had repeated them over and over to himself that morning — he had spoken them aloud, in what had seemed then an unaccountable sincerity, to old Mother Blondin as she had clung to the palings of the cemetery fence that morning. Yes, they were beautiful words — if one could believe.

And here were others! What were these words here? He was staring at an open page before him, staring and staring at it. What were these other words here? It was not that he had never seen them before — but why was the book open at this place now — at these last few words of the *Benedictus*? "*Per viscera misericordiæ Dei nostri... illuminare his qui in tenebris et in umbra mortis sedent: ad dirigendos pedes nostros in viam pacis* — Through the tender mercy of our God... to enlighten those who sit in darkness and in the shade of death: to direct our feet into the way of peace."

Were they but words — mere words — these? They were addressed to him — definitely to him, were they not? He sat in darkness, in an agony of darkness, lost, unable to find his way, and he sat — in the shade of death! Was there a God, a God who had tender mercy, a God — to direct his feet into the way of peace?

The book slipped from his fingers, and dropped to the floor — and, his lips compressed, he stood up from the chair. If there was a God who had mercy, mercy of any kind — it was mercy he asked now. Where was this mercy? Where was this way of peace? Where was — a strange, bewildered, incredulous wonder was creeping into his face. Was that it — the Altar of God? Was that where there was peace — in unto the Altar of God? He had asked for a practical application of the words. Is that what they meant — that he should actually go — in unto the Altar of God — in there in the church — now?

It seemed to stagger him for a moment. Numbly he stooped and picked up the prayer-book, and closed it, and laid it back on the table — and stood irresolute. Something, he was conscious, was impelling him to go there. Well, why not? If there was a God, if there was a God who had tender mercy, if it was that God whose words were suggesting a way of peace — why not put that God to the test! Once, on the afternoon just before he had attempted that man's escape, he had yielded to a previous impulse, and had gone into the church. It had been quiet, still and restful, he remembered; and he remembered that he had come away strangely calmed. But since then a cataclysm had swept over him; then he had been in a state of mind that, compared with now, was one even of peace—but even so, it was quiet, still and restful there, he remembered.

He was crossing the room slowly, hesitantly, toward the door. Well, why not? If there was a God, and this impulse emanated from God—why not put it to the test? If it was all a hollow fraud, a myth, a superstition to which he was weak enough to yield, he would at least be no worse off than to sit here in that chair, or to lie upon the bed and toss the hours away until morning came!

Well, he would go! He stepped softly out into the hall, closed his door behind him, groped his way in the darkness to the front door of the *presbytère*, opened it—and stood still for an instant, listening. Neither Valérie nor her mother, asleep upstairs, had been disturbed he was sure. If they had—well, they would assign no ulterior motive to his going out—it was only that Monsieur le Curé, poor man, did not sleep well!

He closed the door quietly, and went down the steps—and at the bottom paused again. He became suddenly conscious that there was a great quiet and a great serenity in the night—and a great beauty. There were stars, a myriad stars in a perfect sky; and the moonlight bathed the church green in a radiance that made of it a velvet carpet, marvellously wrought in shadows of many hues. There, along the road, a whitewashed cottage stood out distinctly, and still further along another, and yet another—like little fortresses whose tranquillity was impregnable. And the moonlight, and the lullaby of the lapping water on the shore, and the night sounds that were the chirping of the little grass-things, were like some benediction breathed softly upon the earth.

"To direct our feet into the way of peace"—Raymond murmured the words with a sudden overpowering sense of yearning and wistfulness sweeping upon him. And then, as suddenly, he was tense, alert, straining his eyes toward the front of the church. Was that a shadow there that moved, cast perhaps by the swaying branch of some tree? It was a very curious branch if that were so! The shadow seemed to have appeared suddenly from around the corner of the church and to be creeping toward the door. It was too far across the green to see distinctly, even with the moonlight as bright as it was, but it seemed as though he could see the church door open and close again— and now the shadow had disappeared.

Mechanically Raymond rubbed his eyes. It was strange, so very strange that it must surely be only a trick of the imagination. The moonlight was

The Sin That Was His | 185

always deceptive and lent itself easily to hallucinations, and at that distance he certainly could not be sure. And besides, at this hour, after midnight, why should any one go stealing into the church? And yet he could have sworn he had seen the door open! And stare as he would now, the shadow that had crept along the low platform above the church steps was no longer visible.

He hesitated a moment. It was even an added incentive for him to go into the church, but suppose some one was there, and he should be seen? He smiled a little wanly—and stepped forward across the green. Well, what of it! Was he not the Curé of St. Mar-leau? It would be only another halo for the head of the good, young Father Aubert! It would require but a word of explanation from him, he could even tell the truth—and they would call him the *devout*, good, young Father Aubert! Only, instead of entering by one of the main doors, he would go in through the sacristy. He was not even likely to be seen himself in that way; and, if there was any one there, he should be able to discover who it was, and what he or she was doing there.

He passed on along the side of the church, his footsteps soundless on the sward, reached the door of the sacristy, opened it silently, and stepped inside. It was intensely dark here. Treading on tiptoe, he traversed the little room, and finally, after a moment's groping, his fingers closed on the knob of the door that opened on the interior of the church.

A sound broke the stillness. Yes, there was some one out there! Raymond cautiously pulled the door ajar. Came that sound again. It was very loud—and yet it was only the creak of a footstep that seemed to come from somewhere amongst the aisles. It echoed back from the high vaulted roof with a great noise. It seemed to give pause, to terrify with its own alarm whoever was out there, for now as he listened there was silence again.

Still cautiously and still a little wider, Raymond opened the door, and now he could see out into the body of the church—and for a moment, as though gazing upon some mystic scene, he stood there wrapt, immovable. Above the tops of the high, stained windows, it was as though a vast canopy of impenetrable blackness were spread from end to end of the edifice; and slanting from the edge of this canopy in a series of parallel rays the moonlight, coloured into curious solemn tints, filtered across from one wall to the other. And the aisles were like little dark alleyways leading away as into some immensity beyond. And here, looming up, a statue, the figure of some white-robed saint, drew, as it were, a holy light about it, and seemed to take on life and breathe into the stillness a sense of calm and pure and unchanging presence. And the black canopy and the little dark alleyways seemed to whisper of hidden things that kept ward over this abode of God. And there was no sound—and there was awe and solemnity in this silence. And on the altar, very near him, the Altar of God that he had come to seek, the single altar light burned like a tiny scintillating jewel in its setting of moon rays. And there, shadowy against the wall, just outside the chancel rail, was the great cross. There seemed something that spoke of the immutable in that. The first little wooden church above whose doors it had been reared was gone, and there was a church of stone now with a golden, metal cross upon its spire, but this great cross of wood was still here. It was a very precious relic to St. Marleau, and so it hung there on the wall of the new church between the two windows nearest the altar.

And then his eyes, travelling down the length of the cross, fixed upon its base—and the spell that had held him was gone. It was blacker there, very much blacker! There was a patch of blackness there that seemed to move and waver slightly—and it was neither shadow, nor yet the support built out to hold the base of the cross. Some one was crouching there. Well, what should he do? Remain in hiding here, or go out there as the Curé of St. Marleau and see who it was? Something urged him to go; caution bade him remain where he was. He knew a sudden resentment. He had put God to the test—and, instead of peace, he had found a prowler in the church!

Ah—what was that! That low, broken sound—like a sob! Yes, it came again—and the echoes whispered it back from everywhere. It was a woman. A woman was sobbing there at the foot of the cross. Who was it? Came a thought that stabbed with pain. Not Valérie! It could not be Valérie—kneeling there under a load that was beyond her strength! It could not be Valérie in anguish and grief greater than she could bear because—because she loved a man whom she believed to be a priest of God! No—not Valérie! But if it were!

He drew back a little. If it were Valérie she should not know that he had seen. At least he could save her that. He would wait until whoever it was had left the church, and if it were Valérie she would go back to the *presbytère*, and in that way he would know.

And now—what were those words now? She was praying out there as she sobbed. And slowly an amazed and incredulous wonder spread over Raymond's face. No, it was not Valérie! That was not Valérie's voice! Those mumbling, hesitant, uncertain words, as though the memory were pitifully at fault, were not Valérie's. It was not Valérie! He recognised the voice now. It was the old woman on the hill—old Mother Blondin!

And Raymond stared for a moment helplessly out through the crack of the sacristy door which he held ajar, out into those curiously tinted moon rays, and past the altar with its tiny light, to where that dark shadow lay against the wall. Old Mother Blondin! Old Mother Blondin, the heretic, was out there—*praying in the church!* Why? What had brought her there? Old

Mother Blondin who was supposed to be ill in her bed—he had seen her there that morning! She had been sick for the last few days, and worse if anything that morning—and now—now she was here—praying in the church.

What had brought her here? What motive had brought this about, that, with its strength of purpose, must have supplied physical strength as well, for she must almost literally have had to crawl down the hill in her feeble state? Had she too come seeking for—peace! Was it coincidence that they two, who had reached the lees and dregs of that common cup, should be here together, at this strange hour, at the Altar of God! Was it only coincidence— nothing more? Was he ready to believe, would he admit so much, that it was *more* than—coincidence?

A sense of solemnity and of awe that mingled with a sense of profound compassion for old Mother Blon-din sobbing there in her misery took possession of him, and he seemed moved now as by an impulse beyond and outside himself—to go to her—to comfort and soothe her, if he could. And slowly he opened the sacristy door, and stepped out into the chancel, and into the moonlight that fell softly across the altar's edge—and he called her name.

There was a cry, wild, unrestrained—a cry of terror that seemed to swirl about the church, and from the black canopy above that hid the vaulted roof was hurled back in a thousand echoes. But with the cry, as the dark form from against the wall sprang erect, Raymond caught a sharp, ominous cracking sound—and, as he looked, high up on the wall, the arms of the huge cross seemed to waver and begin to tilt forward.

With a bound, as he saw her danger, Raymond cleared the chancel rail, and the next instant had caught at the base of the cross and steadied it. In her terror as she had jumped to her feet, she had knocked against it and forced it almost off the sort of shelf, or ledge, that had been built out from the wall to support it; and at the same time, he could see now, one or more of the wall fastenings at the top had given away. It was very heavy and unmanageable, but he finally succeeded in getting it far enough back into position to make it temporarily secure.

He turned then to face Mother Blondin. She seemed oblivious, unconscious of her escape, though her face in the moonlight held a ghastly colour. She was staring at him with eyes that burned feverishly in their deep sockets. She was not crying now, but there were still tears, undried, that clung to her withered cheeks. One bony hand reached out and clutched at the back of a pew, for she was swaying on her feet; but the other was clenched and knotted—and suddenly she raised it and shook it in his face.

"Yes, it is I! I—Mother Blondin!" she choked. "Mother Blondin—the old hag—the *excommuniée!* You saw me come in—eh? And you have come to put me out—to put old Mother Blondin, the *excommuniée*, out—eh? I have no right here—here—eh? Well, who said I had any right! Put me out—put me out—put me— —-" The clenched hand opened, clawed queerly at her face, as though to clear away something that had gathered before her eyes and would not let her see—and she reeled heavily backward.

Raymond's arm went around her shoulders.

"You are ill, Madame Blondin—ill and weak," he said soothingly. "See"—he half lifted, half supported her into the pew—"sit down here for a moment and rest. I am afraid I frightened you. I am very sorry. Perhaps it would have been better if I had left you by yourself; but I heard you sobbing out here, and I thought that I might perhaps help you—and so I came—and so—you are better now, are you not?—-and so, you see, it was not to drive you out of the church."

She looked at him in a sort of angry unbelief.

"Ah!" she exclaimed fiercely. "Why do you tell me that, eh? Why do you tell me that? I have no right here—and you are a priest. That is your business—to drive me out."

"No," said Raymond gravely; "it is not my business. And I think you would go very far, Madame Blondin, before you would find a priest who would drive you from his church under the circumstances in which I have found you here to-night."

"Well then, I will go myself!" she said defiantly—and made as though to rise.

"No, not yet"—Raymond pressed her quietly back into the seat. "You must rest for a little while. Why, this morning, you know, you were seriously ill in bed. Surely you were not alone in the house to-night, that there was no one to prevent you getting up—I asked Madame Bouchard to— —"

"Madame Bouchard came to spend the night, but I did not want her, and I sent her home," she interrupted brusquely.

"You should not have done that, Madame Blondin," Raymond remonstrated kindly. "But even then, you are very weak, and I do not see how you managed to get here."

Her face set hard with the old stubborn indomitableness that he knew so well.

"I walked!" she said shortly.

Her hands were twisting together in her lap. There was dust covering her skirt thickly.

"And fell," he said.

She did not answer.

"Will you tell me why you came?" he asked.

"Because I was a fool"—her lips were working, her hands kept twisting over each other in her lap.

"I heard you praying," said Raymond gently. "What brought you here to-night, Madame Blondin?"

She shook her head now, and turned her face away.

The moonlight fell on the sparse, gray hair, and the thin, drooping shoulders, and the unkempt, shabby clothing. It seemed to enfold her in an infinite sympathy all its own. And suddenly Raymond found that his eyes were wet. It did not seem so startling and incongruous a thing that she should be here at midnight in the church—at the Altar of God. And yet—and yet why had she come? Something within himself demanded in a strange wistfulness the answer to that question, as though in the answer she would answer for them both, for the two who had no *right* here in this sacred place unless— unless, if there were a God, that God in His own way had meant to—direct their feet into the way of peace.

"Madame Blondin"—his voice was very low, trembling with earnestness—"Madame Blondin, do you believe in God?"

Her hands stopped their nervous movements, and clasped hard one upon the other.

"No!" she cried out sharply. "No—I——" And then her voice faltered, and she burst suddenly into tears. "I—I don't know."

His arm was still about her shoulders, and now his hand tightened a little upon her. She was crying softly. He was silent now—staring before him at that tiny flame burning in the moon rays on the altar. Well, suppose she did! Suppose even Mother Blondin believed, though she would fight on until she was beaten to her knees before she would unconditionally admit it, did that mean anything to him? Mother Blondin had not stood before that altar there with a crucifix upon her breast, and——

She was speaking again—brushing the tears away with the back of her hand.

"Once I did—once I believed," she said. "That was when I was a girl, and—and for a little while afterward. I used to come to the church then, and I used to believe. And then after Pierre died I married Blondin, and after that very soon I came no more. It is forty years—forty years—it was the old church then. The ban came before this one was built—I was never in here before—it is only the old cross there, the cross that was on the old church, that I know.

Forty years is a long time—a long time—I am seventy-two now—seventy-two."

She was crying again softly.

"Yes," said Raymond, and his own voice choked, "and to-night—after forty years?"

"I wanted to come"—she seemed almost to be whispering to herself—"I wanted to come. Blondin said there was no God, but I remembered that when I was a girl—forty years ago—there was a God here. I—I wanted to come and see—and—and I—I don't know—I—I couldn't remember the prayers very well, and so maybe if God is still here He did not understand. Pierre always said there was a God, and he used to come here with me to mass; but Blondin said the priests were all liars, and I began to drink with Blondin, and he said they were all liars when he died, and no one except the ones that came to buy the *whiskey-blanc* would have anything to do with us, and—and I believed him."

"And Pierre?" Raymond asked softly. "Who was Pierre?"

"Pierre?" She turned her head and looked at him—and somehow, perhaps it was the tint of the moon rays, somehow the old, hard face was transfigured, and seemed to glow with untold sweetness, and a smile of tenderness mingled with the tears. "Pierre? Ah, he was a good boy, Pierre. Yes, I have been happy! Who shall say I have not been happy? There were three years of it—three years of it—and then Pierre died. I was eighteen, eighteen on the day that Pierre and I were married. And it was a great day in the village—all the village was *en fête*. You would not believe that! But it is true. It is a long time between eighteen and seventy-two, and I was not like I am now, and Pierre was loved by every one. It is hard to believe, eh? And there are not many now who remember. But there is old Grandmother Frenier. She will tell you that I am telling you the truth about Pierre Letellier."

"*Letellier!*"—it came in a low, involuntary cry from Raymond. Letellier! Where had he heard that name before? What strange stirring of the memory was this that the name had brought? Letellier! Was it—could it be——?

"What is it, monsieur?"—she had caught at his sleeve. "Ah, you had perhaps heard that the Letelliers all moved away from here—and you did not know that I was once a Letellier? They sold everything and went away because of me a few years after I married Blondin."

"Yes," said Raymond mechanically. "But tell me more about yourself and Pierre—and—and those happy years. You had children—a—a son, perhaps?"

"Yes—yes, monsieur!" There was a glad eagerness in her voice—and then a broken sob—and the old eyes brimmed anew with tears. "There was little Jean. He was born just a few months after his father died. He—he was just like Pierre. He was four years old when I married Blondin, and—and when he was ten he ran away."

The altar light, that tiny light there seemed curiously transparent. He could see through it, not to the body of the altar behind it, but through it to a vast distance that did not measure miles, and he could see the interior of a shack whose window pane was thickly frosted and in whose doorway stood a man, and the man was Murdock Shaw who had come to bring Canuck John's dying message—and he could hear Murdock Shaw's words: "'Tell Three-Ace Artie—give good-bye message—my mother and— —' And then he died."

"I do not know where he went"—old Mother Blon-din's faltering voice, too, seemed a vast distance away—"I—I have never heard of him since then. He is dead, perhaps; but, if he is alive, I hope—I hope that he will never know. Yes—there were three years of happiness, monsieur—and then it was finished. Monsieur, I—I will go now."

Raymond's head on his crossed arms was bowed on the back of the pew before him. Letellier! It was the forgotten name come back to him. This was Canuck John's mother—and this was Théophile Blondin's mother—and he had come to St. Marleau to deliver to her a message of death—and he had delivered it in the killing of her other son! Was this the peace that he had come here to seek to-night? Was this the hand of God that had led him here? What did it mean? Was it God who had brought Mother Blondin here to-night? Would it bring her comfort—to believe in God again? Was he here for *that*? Here, that a word from him, whom she thought a priest, might turn the scales and bring her to her God of the many years ago? Was this God's way—to use him, who masqueraded as God's priest, and through whom this woman's son had been killed—was this God's way to save old Mother Blondin?

She touched his arm timidly.

"Are you praying for me, monsieur?" she whispered tremulously. "It—it is too late for that—that was forty years ago. And—and I will go now."

He raised his head and looked at the old, withered, tear-stained face. The question of his own belief did not enter here. If she went now without a word from him, without a priestly word, she went forever. They were beautiful words—and, if one believed, they brought comfort. And she was near, very near to that old belief again. And they were near, very near to his own lips too, those words.

"It is not too late," he said brokenly. "Listen! Do you remember the *Benedictus*? Give me your hand, and we will kneel, and say it together."

She drew back, and shook her head, and tried to speak—but no words came, only her lips quivered.

He held out his hand to her—held it silently there for a long time—and then, hesitantly, she laid her hand in his.

And kneeling there in the pew, old Mother Blondin and Raymond Chapelle, Raymond began the solemn words of the *Benedictus*. Low his voice was, and the tears crept to his eyes as the thin hand clutched and clasped spasmodically at his own. And as he came to the end, the tears held back no longer and rolled hot upon his cheeks.

"... Through the tender mercy of our God... to enlighten those who sit in darkness, and in the shade of death: to direct our feet into the way of peace" — his voice died away.

She was sobbing bitterly. He helped her to her feet as she sought to rise, and, holding tightly to her arm for she swayed unsteadily, he led her down the aisle. And they came to the church door, and out upon the green. And here she paused, as though she expected him to leave her.

"I will walk up the hill with you, Mother Blondin," he said. "I do not think you are strong enough to go alone."

She did not answer.

They started on along the road. She walked very slowly, very feebly, and leaned heavily upon him. And neither spoke. And they turned up the hill. And halfway up the hill he lifted her in his arms and carried her, for her strength was gone. And somehow he knew that when she had left her bed that night to stumble down this hill to the moonlit church she had left it for the last time—save one.

She was speaking again—almost inaudibly. He bent his head to catch the words.

"It is forty years," said old Mother Blondin. "Forty years—it is a long time—forty years."

CHAPTER XX—AN UNCOVERED SOUL

IT hung there precariously. All through the mass that morning Raymond's eyes had kept straying to the great cross on the wall that old Mother Blondin had disturbed the night before. No one else, it was true, had appeared to notice it; but, having no reason to do so, no one else, very probably, had given it any particular attention—nevertheless, a single strand of cord on one end of the horizontal beam was all that now prevented the cross from pitching outward from the wall and crashing down into the body of the church.

The door of the sacristy leading into the chancel was open, and, in the sacristy now, Raymond's eyes fixed uneasily again on the huge, squared timbers of the cross. The support at the base held the weight of course, but the balance and adjustment was gone, and the slightest jar would be all that was necessary to snap that remaining cord above. Massive and unwieldy, the cross itself must be at least seven feet in height; and, though this was of course imagination, it seemed to waver there now ominously, as if to impress upon him the fact that in the cause of its insecurity he was not without a personal responsibility.

He had removed his surplice and stole; Gauthier Beaulieu, the altar boy, had gone; and there was only old Narcisse Pélude, the aged sacristan, who was still puttering about the room. And the church was empty now, save that he could still hear Valérie moving around up there in the little organ loft.

Raymond passed his hand wearily across his eyes. He was very tired. Valérie was lingering intentionally—and he knew why. He had not returned to the *presbytère*, his bed had not been slept in. Valérie and her mother could not have helped but discover that, and they would be anxious, and worried, and perhaps a little frightened—and that was why Valérie was lingering now, waiting for him. He had not dared to leave old Mother Blondin alone through the night. She had been very ill. And he had not gone to any one near at hand, to Madame Bouchard, for instance, to get her to take his place, for that would have entailed explanations which, not on his own account, but for old Mother Blondin's sake, he had not cared to make; and so, when the bell for mass had rung that morning, he had still been at the bedside of the old woman on the hill. And he had left her only then because she was sleeping quietly, and the immediate crisis seemed safely past.

Raymond's eyes, from the cross, rested speculatively for a moment on the bent figure of the aged sacristan. He could make those explanations to Valérie, he could go out there now and in a sort of timely corroboration of the story repair the damage done to the cross, and she would understand; but he could not publicly make those explanations. If it was to be known in the village that old Mother Blondin had come here to the church, it was for old Mother Blondin herself, and for no one else, to tell it. It was the same attitude he had adopted toward her once before. True, Mother Blondin had changed very greatly since then; but a tactless word from any one, a sneer, the suggestion of triumph over her, and the old sullen defiance might well rise supreme again—and old Mother Blondin, he knew now, had not very long to live. Valérie and her mother would very readily, and very sympathetically understand. He could tell Valérie, indeed he was forced to do so in order to explain his own absence from the *presbytère*; but to others, to the village, to old Narcisse Pélude here, since the broken fastenings of the cross must be replaced, old Mother Blondin's name need not be mentioned.

"Narcisse, how long has that great cross hung there on the wall?" he inquired abruptly.

"Ah—the great cross! Yes—Monsieur le Curé!" The old man laid down a vestment that he had been carefully folding, and wagged his head. "It is very old—very old, that cross. You will see how old it is when I tell you it was made by the grandfather of the present Bouchard, whose pew is right underneath it. Grandfather Bouchard was one of the first in St. Mar-leau, and you must know, Monsieur le Curé, that St. Marleau was then a very small place. It was the Grandfather Bouchard who built most of the old wooden church, and there was a little cupola for the bell, and above the cupola was that cross. Yes, Monsieur le Curé, there have been changes in St. Marleau, and— —"

"But how long has it hung there on the wall, Narcisse?" Raymond interrupted with a tolerant smile—Narcisse had been known at times to verge on garrulity!

"But I am telling you, Monsieur le Curé," said the old sacristan earnestly. "We began to build this fine stone church, and when it was finished the little old wooden church was torn down, and we brought the cross here, and it has been here ever since, and that is thirty-two—no, thirty-three years ago, Monsieur le Curé—it will be thirty-three years this coming November."

"And in those thirty-three years," observed Raymond, "I imagine that the cross has remained untouched?"

"But, yes, Monsieur le Curé! Untouched — yes, of course! It was consecrated by Monsignor the Bishop himself — not the present bishop, Monsieur le Curé will understand, but the old bishop who is since dead, and — — "

"Quite so," said Raymond. "Well, come here, nearer to the door, Narcisse. Now, look at the cross very carefully, and see if you can discover why I asked you if it had remained untouched all those years?"

The old man strained his eyes across the chancel to the opposite wall — and shook his head.

"No, Monsieur le Curé, I see nothing — only the cross there as usual."

"Look higher up," prompted Raymond. "Do you not see that all but one of the fastenings are broken, and that it is about to fall?"

"Fall? About to fall?" The old man rubbed his eyes, and stared, and rubbed his eyes again. "Yes — yes — it is true! I see now! The cords have rotted away. It is no wonder — in all that time. I — I should have thought of that long, long ago." He turned a white face to Raymond. "It — it is the mercy of God that it did not happen, Monsieur le Curé, with anybody there! It would have killed Bouchard, and madame, and the children! It would have crushed them to death! Monsieur le Curé, I am a *misérable!* I am an old man, and I forget, but that is not an excuse. Yes, Monsieur le Curé, I am a *misérable!*"

Raymond laid his hand on the old sacristan's shoulder.

"We will see that it does not fall on the excellent Bouchard, or on madame, or on the children," he smiled. "Therefore, bring a ladder and some stout cord, Narcisse, and we will fix it at once."

The old man stared again at the cross for a moment, then started hurriedly toward the sacristy door that gave on the side of the church.

"Yes, Monsieur le Curé — yes — at once," he agreed anxiously. "There is a ladder beside the shed that is long enough. I will get it immediately. I am an old man, and I forget, but I am none the less a *misérable.* If Monsieur le Curé had not happened to notice it, and it had fallen on Bouchard! Monsieur le Curé is very good not to blame me, but I am none the less — — "

The old man, shaking his head, and still talking, had disappeared through the doorway.

Old Narcisse Pélude — the self-styled *misérable!* The old man had taken it quite to heart! Raymond shrugged his shoulders whimsically. Well, so much the better! It was for old Mother Blondin to tell her own story — if she chose! He wondered, with a curious and seemingly unaccountable wistfulness, if she ever would! It had been a night that had left him strangely moved, strangely bewildered, unable even yet to focus his mind clearly and logically upon it. He could tell Valérie of old Mother Blondin, of how the old woman on the hill had come here seeking peace; he could not tell her that he, too, had come in the hope that he might find what old Mother Blondin had sought—at the Altar of God!

Valérie! Yes, he was strangely moved this morning. And now a yearning and an agony surged upon him. Valérie! Between Valérie's coming to him that night in the stillness of the hours just before the dawn, and his coming here to the church last night, there lay an analogy of souls near-spent, clutching at what they might to save themselves. Peace, and the seeking of a way, he had come for; and peace, and the seeking of a way, she had come for then. It seemed as though he could see that scene again—that room in the *presbytère*, and the lamp upon the desk, and that slim, girlish form upon her knees before him; and it seemed as though he could feel the touch again of that soft, dark, silken hair, as she laid his hands upon her bowed head; and it seemed as though he could hear her voice again, as it faltered through the *Pater Noster*: "Hallowed be Thy name... and lead us not into temptation... but deliver us from evil." Had he, in any measure, found what he had sought last night? He did not know. He had knelt and prayed with old Mother Blondin. The *Benedictus*, as he had repeated it, had seemed real. He had known a profound solemnity, and the sense of that solemnity had remained with him, was with him now—and yet he blasphemed that solemnity, and the Altar of God, and this holy place in standing here at this very moment decked out in his stolen *soutane* and the crucifix that hung from his neck! Illogical? Why did he do it then? His eyes were on the floor. Illogical? It was to save his life—it was because he was fighting to save his life. It was not to repudiate the sincerity with which he had repeated the words of the *Benedictus* to old Mother Blondin—it was to save his life. Whatever he had found here, whether a deeper meaning in these holy symbolisms, he had not found the way—no other way but to blaspheme on with his *soutane* cloaked around him. And she—Valérie? Had she found what she had sought that night? He did not know. Refuse to acknowledge it, attempt to argue himself into disbelief, if he would, he knew that when she had knelt there that night in the front room of the *presbytère* she cared. And since then? Had she, in any measure, found what she had sought? Had she crushed back the love, triumphed over it until it remained only a memory in her life? He did not know. She had given no sign. They had never spoken of that night again. Only—only it seemed as though of late there had come a shadow into the fresh, young face, and a shadow into the dark, steadfast eyes, a shadow that had not been there on the night when he had first come to St. Marleau, and she and he had bent together over the wounded man upon the bed.

Subconsciously he had been listening for her step; and now, as he heard her descending the stairs from the organ loft, he stepped out from the sacristy into the chancel, and down into the nave of the church. He could see her now, and she had seen him. She had halted at the foot of the stairs under the gallery at the back of the church. Valérie! How sweet and beautiful she looked this morning! There was just a tinge of rising colour in her cheeks, a little smile, half tremulous, half gay on the parted lips, a dainty gesture of severity and playfulness in the shake of her head, as he approached.

"Oh, Father Aubert," she exclaimed, "you do not know how relieved we were, mother and I, when we saw you enter the church this morning for mass! We—we were really very anxious about you; and we did not know what to think when mother called you as usual half an hour before the mass, and found that you were not there, and that you had not slept in your bed."

"Yes, I know," said Raymond gravely; "and that is what I have come to speak to you about now. I was afraid you would be anxious, but I knew you would understand—though you would perhaps wonder a little—when I told you what kept me away last night. Let us walk down the side aisle there to the chancel, Mademoiselle Valérie, and I will explain."

A bewildered little pucker gathered on her forehead.

"The side aisle, Father Aubert?" she repeated in a puzzled way.

"Yes; come," he said. "You will see."

He led her down the aisle, and, halting before the cross, pointed upward.

"Why, the fastenings, all but one, are broken!" she cried out instantly. "It is a miracle that it has not fallen! What does it mean?"

"It is the story of last night, Mademoiselle Valerie," he answered with a sober smile. "Sit down in the pew there, and I will tell you. I have sent Narcisse for a ladder, and we will repair the damage presently, but there will be time before he gets back. He believes that the fastenings have grown old and rotten, which is true; and that they parted simply from age, which is not quite so much the fact. I have allowed him to form his own conclusions; I have even encouraged him to believe in them."

She was sitting in the pew now. The bewildered little pucker had grown deeper. She kept glancing back and forth from Raymond, standing before her in the aisle, to the broken fastenings of the cross high up on the wall.

"But that is what any one would naturally think," she said slowly. "I thought so myself. I—I do not quite understand, Father Aubert."

"I think you know," said Raymond quietly, "that some nights I do not sleep very well, Mademoiselle Valerie. Last night was one of those. When midnight came I was still wakeful, and I had not gone to bed. I was very restless; I knew I could not sleep, and so I decided to go out for a little while."

"Yes," she said impulsively; "I know. I heard you."

"You heard me?" He looked at her in quick surprise. "But I thought I had been very careful indeed to make no noise. I—I did not think that I had wakened———"

A flush came suddenly to her cheeks, and she turned her head aside.

"I—I was not asleep," she said hurriedly. "Go on, Father Aubert, I did not mean to interrupt you."

Raymond did not speak for a moment. He was not looking at her now—he dared not trust his eyes to drink deeper of that flush that had come with the simple statement that she too had been awake. Valérie! Valérie! It was the silent voice of his soul calling her. And suddenly he seemed to be looking out from his prison land upon the present scene—upon Valérie and the good, young Father Aubert together, looking upon them both, as he had looked upon them together many times. And suddenly he hated that figure in priestly dress with a deadly hate—because Valérie had tossed upon her bed awake, and had not slept; and because, as though gifted with prophetic vision, he could see the shadow in Valérie's fresh, pure face change and deepen into misery immeasurable, and the young life, barely on its threshold, be robbed of youth with its joy and gladness, and with sorrow grow prematurely old.

"You went out, Father Aubert," she prompted. "And then?"

The old sacristan would be back with the ladder very shortly, at almost any minute now—and he had to tell Valérie about old Mother Blondin and the cross before Narcisse returned. He looked up. He found himself speaking at first mechanically, and then low and earnestly, swayed strangely by his own words. And so, standing there in the aisle of the church, he told Valerie the story of the night, of the broken cross, of the broken life so near its end. And there was amazement, and wonder, and surprise in Valerie's face as she listened, and then a tender sympathy—and at the end, the dark eyes, as they lifted to his, were filled with tears.

"It is very wonderful," she said almost to herself. "Old Mother Blondin—it could be only God who brought her here."

Raymond did not answer. The old sacristan had entered the church, and was bringing the ladder down the aisle. It was the sacristan who spoke, catching sight of Valérie, as Raymond, taking one end of the ladder, raised it against the wall beside the cross.

"*Tiens!*" The old man lifted the coil of thin rope which he held, and with the back of his hand mopped away a bead of perspiration from his forehead.

"You have seen then what has happened, mademoiselle! Father Aubert has made light of it; but what will Monsieur le Curé, your uncle, say when he hears of it! Yes, it is true—I am a *misérable*—I do not deserve to be sacristan any longer! It was consecrated by Monsignor the Bishop, that cross, when the church was consecrated, and——"

Raymond took the cord quietly from the old man's hand, and began to mount the ladder. He went up slowly—not that the ladder was insecure, but that his mind and thoughts were far removed from the mere mechanical task which he had set himself to perform. Valérie's words had set that turmoil at work in his soul again. She had not hesitated to say that it was God who had brought old Mother Blondin here. And he too believed that now. Peace he had not found, nor the way, but he believed that now. Therefore he must believe now that there was a God—yes, the night had brought him that. And if there was a God, was it God who had led him, as old Mother Blondin had been led, to fall upon his knees in that pew below there where Valérie now sat, and *pray?* Had he prayed for old Mother Blondin's sake *alone?* Was God partial then? Old Mother Blondin, he knew, even if her surrender were not yet complete, had found the way. He had not. He had found no way—to save that man who was to be hanged by the neck until he was dead—to save Valérie from shame and misery if she cared, if she still cared—to save himself! Old Mother Blondin alone had found the way. Was it because she was the lesser sinner of the two—because he had blasphemed God beyond all recall—because he still dared to blaspheme God—because he had stood again that morning at the altar and had officiated as God's holy priest—because he stood here now in God's house, an impostor, an intruder and a defiler! No way! And yet *through him* old Mother Blondin had found her God again! Was it irony—God's irony—God's answer, irrefutable, to his former denial of God's existence!

No way! Ten feet below him Valérie and the old sacristan talked and watched; the weather-beaten timbers of the great cross were within reach of his hands; there, inside the chancel rail, was the altar—all these things were real, were physically real. It did not seem as though it could be so. It seemed as though, instead, he were taking part in some horrible, and horribly vivid dream-life. Only there would be no awakening! There was no way—he would twist this cord about the iron hooks on the cross and the iron hook on the wall, and descend, and go through another day, and be the good, young Father Aubert, and toss through another night, and wait, clinging to the miserable hope, spurned even by his gambler's instinct, that "something" might happen—wait for the deciding of that appeal, and picture the doomed man in the death cell, and dream his dreams, and watch Valérie from his prison land, and know through the hours and minutes torment and merciless unrest. Yes, he believed there was a God. He believed that God had brought them both here, old Mother Blondin to cling to the foot of the cross, and himself to find her there—but to him there had come no peace—no way. His blasphemy, his desecration of God's altar and God's church had been made to serve God's ends—old Mother Blondin had found the way. But that purpose was accomplished now. How much longer, then, would God suffer this to continue? Not long! To-morrow, the next day, the day after, would come the answer to the appeal—and then he must choose. Choose! Choose what? What was there to choose where—his hands gripped hard on the rung of the ladder. Enough! Enough of this! It was terrible enough in the nights! There was no end to it! It would go on and on—the same ghoulish cycle over and over again. He would not let it master him now, for there would be no end to it! He was here to fix the cross. To fix God's cross, the consecrated cross—it was a fitting task for one who walked always with that symbol suspended from his neck! It was curious how that symbol had tangled up his hands the night his fingers had crept toward that white throat on the bed! Even the garb of priest that he wore God turned to account, and—no! He lifted his hand and swept it fiercely across his eyes. Enough! That was enough! It was only beginning somewhere else in the cycle that inevitably led around into all the rest again.

He fought his mind back to his immediate surroundings. He was above the horizontal arm of the cross now, and he could see and appreciate how narrowly a catastrophe had been averted the night before. It was, as Valérie had said, a miracle that the cross had not fallen, for the single strand of cord that still held it was frayed to a threadlike thinness.

He glanced above him, decided to make the vertical beam, or centre, of the cross secure first by passing the cord around the upper hook in the wall that was still just a little beyond his reach, stepped quickly up to the next rung of the ladder—and lurched suddenly, pitching heavily to one side. It was his *soutane*, the garb of priest, the garb of God's holy priest—his foot had caught in the skirt of his *soutane*. He flung out his hands against the wall to save himself. It was too late! The ladder swayed against the cross—the threadlike fastening snapped—and the massive arms of the cross lunged outward toward him, pushing the ladder back. A cry, hoarse, involuntary, burst from his lips—it was echoed by another, a cry from Valérie, a cry that rang in terror through the church. Two faces, white with horror, looking up at him from below, flashed before his eyes—and he was plunging backward, downward with the ladder—and hurtling through the air behind it, the mighty cross, with arms outspread as though in vengeance and to defy escape, pursued and rushed upon him, and— — There was a terrific crash, the rip and rend and tear of splintering wood—and blackness.

There came at first a dull sense of pain; then the pain began to increase in intensity. There were insistent murmurings; there were voices. He was coming back to consciousness; but he seemed to be coming very slowly, for he could not move or make any sign. His side commenced to cause him agony. His head ached and throbbed as though it were being pounded under quick and never-ending hammer blows; and yet it seemed to be strangely and softly cushioned. The murmurings continued. He began to distinguish words—and then suddenly his brain was cleared, cleared as by some terrific mental shock that struck to the soul, uplifting it in a flood of glory, engulfing it in a fathomless and abysmal misery. It was Valerie—it was Valerie's voice—Valerie whispering in a frightened, terrified, almost demented way—whispering that she *loved* him, imploring him to speak.

"... Oh, will no one come! Can Narcisse find no one! I—I cannot bring him back to consciousness! Speak to me! Speak to me! You must—you shall! It is I who have sinned in loving you. It is I who have sinned and made God angry, and brought this upon you. But God will not let you die—because—because—it was my sin—and—and you would never know. I—I promised God that you would never know. And you—you shall not die! You shall not! You shall not! Speak to me—oh, speak to me!"

Speak to her! Speak to Valerie! Not even to whisper her name—when the blood in a fiery tide whipped through his veins; when impulse born of every fibre of his being prompted him to lift his arms to her face, so close to his that he could feel her breath upon his cheek, and draw it closer, closer, until it lay against his own, and to hold it there, and find her lips, and feel them cling to his! There was a physical agony from his hurts upon him that racked him from head to foot—but there was an agony deeper still that was in his soul. His head was pillowed on her knee, but even to open his eyes and look up into that pure face he loved was denied him, even to whisper a word that would allay her fears and comfort her was denied him. From Valérie's own lips had come the bitterest and dearest words that he would ever hear. He could temporise no longer now. He could juggle no more with his false and inconsistent arguments. Valérie cared, Valérie loved him—as he had known she cared, as he had known she loved him. A moan was on his lips, forced there by a sudden twinge of pain that seemed unendurable. He choked it back. She must not know that he had heard—he must simulate unconsciousness. He could not save her from much now, from the "afterwards" that was so close upon him—but he could save her from this. She should not know! God's cross in God's church... his blasphemy, his sacrilege had been answered... the very garb of priest had repaid him for its profanation and struck him down... and Valérie... Valérie was here... holding him... and Valérie loved him... but

Valérie must not know... it was between Valérie and her God... she must not know that he had heard.

Her hands were caressing his face, smoothing back his hair, bathing his forehead with the water which had been her first thought perhaps before she had sent Narcisse for help. Valérie's hands! Like fire, they were, upon him, torturing him with a torture beyond the bodily torment he was suffering; and like the tenderest, gladdest joy he had ever known, they were. A priest of God—and Valérie! No, it went deeper far than that; it was a life of which this was but the inevitable and bitter culmination—and Valérie. But for that, in a surge of triumphant ecstasy, victor of a prize beyond all price, his arms might have swept out in the full tide of his manhood's strength around her, claiming her surrender—a surrender that would have been his right—a surrender that would have been written deep in love and trust and faith and glory in those dark, tear-dimmed eyes.

And now her hands closed softly, and remained still, and held his face between them—and she was gazing down at him. He could see her, he had no need to open his eyes for that—he could see the sweet, quivering lips; the love, the terror, the yearning, the fear mingling in the white, beautiful face. And then suddenly, with a choked sob, she bent forward and kissed him, and laid her face against his cheek.

"He will not speak to me!"—her voice was breaking. "Then listen, my lover—my lover, who cannot hear—my lover, who will never know. Is it wrong to kiss you, is it making my sin the greater to tell you—you who will not hear. There is only God to know. And out of all my life it is for just this once—for just this once. Afterwards, if you live, I will ask God to forgive—for it is only for this once—this once out of all my life. And—and—if you die—then—then I will ask God to be merciful and—and take me too. You did not know I loved you so, and I had never thought to tell you. And if you live you will never know, because you are God's priest, and my sin is very terrible, but—but I—I shall know that you are somewhere, a big and brave and loyal man, and glad in your life, and—and loved, as all love you here in St. Marleau. All through my life I will love you—all through my life—and—and I will remember that for just this once, for this moment out of all the years, I gave myself to you."

She drew him closer. An agony that was maddening shot through his side as she moved him. If he might only clench his teeth deep in his lips that he might not scream out! But he could not do that for Valeric would see—and Valérie must not know. Tighter and tighter she held him in her strong, young arms—and now, like the bursting wide of flood-gates, there was passion in her voice.

"I love you! I love you! I love you! And I am afraid—and I am afraid! For I am only a woman, and it is a woman's love. Would you turn from me if you knew? No, no—I—I do not know what I am saying—only that you are here with my arms around you—and that—that your face is so pale—and that—and that you will not speak to me."

She was crying. She bent lower until, as a mother clasps a child, his head lay upon her breast and shoulder, and her own head was buried on his breast. And again with the movement came excruciating pain, and now a weakness, a giddy swirling of his senses. It passed. He opened his eyes for an instant, for she could not see him now. He was lying just inside the chancel rail, and almost at the altar's foot. The sunlight streamed through the windows of the church, but they were in shadow, Valérie and he, in a curious shadow—it seemed to fall in a straight line across them both, and yet be spread out in two wide arms that completely covered them. And at first he could not understand, and then he saw that the great cross lay forward with its foot against the wall and the arms upon the shattered chancel rail—and the shadow was the shadow of the cross. What did it mean? Was it there premonitory of a wrath still unappeased, that was still to know fulfilment; or was it there in pity—on Valérie—into whose life he had brought a sorrow that would never know its healing? He closed his eyes again—the giddiness had come once more.

"I—I promised God that he would never know"—she was speaking scarcely above her breath, and the passion was gone out from her voice now, and there was only pleading and entreaty. "Mary, dear and holy Mother, have pity, and listen, and forgive—and bring him back to life. It came, and it was stronger than I—the love. But I will keep my promise to God—always—always. Forgive my sin, if it is not too great for forgiveness, and help me to endure—and—and——" her voice broke in a sob, and was still.

Her lips touched his brow gently; her hands smoothed back his hair. Dizziness and torturing pain were sweeping over him in swiftly alternating flashes. There were beads of agony standing out, he knew, upon his forehead—but they were mingled and were lost in the tears that suddenly fell hot upon him. Valerie! Valerie! God give him strength that he might not writhe, that he might not moan. No, he need not fear that—the pain was not so great now—it seemed to be passing gradually, very gradually, even soothingly, away—there were other voices—they seemed a long way off—there seemed to be footsteps and the closing of a door—and the footsteps came nearer and nearer—but as they came nearer they grew fainter and fainter—and blackness fell again.

CHAPTER XXI—THE CONDEMNED CELL

THE reins lay idly in Raymond's hand. The horse, left to its own initiative, ambled lazily to the crest of a little rise that commanded a view of the town of Tournayville beyond. Raymond's eyes, lifting from the dash-board, ignoring the general perspective, fixed and held on a single detail, to the right, and perhaps a mile away—a high, rectangular, gray stone wall, that inclosed a gray, rectangular stone building.

His eyes reverted to the dash-board. It was nearly two weeks now since he had seen that cold and narrow space with its iron bars, and the figure that huddled on the cot clasping its hands dejectedly between its knees—nearly two weeks. It was ten days since he had been struck down in the church—and in another ten days, over yonder, inside that gray stone wall, a man was to be hung by the neck until he was dead. Ten days forward—ten days backward—ten days.

Ten days! In the ten days just past he had sought, in a deeper, more terrible anguish of mind than even in those days when he had thought the bitterest dregs were already at his lips, for the answer to these ten days to come—for now there was Valerie, Valérie's love, no longer a probability against which he might argue fiercely, desperately with himself, but an actual, real, existent, living thing, glorious and wonderful—and terrible as a hand of death stretching out a pointing finger to the "afterwards." And there was God.

Yes—God! He was still the curé of St. Marleau, still the good, young Father Aubert; but since that morning when he had been struck down at the foot of God's altar he had not entered the church—and he had been no more a priest, profaning that holy place. It was not fear, a craven, superstitious fear that the hand which had struck him once would deal him physical injury again; it was not that—it was—what? He did not know. His mind was chaos there—chaos where it groped for a definite, tangible expression of his attitude toward God. There was a God. It was God who had drawn old Mother Blondin to the church that night, and had made him the instrument of her recovered faith—and the instrument of his own punishment when, in her fright which he had caused, she had loosened the great cross upon the wall.

It was not coincidence, it was not superstition—deep in his consciousness lay the memory of that night when, with the old woman's hand in his, he had knelt and prayed; and deep in his consciousness was the sure knowledge that when he had prayed he had prayed in the presence of God. But he could get no further—it was as though he looked on God from afar off. Here turmoil took command. There was Valérie; the man who was to die; himself; the inflexible, immutable approach, the closing in upon him of that day of final reckoning. And God had shown him no way. He seemed to recognise an avenging God, not one to love. He could not say that he had the impulse to revere as the simple people of St. Marleau had, as Valérie had—and yet since that morning when they had carried him unconscious to the *presbytère* he had not again entered the church, he had not again stood before God's altar in his blasphemous, stolen garb of priest!

Raymond's thumb nail made abstracted little markings on the leather rein in his hand. Yes, that was true; profanation seemed to have acquired a new, and personal, and intimate meaning—and he had not gone. Circumstances had aided him. The solicitude of Madame Lafleur had made it easy for him to linger in bed, and subsequently to remain confined to his room long after his broken ribs, and the severe contusions he had received in his fall, had healed sufficiently to let him get about again. And he had allowed Madame Lafleur to "persuade" him! It had not been difficult as far as the early morning mass was concerned, for, with the curé sick in bed, the mass, it would be expected, would be temporarily dispensed with; but a Sunday had intervened. But even that he had solved. If some one from somewhere must say mass that day, it must be some one who would not by any chance have ever known or met the real Father François Aubert. There was Father Décan, the prison chaplain of Tour-nayville. He had never met Father Décan, even when visiting the jail, but since Father Décan had not recognised the prisoner, Father Décan obviously would have no suspicions of one Raymond Chapelle—and so he had sent a request to Father Décan to celebrate mass on the preceding Sunday, and Father Décan had complied.

The thumb nail bit a little deeper into the leather. Yesterday was the first day he had been out. This morning he had again deliberately dispensed with the mass, but to-day was Saturday—and to-morrow would be Sunday—and to-morrow St. Marleau would gather to hear the good, young Father Aubert preach again! Was God playing with him! Did God not see that he had twisted, and turned, and struggled, and planned that he might not blaspheme and profane God's altar again! Did God not see that he revolted at the thought! And yet God had shown him no other way. What else could he do? What else was there to do? He was still with his life at stake, with the life of another at stake—and there was Valérie—Valérie—Valérie!

A sharp cry of pain came involuntarily to his lips, and found utterance—and startled the horse into a reluctant jogging for a few paces. Valérie! He had scarcely seen her in all those ten days. It was Madame Lafleur who had taken care of him. Valérie had not purposely avoided him—it was not that—only she had gone to live practically all the time at old Mother Blondin's. The old woman was dying. For three days now she had not roused from unconsciousness. This morning she had been very low. By the time he returned she might be dead.

Dead! These were the closing hours of his own life in St. Marleau, the end here, too, was very near—and the closing hours, with sinister, ominous significance, seemed to be all encompassed about and permeated with death. It was not only old Mother Blon-din. There was the man in the death cell, whom he was on his way to see now, this afternoon, who was waiting for death—for death on a dangling rope—for death that was not many days off. Yesterday Father Décan had driven out to say that the prisoner was in a pitiful state of mental collapse, imploring, begging, entreating that Father Aubert should come to him—and so this afternoon Father Aubert, the good, young Father Aubert, was on his way—to the cell of death.

Raymond's lips moved silently. This was the very threshold of the "afterwards"—the threshold of that day—the day of wrath.

"*Dies ilia, dies ira, calamitatis et miserio, dies magna et am ara valde*—That day, a day of wrath, of wasting, and of misery, a great day, and exceeding bitter."

Unbidden had come the words. Set his face was, and white. If all else were false, if God were but the transition from the fairy tales of childhood to the fairy tale of maturity, if religion were but a shell, a beautiful shell that was empty, a storehouse of wonderful architectural beauty that held no treasure within—at least those words were true—a day of wrath, and exceeding bitter. And that day was upon him; and there was no way to go, no turn to take, only the dark, mocking pathways of the maze that possessed no opening, only the dank, slimy walls of that Walled Place against which he beat and bruised his fists in impotent despair. There was the man who was to be hanged—and himself—and Valerie—and he knew now that Valérie loved him.

The horse ambled on through the outskirts of the town. Occasionally Raymond mechanically turned out for a passing team, and acknowledged mechanically the respectful salutation. In his mind a new thought was germinating and taking form. He had said that God-had shown him no way. Was he so sure of that? If God had led him to the church that night, and had brought through him an eleventh hour reversion of faith to old Mother Blondin, and had forced the acceptance of divine existence upon himself, was he so sure that in the breaking of the fastenings of the cross, that it might fall and strike him down, there lay only a crowning punishment, only a thousandfold greater anguish, only bitter, helpless despair, in that it had been the means whereby, from Valérie's own lips, he had come to the knowledge of Valérie's love? Was he so sure of that? Was he so sure that in the very coming to him of the knowledge of her love he was not being shown the way he was to take!

The buckboard turned from the road it had been following, and took the one leading to the jail. Subconsciously Raymond guided the horse now, and subconsciously he was alive to his surroundings and to the passers-by—but his mind worked on and on with the thought that now obsessed him.

Suppose that his choice of saving one of the two lay between this man in the condemned cell and Valerie—which would he choose? He laughed sharply aloud in ironical derision. Which would he choose! It was pitiful, it was absurd—the question! Pitiful? Absurd? Well, but was it not precisely the choice he was called upon to make—to choose between Valérie and the man in the condemned cell? Was that not what the knowledge of her love meant? She loved him; from her own lips, as she had poured out her soul, thinking there was none but God to hear, he had learned the full measure of her love—a love that would never die, deep, and pure, and sinless—a love that was but the stronger for the sorrow it had to bear—a cherished, hallowed love around which her very life had entwined itself until life and love were one for always.

The gray stone walls of the jail, cold, dreary, forbidding, loomed up a little way ahead. The reins were loose upon the dashboard, but clenched in a mighty grip in Raymond's hand. He could save the man in there from death—but he could save Valérie from what would be worse than death to her. He could save her from the shame, the agony, the degradation that would kill that pure soul of hers, that would imbitter, wreck and ruin that young life, if he, the object of her love, should dangle as a felon from the gallows almost before her eyes, or flee, leaving to that love, a felon's heritage. Yes, he could save Valérie from that; and if he could save Valérie from that, what did the man in the condemned cell count for in the balance? The man meant nothing to him—nothing—nothing! It was Valérie! There was the "accident"—so easy, so sure—the "death" of the good, young Father Aubert—the upturned boat—the body supposedly washed out to sea. Long ago, in the first days of his life in St. Marleau, he had worked out the details, and the plan could not fail. There would be her grief, of course; he could not stand between her and her grief for the loss of the one she loved—but it would be a grief without bitterness, a memory without shame.

Did the man in the condemned cell count for anything against that! It would save Valerie, and—his face set suddenly in rigid lines, and his lips drew tight together—and it would save *himself!* It was the one alternative to either giving himself up to stand in the other's place, or of becoming a fugitive, branding himself as such, and saving the condemned man by a confession sent, say, to the Bishop, who, he remembered, knew the real François Aubert personally, and could therefore at once identify the man. Yes, it was the one alternative—and that alternative would save—himself! Wait! Was he sure that it was only Valérie of whom he was thinking? Was he sure that he was sincere? Was he sure there were no coward promptings—to save himself?

For a moment the tense and drawn expression in his face held as he groped in mind and soul for the answer; and then his lips parted in a bitter smile. It was not much to boast of! Three-Ace Artie a coward? Ask of the men of that far Northland whose lives ran hand in hand with death, ask of the men of the Yukon, ask of the men who knew! Gambler, roué, whatever else they might have called him, no man had ever called him coward! If his actual death, rather than his supposititious death, could save Valérie the better, in his soul he knew that he would not have hesitated. Why then should he hesitate about this man! If it lay between Valérie and this man, why should he hesitate! If he would give his own life to save Valérie from suffering and shame, why should he consider this man's life—this man who meant nothing to him—nothing!

Well, had he decided? He was at the jail now. Was he satisfied that this was the way? Yes! Yes—*yes!* He told himself with fierce insistence that it was—an insistence that by brute force beat down an opposition that somehow seemed miserably seeking to intrude itself. Yes—it was the way! There was only the appeal, that one chance to wait for, and once that was refused he would borrow Bouchard's boat—Bouchard's new boat—and to-morrow, or the next day, or the next, whenever it might be, instead of looking for him at mass in church, St. Marleau would look along the shore in search of the body of the good, young Father Aubert.

He tied his horse, and knocked upon the jail gate, and presently the gate was opened.

The attendant touched his cap.

"*Salut,* Monsieur le Curé!" he said respectfully, as he stepped aside for Raymond to enter. "Monsieur le Curé had a very narrow escape. The blessed saints be praised! It is good to see him. He is quite well again?"

"Quite," said Raymond pleasantly.

The man closed the gate, and led the way across a narrow courtyard to the jail building. The jail was pretentious neither in size nor in staff—the man who had opened the gate acted as one of the turnkeys as well.

"It is to see the prisoner Mentone that Monsieur le Curé has come, of course?" suggested the attendant.

"Yes," Raymond answered.

The turnkey nodded.

"*Pauvre diable!* He will be glad! He has been calling for you all the time. It did no good to tell him you were sick, and Father Décan could do nothing with him. He has been very bad—not hard to manage, you understand, Monsieur le Curé—but he does not sleep except when he is exhausted, because he says there is only a little while left and he will live that much longer if he keeps awake. *Tiens!* I have never had a murderer here to be hanged before, and I do not like it. I dream of the man myself!"

Raymond made no reply. They had entered the jail now, and the turnkey was leading the way along a cell-flanked corridor.

"Yes, I dream of him every night, and the job ahead of us—and so does Jacques, the other turnkey." The man nodded his head again; then, over his shoulder: "He has a visitor with him now, Monsieur le Curé, but that will not matter—it is Monsieur l'Avocat, Monsieur Lemoyne, you know."

Lemoyne! Lemoyne—here! Why? Raymond reached out impulsively, and, catching the turnkey's arm, brought the man to a sudden halt.

"Monsieur Lemoyne, you say!" he exclaimed sharply. "What is Monsieur Lemoyne doing here?"

"But—but, I do not know, Monsieur le Curé," the turnkey, taken by surprise, stammered. "He comes often, he is often here, it is the privilege of the prisoner's lawyer. I—I thought that perhaps Monsieur le Curé would care to see him too. But perhaps Monsieur le Curé would prefer to wait until he has gone?"

"No"—Raymond's hand fell away from the other's arm. "No—I will see him. I was afraid for the moment that he might have brought—bad news. That was all."

"Ah, yes, I understand, Monsieur le Curé"—the turnkey nodded once more. "But I do not know. Monsieur Lemoyne said nothing when he came in."

Afraid! Afraid that Lemoyne had brought the answer to that appeal! Well, what if Lemoyne had! Had he, Raymond, not known always what the answer would be, and had he not just decided what he would do when that answer was received—had he not decided that between the man and Valérie there could be no hesitation, no more faltering, or tormenting——

The cell door swung open.

"Enter, Monsieur le Curé!"

The turnkey's voice seemed far away. Mechanically Raymond stepped forward. The door clanged raucously behind him. There came a cry, a choked cry, a strangling cry, that mingled a pitiful joy with terror and despair—and a figure with outstretched arms, a figure with gaunt, white, haggard face was stumbling toward him; and now the figure had flung itself upon its knees, and was clutching at him convulsively with its arms.

"Father—Father François Aubert—father, have pity upon me—father, tell them to have pity upon me!"

And yet he scarcely saw this figure, scarcely heard the voice, though his hands were laid upon the bowed head that was buried in the skirt of his *soutane*. He was looking at that other figure, at Lemoyne, the young lawyer, who stood at the far end of the cell near the iron-barred window. There were tears in Lemoyne's eyes; and Lemoyne held a document in his hand.

"Thank God that you have come, Monsieur le Curé!" Lemoyne said huskily.

"You have"—Raymond steadied his voice—"bad news?"

Lemoyne silently extended the document.

There were a great many words, a great many sentences written on the paper. If he read them all, Raymond was not conscious of it; he was conscious only that, in summary, he had grasped their meaning—*the man must die.*

The man's head was still buried in Raymond's *soutane*, his hands still clasped tightly at Raymond's knees. Raymond did not speak—the question was in his eyes as they met Lemoyne's.

Lemoyne shook his head hopelessly, and, taking the document back from Raymond, returned it slowly to his pocket.

"I will leave you alone with him, Monsieur le Curé—it will be better," he said in a low voice. He stepped across the cell, and for a moment laid his hand on the shoulder of the kneeling man. "Courage, Henri—I will come back to-morrow," he whispered, and passed on to the door.

"Wait!"—Raymond stepped to Lemoyne's side, as the lawyer rattled upon the door for the turnkey. "There—there is nothing more that can be done?" His throat was dry, even his undertone rasped and grated in his own ears. "Nothing?"

"Nothing!" Lemoyne's wet eyes lifted to meet Raymond's, and again he shook his head. "I shall ask, as a matter of course, that the sentence be commuted to life imprisonment—but it will not be granted. It—it would be cruelty even to suggest it to him, Monsieur le Curé." And then, as the door opened, he wrung Raymond's hand, and went hurriedly from the cell.

Slowly Raymond turned away from the door. There was hollow laughter in his soul. A mocking voice was in his ears—that inner voice.

"Well, *that* is decided! Now put your own decision into effect, and have done with this! Have done with it—do you hear! Have done with it—have done with it—once for all!"

His eyes swept the narrow cell, its white walls, the bare, cold floor, the cot with its rumpled blanket, the iron bars on the window that sullenly permitted an oblong shaft of sunlight to fall obliquely on the floor—and upon the figure that, still upon its knees, held out its arms imploringly to him, that cried again to him piteously.

"Father—Father Aubert—help me—tell them to have pity upon me— save me, father—Father François Aubert—save me!"

And Raymond, though he fought to shift his eyes again to those iron bars, to the sunlight's shaft, to anywhere, could not take them from that figure. The man was distraught, stricken, beside himself; weakness, illness, the weeks of confinement, the mental anguish, crowned in this moment as he saw his last hope swept away, had done their work. The tears raced down the pallid cheeks; the eyes were like—like they had been in the courtroom that day— like dumb beast's in agony.

"Soothe him, quiet him," snarled that voice savagely, "and do it as quickly as you can—and get out of here! Tell him about that God that you think you've come to believe is not a myth, if you like—tell him anything that will let you get away—and remember Valérie. Do you think this scene here in this cell, and that thing grovelling on the floor is the sum of human misery? Then picture Valérie nursing shame and horror and degradation in her soul! What is this man to you! Remember Valérie!"

Yes—Valérie! That was true! Only—if only he could avoid the man's eyes! Well, why did not he, Raymond, speak, why did he not act, why did he not do something—instead of standing here impotently over the other, and simply hold the man's hands—yes, that was what he was doing—that was what felt so hot, so feverishly hot—those hands that laced their fingers so frantically around his.

"My son,"—the words were coming by sheer force of will—"do not give way like this. Try and calm yourself. See"—he stooped, and, raising the other by the shoulders, drew him to the cot—"sit here, and——"

"You will not go, father—you will not go?"—the man was passing his hands up and down Raymond's arms, patting them, caressing them, as though to assure and reassure himself that Raymond was there. "They told me that you were hurt, and—and I was afraid, for there is no one else, father—no one else—only—only you—and you are here now—you are here now—and—and you will stay with me, father?"

"Yes," said Raymond numbly.

"Yes, you are here"—it was as though the man were whispering to himself, and a smile had lighted up the wan face. "See, I am not afraid any more, for you have come. Monsieur Lemoyne said that I must die, that there was no hope any more, that—that I would have to be hanged, but you will not let them, father, you will not let them—for you have come now—you have come—Father François Aubert, my friend, you have come."

Raymond's hand, resting on the cot behind the other's back, picked up and clenched a fold of blanket. There was something horrible, abominable, hellish in the man's trustful smile, in the man's faith, that was the faith of a child in the parent's omnipotence, in this man crying upon his own name as a magic talisman that would open to him the gates of life! What answer was there to make? He could not sit here dumb—and yet he could not speak. There were things a *priest* should say—a priest who was here to comfort a man condemned to death, a man who was to be hanged by the neck until he was dead. He should talk to the other of God, of the tender mercy of God, of the life that was to come where there was no more death. But talk to the man like that—when he, Raymond, was sending the other to his doom; when the other, not he, should be sitting here in this *soutane*; when he had already robbed the man of his identity, and even at this moment purposed robbing him of his life! Act Father François Aubert to Father François Aubert here in this prison cell under the shadow of that dangling rope, tell him of God, of God's tender mercy, supplicate to God for that mercy, *pray* with his lips for that mercy while he stabbed the man to death! He shivered, and it seemed as though his fingers would tear and rend through the blanket in the fierceness of their clutch—it was the one logical, natural thing that a priest should say, that he, in his priestly dress, should say! *No!* He neither would nor could! It was hideous! No human soul could touch depths as black as that—and the man was clinging to him—clinging to him—and—-

"*Remember Valérie!*"—it came like a curling lash, that inner voice, curt, brutal, contemptuous. "Are you going to weaken again? Remember what it cost you once—and remember that it is for Valérie's sake this time!"

The strong jaws set together. Yes—Valérie! Yes—he would remember. He would not falter now—he would go through with it, and have done with it. Between this man's life and a lifelong misery for Valerie there could be no hesitation.

"Henri Mentone, my son," he said gravely, "I adjure you to be brave. I have come, it is true, and I will come often, but——"

The words that Raymond's brain was stumbling, groping for, the "something," the "anything" to say, found no expression. The man suddenly appeared to be paying no attention; his head was turned in a tense, listening attitude; there was horror in the white face; and now the other's hands closed like steel bands around Raymond's wrists.

"Listen!" whispered the man wildly. "Listen! Oh, my God—listen!"

Startled, Raymond turned his head about, looking quickly around the cell. There was nothing—there was no sound.

"Don't you hear it!"—the other's voice was guttural and choked now, and he shook fiercely at Raymond's wrists. "I thought it had gone away when you came, but there it is again. I—I thought you had told them to stop! Don't you hear it—don't you hear it! Don't you hear them *hammering!* Listen! Listen! There it is!"

Raymond felt the blood ebb swiftly from his face.

"No—try and compose yourself. There is nothing—nothing, my son—it is only — — — —."

"I tell you, yes!" cried the man frantically. "I hear it! I hear it! You say, no; and I tell you, yes! I have heard it night and day. It comes from there—see!"—he swept one hand toward the barred window, and suddenly, leaping to his feet, dragged at Raymond with almost superhuman strength, forcing Raymond up from the cot and across the cell. "Come, and I will show you! It is out there! They are hammering out there now!"

The man's face was ghastly, the frenzy with which he pulled was ghastly—and now at the window he thrust out his arm through the bars, far out up to the armpit, far out with horrible eagerness, and pointed.

"There! There! You cannot see, but it is just around the corner of the building—between the building and the wall. You cannot see, but it is just around the corner there that they are building it! Listen to them! Listen to them—hammering—hammering—hammering!"

Sweat was on Raymond's forehead.

"Come away!" he said hoarsely. "In the name of God, come away!"

"Ah, you hear it now!"—the condemned man drew in his arm, until his fingers clawed and picked at the bars. "They will not stop, and it is because I cannot remember—because I cannot remember—here—here—here"—he swung clear of the window—and suddenly raising his clenched fists began to beat with almost maniacal fury at his temples. "If I could remember, they would stop—they would — —"

"Henri! My son!" Raymond cried out sharply—and caught at the other's hands. A crimson drop had oozed from the man's bruised skin, and now was trickling down the colourless, working face. "You do not know what you are doing! Listen to me! Listen! Let me go!" — the man wrenched and fought furiously to break Raymond's hold. "They will not stop out there — they are hammering — don't you hear them hammering — and it is because I — I — — " The snarl, the fury in the voice was suddenly a sob. The man was like a child again, helpless, stricken, chidden; and as Raymond's hands unlocked, the man reached out his arms and put them around Raymond's neck, and hid his face upon Raymond's shoulder. "Forgive me, father — forgive me!" he pleaded brokenly. "Forgive me — it is sometimes more than I can bear."

Raymond's arms mechanically tightened around the shaking shoulders; and mechanically he drew the other slowly back to the cot. Something was gnawing at his soul until his soul grew sick and faint. Hell shrieked its abominable approval in his ears, as he sat down upon the cot still holding the other — and shrieked the louder, until the cell seemed to ring and ring again with its unholy mirth, as the man pressed his lips to the crucifix on Raymond's breast.

"Father, I do not want to die" — the man spoke brokenly again. "They say I killed a man. How could I have killed a man, father? See" — he straightened back, and held out both his hands before Raymond's eyes — "see, father, surely these hands have never harmed any one. I cannot remember — I do not remember anything they say I did. Surely if I could remember, I could make them know that I am innocent. But I cannot remember. Father, must I die because I cannot remember? Must I, father" — the man's face was gray with anguish. "I have prayed to God to make me remember, father, and — and He does not answer — He does not answer — and I hear only that hammering — and sometimes in the night there is something that tightens and tightens around my throat, and — and it is horrible. Father — Father François Aubert — tell them to have pity upon me — you believe that I am innocent, don't you — you believe, father — yes, yes!" — he clutched at Raymond's shoulders — "yes, yes, y°u believe — look into my eyes, look into my face — look, father — look — — "

Look! Look into that face, look into those eyes! He could not look.

"My son, be still!" — the words were wrung in sudden agony from Raymond's lips.

He drew the other's head to his shoulder again, and held the other there — that he might not look — that the eyes and the face might be hidden from him. And the form in his arms shook with convulsive sobs, and clung to him, and called him by its own name, and called him friend — this stricken man who was to die — for whom he, Raymond, was building "it" out there under the shadow of the jail wall — and — and — God, he too could hear that *hammering* and — "Fool, remember Valérie!"

The sweat beads multiplied upon Raymond's forehead. His face was bloodless; his grip so tight upon the other that the man cried out, yet in turn but clung the closer. Yes, that voice was right—right—right! It was only that for the moment he was unnerved. It was this man's life for Valérie—this man's life for Valérie. It would only be a few days more, and then it would be over in a second, before even the man knew it—but with Valérie it would be for all of life, and there would be years and years—yes, yes, it was only that he had been unnerved for the instant—it was this man's life for Valérie—if he would give his own life, why shouldn't he give this man's—why shouldn't— —

His brain, his mind, his thoughts seemed suddenly to be inert, to be held in some strangely numbed, yet fascinated suspension. He was staring at the shaft of sunlight that fought for its right against those iron bars to enter this place of death. He stared and stared at it—something—a face—seemed to be emerging slowly out of the sunlight, to be taking form just beyond, just outside those iron bars, to become framed in the gray, pitiless stone of the window slit, to be pressed against those iron bars, to be looking in.

And suddenly he pushed the man violently and without heed from him, until the man fell forward on the cot, and Raymond, lurching upward himself, stood rocking upon his feet. It was clear, distinct now, that face looking in through those iron bars. It was Valerie's face—Valerie's—Valerie's face. It was beautiful as he had never seen it beautiful before. The sweet lips were parted in a smile of infinite tenderness and pity, and the dark eyes looked out through a mist of compassion, not upon him, but upon the figure behind him on the prison cot. He reached out his arms. His lips moved silently—Valérie! And then she seemed to turn her head and look at him, and her eyes swam deeper in their tears, and there was a wondrous light of love in her face, and with the love a condemnation that was one of sorrow and of bitter pain. She seemed to speak; he seemed to hear her voice: "That life is not yours to give. I have sinned, my lover, in loving you. Is my sin to be beyond all forgiveness because out of my love has been born the guilt of murder?"

The voice was gone. The face had faded out of that shaft of sunlight—only the iron bars were there now. Raymond's outstretched arms fell to his side—and then he turned, and dropped upon his knees beside the cot, and hid his face in his hands.

Murder! Yes, it was murder—murder that desecrated, that vilified, that made a wanton thing of that pure love, that brave and sinless love, that Valerie had given him. And he would have linked the vilest and the blackest crime, hideous the more in the Judas betrayal with which he would have accomplished it, with Valerie—with Valerie's love! His hands, locked about his face, trembled. He was weak and nerveless in a Titanic revulsion of soul and mind and body. And horror was upon him, a horror of himself — and yet, too, a strange and numbed relief. It was not he, it was not he as he knew himself, who had meant to do this thing — it was not Raymond Chapelle who had thought and argued that this was the way. See! His soul recoiled, blasted, shrivelled now from before it! It was because his brain had been tormented, not to the verge of madness, but had been flung across that border-line for a space into the gibbering realms beyond where reason tottered and was lost.

He was conscious that the man was sitting upright on the edge of the cot, conscious that the man's hands were plucking pitifully at the sleeve of his *soutane*, conscious that the man was pleading again hysterically: "Father, you will tell them that you know I am innocent. They will believe you, father — they will believe you. They say I did it, father, but I cannot remember, or — or, perhaps, I could make them believe me, too. You will not let me die, father — because — because I cannot remember. You will save me, father" — the man's voice was rising, passing beyond control — "Father François Aubert, for the pity of Christ's love, tell me that you will not let me die — tell me — — "

And then Raymond raised his head. His face was strangely composed.

"Hush, my son" — he scarcely recognised his own voice — it was quiet, low, gentle, like one soothing a child. "Hush, my son, you will not die."

"Father! Father Aubert!" — the man was lurching forward toward him; the white, hollow face was close to his; the burning deep-sunk eyes with a terrible hunger in them looked into his. "I will not die! I will not die! You said that, father? You said that?"

"Hush!" Raymond's lips were dry, he moistened them with his tongue. "Calm yourself now, my son — you need no longer have any fear."

A sob broke from the man's lips. His hands covered his face; he began to rock slowly back and forth upon the cot. He crooned to himself:

"I will not die — I am to live — I will not die — I am to live...."

And then suddenly, in a paroxysm of returning fear, he was on his feet, dragging Raymond up from his knees, and, catching at Raymond's crucifix, lifted it wildly to Raymond's lips.

"Swear it, father!" he cried. "Swear it on the cross! Swear by God's holy Son that I will not die! Swear it on the blessed cross!"

"I swear it," Raymond answered in a steady voice.

There was no sound, no cry now — only a transfigured face, glad with a mighty joy. And then the man's hands went upward queerly, seeking his temples — and the swaying form lay in Raymond's arms.

The man stirred after a moment, and opened his eyes.

"Are you there, father—my friend?" he whispered.

"Yes," Raymond said.

The man's hold tightened, and he sighed like one over-weary who had found repose.

And sitting there upon the edge of the cot, Raymond held the other in his arms—and the sunlight's shaft through the barred window grew shorter—and shadows crept into the narrow cell. At times there came low sobs; at times the man's hand was raised to feel and touch Raymond's face, at times to touch the crucifix on Raymond's breast. And then at last the other moved no more, and the breathing became deep and regular, and a peaceful smile came and lingered on the lips.

And Raymond laid the other gently back upon the cot, and, crossing to the cell door, knocked softly upon it for the turnkey. And as the door was opened, he laid his finger across his lips.

"He is asleep," he said. "Do not disturb him."

"Asleep!"—the turnkey in amazement thrust his head inside the cell; and then he looked in wonder at Raymond. "Asleep—but Monsieur Lemoyne told me of the news when he went out. Asleep—after that! The man who never sleeps!"

But Raymond only shook his head, and did not answer, and walked on down the corridor, and out into the courtyard. It was dusk now. He seemed to be moving purely by intuition. It was not the way—the man was to live. His mind was obsessed with that. It was not the way. There were two ways left—two out of the three.

The turnkey, who had followed in respectful silence, spoke again as he opened the jail gates.

"*Au revoir*, Monsieur le Cure"—he lifted his cap. "Monsieur le Curé will return to-morrow?"

To-morrow! Raymond's hands fumbled with the halter, as he untied the horse. To-morrow! There were two ways left, and the time was short. To-morrow—what would to-morrow bring!

"Perhaps," he said, unconscious that his reply had been long delayed—and found that he was speaking to closed gates, and that the turnkey was gone.

And then Raymond smiled as he seated himself in the buckboard and drove away—the smile a curious twitching of the lips. The turnkey was a tactful man who would not intrude upon Monsieur le Curé's so easily understood sorrow for the condemned man!

He drove on through the town, and turned into the St. Marleau road that wound its way for miles along the river's shore. And as he had driven slowly on his way to the jail, so he drove slowly on his return to the village, the horse left almost to guide itself and to set its own pace.

The dusk deepened, and the road grew dark—it seemed fitting that the road should grow dark. There were two ways left. The jaws of the trap were narrowing—one of the three ways was gone. There were two left. Either he must stand in that other's place, and hang in that other's place; or run for it with what start he could, throw them off his trail if he could, and write from somewhere a letter that would exonerate the other and disclose the priest's identity—-a letter to the Bishop unquestionably, if the letter was to be written at all, for the Bishop, not only because he knew the man personally and could at once establish his identity, but because, in the very nature of the case, with the life of one of his own curés at stake, the Bishop, above all other men, would have both the incentive and the power to act. Two ways! One was a ghastly, ignominious death, to hang by the neck until he was dead—the other was to be a fugitive from the law, to become a hunted, baited beast, fighting every moment with his wits for the right to breathe. There were two ways! One was death—one held a chance for life. And the time was short.

It was the horse that turned of its own accord in past the church, and across the green to the *presbytère*.

He left the horse standing there—Narcisse would come and get it presently—and went up the steps, and entered the house. The door of the front room was open, a light burned upon his desk. Along the hall, from the dining room, Madame Lafleur came hurrying forward smilingly.

"Supper is ready, Monsieur le Curé," she called out cheerily. "Poor man, you must be tired—it was a long drive to take so soon after your illness, and before you were really strong again."

"I am late," said Raymond; "that is the main thing, Madame Lafleur. I put you always, it seems, to a great deal of trouble."

"Tut!" she expostulated, shaking her head at him as she smiled. "It is scarcely seven o'clock. Trouble! The idea! We did not wait for you, Monsieur le Curé, because Valérie had to hurry back to Madame Blondin. Madame Blondin is very, very low, Monsieur le Curé. Doctor Arnaud, when he left this afternoon, said that—but I will tell you while you are eating your supper. Only first—yes—wait—it is there on your desk. Monsieur Labbée sent it over from the station this afternoon—a telegram, Monsieur le Curé."

A telegram! He glanced swiftly at her face. It told him nothing. Why should it!

"Thank you," he said, and stepping into the front room, walked over to the desk, picked up the yellow-envelope, tore it open calmly, and read the message.

His back was toward the door. He laid the slip of paper down upon the desk, and with that curious trick of his stretched out his hand in front of him, and held it there, and stared at it. It was steady — without tremor. It was well that it was so. He would need his nerve now. He had been quite right — the time was short. There remained — *one hour*. In an hour from now, on the evening train, Monsignor the Bishop, who was personally acquainted with Father François Aubert, would arrive in St. Marleau.

CHAPTER XXII—HOW RAYMOND BADE FAREWELL TO ST. MARLEAU

AN hour! There lay an hour between himself—and death. Primal, elemental, savage in its intensity, tigerish in its coming, there surged upon him the demand for life—to live—to fight for self-preservation. And yet how clear his brain was, and how swiftly it worked! Life! There lay an hour between himself—and death. The horse was still outside. The overalls, the old coat, the old hat belonging to the sacristan were still at his disposal in the shed. He would ostentatiously set out to drive to the station to meet the Bishop, hide the horse and buckboard in the woods just before he got there, change his clothes, run on the rest of the way, remain concealed on the far side of the tracks until the train arrived—and, as Monsignor the Bishop descended from one side of the train to the platform, he, Raymond, would board it from the other. There would then, of course, be no one to meet the Bishop. The Bishop would wait patiently no doubt for a while; then Labbée perhaps would manage to procure a vehicle of some sort, or the Bishop might even walk. Eventually, of course, it would appear that Father Aubert had set out for the station and had not since been seen—but it would be a good many hours before the truth began to dawn on any one. There would be alarm only at first for the *safety* of the good, young Father Aubert—and meanwhile he would have reached Halifax, say One could not ask for a better start than that!

Life! With the crisis upon him, his mind held on no other thing. Life—the human impulse to live and not to die! No other thing—but life! It was an hour before the train was due—he could drive to the station easily in half an hour. There was no hurry—but there was Madame Lafleur who, he was conscious, was watching him from the doorway—Madame Lafleur, and Madame Lafleur's supper. He would have need of food, there was no telling when he would have another chance to eat; and there was Madame Lafleur, too, to enlist as an unwitting accomplice.

"Monsieur le Curé"—it was Madame Lafleur speaking a little timidly from the doorway—"it—it is not bad news that Monsieur le Curé has received?"

"Bad news!" Raymond picked up the telegram, and, turning from the desk, walked toward her. "Bad news!" he smiled. "But on the contrary, my dear Madame Lafleur! I was thinking only of just what was the best thing to do, since it is now quite late, and I did not receive the telegram this afternoon, as I otherwise should had I not been away. Listen! Monsignor the Bishop, who is on his way" — Raymond glanced deliberately at the message — "yes, he says to Halifax — who then is on his way to Halifax, will stop off here this evening."

Madame Lafleur was instantly in a flutter of excitement.

"Oh, Monsieur le Curé!" — her comely cheeks grew rosy, and her eyes shone with pleasure. "Oh, Monsieur le Curé — Monsignor the Bishop! He will spend the night here?" she demanded eagerly.

Raymond patted her shoulder playfully, as he led her toward the dining room.

"Yes, he will spend the night here, Madame Lafleur" — it was strange that he could laugh teasingly, naturally. "But first, a little supper for a mere curé, eh, Madame Lafleur — since Monsignor the Bishop will undoubtedly have dined on the train."

"Oh, Monsieur le Curé!" She shook her head at him.

"And then," laughed Raymond, as he seated himself at the table, "since the horse is already outside, I will drive over to the station and meet him."

He ate rapidly, and, strangely enough, with an appetite. Madame Lafleur bustled about him, quite unable to keep still in her excitement. She talked, and he answered her. He did not know what she said; his replies were perfunctory. There was an excuse to be made for going to the shed instead of getting directly into the buckboard and driving off. Madame Lafleur would undoubtedly and most naturally watch him off from the front door. But — yes, of course — that was simple — absurdly simple! Well then, another thing — it would mean at least a good hour to him if the village was not on tiptoe with expectancy awaiting the Bishop's arrival, and thus be ready to start out to discover what had happened to the good, young Father Aubert on the instant that the alarm was given; or, worse still, that any one, learning of the Bishop's expected arrival, should enthusiastically drive over to the station as a sort of self-appointed delegation of welcome, just a few minutes behind himself. In that case anything might happen. No, it would not do at all! Every minute of delay and confusion on the part of St. Marleau, and Labbée, and Madame Lafleur no less than the others, was priceless to him now. He remembered his own experience. It would take Labbée a long time to find a horse and wagon; and Madame Lafleur, on her part, would think nothing of a prolonged delay in his return — if he left her with the suggestion, that the train might be late!

Well, there was no reason why he should not accomplish all this. So far, it was quite evident, since Madame Lafleur had had no inkling of what the telegram contained, that no one knew anything about it; and that Labbée, whom he was quite prepared to credit with being loose-tongued enough to have otherwise spread the news, had not associated the Bishop's official signature — with Monsignor the Bishop! It was natural enough. The telegram was signed simply — "Montigny" — not the Bishop of Montigny.

He had eaten enough — he pushed back his chair and stood up.

"I think perhaps, Madame Lafleur," he said reflectively, "that it would be as well not to say anything to any one until Monsignor arrives." He handed her the telegram. "It would appear that his visit is not an official one, and he may prefer to rest and spend a quiet evening. We can allow him to decide that for himself."

Madame Lafleur adjusted her spectacles, and read the message.

"But, yes, Monsieur le Curé," she agreed heartily. "Monsignor will tell us what he desires; and if he wishes to see any one in the village this evening, it will not be too late when you return. But, Monsieur le Curé" — she glanced at the clock — "hadn't you better hurry?"

"Yes," said Raymond quickly; "that's so! I had!"

Madame Lafleur accompanied him to the front door, carrying a lamp. At the foot of the steps Raymond paused, and looked back at her. It had grown black now, and there was no moon.

"I'll run around to the shed and get a lantern," he called up to her — and, without waiting for a reply, hurried around the corner of the house.

He laughed a little harshly, his lips were tightly set, as he reached the shed door, opened it, and closed it behind him. He struck a match, found and lighted a lantern, procured a small piece of string, tucked the sacristan's overalls, and the old coat and hat swiftly under his *soutane* — and a moment later was back beside the buckboard again.

He tied the lantern in front of the dash-board, and climbed into the seat. Madame Lafleur was still standing in the doorway. He hesitated an instant, as he picked up the reins. The sweet, motherly old face smiled at him. A pang came and found lodgment in his heart. It was like that, standing there in the lamp-lit doorway of the *presbytère*, that he had seen her for the first time -- as he saw her now for the last. He had grown to love the silver-haired little old lady with her heart of gold — and so he looked — and a mist came before his eyes, for this was his good-bye.

"You will be back in an hour?" she called out. "You forget, Madame Lafleur" — he forced himself to laugh in the old playful, teasing way — "that the train is sometimes more than an hour late itself!"

"Yes, that is true!" she said. "*Au revoir*, then, Monsieur le Curé!"

He answered quietly.

"Good-night, Madame Lafleur!"

He drove out across the green, and past the church, and, a short distance down the road, where he could no longer be seen from the windows of the *presbytère*, he leaned forward and extinguished the lantern. He smiled curiously to himself. It was the only act that appeared at all in consonance with escape! He was a fugitive now, a fugitive for life — and a fugitive running for his life. It seemed as though he should be standing up in the buckboard, and lashing at the horse until the animal was flecked with foam, and the buckboard rocked and swayed with a mad speed along the road. Instead — he had turned off and was on the station road now — the horse was labouring slowly up the steep hill. It seemed as though there should be haste, furious haste, a wild abandon in his flight — that there should be no time to mark, or see, or note, as he was noting now, the twinkling lights of the quiet village nestling below him there along the river's shore. It seemed that his blood should be whipping madly through his veins — instead he was contained, composed, playing his last hand with the old-time gambler's nerve that precluded a false lead, that calculated deliberately, methodically, and with deadly coolness, the value of every card. And yet, beneath this nerve-imposed veneer, he was conscious of a thousand emotions that battered and seethed and raged at their barriers, and sought to fling themselves upon him and have him for their prey.

He laughed coldly out into the night. It was not the fool who tore like a madman, boisterously, blindly, into the open that would escape! He had ample time. He had seen to that, even if he had appeared to accept Madame Lafleur's injunction to hurry. He need reach the station but a minute or so ahead of the train. Meanwhile, the minor details — were there any that he had overlooked? What about the *soutane* and the clerical hat, for instance, after he had exchanged them for the sacristan's things? Should he hide them where he left the horse and buckboard in the woods? He shook his head after a moment. No; they would probably find the horse before morning, and they might find the *soutane*. There must be no trace of Father Aubert — the longer they searched the better. And then, more important still, when finally the alarm was spread, the description that would be sent out would be that of a man dressed as a priest. No; he would take them with him, wrap them up in a bundle around a stone, and somewhere miles away, say, throw them from the car into the water as the train crossed a bridge. So much for that! Was there anything else, anything that he — —

A lighted window glowed yellow in the darkness from a little distance away. He had come to the top of the rise. It was old Mother Blondin's cottage.

He had meant to urge the horse into a trot once the level was gained—but instead the horse was forgotten, and the animal plodded slowly forward at the same pace at which it had ascended the hill.

Raymond's eyes were fixed upon the light. Old Mother Blondin's cottage—and in that room, beyond that light, old Mother Blondin, the old woman on the hill, the *excommuniée*, lay dying. And there was a shadow on the window shade—the shadow of one sitting in a chair—a woman's shadow— Valerie!

He stopped the horse, and, sitting there in the buck-board opposite the cottage, he raised his hand slowly and took his hat from his head.

"Go on—fool!"—with a snarl, vicious as the cut of a whip-lash, came that inner voice. "You may have time—but you have none to throw away!"

"Be still!" answered Raymond's soul. "This is my hour. Be still!"

Valerie! That shadow on the window he knew was Valerie—and within was that other shadow, the shadow of death. This was his good-bye to old Mother Blondin, who had drunk of the common cup with him, and knelt with him in the moonlit church, her hand in his, outcasts, sealing a most strange bond—and this was his good-bye to Valérie. Valérie—a shadow there on the window shade. That was all—a shadow—all that she could ever be, nothing more tangible in his life through the years to come, if there were years, than a shadow that did not smile, that did not speak to him, that did not touch his hand, or lift brave eyes to look into his. A shadow—that was all—a shadow. It was brutal, cruel, remorseless, yet immeasurably true in its significance, this good-bye—this good-bye to Valérie—a shadow.

The shadow moved, and was gone; from miles away, borne for a great distance on the clear night air, came faintly the whistle of a train—and Raymond, springing suddenly erect, his teeth clenched together, snatched at the whip and laid it across the horse's back.

The wagon lurched forward, and he staggered with the plunge and jerk—and his whip fell again. And he laughed now—no longer calm—and lashed the horse. It was not time that he was racing, there was ample time, the train was still far away; it was his thoughts—to outrun them, to distance them, to leave them behind him, to know no other thing than that impulse for life that alone until now so far this night had swayed him.

And he laughed—and horse and wagon tore frantically along the road, and the woods were about him now, and it was black, black as the mouth of Satan's pit and the roadway to it were black. He was flung back into his seat— and he laughed at that. Life—and he had doddled along the road, preening himself on his magnificent apathy! Life—and the battle and the fight for it was the blood afire, reckless of fear and of odds, the laugh of defiance, the joy of combat, the clenched fist shaken in the face of hell itself! Life—in the mad rush for it was appeal! On! The wagon reeled like a drunken thing, and the wheels twisted in the ruts; a patch of starlight seeping through the branches overhead made a patch of gloom in the inky blackness underneath, and in this patch of gloom wavering tree trunks, like uncouth monsters as they flitted by, snatched at the wheel-hubs to wreck and overturn the wagon, but he was too quick for them, too quick—they always missed. On! Away from memory, away from those good-byes, away from every thought save that of life—life, and the right to live—life, and the fight to hurl that gibbet with its dangling rope a smashed and battered and splintered thing against the jail wall where they would strangle him to death and bury him in their cursed lime!

On! Why did not the beast go faster! Were those white spots that danced before his eyes a lather of foam on the animal's flanks? On—along the road to life! Faster! Faster! It was not fast enough—for thoughts were swift, and they were racing behind him now in their pursuit, and coming closer, and they would overtake him unless he could go faster—faster! Faster, or they would be upon him, and—*a big and brave and loyal man.*

A low cry, a cry of sudden, overmastering hurt, was drowned in the furious pound of the horse's hoofs, in the rattle and the creaking of the wagon, and in the screech and grinding of the wagon's jolt and swing. And, unconscious that he held the reins, unconscious that he tightened them, his hands, clenched, went upward to his face. There was no black road, no plunging horse, no mad, insensate rush, ungoverned and unguided, no wagon rocking demoniacally through the night—there was a woman who knelt in the aisle of a church, and in her arms she held a man, and across the shattered chancel rail there lay a mighty cross, and the shadow of the cross fell upon them both, and the woman's eyes were filled with tears, and she spoke: "A big and brave and loyal man."

Tighter against his face he pressed his clenched hands, unconscious that the horse responded to the check and gradually slowed its pace. Valérie! The woman was Valerie—and he was the man! God, the hurt of it—the hurt of those words ringing now in his ears! She had given him her all—her love, her faith, her trust. And in return, he— —

The reins dropped from his hands, and his head bowed forward. Life! Yes, there was life this way for him—and for Valerie the bitterest of legacies. He would bequeath to her the belief that she had given her love not only to a felon but to a *coward.* A coward! And no man, he had boasted, had ever called him a coward. Pitiful boast! Life for himself—for Valerie the fuller measure of misery! Yes, he loved Valérie—he loved her with a traitor's and a coward's love!

His lips were drawn together until they were bloodless. In retrospect his life passed swiftly, unbidden before him—and strewn on every hand was wreckage. And here was the final, crowning act of all—the coward's act—the coward afraid at the end to face the ruin he had, disdainful, callous, contemptuous then of consequence, so consistently wrought since boyhood! If he got away and wrote a letter it would save the man's life, it was true; but it was also true that he ran because he was cornered and at the end of his resources, and because what he might write would, in any case, be instantly discovered if he did not run—and to plead his own innocence in that letter, in the face of glaring proof to the contrary, in the face of the evidence he had so carefully budded against another, smacked only of the grovelling whine of the condemned wretch afraid. None would believe him. None! It was paltry, the police were inured to that; all criminals were eager to protest their innocence, and pule out their tale of extenuating circumstances. None would believe him. Valérie would not believe.

Folds of his cheeks were gripped and crushed in his hands until the finger nails bit into the flesh. He *was* innocent. He had not *murdered* that scarred-faced drunken hound—only Valérie would neither believe nor know; and in Valérie's eyes he would stand a loathsome thing, and in her soul would be a horror, and a misery, and a shame that was measured only by the greatness and the depth of the love she had given him, for in that greatness and that depth lay, too, the greatness and the depth of that love's dishonour and that love's abasement. But if—but if— —

For a moment he did not stir or move, his eyes seeing nothing, fixed before him—and then steadily his head came up and poised far back on the broad, square shoulders, and the tight lips parted in a strange and sudden smile. If he drove to the station and met Monsignor the Bishop, and drove Monsignor the Bishop back to St. Marleau—then she would believe. No one else could or would believe him, the proof was irrefutable against him, they would convict him, and the sentence would be death; but she in her splendid love would believe him, and know that she had loved—a man. There had been three ways, but one had gone that afternoon; and then there had been two ways, but there was only one now, the man's way, for the other was the coward's way. And, taking this, he could lift his head and stand before them all, for in Valérie's face and in Valérie's eyes there would not be—-what was worse than death. To save Valérie from what he could—not from sorrow, not from grief, that he could not do—but that she might know that her love had been given where it was held a sacred, a priceless and a hallowed thing, and was not outraged and was not degraded because it had been given to him! To save Valerie from what he could—to save himself in his own eyes from the self-abasing knowledge that through a craven fear he had bartered away his manhood and his self-respect, that through fear he ran, and that through fear he hid, and that through fear, though he was innocent, he dared not stand—a man!

He stopped the horse, and stepped down to the ground; and, searching for a match, found one, and lighted the lantern where it hung upon the dashboard. He was calm now, not with that calmness desperately imposed by will and nerve, but with a calmness that was like to—peace. And, standing there, the lantern light fell upon him, and gleamed upon the crucifix upon his breast. And he lifted the crucifix, and, wondering, held it in his hand, and looked at it. It was here in these woods and on this road that he had first hung it about his neck in insolent and bald denial of the Figure that it bore. It was very strange! He had meant it then to save his life; and now—he let it slip gently from his fingers, and climbed back into the buckboard—and now it seemed, as though strengthening him in the way he saw at last, in the way he was to take, as though indeed it were the way itself, came radiating from it, like a benediction, a calm and holy—peace.

And there was no more any turmoil.

And he picked up the reins and drove on along the road.

CHAPTER XXIII—MONSIGNOR THE BISHOP

THE train had come and gone, as Raymond reached the station platform. He had meant it so. He had meant to avoid the lights from the car windows that would have illuminated the otherwise dark platform; to avoid, if possible, a disclosure in Labbée's, the station agent's, presence. Afterwards, Labbée would know, as all would know—but not now. It was not easy to tell; the words perhaps would not come readily even when alone with Monsignor the Bishop, as they drove back together to the village.

There were but two figures on the platform—Labbée, who held a satchel in his hand; and a tall, slight form in clerical attire.

"Ah, Father Aubert—*salut!*" Labbée called out. "You are late; but we saw your light coming just as the train pulled out, and so——"

"Well, well, François, my son!"—it was a rich, mellow voice that broke in on the station agent.

Raymond stood up and lifted his hat—lifted it so that it but shaded his face the more.

"Monsignor!" he said, in a low voice. "This is a great honour."

"Honour!" the Bishop responded heartily. "Why should I not come, I—but do I sit on this side?"—he had stepped down into the buckboard, as he grasped Raymond's hand.

"Yes, Monsignor"—Raymond's wide-brimmed clerical hat was far over his eyes. The lantern on the front of the dash-board left them in shadow; Labbée's lantern for the moment was behind them, as the station agent stowed the Bishop's valise under the seat. He took up the reins, and with an almost abrupt "goodnight" to the station agent, started the horse forward along the road.

"Good-night!" Labbée shouted after them. "Goodnight, Monsignor!"

"Good-night!" the Bishop called back—and turned to Raymond. "Yes, as I was saying," he resumed, "why should I not come? I was passing through St. Marleau in any case. I have heard splendid things of my young friend, the curé, here. I wanted to see for myself, and to tell him how pleased and gratified I was."

"You are very good, Monsignor," Raymond answered, his voice still low and hurried.

"Excellent!" pursued the Bishop. "Most excellent! I do not know when I have been so pleased over anything. The parish perhaps"—he laughed pleasantly—"would not object if Father Allard prolonged his holiday a little—eh—François, my son?"

Raymond shook his head.

"Hardly that, Monsignor"—he dared indulge in little more than monosyllables—it was even strange the Bishop had not already noticed that his voice was not the voice of Father François Aubert. And yet what did it matter? In a moment, in five minutes, in half an hour, the Bishop would know all—he would have told the Bishop all. Why should he strive now to keep up a deception that he was voluntarily to acknowledge almost the next instant? It was not argument in his mind, not argument again that brought indecision and chaotic hesitancy, it was not that—the way was clear, there was only one way, the way that he would take—? and yet, perhaps because it was so very human, because perhaps he sought for still more strength, because perhaps it was so almost literally the final, closing act of his life, he waited and clung to that moment more, and to that five minutes more.

"Well, well," said the Bishop happily, "we will perhaps have to look around and see if we cannot find for you a parish of your own, my son. And who knows—eh—perhaps we have already found it?"

How queerly the lantern jerked its rays up and down the horse's legs, and cast its shadows along the road! He heard himself speaking again.

"You are very good, Monsignor"—they were the same words with which he had replied before—he uttered them mechanically.

He felt the Bishop's hand close gently, yet firmly, upon his shoulder.

"François, my son"—the voice had suddenly become grave—"what is the matter? You act strangely. Your voice does not somehow seem natural—it is very hoarse. You have a cold perhaps, or perhaps you are ill?"

"No, Monsignor—I am not ill."

"Then—but, you alarm me, my son!" exclaimed the Bishop anxiously. "Something has happened?"

"Yes, Monsignor—something has happened."

How curiously his mind seemed to be working! He was conscious that the Bishop's hand remained in kindly pressure on his shoulder as though inviting his confidence, conscious that the man beside him maintained a sympathetic, tactful silence, waiting for him to speak; but his thoughts for the moment now were not upon the immediate present, but upon the immediate afterwards when his story had been told.

The buckboard rattled on along the road; it entered the wooded stretch — and still went on. When he had told this man beside him all, they would drive into the village. Then presently they would set out for Tournayville, and Monsieur Dupont, and the jail. But before that — there was Valérie. He turned his head still further away — even in the blackness his face must show its ashen whiteness. There was Valérie — Valérie who would believe — but Valérie who was to suffer, and to know agony and sorrow — and he, who loved her, must look into her face and see the smile die out of it, and the quiver come to her lips, and see her eyes fill, while with his own hands he dealt her the blow, which, soften it as he would, must still strike her down. It was the only way — the way of peace. It seemed most strange that peace should lie in that black hour ahead for Valérie and for himself — that peace should lie in death — and yet within him, quiet, undismayed, calm and untroubled in its own immortal truth, was the knowledge that it was so.

Raymond lifted his head suddenly — through the trees there showed the glimmer of a light — as it had showed that other night when he had walked here in the storm. Had they come thus far — in silence! Involuntarily he stopped the horse. It was the light from old Mother Blondin's cottage, and here was the spot where he had stumbled that night over the priest whom he had thought dead, as the other lay sprawled across the road. It was strange again — most strange! He had not deliberately chosen this spot to tell — —

"François, my son — what is it?" — the Bishop's voice was full of deep concern.

For a moment Raymond did not move, and he did not speak. Then he laid down the reins, and, leaning forward, untied the lantern from the dashboard — and, taking off his hat, held up the lantern between them until the light fell full upon his face.

There was a quick and startled cry from the Bishop, and then for an instant — silence. And Raymond looked into the other's face, even as the other looked into his. It was a face full of dignity and strength and quiet, an aged, kindly face, crowned with hair that was silver-white; but the blue eyes that spoke of tranquillity were widened now in amazement, surprise and consternation.

And then the Bishop spoke.

"Something has happened to François," he said, in a hesitant, troubled way, "and you have come from Tournayville to take his place perhaps, or perhaps to—to be with him. Is it as serious as that—and you were loath to break the news, my son? And yet—and yet I do not understand. The station agent said nothing to indicate that anything was wrong, though perhaps he might not have heard; and he called you Father Aubert, though, too, that possibly well might be, for it was dark, and I myself did not see your face. My son, I fear that I am right. Tell me, then! You are a priest from Tournayville, or from a neighbouring parish?"

"I am not a priest," said Raymond steadily.

The Bishop drew back sharply, as though he had been struck a blow.

"Not a priest—and in those clothes!"

"No, Monsignor."

The fine old face grew set and stern.

"And Francois Aubert, then—*where is Father Francois Aubert?*"

"Monsignor"—Raymond's lips were white—"he is in the condemned cell at Tournayville—under sentence of death—he is— —"

"Condemned—to death! François Aubert—condemned to death!"—the Bishop was grasping with one hand at the back of the seat. And then slowly, still grasping at the seat, he pulled himself up and stood erect, and raised his other hand over Raymond in solemnity and adjuration. "In the name of God, what does this mean? Who are you?"

"I am Raymond Chapelle," Raymond answered—and abruptly lowered the lantern, and a twisted smile of pain gathered on his lips. "You have heard the name, Monsignor—all French Canada has heard it." The Bishop's hand dropped heavily to his side.

"Yes, I have heard it," he said sternly. "I have heard that it was a proud name dishonoured, a princely fortune dissolutely wasted. And you are Raymond Chapelle, you say! I have heard this much, that you had disappeared, but after that— —"

Raymond put his head down into his hands, and drew his hands tightly across his face.

"This is the end of the story," he said. "Listen, Monsignor"—he raised his head again. "You have heard, too, of the murder of Théophile Blondin that was committed here a little while ago. It is for that murder that François

Aubert was tried, found guilty, and sentenced to be hanged." He paused an instant, his lips tight. "Monsignor, it is I who killed Théophile Blondin. It is I who, since that night, have lived here as the curé—as Father François Aubert."

How ghastly white the aged face was! As ghastly as his own must be! The other's hands were gripping viselike at his shoulders.

"Are you mad!" the Bishop whispered hoarsely. "Do you know what you are saying!"

"I know"—there was a sort of unnatural calm and finality in Raymond's tones now. "I was on the train the night that Father Aubert came to St. Marleau. I had a message for the mother of a man who was killed in the Yukon, Monsignor. The mother lived here. There was a wild storm that night. There was no wagon to be had, and we both walked from the station. But I did not walk with the priest. You, who have heard of Raymond Chapelle, know why—I despised a priest—I knew no God. Monsignor"—he turned and pointed suddenly—"you see that light through the trees? It is the light I saw that night, as I stumbled over the body of a man lying here in the road. The man was Father Aubert. The limb of a tree had fallen and struck him on the head. I thought him dead. I went over to that house for help."

He paused again. The Bishop's hands, withdrawn,* were clasped now upon a golden crucifix—it was like his own crucifix, only it was larger, much larger than his own. But the Bishop's white face was still close to his; and the blue eyes seemed to have grown darker, and were upon him in a fixed, tense way, as though to read his soul.

"And then?"—he saw the Bishop's lips move, he did not hear the Bishop speak.

At times the horse moved restively; at times there came the chirping of insects from the woods; at times a breeze stirred and whispered through the leaves. Raymond, staring at the yellow flicker of the lantern, set now upon the floor of the buckboard at their feet, spoke on, in his voice that same unnatural calm. It seemed almost as though he himself were listening to some stranger speak. It was the story of that night he told, the story of the days and nights that followed, the story of old Mother Blondin, the story of the cross, the story of the afternoon in the condemned cell, the story of his ride for liberty of an hour ago, the story of his sacrilege and his redemption—the story of all, without reservation, save the story of Valérie's love, for that was between Valérie and her God.

And when he had done, a silence fell between them and endured for a great while.

And then Raymond looked up at last to face the condemnation he thought to see in the other's eyes — and found instead that the silver hair was bare of covering, and that the tears were flowing unchecked down the other's cheeks.

"God's ways are beyond all understanding" — the Bishop seemed to be speaking to himself. He brushed the tears now from his cheeks, as he looked at Raymond. "It is true there is not any proof, and without proof that it was in self-defence, then — — "

"It is the end," said Raymond simply — and, standing up, took the sacristan's old coat from under his *soutane*. "We will drive to the village, Monsignor; and then, if you will, to the jail in Tournayville." Slowly he unbuttoned his *soutane* from top to bottom, and took it off, and laid it over the back of the seat; and, standing there erect, his face white, his eyes half closed, like a soldier in unconditional surrender, he unclasped the crucifix from around his neck, and held it out to the Bishop — and bowed his head.

He felt the Bishop's hands close over his, and over the crucifix, and gently press it back.

"Cling to it, my son" — the Bishop's voice was broken. "It is yours, for you have found it — and, with it, pardon, and the faith that is more precious than life, than the life you are offering to surrender now. It seems as though it were God's mysterious way, the hand of God — the hand of God that would not let you lose your soul. And now, my son, kneel down, for I would pray for a brave man."

A quiet pressure upon his shoulders brought Raymond to his knees. His eyes, were wet; he covered his face with his hands.

"Father, have mercy upon us" — the Bishop's voice was tremulous and low. "Lord, have mercy upon us. Look down in pity upon this man whom Thou hast brought unto Thyself, and who now in expiation of his past offences offers his life that another may not die. Father, grant us Thy divine mercy. Father, show us the way, if there be a way, and if it be Thy will, that he may not drink of this final cup; and if that may not be, then in Thy love continue unto him the strength Thou gavest him to bring him thus far upon his road."

And silence fell again between them. And there was a strange gladness in Raymond's heart that this man, where he had thought no man would, should have believed. It altered no fact, the cold and brutal evidence, clear cut before a jury would not be a scene such as this, for the evidence in the light of logic and before the law would say he *lied*; it held out no hope, he knew that well—but it brought peace again. And so he rose from his knees, and feeling out blindly for the old sacristan's coat, put it on, and spoke to the horse, and the buckboard moved forward.

And a little way along, just around the turn of the road, they came out of the woods in front of old Mother Blondin's cottage. And standing by the roadside in the darkness was a figure. And a voice called out:

"Is that you, Father Aubert? I went to the *presbytère* for you, and mother said you had gone to meet Monsignor. I have been waiting here to catch you on the way back."

It was Valérie.

CHAPTER XXIV—THE OLD
WOMAN ON THE HILL

SHE came forward toward the buckboard, and into the lantern light—and stopped suddenly, looking from Raymond to the Bishop in a bewildered and startled way.

"Why—why, Father Aubert," she stammered, "I—I hardly knew you in that coat. I—Monsignor"—she bent her knee reverently—"I"—her eyes were searching their faces—"I—-"

Raymond's eyes fixed ahead of him, and he was silent. Valérie! Ay, it was the end! He had thought to see her before they should take him to Tournayville—but he had thought to see her alone. And even then he had not known what he should say to her—what words to speak—or whether she should know from him his love. He was conscious that the Bishop was fumbling with his crucifix, as though loath to take the initiative upon himself.

It was Valérie who spoke—hurriedly, as though in a nervous effort to bridge the awkward silence.

"Mother Blondin became conscious a little while ago. She asked for Father Aubert, and—and begged for the Sacrament. I ran down to the *presbytère*, and when mother told me that Monsignor was coming I—-I brought back the bag that my uncle, Father Allard, takes with him to—to the dying. Oh, Monsignor, I thought that perhaps—perhaps—she is an *excommuniée*, Monsignor—but she is a penitent. And when I got back she was unconscious again, and then I came down here to wait by the side of the road so that I would not miss you, for Madame Bouchard is there, and she was to call me if—if there was any change. And so—and so—you will go to her, Monsignor, will you not—and Father Aubert—and—and——" Her lips quivered suddenly, for Raymond's white face was lifted now, and his eyes met hers. "Oh, what is the matter?" she cried out in fear. "Why do you look like that, Father Aubert—and why do you wear that coat, and——"

"My daughter"—the Bishop's grave voice interrupted her. He rose from his seat, and, moving past Raymond, stepped to the ground. "My daughter, Father Aubert is—-"

"No!" — Raymond, too, had stepped to the ground. "No, Monsignor" — his voice caught, then was steadied as he fought fiercely for self-control — "I will tell her, Monsignor."

How clearly her face was defined in the lantern light, how pure it was, and, in its purity, how far removed from the story that he had to tell! And how beautiful it was, even in its startled fear and wonder — the sweet lips parted; the dark eyes wide, disturbed and troubled, as they held upon his face.

"Father Aubert!" — it was a quick cry, but low, and one of apprehension.

"Mademoiselle Valérie" — the words came slowly; it seemed as though his soul faltered now, and had not strength to say this thing — "I am not Father Aubert."

She did not move. She repeated the words with long pauses between, as though she groped dazedly in her mind for their meaning and significance.

"You — are — not — Father — Aubert?"

The Bishop, hands clasped behind his back, his head bowed, had withdrawn a few paces out of the lantern light toward the rear of the buckboard. Raymond's hands closed and gripped upon the wheel-tire against which he stood — closed tighter and tighter until it seemed the tendons in his hand must snap.

"Father Aubert is the man you know as Henri Mentone" — his eyes were upon her hungrily, pleading, searching for some sign, a smile, a gesture of sympathy that would help him to go on — and her hands were clasped suddenly, wildly to her bosom. "When you came upon me in the road that night I had just changed clothes with him. I — I was trying to escape."

She closed her eyes. Her face became a deathly white, and she swayed a little on her feet.

"You — you are not a — a priest?"

He shook his head.

"It was the only way I saw to save my life. He had been struck by the falling limb of a tree. I thought that he was dead."

"To save your life?" — she spoke with a curious, listless apathy, her eyes still closed.

"It was I," he said, "not Father Aubert, who fought with Théophile Blondin that night."

Her eyes were open wide now — wide upon him with terror.

"It was you — *you* who killed Théophile Blondin?" — her voice was dead, scarce above a whisper.

"I caught him in the act of robbing his mother—I had gone to the house for help after finding Father Aubert"—Raymond's voice grew passionate now in its pleading. He must make her believe! He must make her believe! It was the one thing left to him—and to her. "It was in self-defence. He sprang at me, and we fought. And afterwards, when he snatched up the revolver from the *armoire*, it went off in his own hand as I struggled to take it from him. But I could not prove it. Every circumstance pointed to premeditated theft on my part—and murder. And—and my life before that was—was a ruined life that would but—but make conviction certain if I were found there. My only chance lay in getting away. But there was no time—nowhere to go. And so— and so I ran back to where Father Aubert lay, and put on his clothes, meaning to gain a few hours' time that way, and in the noise of the storm I did not hear you coming until it was too late to run."

How mercilessly hard her hands seemed to press at her bosom!

"I—I do not understand"—it was as though she spoke to herself. "There was another—a man who, with Jacques Bourget, tried to have Henri—Henri Mentone escape."

"It was I," said Raymond. "I took Narcisse Pélude's old clothes from the shed."

She cried out a little—like a sharp and sudden moan, it was, as from unendurable pain.

"And then—and then you lived here as—as a priest."

"Yes," he answered.

"And—and to-night?"—her eyes were closed again.

"To-night," said Raymond, and turned away his head, "to-night I am going to—to Tournayville."

"To your death"—it was again as though she were speaking to herself.

"There is no other way," he said. "I thought there was another way. I meant at first to escape to-night when I learned that Monsignor was coming. I took this coat, Narcisse Pélude's old clothes from the shed again, the clothes I wore the night I went to Jacques Bourget, and I meant to escape on the train. But"—he hesitated now, groping desperately for words—he could not tell her of that ride along the road; he had no right to tell her of his love, he saw that now, he had no right to tell her that, to make it the harder, the more cruel for her; he had no right to trespass on his knowledge of her love for him, to let her glean from any words of his a hint of that; he had the right only, for her sake and for his own, that, in her eyes and in her soul, the stain of murder and of theft should not rest upon him—"but"—the words seemed weak, inadequate—"but I could not go. Instead, I gave myself up to Monsignor.

Mademoiselle" — how bitterly full of irony was that word — mademoiselle — mademoiselle to Valérie — like a gulf between them — mademoiselle to Valérie, who was dearest in life to him — "Mademoiselle Valérie" — he was pleading again, his soul in his voice — "it was in self-defence that night. It was that way that Théophile Blondin was killed. I could not prove it then, and — and the evidence is even blacker against me now through the things that I have done in an effort to escape. But — but it was in that way that Théophile Blondin was killed. The law will not believe. I know that. But you — you — " his voice broke. The love, the yearning for her was rushing him onward beyond self-control, and near, very near to his lips, struggling and battling for expression, were the words he was praying God now for the strength not to speak.

She did not answer him. She only moved away. Her white face was set rigidly, and the dark eyes that had been full upon him were but a blur now, for she was moving slowly backward, away from him, toward where the Bishop stood. And she passed out of the lantern light and into the shadows. And in the shadows her hand was raised from her bosom and was held before her face — and it seemed as though she held it, as she had held it in the dream of that Walled Place; that she held it, as she had held it to shut out the sight of his face from her, as she had closed upon him that door with its studded spikes. And like a stricken man he stood there, gripping at the buckboard's wheel. She did not believe him. Valérie did not believe him! There was agony to come, black depths of torment yawning just before him when the numbness from the blow had passed — but now he was stunned. She did not believe him! That man there, whom he had thought would turn with bitter words upon him, had believed him — but Valérie — Valérie — Valérie did not believe him! Ay, it was the end! The agony and the torment were coming now. It was the dream come true. The studded gate clanged shut, and the horror, without hope, without smile, without human word, of that Walled Place with its slimy walls was his, and, over the shrieking of those winged and hideous things, that swaying carrion seemed to scream the louder: "*Dies ila, dies iro* — that day, a day of wrath, of wasting, and of misery, a great day, and exceeding bitter."

He did not move. Through that blur and through the shadows he watched her, watched her as she reached the Bishop, and sank down upon the ground, and clasped her hands around the Bishop's knees. And then he heard her speak — and it seemed to Raymond that, as though stilled by a mighty uplift that swept upon him, the beating of his heart had ceased.

"Monsignor!" she cried out piteously. "Monsignor! Monsignor! It is true that they will not believe him! I was at the trial, Monsignor, I know the evidence, and I know that they will not believe him. He is going to — to his — death — to save that man. Oh, Monsignor — Monsignor, is there no other way?"

Slowly, mechanically, as slowly as she had retreated from him, Raymond moved toward the kneeling figure. The Bishop was speaking now—he had laid his hands upon her head.

"My daughter," he said gently, "what other way would you have him take? It is a brave man's way, and for that I honour him; but it is more, it is the way of one who has come out of the darkness into the light, and for that my heart is full of thankfulness to God. It is the way of atonement, not for any wrong he has done the church, for he could do the church no wrong, for the church is pure and holy and beyond the reach of any human hand or act to soil, for it is God's church—but atonement to God for those sins of sacrilege and unbelief that lay between himself and God alone. And so, my daughter, if in those sins he has been brought to see and understand, and in his heart has sought and found God's pardon and forgiveness, he could do no other thing than that which he has done to-night." The Bishop's voice had faltered; he brushed his hand across his cheek as though to wipe away a tear. "It is God's way, my daughter. There could be no other way."

She rose to her feet, her face covered by her hands.

"No other way"—the words were lifeless on her lips, save that they were broken with a sob. And then, suddenly, she drew herself erect, and there was a pride and a glory in the poise of her head, and her voice rang clear and there was no tremor in it, and in it was only the pride and only the glory that was in the head held high, and in the fair, white, uplifted face. "Listen, Monsignor! I thought he was a priest, and I promised God that he should never know—but to-night all that is changed. Monsignor, does it matter that he has no thought of me! He is going to his death, Monsignor, and he shall not face this alone because I was ashamed and dared not speak. I love him, Monsignor—I love him, and I believe him, and—-"

"*Valérie!*" Raymond's hands reached out to her. Weak he was. It seemed as though in his knees there was no strength. "Valérie!" he cried, and stumbled toward her.

And she put out her hand and held him back for an instant as her eyes searched his face—and then into hers there came a wondrous light.

"I did not know," she whispered. "I did not know you cared."

His arms were still outstretched, and now she came into them, and for a moment she lifted her face to his, and, for a moment that was glad beyond all gladness, he drank with his lips from her lips and from the trembling eyelids. And then the tears came, and she was sobbing on his breast, and with her arms tight about his neck she clung to him—and closer still his own arms enwrapped her—and he forgot—and he forgot—*that it was only for a moment.*

And so he held her there, his face buried in the dark, soft masses of her hair—and he forgot. And then out of this forgetfulness, this transport of blinding joy, there came a voice, low and shaken with emotion—the Bishop's voice.

"There is some one calling from the house."

Raymond lifted up his head. A woman's figure was framed in the now open and lighted doorway of the cottage. It was Madame Bouchard; and now he heard Madame Bouchard as she called again.

"Valerie! Father Aubert! Come! Come quickly! Madame Blondin is conscious again, but she is very weak."

He drew his breath in sharply as one in bitter pain, and then gently he took Valerie's arms from about him, and his shoulders squared. He had had his moment. This was reality now. He heard Valérie cry out, and saw her run toward the cottage.

"Monsignor," he said hoarsely, and, moving back, lifted the *soutane* from the buckboard's seat, "Monsignor, she must not know—and she has asked for me. It is for her sake, Monsignor—that she be not disillusioned in her death, and lose the faith that she has found again. Monsignor, it is for the last time, not to perform any office, Monsignor, for you will do that, but that she may not die in the belief that God, through me, has only mocked her at the end."

"I understand, my son," the Bishop answered simply. "Put it on—and come."

And so Raymond put on the *soutane* again, and they hurried toward the cottage. And at the doorway Madame Bouchard courtesied in reverence to the Bishop, and Raymond heard her say something about the horse, and that she would remain within call; and then they passed on into Mother Blondin's room.

It was a bare room, poor and meagre in its furnishings—a single rag mat upon the floor; a single chair, and upon the chair the black bag that Valerie had brought from the *presbytère*; and beside the rough wooden bed, made perhaps by the Grandfather Bouchard in the old carpenter shop by the river bank, was a small table, and upon the table a lamp, and some cups with pewter spoons laid across their tops.

Extraneous things, these details seemed to Raymond to have intruded themselves upon him as by some strange and vivid assertiveness of their own, for he was not conscious that he had looked about him—that he had looked anywhere but at that white and pitifully sunken face that was straining upward from the pillows, and at Valérie who knelt at the bedside and supported old Mother Blondin in her arms.

"Quick!" Valerie cried anxiously. "Give her a teaspoonful from that first cup on the table. She has been trying to say something, and—and I do not understand. Oh, be quick! It is something about that man in the prison."

The old woman's head bobbed jerkily, as though she fought for strength to hold it up; the eyes, half closed, were dulled; and she struggled, gasping, for her breath.

"Yes—the prison—the man"—the words were almost inarticulate. Raymond, beside her now, was holding the spoonful of stimulant to her lips. She swallowed it eagerly. "I—I lied—I lied—at the trial. Hold me—tighter. Do not let me—go. Not yet—not—not until——" Her body seemed to straighten, then wrench backward, and her eyes closed, and her voice died away.

Raymond felt the Bishop's hand close tensely on his shoulder.

"What is this she says, my son?"

Raymond shook his head.

"I do not know," he said huskily.

The eyes opened again, clearer now—and recognition came into them as they met Raymond's. And there came a smile, and she reached out her hand to him.

"You, father—I—I was afraid you would not come in time. I—I am stronger now. Give Valerie the cup, and kneel, father—don't you remember—like that night in the church—and hold my hand—and—and do not let it go because—because then I—I should be afraid that God—that God would not forgive."

He took her hand between both his own, and knelt beside the bed.

"I will not let it go," he said—and tried to keep the choking from his throat. "What is it that you want to say—Mother Blondin?"

Her fingers twined over his, and clung tighter and tighter.

"That man, father—he—he must not hang. I—I cannot go to God with that on my soul. I lied at the trial—I lied. I hated God then. I wanted only revenge because my son was dead. I said I recognised him again, but—but that is not true, for the light was low, and—and I do not see well—but—but that—that does not matter, father—it is not that—for it must have been that man. But it was not that man who—who tried to rob me—it—it was my own son. That man is innocent—innocent—I tell you—I——" She raised herself wildly up in bed. "Why do you look at me like that, Father Aubert—with that white face—is it too late—too late—and—and—will God not forgive?"

"It is not too late. Go on, Mother Blondin"—it was his lips that formed the words; it was not his voice, it could not be—that quiet voice speaking so softly.

Her face grew calmer. The fear was gone.

"It is not too late—it is not too late—and—and God will forgive," she whispered. "Listen then, father—listen, and pray for me. I—I was sure Théophile had been robbing me. I watched behind the door that night. I saw him go to take the money. And—and then that man came in, and Théophile rushed at him with a stick of wood. The man had—had done nothing. It was in self-defence he fought. And then I—I helped Théophile. It was Théophile who took the revolver to kill him, and—and—it went off in Théophile's hand, and— —" she sighed heavily, and sank back on the pillow.

The room seemed to sway before Raymond—and

Valérie's face, across the bed, seemed to move slowly before him with a pendulum-like movement, and her face was very white, and in it was wonder, and a great dawning hope, and awe. And he put his head down upon the coverlet, but his hands still held old Mother Blondin's hand between them.

And then she spoke again, with greater difficulty now; and somehow her other hand had found Raymond's head, and her fingers played tremblingly through his hair.

"You will tell them, father—and—and this other father here will tell them—and—and Valérie will bear witness—and—and the man will live. And you will tell him, father, how God came again and made me tell the truth because you were good, and—and because you made be believe again in—in you—and God—and— —-"

A broken cry came from Raymond. The scalding tears were in his eyes.

"Hush, my son!"—it was the Bishop's grave and gentle voice. "God has done a wondrous thing tonight."

There was silence in the little room.

And then suddenly Raymond lifted his head—and the room was no more, and in its place was the moonlit church of that other night, and he saw again the old withered face transfigured into one of tender sweetness and ineffable love.

"Pierre, monsieur?"—her mind was wandering now—they were the words she had spoken as she had sat beside him in the pew. "Ah, he was a good boy, Pierre—have you not heard of Pierre Letellier? And there was little Jean—little Jean—he went away, monsieur, and I—I do not know where—where he is—I do not know— —-"

Raymond's voice was breaking, as he leaned forward toward her.

"He is with God, Mother Blondin. Jean—Jean has sent you a message. His last thoughts were of you—his mother."

The old eyes flamed with a dying fire.

"Jean—my son! My little Jean—his—his mother." A smile lighted up her face, and hovered on her lips; and her hand, clinging to Raymond's, tightened.

"Father—I— —" And then her fingers slipped from their hold, and fell away.

The Bishop's arm was around Raymond's shoulders.

"Go now, my son—and you, my daughter," he said gently. "It is very near the end, and the time is short."

Raymond rose blindly from his knees. Mother Blondin was very still, and a pallor, gray and premonitory, had crept into her face. Her eyes were closed. He raised the thin hand, and touched it with his lips—and turned away.

And Valérie passed out of the room with him.

And by the open window of the room beyond, Valérie knelt down, and he knelt down beside her.

It was quiet without—and there was no sound, save now the murmur of the Bishop's voice from the inner room. He was to live—and not to die. To go free! To give himself up—but to be set free—and there were to be the years with Valérie. He could not understand it yet in all its fulness.

Valérie was crying softly. With a great tenderness he put his arm about her.

"It was the *Benedictus*—'into the way of peace'—that you said for her that night," she whispered. "Say it now again, my lover—for her—and for us."

He drew her closer to him, and, with her wet cheek against his own, they repeated the words together.

And after a little time she raised her hands, and held his face between them, and looked into his face for a long while, and there was a great gladness, and a great love, and a great trust in the tear-wet eyes.

"I do not know your name," she said.

"It is Raymond," he answered.